The Best American Mystery Stories 2006

GUEST EDITORS OF
THE BEST AMERICAN MYSTERY STORIES

1997 ROBERT B. PARKER
1998 SUE GRAFTON
1999 ED MCBAIN
2000 DONALD E. WESTLAKE
2001 LAWRENCE BLOCK
2002 JAMES ELLROY
2003 MICHAEL CONNELLY
2004 NELSON DEMILLE
2005 JOYCE CAROL OATES
2006 SCOTT TUROW

The Best American Mystery Stories™ 2006

Edited and with an Introduction
by **Scott Turow**

Otto Penzler, *Series Editor*

HOUGHTON MIFFLIN COMPANY
BOSTON · NEW YORK 2006

Copyright © 2006 by Houghton Mifflin Company
Introduction copyright © 2006 by Scott Turow
All rights reserved

The Best American Series is a registered trademark of Houghton Mifflin Company. *The Best American Mystery Stories* is a trademark of Houghton Mifflin.

No part of this work may be reproduced or transmitted in any form or by any means, electronic or mechanical, including photocopying and recording, or by any information storage or retrieval system without the prior written permission of the copyright owner unless such copying is expressly permitted by federal copyright law. With the exception of nonprofit transcription in Braille, Houghton Mifflin is not authorized to grant permission for further uses of copyrighted selections reprinted in this book without the permission of their owners. Permission must be obtained from the individual copyright owners as identified herein. Address requests for permission to make copies of Houghton Mifflin material to Permissions, Houghton Mifflin Company, 215 Park Avenue South, New York, New York 10003.

Visit our Web site: www.houghtonmifflinbooks.com.

ISSN: 1094-8384
ISBN-13: 978-0-618-51746-6   ISBN-10: 0-618-51746-4
ISBN-13: 978-0-618-51747-3 (pbk.)   ISBN-10: 0-618-51747-2 (pbk.)

Printed in the United States of America

MP 10 9 8 7 6 5 4 3 2 1

These stories are works of fiction. Names, characters, places, and incidents are products of the authors' imagination or are used fictitiously. Any resemblance to actual events, locales, or persons, living or dead, is entirely coincidental.

"Theft" by Karen E. Bender. First published in *Harvard Review*, no. 29. Copyright © 2005 by Karen E. Bender. Reprinted by permission of the author.

"Pirates of Yellowstone" by C. J. Box. First published in *Meeting Across the River*, 2005. Copyright © 2005 by C. J. Box. Reprinted by permission of the author.

"Why Bugsy Siegel Was a Friend of Mine" by James Lee Burke. First published in *The Southern Review*, vol. 41, no. 1, Winter. Copyright © 2005 by James Lee Burke. Reprinted by permission of the author.

"Born Bad" by Jeffery Deaver. First published in *Dangerous Women*, 2005. Copyright © 2005 by Jeffery Deaver. Reprinted by permission of the author.

"Edelweiss" by Jane Haddam. First published in *Creature Cozies*, 2005. Copyright © 2005 by Orania Papazoglou. Reprinted by permission of the author.

"Texas Heat" by William Harrison. First published in *The Texas Review*, Winter 2004/2005. Copyright © 2005 by William Harrison. Reprinted by permission of the author.

"Peacekeeper" by Alan Heathcock. First published in *The Virginia Quarterly Review*, Fall 2005. Copyright © 2005 by Alan Heathcock. Reprinted by permission of the author.

"A.k.a., Moises Rockafella" by Emory Holmes II. First published in *The Cocaine Chronicles*, 2005. Copyright © 2005 by Emory Holmes II. Reprinted by permission of Akashic Books.

"Dust Up" by Wendy Hornsby. First published in *Murder in Vegas*, 2005. Copyright © 2005 by Wendy Hornsby. Reprinted by permission of the author.

"Her Lord and Master" by Andrew Klavan. First published in *Dangerous Women*, 2005. Copyright © 2005 by Andrew Klavan. Reprinted by permission of the author.

"Louly and Pretty Boy" by Elmore Leonard. First published in *Dangerous Women*, 2005. Copyright © 2005 by Elmore Leonard, Inc. Reprinted by permission of the author.

"The Crack Cocaine Diet (Or: How to Lose a Lot of Weight and Change Your Life in Just One Weekend" by Laura Lippman. First published in *The Cocaine Chronicles*, 2005. Copyright © 2005 by Laura Lippman. Reprinted by permission of the author.

"Improvisation" by Ed McBain. First published in *Dangerous Women*, 2005. Copyright © 2005 by Hui Corporation. Reprinted by permission of the author.

"McHenry's Gift" by Mike MacLean. First published in *thuglit.com* #3, 2005. Copyright © 2005 by Mike MacLean. Reprinted by permission of the author.

"Karma" by Walter Mosley. First published in *Dangerous Women*, 2005. Copyright © 2005 by Walter Mosley. Reprinted by permission of the author.

"So Help Me God" by Joyce Carol Oates. First published in *The Virginia Quarterly Review*, Winter 2005. Copyright © 2005 by Ontario Review, Inc. Reprinted by permission of Ontario Review, Inc.

"A Temporary Crown" by Sue Pike. First published in *Murder in Vegas*, 2005. Copyright © 2005 by Sue Pike. Reprinted by permission of the author.

"Smile" by Emily Raboteau. First published in *The Gettysburg Review*, Autumn 2005. Copyright © 2005 by Emily Raboteau. Reprinted by permission of the author.

"Ina Grove" by R. T. Smith. First published in *The Virginia Quarterly Review*, Winter 2005. Copyright © 2005 by R. T. Smith. Reprinted by permission of the author.

"Ringing the Changes" by Jeff Somers. First published in *Danger City*, 2005. Copyright © 2005 by Jeff Somers. Reprinted by permission of the author.

"Vigilance" by Scott Wolven. First published in *Controlled Burn*, 2005. Copyright © 2005 by Scott Wolven. Reprinted by permission of International Creative Management.

Contents

Foreword · ix
Introduction by Scott Turow · xiv

KAREN E. BENDER
    Theft · 1

C. J. BOX
    Pirates of Yellowstone · 18

JAMES LEE BURKE
    Why Bugsy Siegel Was a Friend of Mine · 31

JEFFERY DEAVER
    Born Bad · 45

JANE HADDAM
    Edelweiss · 63

WILLIAM HARRISON
    Texas Heat · 81

ALAN HEATHCOCK
    Peacekeeper · 93

EMORY HOLMES II
    A.k.a., Moises Rockafella · 112

WENDY HORNSBY
    Dust Up · 129

ANDREW KLAVAN
    Her Lord and Master · 144

ELMORE LEONARD
    Louly and Pretty Boy · 154

LAURA LIPPMAN
    The Crack Cocaine Diet (Or: How to Lose a Lot of Weight and Change Your Life in Just One Weekend) · 169

ED MCBAIN
    Improvisation · 180

MIKE MACLEAN
    McHenry's Gift · 197

WALTER MOSLEY
    Karma · 205

JOYCE CAROL OATES
    So Help Me God · 240

SUE PIKE
    A Temporary Crown · 266

EMILY RABOTEAU
    Smile · 278

R. T. SMITH
    Ina Grove · 281

JEFF SOMERS
    Ringing the Changes · 309

SCOTT WOLVEN
    Vigilance · 320

Contributors' Notes · 345
Other Distinguished Mystery Stories of 2005 · 356

Foreword

Now that *Best American Mystery Stories* has reached its first decade, I thought I'd go back and reread the forewords I'd written for the first nine to see if I had anything original to say (which would be a major coup for me at any time). Well, I don't. What I do realize is how much has changed in ten years and how much has not.

Among the changes are that I (stupidly) crowed about not having a computer for the first few volumes. I do now and couldn't live without it. Even though I am a card-carrying Luddite and have a certificate from the Lead Pencil Society on my wall, I should have realized sooner that a computer would help me to be a better correspondent and better able to do research.

It almost seems quaint to read in that first volume that I looked at five hundred stories. My invaluable colleague, Michele Slung, now scans as many as 1,500 mystery stories and double that number of pieces of fiction to determine whether they are eligible for consideration for this genre-specific volume. Don't ask me how she does it; I've never known how she could read that quickly, make such good decisions, and have such extraordinary retention.

The reasons for these dramatically increased numbers are the proliferation of electronic magazines, or e-zines, and the greater access we have to small literary publications.

Literary periodicals are among the most thankless efforts on the planet, as well as the most optimistic. Most are run on a volunteer basis or for wages so miniscule that sharecroppers would be outraged and insulted if given the same pay. They often have tiny circulations of a few hundred copies, and the staff spends as much time fundraising as it does producing these handsomely made books.

Ten years ago, it was a struggle to find these journals. I didn't know where to find them all, didn't know who ran them, and didn't know how to get access to their stories. Further, I have to admit that not everyone involved was as cooperative as one might have wished. The common response to requests for a copy of the magazine was that it didn't publish mystery stories (you could almost hear the sneer jump off the page). That has largely changed, as every edition of this series has featured large numbers of stories culled from the pages of so many of these worthwhile publications. *Story Quarterly, The Harvard Review, The Ontario Review, The Baltimore Review, McSweeney's, TriQuarterly, The Gettysburg Review, Ploughshares, The Chattahoochee Review, Glimmer Train, Epoch, Eureka Literary Magazine, Puerto del Sol, Washington Square,* and *The Georgia Review* are just a few of the journals from which mystery stories have been honored. I am extremely grateful to the editors for their dedication and assistance.

As time goes by, it becomes more apparent that each volume of *Best American Mystery Stories* is a collaboration. The favorite reading of Nat Sobel, the greatest agent in the world, is literary journals, and when he sends a story to me it goes to the top of the pile because he knows a real writer when he reads one. Friends from all parts of the country call or e-mail or send me stories, wanting to be sure I didn't miss something important. My editors at Houghton Mifflin are a dream come true. Never, not once, have they hinted that they'd like more best-selling writers in the book, or a different demographic mix, or stories that would appeal more to older or younger readers, East Coast readers or Southern readers or California readers, male readers or female readers, intelligent readers or those who like it when cuddly kittens solve the crime. Because they have been publishing the most honored and successful anthology in the United States, *Best American Short Stories,* for more than ninety years, they understand it's about the excellence of the writing, that nothing else matters, which is what my guest editors and I have been trying to provide.

Speaking of whom, the contribution of these superb writers should never be underestimated. Only if you, too, are a celebrity can you begin to understand the number of requests made of major authors. Speak to writers' groups, schools, fundraisers, and publishers' events. Go on a book tour and do interviews for radio, television, newspapers, and magazines, as well as in-store signings at the chains — and don't forget the independents. Read this book and provide a quote for the dust jacket. Write a short story for my anthology or an introduction for my book. Write faster, since we have to have a book every year. Then go on a book tour in England, France, Germany, and Australia. And why haven't you finished reading your proofs yet? It's grueling, even though it sounds like fun, and frequently *is* fun. No one is suggesting that being a successful writer is harder work than being a small farmer, a steelworker, or a fireman, but the time drains are enormous. What makes it worse, of course, is that every one of the authors who agreed to be guest editors for the series are really nice people. No kidding — they really are swell. They hate to say no, so find themselves up to their eyeballs with demands that would sink lesser people.

So, in all gratitude and humility, sincere thanks to Robert B. Parker, the first guest editor, and to the cherished friends who followed: Sue Grafton, Ed McBain (the pseudonym of my dear friend Evan Hunter, who sadly passed away last year), Donald E. Westlake, Lawrence Block, James Ellroy, Michael Connelly, Nelson DeMille, Joyce Carol Oates and, of course, one of the finest gentlemen I've ever had the pleasure to know, Scott Turow.

This brings me to an embarrassing confession over which I had no control. The astute reader (and that includes one and all who were sharp enough to add this volume to their libraries) will notice that there are five stories (out of twenty-one) from a single volume. The lamentable fact is that the book, *Dangerous Women,* happens to have been edited by, ah, me. It was my mission to convince as many outstanding writers as possible that it was a good idea to write a story about a *femme fatale* for this book, and I appear to have succeeded too well. When Mr. Turow selected these stories, I demurred, since I am not a complete idiot and recognize the concept of conflict of interest. He pointed out that the best stories of the year were supposed to go into this volume, regardless of who commissioned it, and that pretty much ended the discussion. Two of the stories, Andrew Klavan's "Her Lord and Master" and Jeffery

Deaver's "Born Bad," were nominated for the Edgar Allan Poe award, and I cannot believe that if you read the stories by Elmore Leonard, Ed McBain, and Walter Mosley that you could think them unworthy. Therefore, I'd like to go on record and say that if you see this as a problem, blame the authors for having written too well.

As relentlessly as I work at it, there is always the possibility that I will miss a story, so if you are an author, an editor, a publisher or an interested observer, please feel free to send recommendations to me. (Almost) full disclosure: after 28 years in one location, my bookshop moved in the fall of 2005 and, in all the chaos, an anthology (best left unnamed, lest the editor decide to come after me with an axe, which may be extreme but would have some justification) was overlooked. I am confident that a couple of stories would have received serious consideration for this collection and I'm sick about it. So please, wherever a good mystery story may appear, I'll be delighted to know about it.

Here are the guidelines: any mystery story (defined as any work of fiction in which a crime or the threat of a crime is integral to the theme or the plot) published first in the United States or Canada during the calendar year 2006 is eligible. It must be submitted either as a complete periodical or anthology, or a tear sheet with the name and address of the publication or the editor. If it first appeared in electronic format, it must be submitted in a hard copy, together with the issue number of the e-zine and contact information. Original stories are not eligible.

Last, the drop-dead date for submissions is December 31. It remains unfathomable to me why people decide to submit a story published in April on or around Christmas Day. Last year, no joke, my mailbox brought more than eighty submissions between Christmas and New Year. It also brought more than a score after January 1 with apologetic letters dated December 28 or 29. The book actually has a deadline, so I passed up the opportunity to read them. I want everyone who writes something good to have a fair chance of getting into this series and, trust me, opening the envelope on Christmas Eve gets the reading started with one strike against it. Send the story as soon as it's published. That way you won't forget, and I get to read it wanting to love it rather than murmuring curses at it. Extensive notes are made throughout the year, so don't worry that an early submission will be neglected or forgotten. No submission will be returned. If you refuse to believe the postal service will actually do what it's supposed to do, which is deliver the mail, enclose a self-addressed postcard to receive acknowledgment of delivery. Please do not ask for critiques of your work — that was your editor's job.

All submissions should be sent to Otto Penzler, The Mysterious Bookshop, 58 Warren Street, New York, NY 10007 (please note this is a new address).

O.P.

Introduction

FIRST, A CONFESSION. I have little business being the guest editor of this volume. Although I have always read short stories of every kind with appreciation, I seldom write them. My rate of story production can be measured on a geologic scale, about one every decade. Looking at my predecessors in this role, I would describe all of them as distinguished practitioners of the form. Not so here. In other words, the opinions expressed are not seasoned by an insider's experience. But as is so often true with lawyers, a lack of qualifications will not keep me from speaking.

Let me start, then, by reflecting on the traditional title of this series, *Best American Mystery Stories*. To be sure, some of the stories that appear here, like Walter Mosley's "Karma," are elegant small mysteries, if mystery is taken to have its traditional meaning as a story about the investigation of a puzzling crime. Characteristically, mysteries focus on the detection of the crime's perpetrator, or more broadly, discovering (or revealing) why that enigmatic crime occurred. Andrew Klavan's "Her Lord and Master" is a mystery in that second sense.

But many other stories included here never raise those questions. Instead, what the fictions Otto Penzler and I have chosen hold in common is their subject matter. Every one is about crime — its commission, its aftermath, its anxieties, its effect on character. *Best American Crime Stories* would be equally, if not more, apropos as the title of this book.

In fact, more than any other theme, these stories are portraits, in styles ranging from sly to harrowing, of how crimes occurred —

Introduction xv

the evolution of circumstances so that bad-acting becomes inevitable. "Vigilance" by Scott Wolven or "Ringing the Changes" by Jeff Somers are only two of many possible examples, both gritty and compelling. In fact, more than half the stories here culminate in the commission of one particular offense. So as not to spoil things, I will not name the crime, but let me say if you like all your characters living at the end of a story, this may not be the book for you.

Yet, I would venture that crime is not the only point of intersection between these stories. If you were to compare most of them to those in the companion volume, *Best American Short Stories,* you might feel, more often than not, that they somehow seem different. Despite what some critics contend, the distinction is not in elegance of execution — many of these stories, such as R. T. Smith's "Ina Grove," are technically masterful; nor in the depth of psychological insight — Alan Heathcock's "Peacekeeper" is a moving revelation of the interdependence of an individual and a community; nor in the uniqueness of voice or vision. There are few American stylists as distinctive as Elmore Leonard, whose usual roadside magic is displayed in "Louly and Pretty Boy Floyd." The difference is that the majority of these stories proceed on different assumptions about what a short story is supposed to do when compared to what I'd call "mainstream" contemporary stories that might be taught in a literature class.

If we are seeking the literary heritage of the majority of these stories, we must hark back to the nineteenth century and the quintessential form that was perfected by writers like Hawthorne and Poe in the United States and Guy de Maupassant in France (and sublimely mastered by Chekhov). The classic short story arose as a function of rapid increases in literacy and the far broader circulation that resulted from newspapers and magazines that were, in today's terms, hungry for content. Stories in that era evolved from being anecdotal and diffuse to aiming to create a dominant impression at the end. In pursuit of that goal, they took a conventional form some of us were taught to recognize in grade and high school. They had a beginning, a middle, and an end, meaning they presented a conflict, an exposition, and a resolution. I'll call them three-act stories for convenience. Mysteries are classic three-act stories, which is why naming these volumes *Best American Mystery Stories* is actually very fair.

Most of the stories here adhere, at least roughly, to that framework. They are tales in which the reader wants to know about the situation as much as the character, where the traditional question of suspense — "What happens next?" — is foremost. Laura Lippman's "The Crack Cocaine Diet" or Mike MacLean's "McHenry's Gift" are fine examples in which the denouement in both instances startled, and therefore delighted, me. Often, in stories of this species, we care as much about how the problem is worked out as we do the psychology of the main character. Ed McBain's "Improvisation" is a glimmering case in point, as you'd expect of a story that begins, "'Why don't we kill somebody?' she suggested." "Edelweiss" by Jane Haddam develops the same theme and, intriguingly, comes to a kindred resolution. This is not to suggest that psychological insight is incidental or absent in these stories. Instead, the assumption is that the resolution of conflict will provide a final and telling window into character, and therefore that plot and character are functions of one another. "Dust Up" by Wendy Hornsby and William Harrison's "Texas Heat" employ that strategy to winning effect.

At the beginning of the twentieth century, James Joyce's *Dubliners* abandoned the traditional three-act form of short fiction. Joyce's epochal stories share the narrative approach of modernist poetry, and evolve toward, in Joyce's chosen term, an "epiphany," a moment of realization, for the reader first, and quite often, for the character, too. Emily Raboteau's brief gem, "Smile," is an exquisite exemplar of that approach. The narration evolves only as far as is necessary to achieve that insight. If you ask about the character's circumstances — where she lives, what she does everyday — they are often little changed. To the question, "What happened in the story?" the answer might be, at least outwardly, "Not very much." Karen Bender's potent and fully realized "Theft" provides a splendid illustration of this.

As should be clear, I am a devotee of stories of both kinds, and therefore we've included stories of both schools. Moreover, it is certainly the case that the distinctions I've suggested are not hard and fast ones. For several decades now, the somewhat rigorous boundaries that existed forty years ago between high and low culture in American literature have been breaking down. Looking back, it is not unusual for some stories to appear in both the Best Mystery

Introduction xvii

and Best Short Story volumes. Joyce Carol Oates's "So Help Me God" crosses the borders I've declared, which has been typical of her world-revered body of work for decades now. R. T. Smith's "Ina Grove" is a little bit of everything: it's a mystery by the definition I've included, a searching exploration of individual psychology, and a story with a beginning, middle, and end — several of them in fact. It is also a work of imposing literary art. Indeed, several of these stories are really both fish and fowl. Joyce was determined to wring meaning from the warp and woof of typical daily experience, as opposed to the rare personal cataclysm that crime, for example, represents. Since all of these are crime stories, they are exiles from a pure-blooded Joycean kingdom, but Sue Pike's "A Temporary Crown" or Emory Holmes's "A.k.a., Moises Rockafella" are nonetheless moving portrayals of minds in the grip of decline that come to moments of haunting crystallization.

Conventions are just that. They hold no special spell, except that they give readers a better chance to understand. They are boxes into which we conform our expectations in exchange for the opportunity to make out meaning more plainly. I get aggravated only by the assumption that stories of one kind are "better" than another. Although students of the short story have been worshipping at Joyce's shrine for nearly a century, it is still the three-act story that dominates American narrative. That remains the shape repeated consistently on television and in the movies, as well as in novels, not to mention at the water cooler. When your coworker starts out, "So I met this guy at the health club," what you want to know is what happened next.

More to the point, whatever convention a story originates from, the ultimate measure of its success will be tied to its originality, whether in language (Raboteux and Smith), conception (like Jeffery Deaver's dazzlingly clever "Born Bad"), style (Leonard), or character. On the last point, consider the young Czech immigrants in C. J. Box's "Pirates of Yellowstone," who are of immediate interest because we have not seen them before. That is the great irony — the ultimate function of convention is to provide readers with a series of conditioned expectations that the best work will in some regard then transcend and defy, leading us to new ground. James Lee Burke's "Why Bugsy Siegel Was a Friend of Mine" is an ostensible three-act, but it artfully turns in another direction. Each of these stories exhibits some commendably unique attribute that helps to convincingly project us into a coherent imagined world from which we emerge enlightened in some way about our condition as humans.

SCOTT TUROW

The Best American
Mystery Stories 2006

KAREN E. BENDER

Theft

FROM *Harvard Review*

GINGER KLEIN held all the cash she owned, which came to nine hundred and thirty-four dollars and twenty-seven cents, in an envelope in her red velvet purse. As she waited in line for the first dinner seating on this cruise to Alaska, she fingered the muscular weight of the bills. The ship's ballroom was a large, drab room, tricked into elegance with real silver set out on the linen, sprightly gold foil bows on the walls, white roses blooming briefly in stale water. The room was filled with couples, friends, tour groups, glittering in their sequins, intent on having a good time. The room roared as the guests greeted each other, their faces gilded by the chandeliers' silver haze. Gripping her purse, Ginger watched them and tried to decide where to sit.

Until a few months before, Ginger had been living in a worn pink studio apartment on Van Nuys Boulevard, storing her cash in margarine containers in her refrigerator. She was eighty-two years old and for the last sixty years she had sometimes lived in better accommodations, sometimes worse; this was what she had ultimately earned. On good days she sat with a cup of coffee and the Los Angeles phone book, calling up strangers for contributions to the Fireman's Ball, the Christian Children's Fund, the United Veteran's Relief. Her British accent was her best one; with it, she could keep confused strangers in Canoga Park, Woodland Hills, and Calabasas on the phone. "Congratulations for being the sort of person who will help our cause," she told them, and heard their pleasure in their own generosity. She cashed the checks at different fast cash stores around the San Fernando Valley, presenting them with one of her bountiful collection of false IDs.

One day, she took the wrong bus home. She looked out the window and was staring at a beach that she had never seen before. The water was bright and wrinkled as a piece of blue foil. Surfers scrambled over the dark, glassy waves. The other passengers seemed to believe this was merely a beach, but Ginger felt her heart grow cold. She had succeeded for sixty-five years as a swindler because she always knew which bus to take.

She had actually intended to pay the doctor if the news had been good. The doctor asked her a few questions. He held up a pair of pliers and she had no idea what they were. She returned to the office twice and saw more doctors who wore pert, grim expressions. The diagnosis was a surprise. When he told her, it was one of the few times in her life she reacted as other people did: she covered her face and wept.

"You need to plan," her doctor said. "You have relatives who can take care of you?"

"No," she said.

"Children?"

"No."

"Friends?"

His pained expression aggravated her. "I have many friends," she said because she pitied him.

She listened to him describe the end of her life and what she should expect her friends to do for her. Then Ginger had to stop him. She told the secretary that her checkbook was in the car and left the office without paying the bill.

She tried to come up with a grand scheme that would pay for her future care, but her thoughts were not so ordered and each day she lost something: the word for lemons, the name of her street. Peering out her window at the lamplights that pierced the blue darkness in her apartment complex, she imagined befriending one of her neighbors, but her neighbors were flighty college dropouts, working odd hours, absent, uninterested in her. Ginger did not want to die in a hospital or an institution. Dying in this apartment would mean that she would not be discovered for days; the idea of her body lifeless, but worse, helpless, was intolerable to her.

She was watching television one evening when she saw an ad for a Carnival cruise. Many years ago, she had sat with a man in an airport bar. He had been left by his wife of thirty-six years and was joking about killing himself in a room on a cruise ship. "Someone finds you," he said, on his third bourbon. "A maid, another passenger. Quickly. It's more dignified. You don't just rot."

He was on his way to the Caribbean, desperately festive in his red vacation shirt, festooned with figures of tropical birds. "What an interesting idea," she had said, lightly, deciding that it was time for a game of poker; she got out her rigged cards. When he stumbled off two hours later, she was $150 richer and certain she would never be that hopeless. But now his plan sounded useful to her.

Before she went on her cruise, she wanted to buy a beautiful purse with which to hold the last of her money. Three public buses roaring over the oily freeways led her to the accessories counter at Saks. The red purse sat on the counter like a glowing light. It was simple, a deep red with a rhinestone clasp; when she saw it, she felt her breath freeze in her throat. The salesgirl told her that it was on hold for someone.

"It's mine," said Ginger, her fingers pressing so hard on the glass counter they turned white.

Perhaps it was the hoarse pitch of her voice, or the pity of the salesgirl toward the elderly, but the salesgirl let her buy the purse. In it, Ginger put her cash and also two bottles of sleeping pills. The Caribbean was sold out this time of year, so she spent most of her remaining money on a cruise to Alaska.

She woke up early the first morning of the cruise, restless, trying to remember everything she had ever known. The facts of her life flurried in her head: names of hotel restaurants, the taste of barbecue in Texas versus Georgia, the aqua chiffon dress she had worn at a cocktail party in 1975. She sat at the table, scribbling notes on a pad: *Fake furs on Hollywood Blvd., 1956, cloudy, blue fur hats from the rare Blue Hyena from Alaska, lemon meringue pie at the cafeteria on W. 37th St., New York, 1960s, the seagulls flying on the empty Santa Monica beach at dawn, how much money I made a year, $37,000 from Dr. Chamron in 1987 —*

Magnolia in Los Angeles, she wrote. She remembered the scent of magnolia as she and Evelyn had stepped off the train in Los Angeles when she was fifteen years old. She remembered her sister Evelyn's walk, Evelyn just seventeen then, her walk her first successful con; stepping hard onto her feet, shoulders lifted, she tricked Ginger into believing that she knew what to do. It was 1921 and they walked off the train into Los Angeles, two girls alone, armed with an address for an aunt whom they would never meet.

Finally, Ginger's hand ached and she put down her pen. Scribbling her room number on a paper, she put it in her purse and walked to dinner. She went carefully around the naked ice sculptures of David or Venus that rose, melting, out of bowls of orange punch. Table Sixteen was empty so she sat down, and a silver domed plate floated down in front of her.

She began to eat her salmon when a young woman slid into the seat across from her. Her hair hung down in long, straight sheets, as though flattened by the heat of her own thoughts.

"Darlene Horwitz," she said, holding out her hand for Ginger to shake. She was young, ridiculously young, with the glossy, unmarked skin of a baby. "This is my first cruise."

"Ginger Klein."

"My parents sent me here," said Darlene. "They had enough of my moaning." She looked at Ginger. "I was — well, it's an old story. Pathetic. Have you ever been on a cruise? Is it fun?"

"In the past," said Ginger.

The girl unfolded her napkin onto her lap. "Are you retired? What did you do?" asked the girl.

Ginger leaned across the table and whispered to Darlene, "This is what I do. People have dreams that you want to be part of. I say I can make them come true. One gentleman expressed a desire to sample gelato in Italy. Then I just did it for him, but on his dime. That man was in the field of advertising. I thought of him sitting behind his desk, eating a bag lunch, a little sweaty, and I thought he'd be grateful that I could taste that gelato for him."

This was Evelyn's philosophy, really; she had believed that swindling was generous, as it allowed the suckers a moment to dream. Ginger pushed her seat back slightly. She unfolded her napkin and spread it on her lap.

"I don't understand," said Darlene.

Ginger coughed. Then she said, slowly, "I'm a swindler."

"Oh," said Darlene. She rubbed her face with her hands. Then she laughed. "Should I be hiding my purse? Are you going to steal money from people?"

"No," said Ginger. "I don't need to anymore."

Darlene seemed to want to steer the discussion back to more familiar territory. "What does your family think of your job?" she asked, carefully.

"I haven't talked to them in sixty years," Ginger said. They had lost their parents suddenly, their mother to illness, their father to lust — when their mother had died of tuberculosis, their father left Brooklyn to pursue a stripper in Louisiana. He left a note with some train fare and an address for an aunt in Orange Hills, Los Angeles.

They tried the first phone booth on the street. When the number didn't work there, they tried another. By the fourth phone booth, they realized that there was no neighborhood Orange Hills and there was no aunt. At the time, the girls had between them forty-three dollars.

"You want to know why I'm here?" Darlene asked. She looked dazed, as though she'd just seen something explode. "His name was Warren. One minute we were finishing each other's sentences. The next minute he packed his bags. Now I am twenty-two years old and afraid I will never find the one."

Waiters came out carrying ignited baked Alaskas. Sparklers on the desserts fizzled, and a faint smoky odor filled the air.

"I went to my parents' house," said Darlene. "*Big* mistake, they packed me off to the glaciers to have fun —"

Ginger did not want to spend one moment of this week comforting someone else. She folded her napkin, stood up. "Well," said Ginger, "I hope you have a grand time." Then she turned and walked across the room. The ship was approaching the first glaciers. Sliding down the mountains the ice was rushed and utterly still. The glacial ice was pale blue and huge pieces drifted by, like the ruined bones of a giant. She watched the pale bones of ice float by her and wondered when she would forget her name.

Her awareness had been her great gift: of the best hour to meet the lonely, of the hairstyle that would make her look most innocent, of the raised eyebrow that indicated a person's longing, and of course, the moment when she knew that what a person owned would belong to her. Sitting on a train, she would feel the money, a roll wrapped around her hip, ride the click of the train along the tracks. She sometimes tried to imagine what freedom could feel like, for in its place was an immediate, dangerous urge to chain herself to another. She wanted to be the imposters she claimed to be: the lost cousin, the secret aunt, the high school classmate, the one who had loved from afar. When she acted as these people, she conjured up the feelings she believed she would have; she enjoyed her suckers' gratitude. They saw some goodness in her, and as the night deepened, she sometimes believed she saw their reflections in the dark train windows, sad, unholy ghosts in the glass.

There was a knock on her door at ten A.M. It was the girl from dinner. "Remember me?" she said. "I'm your seatmate. I wanted to go to the chocolate buffet." She clutched her own hands fiercely. "Who wants to gorge on chocolate alone?"

It was the tyranny of the normal, the attempts of regular people to energize their lives. It was ten in the morning and she could hear the rapid footsteps of the other passengers as they rushed to fill their mouths with sweetness. The girl was insistent and Ginger found herself in the long, winding line. All of the passengers appeared to have risen for this experience. To maintain order, a waiter walked through the crowd, doling out, with silver tongs, chunks of milk chocolate to eager hands. Another waiter, dressed as a Kodiak bear, was offering cups of hot chocolate spiked with rum. Many of the passengers had dressed up — in loose-fitting sweatsuits, draping shirts — to celebrate the impending gluttony. There was a radiant excitement in the air.

Darlene was chatty. "After this I go on a diet," the girl said. "A major one. Celery and water for weeks —"

Ginger knew, suddenly, that she herself would never go on another diet. She pressed her hands to her cheeks, her lips, feeling a terrible fierce love for her body. She wanted all the chocolate, fiercely. All. She moved quickly, placing truffles, chocolate-dipped potato chips, macaroons, chocolate torte, mousse, fudge on her tray. She was so hungry she was in pain.

When they sat down, she looked at the girl and she wanted to convince her of something; she wanted to shout into Darlene's ear.

"I've had better than this," she said. "1968. The Academy Awards party at the Sheraton. Truffles everywhere. I said I was a waitress. I said in my off-hours I was working for Montgomery Clift's mother, who was dying of cancer, and could they please contribute to a cancer fund —" She paused. "They were a nice bunch. Generous. I actually have a high opinion of mankind —"

"Did anyone get mad at you?" asked Darlene.

"Mad?" asked Ginger.

"When they realized that you had taken their money —"

Ginger rose halfway in her seat. "Why would I care?" asked Ginger. "Look. You go to a regular job. They tell you what you're worth. Or Warren. You love him and he leaves you and you feel like you're nothing at all. Darling, I don't have to tell my worth to anyone."

Darlene looked down. The longing in the girl's face was like a bright wound.

"What was so good about him anyway?" asked Ginger.

"He said my eyes were pretty," Darlene said. "He also liked listening to the Cherry Tones. He liked to put his hands in my hair —"

This was the material of love? "So fool him into loving you."

"How?" Darlene stared, desolate, at slices of chocolate cake so glossy they appeared to be ceramic.

"What did he want? Pretend to be it," said Ginger.

"He wanted a million dollars."

"So say you've won the lottery," said Ginger. She bit into a truffle.

"But I didn't."

"No one knows what they want until you show them."

Darlene's face was flushed, excited. "But I want him to love the real me —"

"Who do you think you are?" said Ginger. "No one. We all are. That's what I do, notice no ones —"

"I'm not no one," said Darlene, huffily. "I come from a nice suburb in San Diego. My father is a successful pediatrician —"

"So? That's all temporary," said Ginger. "But the noticing, that's yours."

She had never allowed herself weakness, never told anyone how it felt to walk into a new city, how she chose her new name just as the train slowed down. Everyone rushed by, gnarled and worn down by the burden of thwarted love; she was free of that, new. She would wash up in the station bathroom and walk out, erased of her secrets: the fact that everything she did with a man was faked, so the only way she could feel pleasure was to give it to herself; the fact that her broken right hand had healed crooked because she couldn't afford to see a doctor to fix it; the fact that she often ate alone on holidays. In empty coffee shops on Thanksgiving, Ginger looked at the food on her plate, and she knew a strange, burning love for the things the world offered her, real and surprising, again and again.

Evelyn and Ginger rented a room in a Salvation Army and Evelyn began to weep. She curled up on the hard, stained mattress and cried so hard she screamed. Ginger sat beside her, a hand on her shoulder. Sometimes, she had an urge to laugh. Other moments, she wished she could put her hands around Evelyn's throat and strangle her. She was shocked by the private nature of her emotions, and by the fact that Evelyn seemed to believe she was comforting her.

During the day, they walked down Hollywood Boulevard, trying to decide what to do. Their breath smelled, darkly, of bananas. In the light, Evelyn talked rapidly; they both listened with hope to the sound of her voice.

"We will be cigarette girls," Evelyn announced one afternoon.

They walked into sixteen bars before they found one that had jobs for both of them. Every night the two of them strode in wearing black tights and rhinestone loafers, selling cigarettes to heavy, sad-looking men with liquored breath.

Once, Evelyn told Ginger that she tried not to be afraid for five minutes a day. She was impressed that Evelyn could identify when she was afraid, for her own fear floated just outside her skin, like a cloud; she experienced nothing but a heavy numbness. She watched her sister closely, trying to catch her in those precious five minutes when she was clearly not afraid. In those five minutes, Evelyn owned something mysterious, and even the claim of it made Ginger ache to have what she had.

At home, Evelyn's grief metamorphosed into a bloodthirsty envy of the loved, the parented. She wanted their expensive possessions: the jeweled brooches, the feathered hats.

One night, she leaned close to a man clad in a velvet jacket and said, in a husky, unfamiliar voice, "I have a baby at home."

Ginger, walking by with her tray, stopped.

"He is sick," Evelyn said. "Bad stomach. He needs operation. Look. Please." She brought out a wrinkled photo of some stranger's baby. His mouth was open in anguish. "I need just ten more dollars — he cannot eat —"

"All right," he said. He dug into his pocket and handed her a bill. His face was haughty with a perplexing pity, and Ginger stared at it, awed.

Later, she walked with Ginger down the sidewalk and smoothed the bill, like green velvet, in her hands. "I have a baby at home," she said, laughing. She walked down the street, looking down the crowds of people walking down the street, lifted her hands and said, almost gently, "Fools."

The next morning, Ginger sat in her cabin, looking through the nine photographs that she owned. They were souvenirs from fancy occasions, set in cardboard frames so old they felt like flannel. She had kept them because she liked the way she looked in them, as though she had been enjoying herself.

She heard a knock at the door. It was that girl. "I wondered if you wanted some company. Can I come in?" the girl asked.

Darlene was dressed in imitation of a wealthy person. She wore a sequin-trimmed cashmere sweater that Ginger believed she had seen in the cruise gift shop, a strand of pearls, and a pink velvet blazer. Her shoulders were thrust stiffly backward, giving her the posture of a rooster. The girl's earnest quality shone through her garb like the glow of a light bulb through a lampshade.

"Who are you?" asked Ginger.

"I am his dream."

"No," said Ginger. "Don't try so hard. Wear your usual and add an expensive piece of jewelry. Make him guess why."

Darlene shrugged off her blazer and stepped forward too purposefully, like a salesgirl trying to close a deal.

"I can buy you a Rolls Royce," she said, her voice too bright, to the air.

"No, no! Just hint that you went on a trip to — Paris. The four-star hotels have the best sheets. Nothing he can prove," said Ginger.

Darlene looked at the photos laid out.

"So who are these people?" asked Darlene. "Fill me in."

Ginger stood up and picked up a photo. "Here I am on New Year's Eve, 1965," said Ginger. "The presidential suite at the Century Plaza Hotel." She still could see the way the pink shrimp sat on the ice beds, as though crawling through clean snow. "I lit Frank Sinatra's cigarette," said Ginger. "I lent my lipstick to Marilyn Monroe." She remembered the weight of the sequined dress against her skin, the raucous laughter. "Don't I look happy?" she asked.

"I would be happy," said Darlene.

Ginger's mind moved in her skull and she felt her legs crumble. She grabbed hold of a chair and clung to it.

"Whoa! Are you okay?"

She grasped Darlene's hand and felt her body move thickly to the bed.

"What happened? Should I call a doctor?"

"No," said Ginger sharply. "No."

She let Darlene arrange her into a sitting position, her feet up on the bed. Her arms and legs fell open in the obedient posture of the ill. The girl got her a drink of water from the tap and Ginger sipped it. It was sweet.

"Thank you," Ginger said.

They sat. Ginger picked up another photo. "This was when I met the vice president of MGM and had him convinced I was a duchess from Belgium —"

Darlene frowned. Ginger realized that it was the same picture she had just described. "They were all at the party," she said, quickly, "Sinatra and Marilyn and duchesses. It was in Miami. Brazil. The moon was so white it looked blue —"

Darlene looked at her. "I wish I could have been there," she said. She reached out and briefly touched Ginger's hand.

Ginger looked down at the sight of Darlene's hand on her own. At first, the gesture was so startling she viewed it as though it were a sculpture. Then she could not look at Darlene, for Ginger had tears in her eyes.

When Evelyn and Ginger began to lie, the world broke apart, revealing unearthly, beautiful things. They began with extravagant tales of woe: deformed babies, murdered husbands, terminal illnesses. They constructed Hair-Ray caps for bald men, yarmulkes with thin metal inside so that in the sunlight the men's heads would get hot and they would think they were growing hair. They bought nuns' habits at a costume shop and said they were collecting for the construction of a new church.

She remembered particularly one scam in which she wandered through the cavernous Los Angeles train station with a cardboard sign declaring: HELP. MUTE. HALF-BLIND. When strangers came up to her, she wrote on a chalkboard that had chalk attached to it on a string: HELP ME FIND MY SISTER OUTSIDE. She handed the stranger, usually an elderly lady, her purse, an open straw bag. She let the stranger guide her out the door and carefully fell forward so that an envelope inside the purse fell out. Ginger did not pick it up. Then there was Evelyn, running forward, yelling, "Violet!"

Evelyn looked in the purse and said, "Where's your money?"

IN THE PURSE, Ginger wrote.

They looked at the kindly woman holding the purse. "Did you take my blind sister's money?" Evelyn yelled; that was Ginger's cue to weep.

"I didn't," the hapless stranger would protest, but there she was, holding the purse, with a blind mute weeping beside her; they could get ten, twenty, thirty dollars out of the stranger. When the sucker left, Evelyn would walk Ginger around the corner and hug her.

"Good, Violet," she said.

"Thank you," said Ginger, feeling the solidity of her sister's arms around her, and she closed her eyes and let herself breathe.

When Ginger woke up from her nap the following afternoon, she did not know where she was. The dark afternoon light streamed through the mint blue curtains. She shivered and sat up. She flung open a drawer, looking for clues. The room felt as though it were moving. The room service indicated that they were on a ship. Where were they going? She flung open her curtains and saw mountains covered in ice. Her mind was a crumpled ball of paper. She stood up, abruptly, as though that would straighten her thoughts. The phone rang.

"How are you feeling? Do you want to go to the dinner tonight?"

Her heart slowed at the naturalness of the question, at the caller's belief that Ginger would continue this conversation. She remembered that they were on a cruise to Alaska. She also remembered that the girl had said something kind to her.

The room was decorated to flatter the passengers into believing they were traveling in opulence. There were plaster Roman columns, painted gold, topped with bouquets of roses. The waiters' jackets were adorned in rhinestones that said: ALASKA '03. Ginger kept thinking about what the girl had said the night before — that she had wanted to be at the party that Ginger had attended. Ginger wanted her to say more nice things about her life. Outside the large glass windows, the water and sky, black and clear, surrounded the ship.

Tonight, Darlene's hair was slicked up into a topknot and shone, a metallic blond, in the light. Her eyelids gleamed blue, unearthly.

"How are you?" asked Ginger.

"I just want to say . . . I am someone," said Darlene. She looked dazed. "I am going to graduate with a B average in communications." She sat down. "Listen." She closed her eyes. "I left a message on his answering machine. I said, I'll do anything. Let me. I'll change."

"What?" Ginger asked, alarmed.

"I tried to do what you said," she said. "I know how to fool him. I'll keep calling him. I'll be what you said, generous, you're right, I have been selfish —"

"No," said Ginger. "That's not what I meant —"

The girl stared at her with her reptilian eyes. "Then what do I do?" she said, and her voice was hoarse. "Tell me, what do I do?"

Music exploded from a band gathered near the stage. The audience clapped along. "Let's hear where everyone's from, all at once!" the cruise director called. The room rang with hundreds of voices. Los Angeles. Palm Springs. Ottawa. Denver. Orlando. New York. "Welcome aboard!" the cruise director called. "Time to relax. Shake off those fancy duds. We want to make you all a deal. We need a pair of pants. Someone take off a pair! We'll give you fifty dollars! Come on, you'll never see these people again in your life!"

Ginger did not know what to tell the girl, and the sorrow in her eyes was unnerving. Instead, Ginger turned her attention to the stage. She used to love crowds, the way the people in them became one roar, one sound. But now, for the first time, all the people appeared vulnerable to her. Passengers drifted onto the stage, performing various tricks: singing "God Bless America," attempting to juggle, dancing the rumba. They wanted to take off their pants in front of each other or scream out the names of their home cities; they were confused about their place in the world, and they wanted to be told that they did not deserve it. They had everything in common with her.

Yet everyone on the stage also looked pleased to be up there, happy to be briefly bathed in light. They smiled at the sound of cheering, their faces simple in their hunger for recognition. She did not know what to tell Darlene, and suddenly she envied everyone on the stage. She wanted to be with the others, to have a talent, to simply stand in the clear white light.

Ginger raised her hand. The emcee called on her, and she made her way to the stage. The lights glared hard and white in her eyes. Clutching her purse, she felt the weight of her money in it. "Passengers," she called. They stood like sad soldiers before their futures.

"My name is Ginger Klein and I'm going to make you rich. Give me a dollar," she called. "Everyone. A dollar."

They dug into their pockets and a few brought dollars out. She enjoyed watching them obey her. But what was the next step?

"Catch," she called.

She reached into her purse and pulled out a handful of bills. She threw them into the spangled darkness. There were screams of disbelief, laughter. She dug in her purse and tossed out more. The passengers leapt from their seats and dove for the money. They were unhinged, thrilled, alive. Their screams of joy blossomed inside her. Her purse grew lighter and lighter.

After a while, the emcee strode onto the stage and gently moved her off the stage. "Thank you, Ginger Klein!" he yelled. "Best talent of the night, huh?" She paused, wanting to tell them something more, but did not know what it would be. Applause thundered in her chest; she had, somehow, been successful. She walked slowly down the stairs, looking for Darlene. "Darlene," she said, softly, then louder. "I'm here."

She did not see her. Ginger imagined how the girl would walk, carelessly, off the ship by herself at the end of the week. Darlene would join the living pouring toward the shore, clutching her souvenir ivory penguins and Eskimo dolls, going to her future boyfriends and houses and lawns and exercise classes and book clubs and golf games. "Darlene," she said, wanting to walk down the ramp with her, shading her own eyes against the dazzling sunlight, gripping Darlene's arm.

Sometimes, Ginger could hear Evelyn laughing in her sleep, a harsh, broken sound, and she touched her shoulder, trying to feel the joy that her sister could experience most fully in her dreams.

During the day, Evelyn talked about ordinary people, the loved and loving, with too much scorn; Ginger knew that her sister wanted her life to be like theirs. She believed that Evelyn wanted to get rid of her.

One evening in the bar, Evelyn was talking to a man who claimed to work in the movie industry. His hands jabbed the air with the hard confidence of the insecure. He gazed at Evelyn as though he could see a precious light inside of her, and Ginger watched Evelyn's shoulders tremble, delighted, under his gaze. She told him offhand, that she was an orphan. He leaned toward her and took her hands in his.

"I'll take care of you," he said.

Evelyn went home with him that night. The next day, she met Ginger at their room and said, "I am going to go live with him. He loves me and likes the fact that I have no family." She paused; her face was relieved. "You will have to be a secret."

Ginger looked into Evelyn's eyes and saw that this was the most truthful statement she had made in her life. Her own response was the most deceitful. She nodded. "All right," she said.

Evelyn packed her suitcase and was gone, leaving only a lipstick the color of a rose. Ginger waited. Each morning, she put on a new costume, applied Evelyn's lipstick, and murmured the same false pleas to strangers. Ginger made more money without Evelyn. Strangers could see a new emptiness in her eyes that touched them. After two weeks, she tried, briefly, to find Evelyn. She stood outside the walls of the movie studios, waiting to see the man. Her search paralleled her fantasies of what Evelyn would desire; she waited outside of expensive restaurants, wandered through fancy clubs, but as she rushed past the crowded tables, the patrons' faces bloomed up, monstrous, unknown.

It was three weeks before she saw Evelyn again, at the palisades overlooking the Santa Monica beach. Evelyn walked toward Ginger with a curious lightness in her step. She covered her mouth when she laughed. She flicked her wrist at the end of a sentence, as though trying to toss away her words.

"He loves my hair," Evelyn said. "He loves my laugh. Listen."

The sound made Ginger cold. It was difficult to stand straight; the ground was rising like slow, heavy waves.

"You look well. I have to go," said Evelyn. She backed up, as

Theft

though fearful that Ginger would grab onto her. Then she stopped and pulled a small red purse from her pocket. "Here," said Evelyn. She thrust out a purse. "It has two hundred dollars."

"No," said Ginger, stepping back.

She felt her sister shove the purse into her hands and press her fingers around it. "Just take it. Here."

Evelyn quickly ran toward the bus stop. Ginger understood that this would be the last time she saw her. It would be Ginger's own decision to move and not tell her sister where she was going. She sat down for a long time after the bus had pulled off, eyes closed, imagining that the wide blue sky, the gray elephantine palms would be gone when she opened them. When she looked again, the world was still there; Ginger left the purse on the bench and started walking.

The next morning, when she woke up, she did not remember how the crowd had buffeted her like an ocean, how she had finally found a man in a maroon uniform who helped her find her room, but her legs were weak, as though she'd walked a great distance, and her mouth was dry from calling out Darlene's name.

She was trembling, as though she were extremely hungry. She knew what she wanted to do. She wanted to buy a present for Darlene. She wanted to do this simple action: go into a store, select a gift for her, and buy it. That was all. Ginger stood up, wearing the same dress she had the night before, faint with the scent of smoke and alcohol, and walked slowly to the gift shop.

There she stood, surrounded by the store's offerings: the butterfly-sequined blouses, the china statues of noble wildlife, the authentic replica Eskimo fur hats, the jars of glacier-blue rock candy.

"May I help you?" the girl at the counter asked.

Ginger selected a large opal brooch set in a gold snowflake. It was three hundred dollars.

"Beautiful taste," the salesgirl said.

"Hey," said a voice. It was Darlene. "I've been looking all over for you."

The girl stood before her. Ginger put down the brooch.

"Are you all right?" asked Darlene. "Who's that for?" she said, glancing at the brooch.

Ginger looked at her. "You," she said.

"That will be three hundred and fifteen dollars and seventy-three cents," said the salesgirl.

Ginger put her hand into her red velvet purse. There was nothing in it but the silk lining. She shook out her purse. Now she had one dollar and thirty-seven cents.

"I have no money," she said, softly.

"Is it in your room?" the salesgirl asked.

"This is all I have," Ginger said.

She pushed her hand deep into the purse, feeling its emptiness. Her coins fell onto the floor. "You don't have to buy me anything," said Darlene.

The lights were too bright, as though someone had turned them all on at once.

"I want to buy it," said Ginger. "Don't you understand? I want to."

She stood, swaying a little, aggravated that Darlene did not recognize her goodness. Darlene squinted at her, as though Ginger had begun to disappear.

"What are you looking at?" she asked Darlene. She lurched toward her. "What?"

"Hold on," said Darlene, looking at the salesgirl. "I'll be right back." She backed up and began to hurry down the hallway.

"Where is she going?" asked Ginger. She stepped toward the door. Then Ginger went into the hallway and began to follow her.

An elderly couple floated toward her. The woman wore a white brimmed sunhat and the man wore a camera around his neck. "Thief," Ginger whispered. She passed the maid clutching armfuls of crumpled sheets. "Thief," she said. The maid turned around. Ginger began to walk onto the deck, the sunlight brilliant and cold on her arms. She staggered through the crowd in their pale sweatsuits. "Thief!" she yelled. She believed one side of her was becoming heavy. Her heart banged in her throat. Her voice was flat and loud. She heard the jingle of ice cubes in people's drinks. "My money!" she yelled. Her voice was guttural, unrecognizable to her. "Give me my money!"

The girl was running up to her.

"Thief," she yelled.

The girl blinked. "What?" she asked.

"Thief," said Ginger. She wanted to say the word over and over.

Ginger's face was warm; she was exhilarated by the act of accusation. She had forgotten the girl's name. It had simply disappeared from her. "I know who you are." Her knees buckled. The girl grabbed her arm.

"Call a doctor!" the girl yelled. "Quick."

The ocean was moving by very quickly, and Ginger stared, unblinking, at the bright water until she was unsure whether she was on the deck looking at the water or in the water looking up at the light.

The girl's firm grip made her feel calmer. Ginger did not remember her name, did not know who this friend was, did not know who had loved her and whom she had loved. She leaned toward the glaring blue world, the water and ice and sky and she felt as though she were part of it.

"You're not what you say," murmured the girl. "I don't believe you. You're not a swindler. You're a nice old lady. It was all a joke, wasn't it —"

Ginger breathed more slowly and clutched the girl's arm. She saw everything in that moment: saw the trees on the shore giving up their leaves to the aqua sky, the ocean shimmering into white cloud, and the passengers' breath becoming rain. She felt the vibrations of the ship's motor in her throat. She stood, with the other passengers, looking. Through the clear, chill water, the ship moved north.

C. J. BOX

Pirates of Yellowstone

FROM *Meeting Across the River*

IT WAS COLD in Yellowstone Park in early June, and dirty tongues of snow glowed light blue in the timber from the moonlight. The tires of the van hissed by on the road.

"Look," Vladdy said to Eddie, gesturing out the window at the ghostly forms emerging in the meadow, "elks."

"I see 'em every night," the driver said. "They like to eat the willows. And you don't say 'elks.' You say 'elk.' Like in 'a herd of elk.'"

"My pardon," Vladdy said, self-conscious.

The driver of the van was going from Mammoth Hot Springs in the northern part of the park to Cody, Wyoming, out the east entrance. He had told them he had to pick up some people at the Cody airport early in the morning and deliver them to a dude ranch. The driver was one of those middle-aged Americans who dressed and acted like it was 1968, Vladdy thought.

The driver thought he was cool, giving a ride to Vladdy and Eddie, who obviously looked cold and out of place and carried a thick metal briefcase and nothing else. The driver had long curly hair on the side of his head with a huge mustache that was turning gray. He had agreed to give them a ride after they waved him down on the side of the road. The driver lit up a marijuana cigarette and offered it to them as he drove. Eddie accepted. Vladdy declined. He wanted to keep his head clear for what was going to happen when they crossed the huge park and came out through the tunnels and crossed the river. Vladdy had not done business in America yet, and he knew that Americans could be tough and ruthless in business. It was one of the qualities that had attracted Vladdy in the first place.

"Don't get too high," Vladdy told Eddie in Czech.

"I won't," Eddie said back. "I'm just a little scared, if that's all right with you. This helps."

"I wish you wouldn't wear that hat," Vladdy said. "You don't look professional."

"I look like Marshall Mathers, I think. Slim Shady," Eddie said, touching the stocking cap that was pulled over his eyebrows. He sounded a little hurt.

"Hey, dudes," the driver said over his shoulder to his passengers in the back seat, "speak American or I'm dropping you off on the side of the road. Deal?"

"Of course," Vladdy said, "we have deal."

"You going to tell me what's in the briefcase?" The driver asked, smiling to show that he wasn't making a threat.

"No, I think not," Vladdy said.

Vladimir and Eduard were branded "Vladdy" and "Eddie" by the man in the human resources office for Yellowstone in Gardiner, Montana, when they showed up to apply for work three weeks before and were told that there were no job openings. Vladdy had explained that there must have been some kind of mix-up, some kind of misunderstanding, because they had been assured by the agent in Prague that both of them had been accepted to work for the official park concessionaire for the whole summer and into the fall. Vladdy showed the paperwork that allowed them to work on a visa for six months.

Yellowstone, like a microcosm of America, was a place of wonders, and it sought Eastern Europeans to work making beds, washing dishes, and cleaning out the muck from the trail horses, jobs that American workers didn't want or need. Many Czechs Vladdy and Eddie knew had come here, and some had stayed. It was good work in a fantastic place, "a setting from a dream of nature," as Vladdy put it. But the man at human resources said he was sorry, that they were overstaffed, and that there was nothing he could do until somebody quit and a slot opened up. Even if that happened, the nonhiring man said, there were people on the list in front of them.

Vladdy had explained in his almost-perfect English, he thought, that he and Eddie didn't have the money to go back. In fact, he told the man, they didn't even have the money for a room to wait in. What they had was on their backs — cracked black leather jackets, ill-fitting clothes, street shoes. Eddie wore the stocking cap because he liked Eminem, but Vladdy preferred his slicked-back hair look. They looked nothing like the other young people their age they saw in the office and on the streets.

"Keep in touch," the hiring man had told Vladdy. "Check back every few days."

"I can't even buy cigarettes," Vladdy had pleaded.

The man felt sorry for them and gave them a twenty-dollar bill out of his own wallet.

"I told you we should have gone to Detroit," Eddie said to Vladdy in Czech.

Vladdy pressed his forehead against the cold glass of the van window as they drove. The metal briefcase was on the floor, between his legs.

He had not yet seen the whole park since he had been here, and it was something he very much wanted to do. He had read about the place since he was young and watched documentaries on it on television. He knew there were three kinds of thermal activity: geysers, mud pots, and fumaroles. He knew there were over ten thousand places where the molten core of the earth broke through the thin crust. He knew that the park was the home of bison, elk, mountain sheep, and many fishes. People from all over the world came here to see it, smell it, feel it. Vladdy was still outside of it, though, looking in, like Yellowstone Park was still on a television show and not right in front of him. He wouldn't allow himself to become a part of this place yet. That would come later.

Eddie was talking to the driver, talking too much, Vladdy thought. Eddie's English was very poor. It was embarrassing. Eddie was telling the driver about Prague, about the beautiful women there. The driver said he always wanted to go to Prague. Eddie tried to describe the buildings but was doing a bad job of it.

"I don't care about buildings," the driver said. "Tell me about the women."

*

The girl, Cherry, would be angry with him at first, Vladdy knew that. While she was at work at the motel that day, Vladdy had sold her good stereo and DVD unit to a man in a pawn shop full of rifles for $115, less $90 for a .22 pistol with a broken handgrip. But when she found out why he had done it, he was sure she would come around. The whole thing was kind of her idea in the first place, after all.

Vladdy and Eddie had spent that first unhappy day after meeting the nonhiring man in a place called K-Bar Pizza in Gardiner, Montana. They sat at a round table and were so close to the human resources building that when the door to the K-Bar opened they could see it out there. Vladdy had placed the twenty-dollar bill on the table and ordered two tap beers, which they both agreed were awful. Then they ordered a Budweiser, which was nothing like the Czechoslovakian Budweiser, and they laughed about that. Cherry was their waitress. She told Vladdy she was from Kansas, some place like that. He could tell she was uncomfortable with herself, with her appearance, because she was a little fat and had a crooked face. She told Vladdy she was divorced, with a kid, and she worked at the K-Bar to supplement her income. She also had a job at a motel, servicing rooms. He could tell she was flattered by his attention, by his leather jacket, his hair, his smile, his accent. Sometimes women reacted this way to him, and he appreciated it. He didn't know if his looks would work in America, and he still didn't know. But they worked in Gardiner, Montana. Vladdy knew he had found a friend when she let them keep ordering even though the twenty dollars was spent, and she didn't discourage them from staying until her shift was over.

Cherry led them down the steep, cracked sidewalks and down an alley to an old building backed up to the edge of a canyon. Vladdy looked around as he followed. He didn't understand Gardiner. In every direction he looked, he could see only space. Mountains, bare hillsides, an empty valley going north, under the biggest sky he had ever seen. Yet Gardiner was packed together. Houses almost touched houses, windows opened up to other windows. It was like a tiny island in an ocean of . . . nothing. Vladdy decided he would find out about this.

She made them stand in the hallway while she went in to check to make sure her little boy was in bed, then she let them sleep in the front room of her two-bedroom apartment. That first night, Vladdy waited until Eddie was snoring and then he padded across the linoleum floor in his bare feet and opened Cherry's bedroom door. She was pretending she was asleep, and he said nothing, just stood there in his underwear.

"What do you want?" Cherry asked him sleepily.

"I want to pleasure you," he whispered.

"Don't turn on the light," she said. "I don't want you to look at me."

Afterward, in the dark, Vladdy could hear the furious river below them in the canyon. It sounded so raw, like an angry young river trying to figure out what it wanted to be when it grew up.

While Eddie and Vladdy checked back with the nonhiring man every morning, Vladdy tried to help out around the house since he had no money for rent. He tried to fix the dripping faucet but couldn't find any tools in the apartment besides an old pair of pliers and something cheap designed to slice potatoes. He mopped the floors, though, and washed her windows. He fixed her leaking toilet with the pliers. While he did this, Eddie sat on the couch and watched television, MTV mostly. Cherry's kid, Tony, sat with Eddie and watched and wouldn't even change out of his pajamas and get dressed unless Vladdy told him to do so.

Vladdy was taking the garbage out to the Dumpster when he first saw Cherry's neighbor, a man whose name he later learned was Bob. Vladdy thought it was funny, and very American, to have a one-syllable name like "Bob." It made him laugh inside.

Bob pulled up to the building in a dark, massive four-wheel-drive car. The car was mud-splashed, scratched, and dented, even though it didn't look very old. It was a huge car, and Vladdy recognized it as a Suburban. Vladdy watched as Bob came out of the car. Bob had a hard, impatient look on his face. He wore dirty blue jeans, a sweatshirt, a fleece vest, and a baseball cap, like everyone else did in Gardiner.

Bob stepped away from the back of the Suburban, slammed both doors, and locked it with a remote. That's when Vladdy first saw the metal briefcase. It was the briefcase Bob was retrieving from the back of the Suburban.

And with that, Bob went into the building.

That night, after Eddie and Tony had gone out to bring back fried chicken from the deli at the grocery store for dinner, Vladdy asked Cherry about her neighbor, Bob. He described the metal briefcase.

"I'd stay away from him, if I was you," Cherry said. "I've got my suspicions about that Bob."

Vladdy was confused.

"I hear things at the K-Bar," Cherry said. "I seen him in there a couple of times by himself. He's not the friendliest guy I've ever met."

"He's not like me," Vladdy said, reaching across the table and brushing a strand of her hair out of her eyes.

Cherry sat back in the chair and studied Vladdy. "No, he's not like you," she said.

After pleasuring Cherry, Vladdy waited until she was asleep before he crept through the dark front room where Eddie was sleeping. Vladdy found a flashlight in a drawer in the kitchen and slipped outside into the hallway. He went down the stairs in his underwear, went outside, and approached the back of the Suburban.

Turning on the flashlight, he saw rumpled clothing, rolls of maps, hiking boots, and electrical equipment with dials and gauges. He noticed a square of open carpet where the metal briefcase sat when Bob wasn't carrying it around. He wondered if Bob wasn't some kind of engineer, or a scientist of some kind. He wondered where it was that Bob went every day to do his work, and what he kept in the metal briefcase that couldn't be left with the rest of his things.

Vladdy had taken classes in geology and geography and chemistry. He had done well in them, and he wondered if maybe Bob needed some help, needed an assistant. At least until a job opened up in the park.

Cherry surprised them by bringing two bottles of Jack Daniel's home after her shift at the K-Bar, and they had whiskey on ice while they ate Lean Cuisine dinners. They kept drinking afterward at the table. Vladdy suspected that Cherry had stolen the bottles from behind the bar but said nothing because he was enjoying himself and he wanted to ask her about Bob. Eddie was getting pretty drunk and was telling funny stories in Czech that Cherry and Tony didn't understand. But the way he told them made everyone laugh. Tony said he wanted a drink, too, and Eddie started to pour him one until Vladdy told Eddie not to do it. Eddie took his own drink to the couch, sulking, the evening ruined for him, he said.

"Cherry," Vladdy said, "I feel bad inside that I cannot pay rent."

Cherry waved him off. "You pay the rent in other ways," she laughed. "My floor and windows have never been cleaner. Not to mention your other . . . services."

Vladdy looked over his shoulder to make sure Tony hadn't heard his mother.

"I am serious," Vladdy said, trying to make her look him in the eyes. "I'm a serious man. Because I don't have a job yet, I want to work. I wonder maybe if your neighbor Bob needs an apprentice in his work. Somebody who would get mud on himself if Bob doesn't want to."

Cherry shook her head and smiled, and took a long time to answer. She searched Vladdy's face for something that Vladdy hoped his face had. When she finally spoke, her voice was low, for a change. She leaned her head forward, toward Vladdy.

"I told you I'd heard some things about Bob at the K-Bar," she said softly. "I heard that Bob is a bio pirate. He's a criminal."

"What is this bio pirate?"

He could smell her whiskey breath, but he bent closer. "In Yellowstone, in some of the hot pots and geysers, there are rare microorganisms that can only be found here. Our government is studying some of them legitimately, trying to find out if they could be a cure for cancer, or maybe a bioweapon, or whatever. It's illegal to take them out of the park. But the rumor is there are some people stealing the microbes and selling them. You know, bio pirates."

Vladdy sat back for a moment to think. Her eyes burned into his as they never had before. It was the whiskey, sure, but it was something else.

"The metal briefcase," Vladdy whispered. "That's where he keep the microbes."

Cherry nodded enthusiastically. "Who knows what they're worth? Or better yet, who knows what someone would pay us to give them back and not say anything about it?"

Vladdy felt a double-edged chill, of both excitement and fear. This Cherry, he thought, she didn't just come up with this. She had been thinking about it for a while.

"Next time he's at the K-Bar, I'll call you," she said. "He doesn't bring his briefcase with him there. He keeps it next door, in his apartment, when he goes out at night. That's where it will be when I call you."

"Hey," Tony called from the couch, "what are you two whispering about over there?"

"They talk *fornication*," Eddie said with a slur, making Tony laugh. As far as Vladdy knew, it was Eddie's first American sentence.

Vladdy was wiping the counter clean with Listerine — he loved Listerine and thought it was the best disinfectant in the entire world — when the telephone rang. A bolt shot up his spine. He looked around. Eddie and Tony were watching television.

It was Cherry. "He's here at the K-Bar, and he ordered a pitcher just for himself. He's settling in for a while."

"Settling in?" Vladdy asked, not understanding.

"Jesus," she said. "I mean he'll be here for a while. Which means his briefcase is in his apartment. Come on, Vladdy."

"I understand," Vladdy said.

"Get over there," Cherry said. "I love you."

Vladdy had thought about this, the fact that he didn't love Cherry. He liked her, he appreciated her kindness, he felt obligated to her, but he didn't love her at all. So he used a phrase he had heard in the grocery store.

"You bet," he said.

Hanging up, he asked Eddie to take Tony to the grocery store and get him some ice cream. Eddie winked at Vladdy as they left, because Vladdy had told Eddie about the bio pirates.

The metal briefcase wasn't hard to find, and the search was much easier than shinnying along a two-inch ridge of brick outside the window in his shiny street shoes with the mad river roaring somewhere in the dark beneath him. He was happy that Bob's outside window slid open easily, and he stepped through the open window into Bob's kitchen sink, cracking a dirty plate with his heel.

It made some sense that the metal case was in the refrigerator, on large shelf of its own, and he pulled it out by the handle, which was cold.

Back in Cherry's apartment, he realized he was still shivering, and it wasn't from the temperature outside. But he opened the briefcase on the kitchen table. Yes, there were glass vials filled with murky water. Cherry was right. And in the inside of the top of the briefcase was a taped business card. There was Bob's name and a cell phone number on the business card.

Vladdy poured the last of the Jack Daniel's that Cherry had stolen into a water glass and drank most of it. He waited until the burn developed in his throat before he dialed.

"What?" Bob answered. Vladdy pictured Bob sitting at a table in the K-Bar. He wondered if Cherry was watching.

"I have an important briefcase, full of water samples," Vladdy said, trying to keep his voice deep and level. "I found it in your flat."

"Who in the hell are *you*? How did you get my number?"

Vladdy remembered a line from an American movie he saw at home. "I am your worst nightmare," he said. It felt good to say it.

"Where are you from that you talk like that?" Bob asked. "How in the hell did you get into my apartment?"

Vladdy didn't answer. He didn't know what to say.

"Damn it," Bob said, "what do you want?"

Vladdy breathed deeply, tried to stay calm. "I want two thousand dollars for your metal briefcase, and I won't say a word about it to anyone."

"Two thousand?" Bob said, in a dismissive way that instantly made Vladdy wish he had asked for ten thousand, or twenty thousand. "I don't have that much cash on me. I'll have to get it in Cody tomorrow, at my bank."

"Yes, that would be fine," Vladdy said.

Silence. Thinking. Vladdy could hear something in the background, probably the television above the bar.

"Okay," Bob said. "Meet me tomorrow night at eleven P.M. on the turnout after the tunnels on the Buffalo Bill Dam. East entrance, on the way to Cody. Don't bring anybody with you, and don't tell anyone about this conversation. If you do, I'll know."

Vladdy felt an icy hand reach down his throat and grip his bowels. This was real, after all. This was American business, and he was committed. *Stay tough,* he told himself.

"I have a partner," Vladdy said. "He comes with me."

More silence. Then a sigh. "Him only," the man said. "No one else."

"Okay."

"I'll be in a dark Suburban, parked in the turnout."

"Okay." Vladdy knew the vehicle, of course, but he couldn't give that away.

"If you show up with more than your partner, or if there are any other vehicles on the road, this deal is over. And I mean over in the worst possible sense. You understand?"

Vladdy paused, and the telephone nearly slipped out of his sweaty hand like a bar of soap.

"Okay," Vladdy said. When he hung up the telephone it rattled so hard in the cradle from his hand that it took him two tries.

Vladdy and Eddie sat in silence on the couch and listened as Bob crashed around in his apartment next door. Had Vladdy left any clues next door, he wondered? Eddie looked scared and had the broken .22 pistol on his lap. After an hour, the crashing stopped. Vladdy and Eddie watched Cherry's door, praying that Bob wouldn't realize they were there and smash through it.

"I think we're okay," Vladdy said, finally. "He doesn't know who took it."

Vladdy kept his cheek pressed against the cold window as they left Yellowstone Park. He closed his eyes temporarily as the van rumbled through the east entrance, then opened them and noted the sign that read ENTERING SHOSHONE NATIONAL FOREST.

Eddie was still talking, still smoking. He had long ago worked his way into the front so he sat next to the driver. A second marijuana cigarette had been passed back and forth. The driver was talking about democracy versus socialism and was for the latter. Vladdy thought the driver was an idiot, an idiot who pined for a forgotten political system that had never, ever worked, and a system that

Vladdy despised. But Vladdy said nothing, because Eddie wouldn't stop talking, wouldn't quit agreeing with the driver.

They went through three tunnels lit by orange ambient light, and Vladdy stared through the glass. The Shoshone River serpentined below them, reflecting the moonlight. They crossed it on a bridge.

"Let us off here," Vladdy said, as they cleared the last tunnel and the reservoir sparkled beneath the moon and starlight to the right as far as he could see.

The driver slowed, then turned around in his seat. "Are you sure?" he asked. "There's nothing out here except for the dam. It's another half-hour to Cody and not much in between."

"This is our place," Vladdy said. "Thank you for the drive."

The van braked and stopped.

"Are you sure?" the driver asked.

"Pay him, Eddie," Vladdy said, sliding across the seat toward the door with the metal briefcase. He listened vaguely as the driver insisted he needed no payment and as Eddie tried to stuff a twenty in the driver's pocket. Which he did, eventually, and the van pulled away en route to Cody, which was a cream-colored smudge in the distance, like an inverted half-moon against the dark eastern sky.

"What now?" Eddie asked, and Vladdy and Eddie walked along the dark shoulder of the road, crunching gravel beneath their shoes.

"Now?" Vladdy said in English, "I don't know. You've got the gun in your pants, right? You may need to use it as a threat. You've got it, right?" Eddie did a hitch in his step, as he dug through his coat. "I got it, Vladdy," Eddie said, "but it is small."

Vladdy's teeth began to chatter as they approached the pullout and he saw the Suburban. The vehicle was parked on the far side of the lot, backed up against the railing of the dam. The car was dark.

"Are you scared?" Eddie asked. He was still high.

"Just cold," Vladdy lied.

Vladdy's legs felt weak, and he concentrated on walking forward toward the big car.

Vladdy said, "Don't smile at him. Look tough."

"*Tough*," Eddie repeated.

Vladdy said to Eddie, "I told you to look professional but you look like Eminem."

"Slim Shady is my *man*," Eddie whined.

At twenty yards, the headlights blinded them. Vladdy put his arm up to shield his eyes. Then the headlights went out and he heard a car door open and slam shut. He couldn't see anything now but heard fast-moving footfalls coming across the gravel.

Vladdy's eyes readjusted to the darkness in time to see Bob raise a pistol and shoot Eddie point-blank in the forehead, right through his stocking cap. Eddie dropped straight down as if his legs had been kicked out from under him, and he landed in a heap.

"Some fuckin' nightmare," Bob said, pointing the pistol at Vladdy. "Where are you boys *from*?"

Instinctively, Vladdy fell back. As he did so, he raised the metal briefcase and felt a shock through his hand and arm as a bullet smashed into it. On the ground, Vladdy heard a cry and realized that it had come from inside of him. He thrashed and rolled away, and Bob cursed and fired another booming shot into the dirt near Vladdy's ear.

Vladdy leaped forward and swung the briefcase as hard as he could, and by pure chance it hit hard into Bob's kneecaps. Bob grunted and pitched forward, nearly onto Vladdy. In the dark, Vladdy had no idea where Bob's gun was, but he scrambled to his feet and clubbed at Bob with the briefcase.

Bob said, "Stop!" but all Vladdy could see was the muzzle flash on Eddie's face a moment before.

"Stop! I've got the —" Vladdy smashed the briefcase down as hard as he could and stopped the sentence. Bob lay still.

Breathing hard, Vladdy dropped the briefcase and fell on top of Bob. He tore through Bob's clothing and found the gun that shot Eddie. Bob moaned, and Vladdy shot him in the eye with it.

With tears streaming down his face, Vladdy buckled Eddie's and Bob's belts together and rolled them off of the dam. He heard the bodies thump onto some rocks and then splash into the reservoir. He threw the pistol as far as he could and it went into the water with a *ploop*. The briefcase followed.

He found a vinyl bag on the front seat of the Suburban that bulged with two thousand dollars in cash. It puzzled Vladdy for a moment, but then it made sense. Bob had flashed his lights to see who had taken his briefcase. When he saw two out-of-place guys like Vladdy and Eddie — *especially* Eddie — Bob made his choice not to pay.

Vladdy drove back through Yellowstone Park in the Suburban, thinking of Eddie, thinking of what he had done. He would buy some new clothes, new shoes, one of those fleece vests. Get a baseball cap, maybe.

He parked on a pullout on the northern shore of Yellowstone Lake and watched the sun come up. Steam rose from hot spots along the bank, and a V of Canada geese made a long graceful descent onto the surface of the water.

He felt a part of it, now.

A setting from a dream of nature, he thought.

JAMES LEE BURKE

Why Bugsy Siegel Was a Friend of Mine

FROM *The Southern Review*

IN 1947 NICK HAUSER AND I had only two loves in this world — baseball and Cheerio yo-yo contests. That's how we met Benny, one spring night after a doubleheader out at Buffalo Stadium on the Galveston Freeway. His brand-new Ford convertible, a gleaming maroon job with a starch-white top, whitewall tires, and blue-dot taillights, was stuck in a sodden field behind the bleachers. Benny was trying to lift the bumper while his girlfriend floored the accelerator, spinning the tires and blowing streams of muddy water and torn grass back in his face.

He wore a checkered sports coat, lavender shirt, hand-painted necktie, and two-tone shoes, all of it now whipsawed with mud. But it was his eyes, not his clothes, that you remembered. They were a radiant blue and literally sparkled.

"You punks want to earn two bucks each?" he said.

"Who you calling a punk?" Nick said.

Before Benny could answer, his girlfriend shifted into reverse, caught traction, and backed over his foot.

He hopped up and down, holding one shin, trying to bite down on his pain, his eyes lifted heavenward, his lips moving silently.

"Get in the fucking car before it sinks in this slop again!" his girlfriend yelled.

He limped to the passenger side. A moment later they fishtailed across the grass past us. Her hair was long, blowing out the window, the pinkish red of a flamingo. She thumbed a hot cigarette into the darkness.

"Boy, did you check out that babe's bongos? Wow!" Nick said.

But our evening encounter with Benny and his girlfriend was not over. We were on the shoulder of the freeway, trying to hitch a ride downtown, flicking our Cheerios under a streetlamp, doing a whole range of upper-level yo-yo tricks — Round the World, Shoot the Moon, Rock the Cradle, and the Atomic Bomb — when the maroon convertible roared past us, blowing dust and newspaper in our faces.

Suddenly the convertible cut across two lanes of traffic, made a U-turn, then a second U-turn, horns blowing all over the freeway, and braked to a stop abreast of us.

"You know who I am?" Benny said.

"No," I replied.

"My name is Benjamin Siegel."

"You're a gangster," Nick said.

"He's got you, Benny," the woman behind the wheel said.

"How you know that?" Benny said.

"We heard your name on *Gangbusters*. Nick and me listen every Saturday night," I said.

"Can you do the Chinese Star?" he asked.

"We do Chinese Stars in our sleep," Nick said.

"Get in," Benny said, pulling back the leather seat.

"We got to get home," I said.

"We'll take you there. Get in," he said.

We drove out South Main, past Rice University and parklike vistas dense with live oak trees, some of them hung with Spanish moss. To the south, heat lightning flickered over the Gulf of Mexico. Benny bought us fried chicken and ice cream at Bill Williams Drive-In, and while we ate, his girlfriend smoked cigarettes behind the wheel and listened to the radio, her thoughts known only to herself, her face so soft and lovely in the dash light I felt something drop inside me when I stole a look at it.

Benny popped open the glove box and removed a top-of-the-line chartreuse Cheerio yo-yo. Behind the yo-yo I could see the steel surfaces of a semiautomatic pistol. "Now show me the Chinese Star," he said.

He stood with us in the middle of the drive-in parking lot, watching Nick and me demonstrate the intricate patterns of the most difficult of all the Cheerio competition tricks. Then he tried it himself. His yo-yo tilted sideways, its inner surfaces brushing against the string, then twisted on itself and went dead.

"The key is candle wax," I said.

"Candle wax?" he said.

"Yeah, you wrap the string around a candle and saw it back and forth. That gives you the spin and the time you need to make the pattern for the star," I said.

"I never thought of that," he said.

"It's a breeze," Nick said.

"Benny, give it a rest," his girlfriend said from inside the car.

Fifteen minutes later we dropped off Nick at his house on the dead-end street where I used to be his neighbor. It was a wonderful street, one of trees and flowers and old brick homes, and a horse pasture dotted with live oaks beyond the canebrake that enclosed the cul-de-sac. But when my father died my mother and I were evicted, and we moved across Westheimer and took up residence in a neighborhood where every sunrise broke on the horizon like a testimony to personal failure.

Benny's girlfriend pulled to a stop in front of my house. Benny looked at the broken porch and orange rust on the screens. "This is where you live?" he asked.

"Yeah," I said, my eyes leaving his.

He nodded. "You need to study hard, make something of yourself. Go out to California, maybe. It's the place to be," he said.

Our next-door neighbors were the Dunlops. They had skin like pig hide and heads with the knobbed ridges of coconuts. The oldest of the five boys was executed in Huntsville Pen; one did time on Sugarland Farm. The patriarch of the family was a security guard at the Southern Pacific train yards. He covered all the exterior surfaces of his house, garage, and tool shed with the yellow paint he stole from his employer. The Dunlops even painted their car with it. Then, through a fluke no one could have anticipated, they became rich.

One of the girls had married a morphine addict who came from an oil family in River Oaks. The girl and her husband drove their Austin-Healey head-on into a bus outside San Antonio, and the Dunlops inherited two hundred thousand dollars and a huge chunk of rental property in their own neighborhood. It was like giving a tribe of pygmies a nuclear weapon.

I thought the Dunlops would move out of their dilapidated two-story frame house, with its piles of dog shit all over the backyard, but instead they bought a used Cadillac from a mortuary, covered their front porch with glitter-encrusted chalk animals and icons from an amusement park, and continued each morning to piss out the attic window onto my mother's car, which looked like it had contracted scabies.

As newly empowered landlords, the Dunlops cut no one any slack, did no repairs on their properties, and evicted a Mexican family who had lived in the neighborhood since the middle of the Depression. Mr. Dunlop also seized upon an opportunity to repay the parochial school Nick and I attended for expelling two of his sons.

Maybe it was due to the emotional deprivation and the severity of the strictures imposed upon them, or the black habits they wore in ninety-degree humidity, but a significant number of the nuns at school were inept and cruel. Sister Felicie, however, was not one of these. She was tall and wore steel-rimmed glasses and small black shoes that didn't seem adequate to support her height. When I spent almost a year in bed with rheumatic fever, she came every other day to the house with my lessons, walking a mile, sometimes in the hottest of weather, her habit powdered with ash from a burned field she had to cross.

But things went south for Sister Felicie. We heard that her father, a senior army officer, was killed on Okinawa. Some said the soldier was not her father but the fiancé she had given up when she entered the convent. Regardless, at the close of the war a great sadness seemed to descend upon her.

In the spring of '47 she would take her science class on walks through the neighborhood, identifying trees, plants, and flowers along the way. Then, just before 3 P.M., we would end up at Costen's Drug Store, and she would let everyone take a rest break on the benches under the awning. It was a grand way to end the school day because on some afternoons the Cheerio yo-yo man would arrive at exactly 3:05 and hold competitions on the corner.

But one day, just after the dismissal bell had rung across the street, I saw Sister Felicie walk into the alleyway between the drug store and Cobb's Liquors and give money to a black man who had an empty eye socket. A few minutes later I saw her upend a small bottle of fortified wine, what hobos used to call short-dogs, then drop it surreptitiously into a trash can.

She turned and realized I had been watching her. She walked toward me, between the old brick walls of the buildings, her small shoes clicking on pieces of gravel and bottle caps and broken glass, her face stippled with color inside her wimple. "Why aren't you waxing your string for the Cheerio contest?" she said.

"It hasn't started yet, Sister," I replied, avoiding her look, trying to smile.

"Better run on now," she said.

"Are you all right, Sister?" I said, then wanted to bite off my tongue.

"Of course I'm all right. Why do you ask?"

"No reason. None. I just don't think too good sometimes, Sister. You know me. I was just —"

But she wasn't listening now. She walked past me toward the red light at the corner, her habit and beads swishing against my arm. She smelled like camphor and booze and the lichen in the alley she had bruised under her small shoes.

Two days later the same ritual repeated itself. Except this time Sister Felicie didn't empty just one short-dog and head for the convent. I saw her send the black man back to Cobb's for two more bottles, then she sat down on a rusted metal chair at the back of the alley, a book spread on her knees as though she were reading, the bottles on the ground barely hidden by the hem of her habit.

That's when Mr. Dunlop and his son Vernon showed up. Vernon was seventeen and by law could not be made to attend school. That fact was a gift from God to the educational system of southwest Houston. Vernon had half-moon scars on his knuckles, biceps the size of small muskmelons, and deep-set simian eyes that focused on other kids with the moral sympathies of an electric drill.

Mr. Dunlop was thoroughly enjoying himself. First, he announced to everyone within earshot he was the owner of the entire corner, including the drug store. He told the Cheerio yo-yo man to beat it and not come back, then told the kids to either buy something inside the store or get off the benches they were loitering on.

His face lit like a jack-o'-lantern's when he saw Sister Felicie emerge from the alley. She was trying to stand straight, and not doing a very good job of it, one hand touching the brick wall of the drug store, a drop of sweat running from the top edge of her wimple down the side of her nose.

"Looks like you got a little bit of the grog in you, Sister," Mr. Dunlop said.

"What were you saying to the children?" she asked.

"Oh, her ladyship wants to know that, does she? Why don't we have a conference with the pastor and hash it out?" Mr. Dunlop said.

"Do as you wish," Sister replied, then walked to the red light with the cautious steps of someone aboard a pitching ship.

Mr. Dunlop dropped a buffalo nickel into a pay phone, an unlit cigarette in the corner of his mouth. His head was shaved bald, his brow knurled, one eye recessed and glistening with pleasure when someone picked up on the other end. "Father?" Mr. Dunlop said.

His son Vernon squeezed his scrotum and shot us the bone.

The Cheerio yo-yo man did not come back to the corner and Sister Felicie disappeared from school for a week. Then one Monday morning she was back in class, looking joyless and glazed, as though she had just walked out of an ice storm.

That afternoon Benny and his girlfriend pulled into my driveway while I was picking up the trash Vernon and his brothers had thrown out of their attic window into the yard. "I can't get the Atomic Bomb right. Get in the car. We'll pick up your friend on the way out," he said.

"Way where?" I said.

"The Shamrock. You want to go swimming and have some eats, don't you?" he said.

"I'll leave my mom a note," I said.

"Tell her to come out and join us."

That definitely will not flush, I thought, but did not say it.

Benny had said he couldn't pull off the yo-yo trick called the Atomic Bomb. The truth was he couldn't even master Walk the Dog. In fact, I couldn't figure why a man with his wealth and criminal reputation would involve himself so intensely with children's games. After Nick and I went swimming, we sat on the balcony of Benny's suite, high above the clover-shaped pool of the Shamrock Hotel, and tried to show him the configurations of the Atomic Bomb. It was a disaster. He would spread the string between his fingers, then drop the yo-yo through the wrong spaces, knotting the string, rendering it useless. He danced up and down on the balls of his feet in frustration.

"There's something wrong with this yo-yo. I'm gonna go back to the guy who sold it to me and stuff it down his throat," he said.

"He's full of shit, kids," his girlfriend said through the open bathroom door.

"Don't listen to that. You're looking at the guy who almost blew up Mussolini," he said to us. Then he yelled through the French doors into the suite, "Tell me I'm full of shit one more time."

"You're full of shit," she yelled back.

"That's what you got to put up with," he said to us. "Now, teach me the Atomic Bomb."

Blue-black clouds were piled from the horizon all the way to the top of the sky, blooming with trees of lightning that made no sound. Across the street we could see oil rigs pumping in an emerald green pasture and a half dozen horses starting to spook at the weather. Benny's girlfriend came out of the bathroom, dressed in new jeans and a black and maroon cowboy shirt with a silver stallion on the pocket. She drank from a vodka collins, and her mouth looked cold and hard and beautiful when she lowered the glass.

"Anybody hungry?" she said.

I felt myself swallow. Then, for reasons I didn't understand, I told her and Benny what Mr. Dunlop had done to Sister Felicie. Benny listened attentively, his handsome face clouding, his fingers splaying his knotted yo-yo string in different directions. "Say all that again? This guy Dunlop ran off the Cheerio man?" he said.

It was almost Easter and at school that meant the Stations of the Cross and a daily catechism reminder about the nature of disloyalty and human failure. When he needed them most, Christ's men bagged it down the road and let him take the weight on his own. I came to appreciate the meaning of betrayal a little better that spring.

I thought my account of Mr. Dunlop's abuse of Sister Felicie and the Cheerio man had made Benny our ally. He'd said he would come by my house the next night and straighten out Mr. Dunlop and anyone else who was pushing around kids and nuns and yo-yo instructors. He said these kinds of guys were Nazis and should be boiled into lard and poured into soap molds. He said, "Don't worry, kid. I owe you guys. You taught me the Atomic Bomb and the Chinese Star."

The next day, after school, when I was raking leaves in the yard,

Vernon used his slingshot to shoot me in the back with a marble. I felt the pain go into the bone like a cold chisel.

"Got a crick?" he said.

"Yeah," I said, mindlessly, squeezing my shoulders back, my eyes shut.

"How about some hair of the dog that bit you?" he said, fishing another marble out of his shirt pocket.

"You screwed with Benny Siegel, Vernon. He's going to stuff you in a toilet bowl," I said.

"Yeah? Who is Benny Sea Gull?"

"Ask your old man. Oh, I forgot. He can't read, either."

Vernon's fist came out of the sky and knocked me to the ground. I felt the breath go out of my chest as though it were being sucked into a giant vacuum cleaner. Through the kitchen window, I could see my mother washing dishes, her face bent down toward the sink. Vernon unbuckled my belt, worked the top button loose on my jeans, and pulled them off my legs, dragging me through the dust. The clouds, trees, garage, alleyway, even the dog dumps, spun in circles around me. Vernon pulled one of my pants legs inside out and used it to blow his nose.

Benny and his girlfriend did not show up at my house that night. I called the Shamrock Hotel and asked for his room.

"There's no one registered here by that name," the clerk said.

"Has he checked out?"

There was a pause. "We have no record of a guest with that name. I'm sorry. Thank you for calling the Shamrock," the clerk said, and hung up.

The next day at recess I saw Sister Felicie sitting on a stone bench under a live oak in a garden behind the church. Her black habit was spangled with sunlight, and her beads lay across her open palm as though the wind had robbed her of her concentration. Her face looked like ceramic, polished, faintly pink, not quite real. She smelled of soap or perhaps shampoo in her close-cropped hair, which was covered with a skullcap and veil that must have been unbearable in the summer months.

"You're supposed to be on the playground, Charlie," she said.

"I told Benny Siegel what Mr. Dunlop did to you. He promised to help. But he didn't show up last night," I said.

"What are you talking about?"

"Benny is a gangster. Nick and I have been teaching him yo-yo tricks. He built a casino in Nevada."

"I'm convinced you'll be a great writer one day," she said, and for the first time in weeks she smiled. "You're a good boy, Charlie. I may not see you again, at least for a while. But you'll be in my prayers."

"Not see you?"

"Run along now. Don't hang out with too many gangsters."

She patted me on top of the head, then touched my cheek.

Benny had shown Nick and me color photographs of the resort hotel and gambling casino he had built in the desert. He also showed us a picture of him and his girlfriend building a snowman in front of a log cabin in west Montana. In the photograph she was smiling and looked much younger, somehow innocent among evergreens that rang with winter light. She wore a fluffy pink sweater and knee-length boots stitched with Christmas designs.

I kept wanting to believe Benny would call or come by, but he didn't. I dreamed about a building in a desert, its exterior scrolled with neon, a grassy pond on one side of it where flamingos stood in the water, arching their necks, pecking at the insects in their feathers.

I put away my Cheerio yo-yo and no longer listened to ballgames at Buffalo Stadium. I refused to eat, without understanding why, threw my lunch in a garbage can on the way to school, and fantasized about hurting Vernon Dunlop.

"We'll set fire to his house," Nick said.

"Serious?" I said, looking up from the box of shoes we were shining in his garage.

"It's a thought," he replied.

"What if somebody gets killed?"

"That's the breaks when you're white trash," Nick said. He grinned, his face full of play. He had a burr haircut and the overhead light reflected on his scalp. Nick was a good boxer, swallowed his blood in a fight, and never let anyone know when he was hurt. Secretly I always wished I was as tough as he was.

He and I had a shoeshine route. We collected shoes from all over the neighborhood and shined them for ten cents a pair, using only one color polish — brown; home delivery was free. Nick peeled open a Milky Way and bit into it. He chewed thoughtfully, then offered the candy bar to me. I shook my head.

"You got to eat," he said.

"Who says?" I replied.

"You make me sad, Charlie," he said.

My father was an old-time pipeline man whose best friend was killed by his side on the last day of World War I. He read classical literature, refused to mow the lawn under any circumstances, spent more days than he should have in the beer joint, attended church irregularly, and contended there were only two facts you had to remember about the nature of God: that He had a sense of humor and, as a gentleman, He never broke His word.

The last part always stuck with me.

Benny had proved himself a liar and a bum. My sense of having been used by him seemed to grow daily. My mother could not make me eat, even when my hunger was eating its way through my insides like a starving organism that had to consume its host in order to survive. I had bed spins when I woke in the morning and vertigo when I rode my bike to school, wobbling between automobiles while the sky, trees, and buildings around me dissolved into a vortex of atomic particles.

My mother tried to tempt me from my abstinence with a cake she baked and the following day with a codfish dinner she brought from the cafeteria, wrapped in foil, butter oozing from an Irish potato that was still hot from the oven.

I rushed from the house and pedaled my bike to Nick's. We sat inside the canebrake at the end of our old street, while the day cooled and the evening star twinkled in the west. There was a bitter taste in my mouth, like the taste of zinc pennies.

"You miss your dad?" Nick asked.

"I don't think about it much anymore. It was an accident. Why go around feeling bad about an accident?" I replied, turning my face from his, looking at the turquoise rim along the bottom of the sky.

"My old man always says your dad was stand-up."

"Benny Siegel treated us like jerks, Nick," I said.

"Who cares about Benny Siegel?"

I didn't have an answer for him, nor could I explain why I felt the way I did.

I rode my bike home in the dusk, then found a heavy rock in the alley and threw it against the side of the Dunlops's house. It struck the wood so hard the glass in the windows rattled. Vernon came out on the back porch, eating a piece of fried chicken, his body silhouetted in the kitchen light. He wore a strap undershirt and his belt was unbuckled, hanging loosely over his fly.

"You're lucky, dick wipe. I got a date tonight. But wait till tomorrow," he said. He shook his chicken bone at me.

I couldn't sleep that night. I had terrible dreams about facing Vernon in the morning. How could I have been so foolish as to actually assault his house? I wished I had taken the pounding right then, when I was in hot blood and not trembling with fear. I woke at 2 A.M. and threw up in the toilet, then went into the dry heaves. I lay in bed, my head under the pillow. I prayed an asteroid would crash into our neighborhood so I wouldn't have to see the sunrise.

At around five o'clock I fell asleep. Later I heard wind rattle the roof, then a loud knocking sound like a door slamming repeatedly on a doorjamb. When I looked out my window screen I could see fog on the street and a maroon convertible with whitewall tires parked in front of the Dunlops's house. An olive-skinned man with patent leather hair parted down the middle, wearing a clip-on bow tie and crinkling white shirt, sat in the passenger seat. I rubbed my eyes. It was the Cheerio man Mr. Dunlop had run off from the parking lot in front of Costen's Drug Store. Then I heard Benny's voice on the Dunlops's porch.

"See, you can't treat people like that. This is the United States, not Mussoliniville. So we need to walk out here and apologize to this guy and invite him back to the corner by the school. You're good with that, aren't you?"

There was a gap in the monologue. Then Benny's voice resumed. "You're not? You're gonna deny kids the right to enter Cheerio yo-yo contests? You think all those soldiers died in the war for nothing? That's what you're saying? You some kind of Nazi pushing around little people? Look at me when I'm talking, here."

Then Benny and Mr. Dunlop walked out to the convertible and

talked to the Cheerio man. A moment later Benny got behind the wheel and the convertible disappeared in the fog.

I fell sound asleep in the deep blue coolness of the room, with a sense of confidence in the world I had not felt since the day the war ended and Kate Smith's voice sang "God Bless America" from every radio in the neighborhood.

When I woke, it was hot and bright outside, the wind touched with dust and the stench of melted tar. I told my mother of Benny Siegel's visit to the Dunlops.

"You must have had a dream, Charlie. I was up early. I would have heard," she said.

"No, it was Benny. His girlfriend wasn't with him, but the Cheerio man was."

She smiled wanly, her eyes full of pity. "You've starved yourself and you break my heart. Nobody was out there, Charlie. *Nobody,*" she said.

I went out to the curb. No one ever parked in front of the Dunlops's house, and because the sewer drain was clogged, a patina of mud always dried along the edge of the gutter after each rain. I walked out in the street so I wouldn't be on the Dunlops's property, my eyes searching along the seam between the asphalt and the gutter. But I could see no tire imprint in the gray film left over from the last rain. I knelt down and touched the dust with my fingers.

Vernon opened his front door and held it back on the spring. He was bare-chested, a pair of sweatpants hanging below his navel. "Losing your marbles, frump?" he asked.

By noon my skin was crawling with anxiety and fear. Worse, I felt an abiding shame that once again I had been betrayed by my own vanity and foolish trust in others. I didn't care anymore whether Vernon beat me up or not. In fact, I wanted to see myself injured. Through the kitchen window I could see him pounding dust out of a rug on the clothesline with a broken tennis racquet. I walked down the back steps and crossed into his yard. "Vernon?" I said.

"Your butt-kicking appointment is after lunch. I'm busy right now. In the meantime, entertain yourself by giving a blowjob to a doorknob," he replied.

"This won't take long," I said.

He turned around, exasperated. I hit him, hard, on the corner of the mouth, with a right cross that Nick Hauser would have been proud of. It broke Vernon's lip against his teeth, whipping his face sideways, causing him to drop the racquet. He stared at me in disbelief, a string of spittle and blood on his cheek. Before he could raise his hands, I hit him again, this time square on the nose. I felt it flatten and blood fly under my knuckles, then I caught him in the eye and throat. I took one in the side of the head and felt another slide off my shoulder, but I was under his reach now and I got him again in the mouth, this time hurting him more than he was willing to live with.

He stepped back from me, blood draining from his split lip, his teeth red, his face twitching with shock. Out of the corner of my eye, I saw his father appear on the back porch.

"Get in here, boy, before I whup your ass worse than it already is," Mr. Dunlop said.

That afternoon Nick Hauser and I went to a baseball game at Buffalo Stadium. When I came home my mother told me I had received a long-distance telephone call. This was in an era when people only called long-distance to inform family members that a loved one had died. I called the operator and was soon connected to Sister Felicie. She told me she was back at Our Lady of the Lake, the college in San Antonio where she had trained to become a teacher.

"I appreciate what your friend has tried to do, but would you tell him everything is fine now, that he doesn't need to act on my behalf anymore?" she said.

"Which friend?" I asked.

"Mr. Siegel. He's called the archdiocese twice." I heard her laugh, then clear her throat. "Can you do that for me, Charlie?"

But I never saw Benny or his girlfriend again. In late June I read in the newspaper that Benny had been at her cottage in Beverly Hills, reading the *L. A. Times,* when someone outside propped an M-1 carbine across the fork of a tree and fired directly into Benny's face, blowing one eye fifteen feet from his head.

Years later I would read a news story about his girlfriend, whose nickname was the Flamingo, and how she died by suicide in a snowbank in Austria. I sometimes wondered if in those last moments of her life she tried to return to that wintertime photograph of her and Benny building a snowman in west Montana.

Vernon Dunlop never bothered me again. In fact, I came to have a sad kind of respect for the type of life that had been imposed upon him. Vernon was killed at the Battle of Inchon during the Korean War. Nick Hauser and I became schoolteachers. The era in which we grew up was a poem and Bugsy Siegel was a friend of mine.

JEFFERY DEAVER

Born Bad

FROM *Dangerous Women*

> *Sleep, my child, and peace attend thee,*
> *All through the night. . . .*

THE WORDS OF THE LULLABY looped relentlessly through her mind, as persistent as the clattering Oregon rain on the roof and window.

The song that she'd sung to Beth Anne when the girl was three or four seated itself in her head and wouldn't stop echoing. Twenty-five years ago, the two of them: mother and daughter, sitting in the kitchen of the family's home outside Detroit, Liz Polemus, hunching over the Formica table, the frugal young mother and wife, working hard to stretch the dollars.

Singing to her daughter, who sat across from her, fascinated with the woman's deft hands.

> *I who love you shall be near you,*
> *All through the night.*
> *Soft the drowsy hours are creeping.*
> *Hill and vale in slumber sleeping.*

Liz felt a cramp in her right arm — the one that had never healed properly — and realized she was still gripping the receiver fiercely at the news she'd just received. That her daughter was on her way to the house.

The daughter she hadn't spoken with in more than three years.

> *I my loving vigil keeping,*
> *All through the night.*

Liz finally replaced the telephone and felt blood surge into her arm, itching, stinging. She sat down on the embroidered couch that had been in the family for years and massaged her throbbing forearm. She felt lightheaded, confused, as if she wasn't sure the phone call had been real or a wispy scene from a dream.

Only the woman wasn't lost in the peace of sleep. No, Beth Anne was on her way. A half-hour and she'd be at Liz's door.

Outside, the rain continued to fall steadily, tumbling into the pines that filled Liz's yard. She'd lived in this house for nearly a year, a small place miles from the nearest suburb. Most people would've thought it too small, too remote. But to Liz it was an oasis. The slim widow, mid-fifties, had a busy life and little time for housekeeping. She could clean the place quickly and get back to work. And while hardly a recluse, she preferred the buffer zone of forest that separated her from her neighbors. The minuscule size also discouraged suggestions by any male friends that, hey, got an idea, how 'bout I move in? The woman would merely look around the one-bedroom home and explain that two people would go crazy in such cramped quarters; after her husband's death she'd resolved she'd never remarry or live with another man.

Her thoughts now drifted to Jim. Their daughter had left home and cut off all contact with the family before he died. It had always stung her that the girl hadn't even called after his death, let alone attended his funeral. Anger at this instance of the girl's callousness shivered within Liz but she pushed it aside, reminding herself that whatever the young woman's purpose tonight there wouldn't be enough time to exhume even a fraction of the painful memories that lay between mother and daughter like wreckage from a plane crash.

A glance at the clock. Nearly ten minutes had sped by since the call, Liz realized with a start.

Anxious, she walked into her sewing room. This, the largest room in the house, was decorated with needlepoint of her own and her mother's and a dozen racks of spools — some dating back to the fifties and sixties. Every shade of God's palette was represented in those threads. Boxes full of *Vogue* and Butterick patterns too. The centerpiece of the room was an old electric Singer. It had none of the fancy stitch cams of the new machines, no lights or complex gauges or knobs. The machine was a forty-year-old, black-enameled workhorse, identical to the one that her mother had used.

Liz had sewed since she was twelve and in difficult times the craft sustained her. She loved every part of the process: buying the fabric, hearing the *thud thud thud* as the clerk would turn the flat bolts of cloth over and over, unwinding the yardage (Liz could tell the women with near-perfect precision when a particular amount had been unfolded). Pinning the crisp, translucent paper onto the cloth. Cutting with the heavy pinking shears, which left a dragon-tooth edge on the fabric. Readying the machine, winding the bobbin, threading the needle . . .

There was something so completely soothing about sewing: taking these substances — cotton from the land, wool from animals — and blending them into something altogether new. The worst aspect of the injury several years ago was the damage to her right arm, which kept her off the Singer for three unbearable months.

Sewing was therapeutic for Liz, yes, but more than that, it was a part of her profession and had helped her become a well-to-do woman; nearby were racks of designer gowns, awaiting her skillful touch.

Her eyes rose to the clock. Fifteen minutes. Another breathless slug of panic.

Picturing so clearly that day twenty-five years ago — Beth Anne in her flannel jammies, sitting at the rickety kitchen table and watching her mother's quick fingers with fascination as Liz sang to her.

Sleep, my child, and peace attend thee . . .

This memory gave birth to dozens of others and the agitation rose in Liz's heart like the water level of the rain-swollen stream behind her house. Well, she told herself now firmly, don't just sit here . . . do something. Keep busy. She found a navy-blue jacket in her closet, walked to her sewing table, then dug through a basket until she found a matching remnant of wool. She'd use this to make a pocket for the garment. Liz went to work, smoothing the cloth, marking it with tailor's chalk, finding the scissors, cutting carefully. She focused on her task but the distraction wasn't enough to take her mind off the impending visit — and memories from years ago.

The shoplifting incident, for instance. When the girl was twelve.

Liz recalled the phone ringing, answering it. The head of security at a nearby department store was reporting — to Liz's and Jim's shock — that Beth Anne had been caught with nearly a thousand dollars' worth of jewelry hidden in a paper bag.

The parents had pleaded with the manager not to press charges. They'd said there must've been some mistake.

"Well," the security chief said skeptically, "we found her with five watches. A necklace too. Wrapped up in this grocery bag. I mean, that don't sound like any mistake to me."

Finally, after much reassurance that this was a fluke and promises she'd never come into the store again, the manager agreed to keep the police out of the matter.

Outside the store, once the family was alone, Liz turned to Beth Anne furiously. "Why on earth did you do that?"

"Why not?" was the girl's singsong response, a snide smile on her face.

"It was stupid."

"Like I care."

"Beth Anne . . . why're you acting this way?"

"What way?" the girl'd asked in mock confusion.

Her mother had tried to engage her in a dialogue — the way the talk shows and psychologists said you should do with your kids — but Beth Anne remained bored and distracted. Liz had delivered a vague, and obviously futile, warning and had given up.

Thinking now: You put a certain amount of effort into stitching a jacket or dress and you get the garment you expect. There's no mystery. But you put a thousand times *more* effort into raising your child and the result is the opposite of what you hope and dream for. This seemed so unfair.

Liz's keen gray eyes examined the wool jacket, making sure the pocket lay flat and was pinned correctly into position. She paused, looking up, out the window toward the black spikes of the pine, but what she was seeing were more hard memories of Beth Anne. What a mouth on that girl! Beth Anne would look her mother or father in the eye and say, "There is no goddamn way you're going to make me go with you." Or, "Do you have *any* fucking clue at all?"

Maybe they should've been stricter in their upbringing. In Liz's family you got whipped for cursing or talking back to adults or for not doing what your parents asked you to do. She and Jim had never spanked Beth Anne; maybe they *should've* swatted her once or twice.

One time, somebody had called in sick at the family business — a warehouse Jim had inherited — and he needed Beth Anne to help out. She'd snapped at him, "I'd rather be dead than go back inside that shithole with you."

Her father had backed down sheepishly but Liz stormed up to her daughter. "Don't talk to your father that way."

"Oh?" the girl asked in a sarcastic voice. "How *should* I talk to him? Like some obedient little daughter who does everything he wants? Maybe that's what he wanted but it's not who he got." She'd grabbed her purse, heading for the door.

"Where are you going?"

"To see some friends."

"You are not. Get back here this minute!"

Her reply was a slamming door. Jim started after her but in an instant she was gone, crunching through two-month-old gray Michigan snow.

And those "friends"?

Trish and Eric and Sean . . . Kids from families with totally different values from Liz's and Jim's. They tried to forbid her from seeing them. But that, of course, had no effect.

"Don't tell me who I can hang out with," Beth Anne had said furiously. The girl was eighteen then and as tall as her mother. As she walked forward with a glower, Liz retreated uneasily. The girl continued, "And what do you know about them anyway?"

"They don't like your father and me — that's all I need to know. What's wrong with Todd and Joan's kids? Or Brad's? Your father and I've known them for years."

"What's *wrong* with them?" the girl muttered sarcastically. "Try, they're losers." This time grabbing both her purse and the cigarettes she'd started smoking, she made another dramatic exit.

With her right foot Liz pressed the pedal of the Singer and the motor gave its distinctive grind, then broke into *clatta clatta clatta* as the needle sped up and down, vanishing into the cloth, leaving a neat row of stitches around the pocket.

Clatta clatta clatta . . .

In middle school the girl would never get home until seven or eight and in high school she'd arrive much later. Sometimes she'd stay away all night. Weekends too she just disappeared and had nothing to do with the family.

Clatta clatta clatta. The rhythmic grind of the Singer soothed Liz somewhat but couldn't keep her from panicking again when she looked at the clock. Her daughter could be here at any minute.

Her girl, her little baby . . .

Sleep, my child . . .

And the question that had plagued Liz for years returned now: What had gone wrong? For hours and hours she'd replay the girl's early years, trying to see what Liz had done to make Beth Anne reject her so completely. She'd been an attentive, involved mother, been consistent and fair, made meals for the family every day, washed and ironed the girl's clothes, bought her whatever she needed. All she could think of was that she'd been too strongminded, too unyielding in her approach to raising the girl, too stern sometimes.

But this hardly seemed like much of a crime. Besides, Beth Anne had been equally mad at her father — the softie of the parents. Easygoing, doting to the point of spoiling the girl, Jim was the perfect father. He'd help Beth Anne and her friends with their homework, drive them to school himself when Liz was working, read her bedtime stories, and tuck her in at night. He made up "special games" for him and Beth Anne to play. It was just sort of parental bond that most children would love.

But the girl would fly into rages at him too and go out of her way to avoid spending time with him.

No, Liz could think of no dark incidents in the past, no traumas, no tragedies that could have turned Beth Anne into a renegade. She returned to the conclusion that she'd come to years ago: that — as unfair and cruel as it seemed — her daughter had simply been born fundamentally different from Liz; something had happened in the wiring to make the girl the rebel she was.

And looking at the cloth, smoothing it under her long, smooth fingers, Liz considered something else: rebellious, yes, but was she a *threat* too?

Liz now admitted that part of the ill ease she felt tonight wasn't only from the impending confrontation with her wayward child; it was that the young woman scared her.

She looked up from her jacket and stared at the rain spattering her window. Her right arm tingling painfully, she recalled that terrible day several years ago — the day that drove her permanently from Detroit and still gave her breathless nightmares. Liz had walked into a jewelry store and stopped in shock, gasping as she saw a pistol swinging toward her. She could still see the yellow flash as the man pulled the trigger, hear the stunning explosion, feel the numbing shock as the bullet slammed into her arm, sending her sprawling on the tile floor, crying out in pain and confusion.

Her daughter, of course, had nothing to do with that tragedy. Yet Liz had realized that Beth Anne was just as willing and capable of pulling the trigger as that man had done during the robbery; she had proof her daughter was a dangerous woman. A few years ago, after Beth Anne had left home, Liz had gone to visit Jim's grave. The clay was foggy as cotton and she was nearly to the tombstone when she realized that somebody was standing over it. To her shock she realized it was Beth Anne. Liz eased back into the mist, heart pounding fiercely. She debated for a long moment but finally decided that she didn't have the courage to confront the girl and decided to leave a note on her car's windshield.

But as she stepped to the Chevy, fishing in her handbag for a pen and some paper, she glanced inside and her heart shivered at the sight: a jacket, a clutter of papers, and half-hidden beneath them a pistol and some plastic bags, which contained white powder — drugs, Liz assumed.

Oh, yes, she now thought, her daughter, little Beth Anne Polemus, was very capable of killing.

Liz's foot rose from the pedal and the Singer fell silent. She lifted the clamp and cut the dangling threads. She pulled it on and slipped a few things into the pocket, examined herself in the mirror, and decided that she was satisfied with the work.

Then she stared at her dim reflection. Leave! a voice in her head said. She's a threat! Get out now before Beth Anne arrives.

But after a moment of debate Liz sighed. One of the reasons she'd moved here in the first place was that she'd learned her daughter had relocated to the Northwest. Liz had been meaning to try to track the girl down but had found herself oddly reluctant to do so. No, she'd stay, she'd meet with Beth Anne. But she wasn't going to be stupid, not after the robbery. Liz now hung the jacket on a hanger and walked to the closet. She pulled down a box from the top shelf and looked inside. There sat a small pistol. "A ladies' gun," Jim had called it when he gave it to her years ago. She took it out and stared at the weapon.

Sleep, my child . . .
All through the night.

Then she shuddered in disgust. No, she couldn't possibly use a weapon against her daughter. Of course not.

The idea of putting the girl to sleep forever was inconceivable.

And yet . . . what if it were a choice between her life and her daughter's? What if the hatred within the girl had pushed her over the edge?

Could she kill Beth Anne to save her own life?

No mother should ever have to make a choice like this one.

She hesitated for a long moment, then started to put the gun back. But a flash of light stopped her. Headlights filled the front yard and cast bright yellow cat's eyes on the sewing room wall beside Liz.

The woman glanced once more at the gun and, rather than put it away in the closet, set it on a dresser near the door and covered it with a doily. She walked into the living room and stared out the window at the car in her driveway, which sat motionless, lights still on, wipers whipping back and forth fast, her daughter hesitating to climb out; Liz suspected it wasn't the bad weather that kept the girl inside.

A long, long moment later the headlights went dark.

Well, think positive, Liz told herself. Maybe her daughter had changed. Maybe the point of the visit was reaching out to make amends for all the betrayal over the years. They could finally begin to work on having a normal relationship.

Still, she glanced back at the sewing room, where the gun sat on the dresser, and told herself: Take it. Keep it in your pocket.

Then: No, put it back in the closet.

Liz did neither. Leaving the gun on the dresser, she strode to the front door of her house and opened it, feeling cold mist coat her face.

She stood back from the approaching silhouetted form of the

slim young woman as Beth Anne walked through the doorway and stopped. A pause, then she swung the door shut behind her.

Liz remained in the middle of the living room, pressing her hands together nervously.

Pulling back the hood of her windbreaker, Beth Anne wiped rain off her face. The young woman's face was weathered, ruddy. She wore no makeup. She'd be twenty-eight, Liz knew, but she looked older. Her hair was now short, revealing tiny earrings. For some reason, Liz wondered if someone had given them to the girl or if she'd bought them for herself.

"Well, hello, honey."

"Mother."

A hesitation then a brief, humorless laugh from Liz. "You used to call me 'Mom.'"

"Did I?"

"Yes. Don't you remember?"

A shake of the head. But Liz thought that in fact she did remember but was reluctant to acknowledge the memory. She looked her daughter over carefully.

Beth Anne glanced around the small living room. Her eye settled on a picture of herself and her father together — they were on the boat dock near the family home in Michigan.

Liz asked, "When you called you said somebody told you I was here. Who?"

"It doesn't matter. Just somebody. You've been living here since . . ." Her voice faded.

"A couple of years. Do you want a drink?"

"No."

Liz remembered that she'd found the girl sneaking some beer when she was sixteen and wondered if she'd continued to drink and now had a problem with alcohol.

"Tea, then? Coffee?"

"No."

"You knew I moved to the Northwest?" Beth Anne asked.

"You always talked about the area, getting away from . . . well, getting out of Michigan and coming here. Then after you moved out you got some mail at the house. From somebody in Seattle."

Beth Anne nodded. Was there a slight grimace too? As if she was angry with herself for carelessly leaving a clue to her whereabouts. "And you moved to Portland to be near me?"

Liz smiled. "I guess I did. I started to look you up but I lost the nerve." Liz felt tears welling in her eyes as her daughter continued her examination of the room. The house was small, yes, but the furniture, electronics, and appointments were the best — the rewards of Liz's hard work in recent years. Two feelings vied within the woman: She half-hoped the girl would be tempted to reconnect with her mother when she saw how much money Liz had but, simultaneously, she was ashamed of the opulence; her daughter's clothes and cheap costume jewelry suggested she was struggling.

The silence was like fire. It burned Liz's skin and heart.

Beth Anne unclenched her left hand and her mother noticed a minuscule engagement ring and a simple gold band. The tears now rolled from her eyes. "You — ?"

The young woman followed her mother's gaze to the ring. She nodded.

Liz wondered what sort of man her son-in-law was. Would he be someone soft like Jim, someone who could temper the girl's wayward personality? Or would he be hard? Like Beth Anne herself?

"You have children?" Liz asked.

"That's not for you to know."

"Are you working?"

"Are you asking if I've changed, Mother?"

Liz didn't want to hear the answer to this question and continued quickly, pitching her case. "I was thinking," she said, desperation creeping into her voice, "that maybe I could go up to Seattle. We could see each other . . . We could even work together. We could be partners. Fifty-fifty. We'd have so much fun. I always thought we'd be great together. I always dreamed —"

"You and me working together, Mother?" She glanced into the sewing room, nodded toward the machine, the racks of dresses. "That's not my life. It never was. It never could be. After all these years, you really don't understand that, do you?" The words and their cold tone answered Liz's question firmly: No, the girl hadn't changed one bit.

Her voice went harsh. "Then why're you here? What's your point in coming?"

"I think you know, don't you?"

"No, Beth Anne, I *don't* know. Some kind of psycho revenge?"

"You could say that, I guess." She looked around the room again. "Let's go."

Liz's breath was coming fast. "Why? Everything we ever did was for you."

"I'd say you did it *to* me." A gun appeared in her daughter's hand and the black muzzle lolled in Liz's direction. "Outside," she whispered.

"My God! No!" She inhaled a gasp, as the memory of the shooting in the jewelry store came back to her hard. Her arm tingled and tears streaked down her cheeks.

She pictured the gun on the dresser.

Sleep, my child . . .

"I'm not going anywhere!" Liz said, wiping her eyes.

"Yes, you are. Outside."

"What are you going to do?" she asked desperately.

"What I should've done a long time ago."

Liz leaned against a chair for support. Her daughter noticed the woman's left hand, which had eased to within inches of the telephone.

"No!" the girl barked. "Get away from it."

Liz gave a hopeless glance at the receiver and then did as she was told.

"Come with me."

"Now? In the rain."

The girl nodded.

"Let me get a coat."

"There's one by the door."

"It's not warm enough."

The girl hesitated, as if she was going to say that the warmth of her mother's coat was irrelevant, considering what was about to happen. But then she nodded. "But don't try to use the phone. I'll be watching."

Stepping into the doorway of the sewing room, Liz picked up the blue jacket she'd just been working on. She slowly put it on, her eyes riveted to the doily and the hump of the pistol beneath it. She glanced back into the living room. Her daughter was staring at a framed snapshot of herself at eleven or twelve standing next to her father and mother.

Quickly she reached down and picked up the gun. She could turn fast, point it at her daughter. Scream to her to throw away her own gun.

> *Mother, I can feel you near me.*
> *All through the night...*
> *Father, I know you can hear me.*
> *All through the night...*

But what if Beth Anne *didn't* give up the gun?
What if she raised it, intending to shoot?
What would Liz do then?
To save her own life could she kill her daughter?

> *Sleep, my child...*

Beth Anne was still turned away, examining the picture. Liz would be able to do it — turn, one fast shot. She felt the pistol, its weight tugging at her throbbing arm.

But then she sighed.

The answer was no. A deafening no. She'd never hurt her daughter. Whatever was going to happen next, outside in the rain, she could never hurt the girl.

Replacing the gun, Liz joined Beth Anne.

"Let's go," her daughter said and, shoving her own pistol into the waistband of her jeans, she led the woman outside, gripping her mother roughly by the arm. This was, Liz realized, the first physical contact in at least four years.

They stopped on the porch and Liz spun around to face her daughter. "If you do this, you'll regret it for the rest of your life."

"No," the girl said. "I'd regret *not* doing it."

Liz felt a spatter of rain join the tears on her cheeks. She glanced at her daughter. The young woman's face was wet and red too, but this was, her mother knew, solely from the rain; her eyes were completely tearless. In a whisper she asked, "What've I ever done to make you hate me?"

This question went unanswered as the first of the squad cars pulled into the yard, red and blue and white lights igniting the fat raindrops around them like sparks at a Fourth of July celebration. A man in his thirties, wearing a dark windbreaker and a badge around his neck, climbed out of the first car and walked toward the house, two uniformed state troopers behind him. He nodded to Beth Anne. "I'm Dan Heath, Oregon State Police."

The young woman shook his hand. "Detective Beth Anne Polemus, Seattle PD."

"Welcome to Portland," he said.

She gave an ironic shrug, took the handcuffs he held and cuffed her mother's hands securely.

Numb from the cold — and from the emotional fusion of the meeting — Beth Anne listened as Heath recited to the older woman, "Elizabeth Polemus, you're under arrest for murder, attempted murder, assault, armed robbery, and dealing in stolen goods." He read her her rights and explained that she'd be arraigned in Oregon on local charges but was subject to an extradition order back to Michigan on a number of outstanding warrants there, including capital murder.

Beth Anne gestured to the young OSP officer who'd met her at the airport. She hadn't had time to do the paperwork that'd allow her to bring her own service weapon into another state so the trooper had loaned her one of theirs. She returned it to him now and turned back to watch a trooper search her mother.

"Honey," her mother began, the voice miserable, pleading.

Beth Anne ignored her and Heath nodded to the young uniformed trooper, who led the woman toward a squad car. But Beth Anne stopped him and called, "Hold on. Frisk her better."

The uniformed trooper blinked, looking over the slim, slight captive, who seemed as unthreatening as a child. But, with a nod from Heath, he motioned over a policewoman, who expertly patted her down. The officer frowned when she came to the small of Liz's back. The mother gave a piercing glance to her daughter as the officer pulled up the woman's navy-blue jacket, revealing a small pocket sewn into the inside back of the garment. Inside was a small switchblade knife and a universal handcuff key.

"Jesus," whispered the officer. He nodded to the policewoman, who searched her again. No other surprises were found.

Beth Anne said, "That was a trick I remember from the old days. She'd sew secret pockets into her clothes. For shoplifting and hiding weapons." A cold laugh from the young woman. "Sewing and robbery. Those're her talents." The smile faded. "Killing too, of course."

"How could you do this to your mother?" Liz snapped viciously. "You Judas."

Beth Anne watched, detached, as the woman was led to a squad car.

Heath and Beth Anne stepped into the living room of the house. As the policewoman again surveyed the hundreds of thousands of dollars of stolen property filling the bungalow, Heath said, "Thanks, Detective. I know this was hard for you. But we were desperate to collar her without anybody else getting hurt."

Capturing Liz Polemus could indeed have turned into a bloodbath. It had happened before. Several years ago, when her mother and her lover, Brad Selbit, had tried to knock over a jewelry store in Ann Arbor, Liz had been surprised by the security guard. He'd shot her in the arm. But that hadn't stopped her from grabbing her pistol with her other hand and killing him and a customer and then later shooting one of the responding police officers. She'd managed to escape. She'd left Michigan for Portland, where she and Brad had started up her operation again, sticking with her forte — knocking over jewelry stores and boutiques selling designer clothes, which she'd use her skills as a seamstress to alter and then would sell to fences in other states.

An informant had told the Oregon State Police that Liz Polemus was the one behind the string of recent robberies in the Northwest and was living under a fake name in a bungalow here. The OSP detectives on the case had learned that her daughter was a detective with the Seattle police department and had helicoptered Beth Anne to the Portland airport. She'd driven here alone to get her mother to surrender peacefully.

"She was on two states' ten-most-wanted lists. And I heard she was making a name for herself in California too. Imagine that — your own mother." Heath's voice faded, thinking this might be indelicate.

But Beth Anne didn't care. She mused, "That was my childhood — armed robbery, burglary, money laundering ... My father owned a warehouse where they fenced the stuff. That was their front — they'd inherited it from his father. Who was in the business too, by the way."

"Your *grandfather*?"

She nodded. "That warehouse ... I can still see it so clear. Smell it. Feel the cold. And I was only there once. When I was about eight, I guess. It was full of perped merch. My father left me in the office alone for a few minutes and I peeked out the door and saw him and one of his buddies beating the hell out of this guy. Nearly killed him."

"Doesn't sound like they tried to keep anything very secret from you."

"Secret? Hell, they did everything they could to get me *into* the business. My father had these special games, he called them. Oh, I was supposed to go over to friends' houses and scope out if they had valuables and where they were. Or check out TVs and VCRs at school and let him know where they kept them and what kind of locks were on the doors."

Heath shook his head in astonishment. Then he asked, "But you never had any run-ins with the law?"

She laughed. "Actually, yeah — I got busted once for shoplifting."

Heath nodded. "I copped a pack of cigarettes when I was fourteen. I can still feel my daddy's belt on my butt for that one."

"No, no," Beth Anne said. "I got busted *returning* some crap my mother stole."

"You what?"

"She took me to the store as cover. You know, a mother and daughter wouldn't be as suspicious as a woman by herself. I saw her pocket some watches and a necklace. When we got home I put the merch in a bag and took it back to the store. The guard saw me looking guilty, I guess, and he nailed me before I could replace anything. I took the rap. I mean, I wasn't going to drop a dime on my parents, was I? . . . My mother was so mad . . . They honestly couldn't figure out why I didn't want to follow in their footsteps."

"You need some time with Dr. Phil or somebody."

"Been there. Still am."

She nodded as memories came back to her. "From, like, twelve or thirteen on, I tried to stay as far away from home as I could. I did every after-school activity I could. Volunteered at a hospital on weekends. My friends really helped me out. They were the best . . . I probably picked them because they were one-eighty from my parents' criminal crowd. I'd hang with the National Merit scholars, the debate team, Latin club. Anybody who was decent and normal. I wasn't a great student but I spent so much time at the library or studying at friends' houses I got a full scholarship and put myself through college."

"Where'd you go?"

"Ann Arbor. Criminal justice major. I took the CS exam and landed a spot on Detroit PD. Worked there for a while. Narcotics mostly. Then moved out here and joined the force in Seattle."

"And you've got your gold shield. You made detective fast." Heath looked over the house. "She lived here by herself? Where's your father?"

"Dead," Beth Anne said matter-of-factly. "She killed him."

"*What?*"

"Wait'll you read the extradition order from Michigan. Nobody knew it at the time, of course. The original coroner's report was an accident. But a few months ago this guy in prison in Michigan confessed that he'd helped her. Mother found out my father was skimming money from their operation and sharing it with some girlfriend. She hired this guy to kill him and make it look like an accidental drowning."

"I'm sorry, Detective."

Beth Anne shrugged. "I always wondered if I could forgive them. I remember once, I was still working Narc in Detroit. I'd just run a big bust out on Six Mile. Confiscated a bunch of smack. I was on my way to log the stuff into Evidence back at the station and I saw I was driving past the cemetery where my father was buried. I'd never been there. I pulled in and walked up to the grave and tried to forgive him. But I couldn't. I realized then that I never could — not him or my mother. That's when I decided I had to leave Michigan."

"Your mother every remarry?"

"She took up with Selbit a few years ago but she never married him. You collared him yet?"

"No. He's around here somewhere but he's gone to ground."

Beth Anne gave a nod toward the phone. "Mother tried to grab the phone when I came in tonight. She might've been trying to get a message to him. I'd check out the phone records. That might lead you to him."

"Good idea, Detective. I'll get a warrant tonight."

Beth Anne stared through the rain, toward where the squad car bearing her mother had vanished some minutes ago. "The weird part was that she believed she was doing the right thing for me, trying to get me into the business. Being a crook was her nature; she thought it was my nature too. She and dad were born bad. They couldn't figure out why I was born good and wouldn't change."

"You have a family?" Heath asked.

"My husband's a sergeant in Juvenile." Then Beth Anne smiled. "And we're expecting. Our first."

"Hey, very cool."

"I'm on the job until June. Then I'm taking an LOA for a couple of years to be a mom." She felt an urge to add, "Because children come first before anything." But, under the circumstances, she didn't think she needed to elaborate.

"Crime Scene's going to seal the place," Heath said. "But if you want to take a look around, that'd be okay. Maybe there's some pictures or something you want. Nobody'd care if you took some personal effects."

Beth Anne tapped her head. "I got more mementos up here than I need."

"Got it."

She zipped up her windbreaker, pulled the hood up. Another hollow laugh.

Heath lifted an eyebrow.

"You know my earliest memory?" she asked.

"What's that?"

"In the kitchen of my parents' first house outside of Detroit. I was sitting at the table. I must've been three. My mother was singing to me."

"Singing? Just like a real mother."

Beth Anne mused, "I don't know what song it was. I just remember her singing to keep me distracted. So I wouldn't play with what she was working on at the table."

"What was she doing, sewing?" Heath nodded toward the room containing a sewing machine and racks of stolen dresses.

"Nope," the woman answered. "She was reloading ammunition."

"You serious?"

A nod. "I figured out when I was older what she was doing. My folks didn't have much money then and they'd buy empty brass cartridges at gun shows and reload them. All I remember is the bullets were shiny and I wanted to play with them. She said if I didn't touch them she'd sing to me."

This story brought the conversation to a halt. The two officers listened to the rain falling on the roof.

Born bad...

"All right," Beth Anne finally said, "I'm going home."

Heath walked her outside and they said their good-byes. Beth Anne started the rental car and drove up the muddy, winding road toward the state highway.

Suddenly, from somewhere in the folds of her memory, a melody came into her head. She hummed a few bars out loud but couldn't place the tune. It left her vaguely unsettled. So Beth Anne flicked the radio on and found Jammin' 95.5, filling your night with solid-gold hits, party on, Portland . . . She turned the volume up high and, thumping the steering wheel in time to the music, headed north toward the airport.

JANE HADDAM

Edelweiss

FROM *Creature Cozies*

Looking at her now, you'd never guess that Edelweiss was once an abandoned cat, dumped at the back door of the Naugy Doggy pet shop in Naugatuck, Connecticut, with the rest of a litter of kittens that nobody seemed to want. These days, she's fat, furry, and arrogant, and her dietary requirements resemble the main menu at the Golden Door spa. Unfortunately, she doesn't much like having her picture taken — she seems to think the camera flash is an unspeakable indignity — and she's iffy on small boys, especially the one in our house. Taking this picture required a whole role of film, the help of a few friends, and banishing my younger son to his room. When the photo session was over, she installed herself under my coffee table and refused to come out until the turkey in the oven was done. Maybe she should have her name changed to Greta Garbo.
— JANE HADDAM

THAT MORNING, the air was hot and muggy and thick, the way it can be only in central Florida in the winter, and Miss Caroline Edgerton was taking her cat to work. Shelley Altman saw them coming out of Miss Edgerton's front door at seven forty-five in the morning, the earliest Shelley had ever seen Miss Edgerton head to work. By now, Shelley knew everything there was to know about "Miss Caroline," as the paperboy called her, right down to the size of her underwear and the pattern she preferred at Victoria's Secret. It was funny to think of Miss Edgerton shopping at Victoria's Secret. She was sixty if she was a day, and she was probably a virgin on top of it. Shelley hadn't found any birth control any of the last three times she'd searched the house. She'd been particularly looking for it, too, because Amanda absolutely insisted that that was one thing they needed to know. Was Miss Edgerton a virgin? Was she a lesbian? Was she anything at all besides a dried up old prune of a hag who had dedicated her life to making things miserable for girls who were younger than she was and prettier than she had ever been? It mattered, Amanda said, because the answers might change their minds about what they had decided to do. It was one thing to murder a woman who was nothing more than a waste of light and air. It was something else to murder a tragic victim of life's circumstances. Maybe Miss Edgerton had once had a lover who had died in a war — Vietnam or World War II, whichever. Maybe Miss Edgerton had always wished and hoped for a lover but had been too poor or too ugly to get one. Maybe Miss Edgerton was pining right now for some young man at her office, who would never look at her because she was far too old. Whatever it was, they had to find out, just in case it made her less than the best of candidates. It wasn't as if they were shy of people who deserved to be dead. Matahatchee was full of them. Amanda could name six right off the top of her head, and that was without going any farther afield than Main Street.

Out in the driveway next door, Miss Caroline Edgerton had put her cat very carefully into the cat carrier that she kept in the back seat for whenever she needed it. Her cat was named Edelweiss, because it was as purely white as some silly flower that grew in Switzerland, and it didn't like going into the carrier for any reason whatsoever. Shelley was always a little surprised that Miss Edgerton didn't take her cat to work *every* day. She surely lived with it like it was surgically attached when she was home. Sometimes, when Shelley looked into the windows at night, Miss Edgerton would be sitting in the big club chair in the living room with Edelweiss draped around her neck like a feather boa, the both of them watching something mind-numbingly boring on PBS. Shelley didn't care if Miss Edgerton was somebody who had had a tragic life. She hated Miss Edgerton with everything inside herself, much the way she also hated Mrs. Keller who taught English at school and Mrs. Partree who ran that youth group at the Methodist church. Shelley's parents went to the Methodist church. They made Shelley go with them. Twice a year they made Shelley go on a Bible retreat with the youth group, too. By now, Shelley had read through the really *good* parts of the Bible almost as often as she had watched *Natural Born Killers* — but only because she wasn't allowed to watch *Natural Born Killers* in the house.

Miss Edgerton had Edelweiss safely in the cat carrier and the cat carrier safely on the floor of the back seat of the car. That was the safest place for Edelweiss to be if there was ever a car accident. Miss Edgerton came around front and got in behind the wheel. Her car was a trim little Volvo sedan, in navy blue, which matched her business suit today. Miss Edgerton always looked businesslike, even though she didn't work at anything any more important than being a secretary.

Shelley moved away from her bedroom window and sat down on her bed. Her school clothes were hung on her closet door. Her makeup was laid out on the vanity table in front of the beveled mirror that was supposed to be good for making sure you covered up your flaws and imperfections. Her fingernails were bright green. It seemed impossible to her that she should have to get up and go out and spend the day at Matahatchee High School, where she was only a sophomore and not considered very important by the other girls in her class. Amanda was important. Amanda was so important, she was already a varsity cheerleader, and secretary of the student council, and a member of the Key Club. Once a month, at least, Amanda had her picture in the *Matahatchee Echo*, which was the school newspaper. Amanda was a peer tutor. Amanda was an anger management peer counselor. Amanda sang in the choir at church. Sometimes, when Shelley thought about killing somebody, Amanda seemed to be the very best one to kill. Then Shelley would think about Miss Edgerton and change her mind. It was just that the waiting was making her crazy. It got to the point sometimes when she couldn't seem to make herself think. Now she got up and got her bright blue halter-top off its hanger and started to put it on. She didn't know if she was glad to live in a place where it almost never got cold. She hated halter-tops. They made her feel as if someone were about to scrape away her skin.

School made Shelley feel as if she were already dead. It took her forever to get dressed to go there, and then it took her forever to walk the six long blocks that got her to its front door. To pass the time, she went looking for Miss Caroline Edgerton on Main Street, through the front window in the offices of Carmeth, Brane, and DeVoe, where she worked. Sometimes Miss Edgerton sat at the front desk there and answered the phone for hours. When she had the cat with her, the cat sat on the desk near the phone and looked up every time it rang. Sometimes the cat draped itself over the phone, as if it were a chicken and the phone was its egg. When it was like that and the phone rang, Miss Edgerton would lift the cat gently so that she could pick up the phone. She was never angry or impatient with the cat. She was better to Edelweiss than most parents were to their children. She was certainly better to Edelweiss than Shelley's parents were to Shelley. This morning, though, neither Miss Edgerton nor the cat was anywhere to be seen. The woman behind the front desk was young and weighted down under a cascade of falls and hairpieces. Shelley went around the back to make sure Miss Edgerton's car was in the parking lot — it was, right next to the bright red Porsche that belonged to Mr. DeVoe — and then she went to school, thinking about palm trees as she went. Amanda came from New York State someplace. She'd never seen a palm tree in person until her parents had moved here when she was still in junior high. Palm trees were the first thing she and Shelley had talked about, in Shelley's backyard, on the day they met.

"They don't look like real trees at all," Amanda had said, and then she'd seen Miss Caroline Edgerton come out her back door to potter around in her yard.

Shelley went to her locker and stowed away most of her books in it. She brought books home every night, because if she didn't, her parents screamed at her, her mother especially. They gave her lectures about how she would never amount to anything, and how she'd end up like those homeless people who slept every night on Segovia Avenue. She brought the books home, and she laid them out across the desk in her bedroom, but that was all she did with them. If she had homework and knew about it, she ignored it. Mostly she didn't have homework, because if you weren't in the college track, the teachers didn't see any point in giving any. She did go to class. Not going was the surest way to get the principal to call your parents, and Shelley lived to make sure she wasn't bothered by her parents.

She got her English book — *Explorations in Literature,* a complete bore — and headed down the hall to her homeroom. She would have skipped homeroom if she could have. It was nothing but sitting in a sea of people who didn't want to talk to her and listening to announcements about things she wouldn't touch with a ten-foot pole. Chess Club. Glee Club. Future Teachers of America. Homeroom, though, was the one thing she could not skip, not ever. If you skipped that, you were counted absent for the entire day.

She was just adjusting the strap on her shoulder bag for the fiftieth time when she saw Amanda in the hall, and for the first few moments she didn't pay attention. Amanda didn't much like talking to her in school. Usually, they passed each other in the halls without even saying hello, and saved their conversations for after school, in their own bedrooms. Their houses were only across the street from each other. Shelley started to go on by and take her seat in Room 122, but Amanda snaked out her hand and grabbed her elbow.

"Go to the girls' room," Amanda said. "I'll meet you there."

Shelley hesitated. It really *wasn't* all right to miss homeroom, although having to go to the bathroom was usually a good enough excuse for being tardy. She looked through the window in the door at Miss Carroll, who was wearing a sleeveless dress and a crucifix. She wore the crucifix because somebody's father objected to the school board that they had a "Satanist" teaching in Matahatchee, by which it turned out he meant a Catholic. Shelley prodded at her hair. The school's air-conditioning was only half working. Her hair was full of sweat.

"Go ahead," Amanda said. "This is important."

Miss Carroll looked up and saw Shelley standing outside the door. Shelley made hand motions meant to explain that she was heading to the bathroom. Miss Carroll nodded. In Shelley's imaginary universe — the one where she and Amanda were masterminds, committing murder after murder, whenever they felt it was necessary — Miss Carroll was the second to go.

In the girls' room, Amanda was standing near the sinks, putting on lipstick. She put on makeup four or five times a day. Her hair never looked full of sweat. Today she was wearing the short little kick-pleat skirt that was practically the uniform of the Key Club. If anybody wore one just like it who didn't belong, the Key Club girls ganged up on her on the athletic field and made sure it would never happen again.

Shelley put down her books on a corner of the sink. She didn't want to put on makeup. She didn't want to look in the mirror at all.

Mirrors made it impossible to forget that she had acne running all across the ridge of her jaw.

"What is it?" she asked, folding her arms across her chest. "I thought I wasn't supposed to talk to you here. I thought it would compromise the operation."

"You aren't supposed to talk to me in public," Amanda said. "It *would* compromise the operation. If everybody knew we were friends, they'd guess right away."

"They'd guess about Miss Edgerton? Why? Why would our being friends mean we'd done something to —"

"Shh," Amanda said. She abandoned the lipstick for some kind of powder. When Shelley put on makeup, it seemed to clot up on her skin. In a few hours, she looked as if she were walking around with pieces of plaster clinging to her face. Amanda's makeup didn't even look like makeup. When Amanda's makeup had been on Amanda for a few hours, it just seemed to disappear.

"I don't think it has anything to do with Miss Edgerton," Shelley said. "I think that's just a big cover so that you don't have to talk to me in front of your popular friends. I mean, for God's sake. What is that? Amanda the supercheerleader."

Amanda had gone from powder to something for her eyebrows. "You could be popular, too, if you put in a little effort. I don't know what's wrong with you that you want to be by yourself all the time."

"I don't want to be by myself all the time. I want to be with you."

"Well, that wouldn't make much sense, under the circumstances. Especially today. Did you see her? She's here."

"Who's here?"

"Miss Edgerton," Amanda said. "Mr. DeVoe is here doing something or the other, and she's come with him. She brought her cat, too. It's in with Miss Lazio in the secretaries' place, you know, the big room in front of the principal's office. Anyway, she's here, and I hung around the office for a little and from what I heard, she's going to be here until noon."

"Why?"

"I don't know. Some legal thing having to do with the school, I'd guess. Mr. DeVoe is a lawyer. She's a lawyer's secretary. What does it matter?"

"That's what I want to know," Shelley said. "What does it matter? Why should we care where she is or what she does?"

Amanda stopped putting on makeup. "You must be joking. You know why we care."

"I meant why should we care where she is or what she does today?" Shelley said. "I'm not a complete idiot, Amanda. I know why we care in the long run. But what does it matter if she's here today?"

"Well," Amanda said. "I was thinking. It might be the perfect chance."

"The perfect chance for what?"

"For us to do what we want to do. Think about it. You live next door to her, right? She knows who you are?"

"Of course she does," Shelley said. "She knows who you are, too. You live right across the street."

"But she doesn't know me that well. We only moved here a couple of years ago. She's known you forever."

"So?"

"So, you could ask her for a ride. You could go out to the parking lot, and run into her, and ask her for a ride somewhere."

"Where?"

"I don't know." Amanda sounded impatient. "Make something up. Make somewhere up. How about out to Grandview Park?"

"It's a swamp," Shelley said.

"So?" Amanda said.

"Why would I want to go there? Why would she go out of her way to drive me out there? You aren't making any sense."

Amanda's makeup things were spread all across the stainless steel shelf under the face mirror above the sinks. She opened her bag under the shelf and swept all the jars and tubes and bottles out of sight. She looked angry, the way only Amanda could look angry — as if she had every right to expect you to do what she wanted you to do, and you were being evil to refuse her.

"Listen," Amanda said. "This was your idea as much as mine. You wanted this as much as I ever did. If you're not interested anymore, just tell me."

"Of course I'm interested," Shelley said.

"Well, then. I'm going to be out at Grandview Park at twelve thirty this afternoon. You ask Miss Edgerton for a ride and get her out there and meet me. I don't care what you tell her. Just be there. Or we can call the whole thing off."

"You couldn't do it without me," Shelley said. "If you tried, I'd know it was you. I could go to the police and say it was you."

"Meet me out there," Amanda said again. Then she tossed her hair against her back, picked up her shoulder bag, and flounced out of the girls' room. If the door hadn't been on an air hinge, she would have made it slam.

Once she was gone, Shelley took a look at herself in the mirror. There really was a line of acne along her jaw. Her cheeks really were as puffy and round as a chipmunk's. Everything the other girls said about her was true, except that she wasn't actually stupid. If Amanda couldn't do it on her own, she couldn't, either, and she wanted to do it very much. She very certainly didn't want to give it up.

Still, for a while there that morning, Shelley did think she'd give it up. At least, she'd give it up for now, and lay low for a year or two, until she was old enough to get out of Matahatchee, and go someplace where nobody had ever heard of her or of Amanda Marsh. It was depressing to walk through school all day watching Amanda in the middle of crowds of people, all of them looking like they'd just stepped off the cover *of Seventeen* magazine. It was even more depressing to hear Amanda's name called out in homeroom for the honor roll the third time already this year. It seemed to Shelley that there should be some kind of balance. Pretty girls should be stupid girls. Not-so-pretty girls should be smart girls. That was the way it was in the movies, except that in the movies even the not-so-pretty girls were prettier than Shelley was, and they always blossomed into beautiful girls as soon as anybody paid any attention to them.

Shelley was not blossoming into beautiful, and by third period, she was already in trouble with three different teachers. She had forgotten her business math homework for the third time this week. She got caught talking in English class when the teacher was trying to read a poem. She got caught walking in the hall chewing gum, which had recently become verboten at Matahatchee High School, along with guns, knives, and charm bracelets. Charm bracelets were suspected of being vehicles for carrying gang symbols, although there had never been a gang of any kind at Matahatchee that anybody could remember. The trouble in English was stupid, too. The poem was this thing called "The Emperor of Ice Cream," and if anybody had ever been able to make sense out of it, Shelley would gladly eat cow dung. Holding the pink slips that meant she was due in the office during lunchtime to discuss the "appropriate discipline," wandering through the west wing corridor on the way to her study hall, Shelley found herself thinking about Miss Edgerton again. Miss Edgerton, who always wore the right thing at the right time. Miss Edgerton, who was always organized and polite. Miss Edgerton, whose car was always clean and whose clothes were always pressed. In some odd way that Shelley could not pin down, Miss Edgerton seemed to be at the root of all the trouble in the world, of all the trouble for people like Shelley. For some reason, she reminded Shelley of Amanda, all grown up.

It was the pink slips that decided it, in the end. Shelley had the pink slips and had to take them to the office. Miss Edgerton was in that very same office, doing some kind of work for the lawyer who was working for the Board of Education. Something. Shelley couldn't remember. She only knew that as she made her way toward the center of the building, she felt better than she had in hours. She felt lightheaded and secure.

She'd expected to have to look around to find Miss Edgerton — in a back office, maybe, or closeted with the principal — but Miss Edgerton was right out front at a desk, next to Miss Lazio, and the cat was with her. Or rather, the cat was lying across a pile of papers, curled around a crystal paperweight that Shelley didn't remember ever seeing before. Maybe it belonged to Miss Edgerton, or the cat, and Miss Edgerton had brought it along to keep the cat happy. Miss Lazio was certainly happy. She reached across to Miss Edgerton's desk every once in a while to stroke Edelweiss's back, and Edelweiss curled around to nuzzle the fingers when they came close. It was, Shelley thought, completely nauseating. They treated that cat the way they should have treated a child, except that neither of them had children. They probably didn't even want them. Maybe Amanda was right. Maybe Miss Edgerton was a lesbian. Maybe Miss Lazio was her lover. Shelley seemed to be full of maybes today. It made no sense. She wished she could take off for the rest of the day and spend her time downtown, where there was nothing to do, but where nobody was watching her.

Miss Edgerton and Miss Lazio both looked up when she came into the office. Miss Lazio looked at the little clutch of pink slips with a frown. Miss Lazio was nowhere near as annoying as Miss Edgerton, because she was younger, and not so perfect. Her hair was forever falling out of the clips she used to try to hold it back.

"Well," she said, as Shelley pushed her way up to the counter that separated the desks from the waiting area. "You seem to have been busy today. Let me see what you've got."

She got out from behind her desk and came to where Shelley was standing. At the desk with the cat on it, Miss Edgerton sat still, staring. The cat was snaking around as if it were trying to rub itself rich. It was so white, it made everything near it look darker.

"I know you, don't I?" Miss Edgerton said finally. "You live next door to me."

"That's right," Shelley said.

Miss Lazio had gone through each of the pink slips. "I don't want you to think she's some kind of juvenile delinquent," she said. "These are all minor enough. They always are, with Shelley."

"That's right," Miss Edgerton said. "Shelley Altman. When you were younger, you used to play the piano."

"I gave it up in fifth grade," Shelley said.

"That's a pity. It's a fine talent, playing the piano. When I was younger, almost every girl learned. You should have had more ambition."

"I like your cat," Shelley said.

Miss Edgerton brightened and put out a hand to let Edelweiss nuzzle against it. The two of them together looked like some kind of joke: the old maid and her cat. Miss Edgerton had long fingers with blunt, well-tended nails. Her nail polish was clear and uneventful. Shelley wondered, suddenly, which of the Victoria's Secret underwear sets she was wearing today.

"It can't be helped," Miss Lazio was saying. "Shelley? Are you listening? It can't be helped. We've got the curricular plan for next year to get out of this office today. I've got Caroline here to help us with the legal documents we have to file. There's just not going to be anybody free to talk to you about these until tomorrow. It would be different if you'd done something really serious. I could have sent you to Mr. Borden if you'd vandalized some property or threatened another student with bodily harm. But this —" Miss Lazio waved it all away with one hand. "This is barely worth talking about. You'll have to come back tomorrow and talk to somebody then."

"All right," Shelley said.

"I don't think it would have been better if she had vandalized property," Miss Edgerton said.

Miss Lazio brushed hair out of her face. "Just let it go," she said. "I'll charge these off on the book. You can forget all about them. Except the homework, of course, and that's up to your teacher. Why you girls don't do homework is more than I can understand. But then, I don't understand anything anymore, do I? We didn't have air-conditioning when I went to high school. We got hot, that was all, and we learned to live with it. They never learn to live with anything."

"I like your cat," Shelley said again.

Miss Edgerton smiled. Then she leaned over and picked up Edelweiss and laid her across her shoulder. The cat purred and stretched and yawned.

"I like my cat, too," Miss Edgerton said. "Nobody can be completely without sense if they truly love a cat."

Lunch was at eleven o'clock. Shelley didn't eat it. After she was finished in the office, she went down the corridor and out the side door, to the teachers' parking lot. She looked up and down the rows until she found Miss Edgerton's car. Then she walked through the planters until she was standing beside it. It had not changed since the last time she'd seen it. There was no reason why she should have expected it would. It was still dark blue, and it still had the cat carrier in the back seat. The carrier's door was propped open now, though, to make it easier for Miss Edgerton to get Edelweiss inside it when it was time to go. All the doors were locked, and the trunk was locked, too. Shelley tried it. Whatever she was going to do next, she wouldn't be able to hide in the back seat or the trunk until Miss Edgerton decided to go home.

She walked around the car a few times. She sat down on the concrete bumper that defined the parking space inside its two white border lines. The teachers' parking lot was full of these bumpers, although the student parking lot had none. Shelley had no idea what they were for. She didn't know how to drive, and it if was up to her mother, she never would.

She walked around the car again, and again, and again. She felt dizzy, but she didn't want to stop. She thought of going into Miss

Edgerton's house when Miss Edgerton wasn't there, but the cat was. She'd been doing that long before Amanda had moved to Matahatchee and had come up with the idea of killing off Miss Edgerton, and not just Miss Edgerton, but lots of people, all the people who deserved to die. Shelley would have thought of it on her own, though, eventually, because when she was in Miss Edgerton's house and it was quiet and cool and dark, she sometimes imagined Miss Edgerton dead, on the floor, on the couch, stone cold and unable ever to come back to life again. Every once in a while, she even dreamed of it. She turned over in bed and there she was, in her head, in that house, with the body cold in the bathtub or the garage or someplace else out of the way. She sat down at the kitchen table, and Edelweiss came up to sit in her lap. She lay down in the big queen-size sleigh bed — why did Miss Edgerton have a bed that size, when she was the only one who ever slept in it? — and Edelweiss came to lie across her stomach. It was not stupid to love a cat, Shelley thought, if you loved it the right way. It was only stupid to treat a cat as a child. She was sure she would never treat Edelweiss as a child, if Edelweiss was her own. The only problem would be her parents, who did not like the idea of a pet in the house. They didn't like the idea of Edelweiss, either. When Edelweiss came across the yard to look for Shelley, Shelley's mother would shoo it back home. *Cats bring lice,* Shelley's mother always said. Then she gave Shelley a lecture on why it was more important, and more Christian, to love your fellow human beings instead of a cat.

The best thing, Shelley thought, would be to kill Miss Edgerton where nobody could see it and to hide the body where nobody could find it. That way, it could be months before someone came along to do something about the house, or the cat. She wouldn't even have to worry about the grass growing out of control. Miss Edgerton didn't have grass. She had pebbles in decorative colors, the way a lot of people did, so that they didn't have to look at brown and dying lawns during the long months of water rationing in the summer.

Shelley got up from where she was sitting, walked around the car again, and sat down again. When she put her hands into the thick warm air, she could feel Edelweiss's fur on her fingers. Buried in the white like that, her fingers looked as dark as sand.

*

It was ten minutes after twelve when Miss Edgerton came out of the building and headed for her car. Shelley was still there, in the parking lot, making no sense at all, and for a single frightened moment she thought that Miss Edgerton would not be alone. Mr. DeVoe would be with her, surely, or Miss Lazio would walk her out. That was the kind of thing adults did with each other. Shelley looked around, but the parking lot was deserted. So was the space at Miss Edgerton's back. There was only Miss Edgerton, carrying the cat.

"Miss Altman?" Miss Edgerton said.

Shelley had only been called "Miss Altman" before by teachers — schoolteachers or Sunday-school teachers — and then because she was about to be in trouble. She blushed four shades of red and looked directly into Edelweiss's eyes. He looked miserable. He looked as if he knew what was about to happen to him. And why shouldn't he know? He'd probably been put in the car, and the cat carrier, often enough.

"I wasn't doing anything," Shelley said. "I was just — just —"

"Just what?"

"Just looking for somebody to give me a ride. Out to Grandview Park."

"Grandview Park?" Miss Edgerton blinked. She had her keys in one hand. She had Edelweiss in the other, tucked under her arm like a loaf of bread. She got the back passenger door open and reached for the cat carrier. "Why ever would you want to go to Grandview Park?"

If Edelweiss had been her own cat, Shelley would never have put her in the cat carrier. She wouldn't even put her in the car, if she didn't like to drive places. She stared stupidly as Miss Edgerton got Edelweiss into the carrier. Why ever would she want to go to Grandview Park?

"Shelley?" Miss Edgerton said. "Why do you want to go to Grandview Park?"

"Oh," Shelley said. "Well. My mother's there. For the afternoon. You know. She does nature stuff."

"Does she? I wasn't aware of that."

"Oh, yeah. She does. She always has. You know. Since college. She went to Agnes Scott, did you know that?"

"No." Edelweiss was hunched down in the carrier, making a noise like an angry purr. Shelley had to hold herself back from trying to rescue her.

"Well," Shelley said. "She did. Go to Agnes Scott. And now she does nature stuff. And she's out at Grandview and I'm supposed to meet her there. Except my ride isn't here."

"Who is your ride?" Miss Edgerton asked. "Possibly we could phone him." She reached into her bag and came out with a cell phone.

"I don't know her name," Shelley said quickly. "It's somebody my mom knows at the Methodist church. I mean, I know her first name. It's Elizabeth. I just don't know her last one. If you see what I mean."

"I see that this seems to be a very disorganized undertaking," Miss Edgerton said. "Are you always this confused about your plans? Is your mother always this confused? She keeps such a nice house. I wouldn't have imagined she wasn't meticulous about her arrangements."

"There's never been any problem before," Shelley said, wondering when, exactly, this before was supposed to have taken place. The last time she'd been out to Grandview Park, she'd been ten years old and on a hike with the United Methodist Church's Girl Scout troop. That was when her mother was still insisting that she belong to the Girl Scouts, before it turned out the Girl Scouts didn't have anything against atheists joining, or gays. Then Shelley's mother had gone on a long tirade about how she should have known it all along. Girl Scouts were always such tomboys. They hiked and tied knots. They were as masculine as lady wrestlers.

Miss Edgerton was standing by the side of her car. She had her keys in her hand. She had her jacket over her shoulders as if the day was a cool one instead of a lethally hot one. She squinted in the sun.

"I suppose there's no reason for me not to drop you off, if you have to go," she said. "But I do worry about what your mother is likely to say. I'm sure she doesn't want you driving around with strangers."

"You're not a stranger," Shelley said. "You live next door."

"Yes," Miss Edgerton said. Then she got in behind the wheel and popped the locks on the two doors that were still closed.

Shelley closed the door next to Edelweiss's cat carrier and opened the one to the front passenger seat. Behind her, she could hear the cat making that same low growl, miserable and angry.

Shelley knew she would be miserable and angry, too, if somebody had put her in a cage.

It got too much to listen to after a while. Shelley could hear the low tortured growl over the sound of the Volvo's engine, even over the hum of National Public Radio, which seemed to have nothing else on it except people talking endlessly about things that didn't make much sense. All the radio stations Shelley had ever listened to either played music or Rush Limbaugh. When Rush Limbaugh talked, he sounded excited, not hushed and secretive like these people here. Shelley tried to concentrate on the conversation — about gardening, and whether it was better to grow vegetables or flowers — but finally she couldn't stand it anymore. She had to make Miss Edgerton stop.

"It's not as if I mean to make the cat suffer," Miss Edgerton said. "I put her in the back like that because it's the best place for her. She's safe there. If I put her up on the seat, she rocks the carrier until it falls over."

"It's all right," Shelley said. They had stopped near the curb on one of those long stretches of two-lane road that were everywhere in this part of Florida. Palm trees lined the sidewalks on both sides, but nothing else did. Shelley looked around as she was getting the cat carrier out to put on her lap in the front seat, and there was nothing to see. The nearest house was blocks away, except you couldn't call it blocks because there weren't any blocks. The nearest gas station was half a mile down the road. She shut the back door and climbed into her seat with the cat carrier in her hands. She got her seat belt on and her arms around the carrier. She could put her fingers through the grille at the carrier's front, the little cage part. Edelweiss nipped at her, causing no pain.

"She really is quite all right in the back," Miss Edgerton said. "She doesn't like it, it's true, but we can't always like all the things we have to do. I'm sure you don't like all the things you have to do."

"She doesn't know any better," Shelley said, although that was not what she meant. Edelweiss seemed to her to know better than just about anybody.

Miss Edgerton got back on the road. It wasn't very far to Grandview Park now. If Shelley had ignored the noise, the cat would not have had to suffer any longer than a few more minutes. Still,

Shelley felt better. Edelweiss had stopped nipping her fingers and begun to nuzzle them. She had stopped making that noise that sounded like agony.

Grandview Park announced itself with a tall gate that was always open, with a latticework arch above it that spelled out its name in metal letters. Miss Edgerton turned the Volvo into the drive and went in for the five hundred or so feet that were possible before all traffic had to stop. It was not really a park. It was a "wilderness area," designated as such by the federal government, and set aside to remain completely undeveloped. Like the Everglades, its only purpose was to exist. Shelley got out of the car and looked around. There was no sign of Amanda she could see. There was no sign of anything except a narrow trail leading in through the Spanish moss and the high grass. Shelley shifted from one foot to the other, unsure what to do.

Miss Edgerton got out of the car. "Your mother doesn't seem to be here. There's no car parked anywhere I can see."

"It's probably parked around the other side."

"Let's go there, then."

"Oh, no," Shelley said. "That's not necessary. I know where she goes. It's easy enough to reach from here. It's just —"

"Yes?"

"Well, if you wouldn't mind, walking in with me? I get a little spooked by the stuff, you know. Bugs and things. And there are alligators."

"If there are alligators, you shouldn't go in at all."

"Oh, the alligators aren't roaming around loose. I mean, they are, but they live at the bottom of this clifflike thing, you know, and they never come out where they're going to bother you. My mother comes out here bird-watching and stuff all the time."

Shelley rubbed the side of her face. She had no idea what she was saying. The park could be crawling with alligators. There could be an alligator behind every bush. She really did not remember, in any detail, the last time she had been here, except that she had sat down on a path and cried when she found out they hadn't brought any Coke. She should have brought a different kind of coke. That would have been the best idea. She looked around. She wished she knew where Amanda was. She wondered if she could do this on her own, and then decided she had to. If she had closed her eyes at just that moment, she could have seen Miss Edgerton dead again, this time on the overgrown grass, with alligators coming toward her.

Miss Edgerton looked from one side of her to the other, and then up the path. There was nothing to see there. The trees were too thick. So was the grass. So was the Spanish moss. When you looked up the path, all you saw was darkness.

"We'll bring Edelweiss," Miss Edgerton said suddenly. "I don't like to leave her in the car very long in this heat. She'll get dehydrated. Bring me the carrier now, and show me the way your mother will have gone. We'll walk for a while, but if we don't find her soon we'll go back. I'm not going to have you wandering around a swamp in central Florida on your own."

Shelley snatched Edelweiss in the carrier and came around the side of the car. Miss Edgerton took the carrier and nodded toward the path.

"You lead," Miss Edgerton said. "You're the one who knows where we're going. And call out. Maybe your mother will hear us and show us some mercy."

"Right," Shelley said, looking back at Edelweiss in the carrier. All she could see were the eyes in white fir, eyes as black as the asphalt pebbles that sucked up onto the road every year in the worst heat of the summer.

She turned toward the path and started in, her stomach turning, her head full of fuzz. Now that the moment was here, she could barely think at all. She needed Amanda to be here, and Amanda was not. Amanda would know what to do. As it was, all Shelley could manage was to walk steadily forward, into the trees, into the brush, and to imagine, as she had always imagined. For some reason, though, she couldn't seem to imagine Miss Edgerton dead — she couldn't imagine Miss Edgerton at all. It was as if Miss Edgerton had never existed. All Shelley could concentrate on was the light on Edelweiss's face as she let her out of the cat carrier and into the daylight. You shouldn't keep an animal caged, Shelley thought, you really shouldn't. Not even to ride in a car. If there was no way for Edelweiss to be safe in a car without a carrier, then she and Edelweiss would walk everywhere they went. They would start by walking home, as soon as Miss Edgerton was dead.

You shouldn't keep an animal caged, Shelley told herself virtuously, one more time. And then something hit her hard, on the back of the head.

Farther back on the path, Miss Edgerton stopped and put the cat carrier down next to her feet. She had seen the poker arch and Shelley's body fall, but she hadn't witnessed the details of the wound, and she had no intention of doing so. That was why she had her helpers in the first place. She needed someone to handle the messy parts, and she had never much cared for the sight of blood. Now she waited patiently while Amanda walked farther up the path and threw the poker into the brush. Then she came back into view, stripping off her white cotton gloves. There was a time when women everywhere wore white cotton gloves as automatically as they wore panties, but those days were dead and gone, and Miss Edgerton knew it.

"Well," she said.

"She wasn't paying any attention," Amanda said.

"They never do," Miss Edgerton said. "They get distracted by the cat. I'd better give you a lift home, or people will start wondering where you are."

She turned around and went back down the path, toward her car. She did not look back at Amanda, and would not have, no matter what she thought the girl was doing. She got to the car and put the cat carrier in the back seat, where it belonged. She got behind the wheel and waited. Amanda would want to look at the body, to prod it, to make sure of it. She'd been at this only six months, and this was only her third adventure.

Miss Edgerton could remember when *she* had been at this for only six months — but that was decades ago, and she had been younger then.

WILLIAM HARRISON

Texas Heat

FROM *The Texas Review*

CARLA MET HIM FIRST: an oddly handsome, tall, grinning cowboy type with large red hands. He introduced himself as Boomer Smith and said he grew up in Harlingen and the valley, but moved around these days chasing deals. He wanted a nice house out in the hill country, he said, with a pool, a view, and, if possible, stables.

Carla told her partner, Mary Beth, about him. They owned a small realty company, Lantana, out on Highway 290, west of Austin, and specialized in small ranches.

"He bring a letter from a bank?" Mary Beth asked. "He sounds too good to be true."

"Said he'd pay cash. But he also said we could check his credit, though I haven't done it. I think we're talking a buyer who'll spend a million or two."

"You like him?"

"Kinda. Once or twice this look came over his face, though."

"What sort of look?"

"Like he definitely might want to get in my pants."

"Carla, we're having a lousy month and you know it. You might have to sacrifice your body."

"Tell me about it," Carla answered, and they shared a snort of laughter.

Mary Beth and Carla decided in college that they could run a successful real estate business together, but since that time they had suffered failed marriages, money problems, heartbreaks, and heavy competition from the larger real estate firms in both Austin and over in Blanco County. They struggled to pay rent on their office building, a washed-out abode with noisy plumbing set back in a grove of scrub oaks and windblown mesquite trees halfway out toward Dripping Springs. Mary Beth had a nine-year-old son with asthma, Luke, who sat on the bench for his Little League team and Carla had a demanding mother with too many cats and a series of bad hairdressers who cut too much off. Even so, both Carla and Mary Beth danced the salsa at Miguel's, the Texas Two-Step at the Broken Spoke, and up close on Sixth Street with assorted telephone linemen, executives, former halfbacks and dull professors. They traded date notes after occasions at Threadgill's or the Oasis and agreed on just one general rule between them: no musicians.

They also took care. At the clubs or in business they worried about men.

When they met male clients at isolated houses or ranch property they went as a team, a caution against unwanted sexual advances. They vowed to watch out for each other, figuring they lived in a masculine ethos: beer and barbeque, football and bullshit, kisses and violence.

Boomer Smith, of course, had a shy, goofy, awkward way about him and wouldn't even meet their gaze. Carla felt motherly toward him because his Stetson was somehow tilted wrong and he moved clumsily, bumping chairs and desks with his hip, fumbling, grinning, and getting out of sync even in his best moments.

"How can he go around making deals? He hardly talks!" Mary Beth observed while they waited to show him the first property.

"Maybe he does all right with the guys," Carla offered. "He was probably the nerdy valedictorian in high school. Straight A's and a member, you know, of the model airplane club."

He arrived an hour late after their part-time secretary, Maria, had gone home for the day. Held up at the Driskill Hotel, he told them, and very sorry. He brought them each a single rose and offered to take them to dinner as compensation, but still wouldn't look directly at either of them.

They drove out to a small ranch near Driftwood. On the way Mary Beth asked if he meant to raise cattle and he said, "No, maybe horses," yet he admitted he didn't ride. Carla asked if he had a family and he said, "No, I'm single and mean to stay that way." He snapped off that last reply, so that five minutes of silence ensued. Later, the little ranch looked overgrown and wrong.

"Maybe if you could give us an idea of how much you intend to spend," Carla ventured cautiously. "I mean, if this place is just too small, what do you have in mind?"

"I mean to impress," he instructed them, and that cryptic reply — as they later discussed with one another — was curiously worded and spoken. His voice actually changed when he said it. The drawl vanished. He seemed more out of place than ever, a lost outsider employing a strangely arch diction.

At the Salt Lick, though, a big barbecue hangout on a nearby farm road, they relaxed. Boomer bought a case of Budweiser, laughed for the first time, and began to tell stories: one about his mother, who lived near Alpine and owned a pet kangaroo, and another about an uncle who lived in a maze of trailers in the middle of nowhere near Amarillo. In such tales his drawl returned and he became an affable and earnest country boy.

"Six trailers." he said about his uncle's place. "Two of 'em big doublewides. Lashed together with cable, so they won't blow off in a dust storm!" In their accompanying laughter they forgave him his peculiarities and he fit, clearly, Carla's view of him as a former high school nerd, the one with the nutty family, the one who never knew what to do with his hands. While they ate peach cobbler and pecan pie with their coffee, later, Mary Beth went on about her little boy, Luke, who didn't fit in at school and who occasionally whined that he wanted to live with his drunken daddy. Boomer offered that Mary Beth seemed practical and sure of herself and that she could undoubtedly accomplish more with him than any man. When she smiled at this flattery he went on, saying that a young boy needs his mother, ask any psychologist, and if the teenager, later, needed a stronger hand, then maybe the father. "But for now, Mary Beth, have confidence in your intuitions," and he placed a big red hand over hers as big, moist, inebriated tears appeared in her eyes.

"I think Boomer's just wonderful," Mary Beth said, turning suddenly to Carla, who watched all this over the rim of her coffee cup.

"He's fine," Carla replied. "But when you drink beer, Mary Beth, you have a tendency to fall in love, to believe in gurus, or to want plastic surgery."

Minutes later they reeled through the parking lot arm in arm beneath a gaudy display of stars in a moonless sky. Boomer forgot his Stetson, so Mary Beth volunteered to retrieve it, leaving Carla alone with him. She leaned against the rail fence and gazed up at the Milky Way — a down-home name for a galaxy, she commented — and Boomer moved beside her. For a moment she thought he might try to kiss her, and then she wondered if he intended to say something, but he remained wordless and didn't make a move. When Mary Beth came back wearing the Stetson down over her ears and grinning, he moved off sideways, awkwardly, in retreat. They were soon all talking at once and driving back.

A few days went by. Clients materialized, including a young couple with only a thousand dollars for a down payment. When Boomer phoned again, Carla told him about a spread at the edge of Blanco County, a working horse ranch whose owners agreed to let him look at it. No, he said, he didn't want to deal with occupants, not with anybody *except* Carla and Mary Beth themselves.

"Maybe you can drive by the ranch and look at it," Carla suggested. "I'll give you directions. If you like it, we'll arrange to see it when the owners are away."

He agreed.

But he also said that he had business in Galveston, so another week passed before they heard from him again.

Carla lived in an apartment just off the Mopac: four big rooms furnished with light pine furniture and lots of gadgets — an espresso machine, an ice-cream maker, a big music center, a forty-one-inch TV, and dozens of novelty clocks, mobiles, and sculptures that turned on rotating pedestals. That week she and Mary Beth attended another Little League game, watching Luke sit in the dugout, then play right field after the score was decided. Afterward, walking away from the concession stand, Carla thought she saw Boomer's big dark Lincoln Continental, and she walked halfway across the parking lot to make sure. It was somebody else's car. Later, she fretted over the mistake.

When Boomer came back he gave Carla a friendship ring. Just an item bought in Galveston, he said, but it was too extravagant: a sapphire of about a half-carat. "Payment for all the work you've been doing," he said, and he gently pushed away her hand when she tried to give it back.

"To tell the truth, I bought it secondhand," he admitted, not looking at her. "It was a genuine bargain. You take it. Please."

They were at the office on Maria's day off. Carla had been typing out a contract for the young couple, who were probably going to be turned down by loan officers. The toilet down the hallway made an embarrassing noise.

"Did you drive over and look at that ranch in Blanco County?" Carla asked, trying the ring on her finger. It was a dazzling gift, bigger than the wedding ring she once wore, and she couldn't analyze the nervousness she felt.

"Didn't go by," he said of the ranch in question. "But I saw another place over that way. Just off Highway 165. A vacant house that looks new with good grassland."

"I'll find out who handles it and set up an appointment," she told him, and at that point Mary Beth and Luke drove up, the windshield of her green Toyota flashing at them. Carla felt strange and caught, especially moments later when she showed Mary Beth the ring and tried to explain why she couldn't accept it, yet had. Boomer hunched down and talked to Luke while Carla followed Mary Beth back to the toilet, where they jiggled the handle, grinned, gave each other looks, and tried to cope with their client.

"It's just an inappropriate gift," Carla said of the ring. "What do you suppose he thinks it means?"

"Honey, accept it," Mary Beth advised. "When he chooses a house, we'll sell the damn thing and split the profit as part of our commission."

"He wants to get me in bed, I just know it," Carla sighed.

"Well, sure he does. You're a looker and he's clumsy as a goose. He didn't know what to do, so he just bought that damn ring."

When they emerged, Boomer was showing Luke how to throw a curve ball and, somehow, baseball made everything natural again. Mary Beth actually flirted, bumping Boomer with her hip, and they all grinned and went out for burgers. At the Dairy Dip, Boomer played pinball and, later, showed Luke a switchblade knife with a curved ivory handle, but something happened so that Luke came over with his root beer float and sat beside his mother as if he didn't want anything more to do with Boomer.

"What happened, Honey?" Mary Beth asked, but Luke wouldn't respond.

"Did Boomer hurt your feelings?" Carla persisted, but Luke just crushed his baseball cap in his fist — a pinstripe cap in the New

York Yankees style — and sucked the straw of his empty root beer float. Meanwhile, Boomer slapped the sides of the pinball machine, his face and raw hands illumined in its glow.

"What, Luke? Tell me," his mother kept on.

"Oh, it's some male conspiracy thing," Carla decided, so they let it go.

The weekend arrived and Carla continued to fret. It was illegal to run a credit report, but she considered it. She didn't want to ask Boomer to allow himself to be investigated because she might offend him and lose a sale. Too awkward, she told herself, yet her skepticism annoyed her, especially since she had accepted the ring. She scolded herself for having doubts.

The weather turned hotter.

According to the listing information, the house out on 165 had sixteen adjoining acres, no pool, no stable, and no view, but Boomer wanted to see it that weekend, so Carla made arrangements. Mary Beth would attend another Little League game with Luke, Carla would show another house to the young couple with only a thousand dollars, then they would meet Boomer out in the hill country late on Saturday.

A wind blew up, but hot: swirls of dust in the flats, trees bending on the ridges, great pavilions of cloud rising on the southern zephyrs. Deadly humidity, too: Carla's blouse stuck to her back and the young couple perspired and whined. She wanted Boomer to write a big fat check, so she could go off to the mountains, up in New Mexico, say, where the nights turned cold even in summertime.

She drove west behind an old slow pickup and couldn't pass in the traffic, then turned off on a farm road quivering with a mirage of rising heat. The twang of an irritating guitar jangled her nerves, so she turned off the radio.

Following another realtor's instructions she found the house: an angular rock, cypress, and glass monstrosity — no architect would do such a thing — along a dry creek bed in a stand of live oak and cottonwood trees. The house could barely be seen from the highway and she wondered how Boomer had found it, but there he was, waiting, leaning against his big Continental beside a rock archway and gate, grinning and waving. He had sweated through his T-shirt and his Stetson was pushed back on his head.

"Found me," he said, as Carla got out of her car.

"Lordy, I feel like I've driven all day," she managed in reply, and she manufactured a smile. The heat bore down on them.

"The house is already open," Boomer told her. "I peeked inside."

With that they started up the flagstone walkway. She felt relieved to be rid of the young couple and confident that Mary Beth and Luke would soon be along.

"You know, I like this place," he said when they stood in the living room.

"Nice," Carla agreed, though she didn't completely mean it.

The high windows let in a brass-colored and stifling heat of late afternoon.

"It's nothing like I wanted," he admitted. "But it has a good feel to it."

"This happens a lot," she said, as they made their way toward the kitchen. "A client will have a very specific idea about what he wants, then buy something completely different. Just goes to show."

"I'm not anybody's usual client," Boomer reminded her, and his voice did that thing again: formality crept in in an aloof arch tone.

"No, I don't want to imply that you are. You're one of a kind, Boomer, really, I mean it."

"Hey, you're not wearing the ring."

"It's in my purse. I intend to have it sized right away."

They admired the kitchen and breakfast nook decorated with bright Mexican tiles, then they stepped outside on the wide deck across the back of the house. At one corner of the deck an outdoor shower surrounded by glass brick emptied into a drain that led through the cottonwood grove to the dry creek. Boomer stepped inside the shower and found that the water could be turned on.

"Look at this! Nice, huh?"

"It's a great outdoor shower," Carla agreed.

"Tell you what. Let's take a shower and cool off."

"You go ahead," she managed, and that nervous laugh came out of her. Before she knew it, he began to skin out of his T-shirt and sat down abruptly on a wooden bench to remove his boots.

"Now come on, don't leave," he instructed her. "At least stand guard, so Mary Beth doesn't barge in on me." He had a wide grin and as he fumbled with his belt his effort seemed frantic, childlike, as though his big hands couldn't keep up with his enthusiasm.

She watched until he began to stumble around in his jeans, trying to get them off, then she turned away, laughing, and thinking, no, you're certainly not the usual client, you're a doofus, you're too much, and she caught a glimpse of his bare butt as he entered the shower stall. Above the glass bricks, then, she could see his grinning face and the curve of the chrome showerhead.

"Whoa!" he yelled when the water came on. "That's cold!"

"I'll bet it's nice," she called to him. He made a noise like a goat and ran his long fingers through his hair.

When she started to leave, he once again called her back, saying, "You know, I think I'll buy this place. I'd have to add a stable, but it could be small. I only intend to keep a coupla horses."

She found herself getting used to this silliness of his: talking business while buck-naked underneath a shower.

"You haven't even seen the upstairs," she reminded him.

"Five bedrooms, five baths, all tucked away, very private. I like it. You know, I think I'll make out a check."

She began to feel lightheaded. Cash, a solid commission. Then he started talking about an apartment in Austin, too: Something close to the center for nights he might want to stay in town. She sat down on the wooden bench while he yelled out his thoughts. Was there anything for sale around Town Lake? Some real nice condos?

"Carla, are you there?"

"Right here," she said, standing up again, so he could see her. "Standing guard as ordered."

"Just drape my T-shirt over the stall," he said. "I'll dry with it. And if you don't mind, lay my jeans over the side, too."

While he dressed, she suggested that he should make a low bid on the house, but he rejected that. No, the asking price seemed fair, he said, and they went back to a discussion of condos. Maybe something around the university, he added. He liked to watch the kids come and go.

By the time he came out of the shower, dressed, they were laughing so naturally that when he suggested that she should hop into the cold water, too, she considered it.

"I won't watch, promise," he told her. "In fact, I'll go get a big ol' beach towel outta my car. I bought it in Galveston, never used it, and you can dry off with it afterward."

"Well, maybe," she allowed, and by now, somehow, all of Boomer's unpredictability was part of a general charm.

"We'll do it this way," he said. "Wait until I bring the towel to you, then I'll go away again. I'll go wait for Mary Beth and Luke and when you're finished you can show me upstairs. Or we can walk off some of the land. How about it?"

"Sounds okay," she agreed. "I'll wait for you."

He hurried off and while he was gone Carla listened to a dove's familiar call from the glade. The sun sank low behind the cottonwoods and the last of the wildflowers — so lush in the springtime that they blanketed the hillsides — now filled what remained of the day with their sweet decay. She wondered if someone like Boomer could possibly become her fate: an odd guy, never quite on cue. The money, of course, would make a difference, and she speculated for a moment about a life where sapphires came as easily as Cracker Jack prizes. Awkward endearments would be the routine, not romance, she knew, but romance never worked anyway. And she wanted somebody to love and care for; her mother had sensed the vacuum in her life, so had become too demanding and the only things that moved in her apartment were the mechanical sculptures. Such thoughts — and a chorus of dove calls from the darkening trees — occupied her until Boomer came back with the beach towel, grinned, shuffled his feet, backed away, and excused himself.

"You just take your time," he assured her. "I'll be out front. When you're all done, you can show me the rest of the house."

After he disappeared she stripped off quickly, left her clothes draped over the stall, stepped in, and turned on the tap. A little shriek came out of her when the cold water hit her skin, then she stood there, getting used to it, and noting that the beach towel said *Welcome to Biloxi*, so that she wondered how Boomer came to buy such a thing in Galveston.

She wished she had soap. Then, holding her face up to the spray, her thoughts going nowhere in particular, she felt his arms encircle her.

"Boomer!" she cried out with another burst of nervous laughter. "You lied to me, you devil!" And to herself: Okay, here it is, deal with it, stupid, because you're bare-assed and helpless.

She spoke to him again, but he didn't answer and she could feel his naked body pressed against her backside, feel his chest rising and falling with excited breathing, and feel, distinctly, his pubic hair pressed against her hip. He turned her slightly, cupping a breast in his giant hand, saying nothing, and she felt him trembling as if all his timid wires had come loose.

A moment passed, then she said softly, "There, Boomer, steady," and she felt strangely motherly and helpful as if he hadn't deceived her, as if he hadn't circled back and slipped out of his clothes again. She took his free hand in hers and felt its shudder. For all his boldness he was sexually frightened, she sensed, and in this knowledge her own fear lessened.

"Boomer?" she murmured again, gently, urging him to say something. But he kept his silence. She knew she couldn't fully express her apprehension: He had stepped over the line into this heavy sexual move, but couldn't go on. Dozens of times in her life Carla had experienced this, a sad thing, really: The aggressive mating male often boldly lurches forward into an embarrassing sexual paralysis and requires soothing out.

"Boomer? There, it's all right," she heard herself say.

"Very well," he said in rasp. And his voice became strangely formal again, clipped, the Texas drawl gone. "Touch me."

With this request — or was it a command — she felt curiously in charge and decided to obey. As he bent forward, dipping his head into the stream of water so that his lips touched her shoulder, she let her fingers move down his body. He was limp and pitiful, nothing there at all, and she decided that the cold water pouring over them caused this so began to lead him out of the stall. She even managed a smile and let him gawk at her nakedness, then she saw that her clothes were gone. "Boomer, Honey," she said gently and carefully, "where are my clothes?" and she managed to still keep her calm although this was definitely a little crazy.

"You're very pretty naked," he told her, and his voice was someone else who used considerably more proper diction. "I knew you would be."

"Here, let me get the towel," she said, and she pulled it off the stall as he led her by the hand. They padded across the deck, leaving wet footprints, passing through the tiled kitchen and into the den where he took the towel from her and spread it onto the plush carpet. Fine, all right, he's gaining confidence, she told herself, and we're going to do it now, okay, and she thought about her sexual history — how many boys and men? Fifteen? A husband and two lovers of some duration and all the others — and she decided that she hadn't been promiscuous, not really, maybe it was sixteen or twenty, it was the way of the world, the adventure and the desperation, and she settled on the towel and pulled Boomer down beside her. Pressed against him, she could still feel his indecisiveness so she tried to kiss him — to say, yes all right, with a kiss — but he wouldn't have it.

And where was Mary Beth? And the only sounds now were the distant three-part notes of the dove and his labored breathing, that deep rasp, and he turned her on her side and settled himself against her thigh and began grinding himself against her, so that she thought, no, wait, should I help him out here? And from his mouth came a deep *n* sound, an unexpected, doleful, creepy subtext to his breathing: "Nnnnn, Nnnnn." She felt her lower lip tremble and knew she might cry, but held on.

He had no erection, but moved against her thigh in a wild impersonation of the act, and she felt her heart go out to him even as she wanted to weep for herself. She prayed to the wall, oh, God, please, don't let him be the one, and she didn't even know what she meant, exactly, but the prayer spilled out of her along with a sob. She clasped her hand over her mouth, so he wouldn't hear her cry, and his movement went on and on, accompanied by that same "Nnnnn" that he made with his teeth clenched and in what seemed to be a prolonged agony that he couldn't release.

At last something in him was finished and he lay beside her, his arm draped across her rib cage, and she fought for control, trying to recover, until finally she managed, to say, "Boomer? If it's all right now, I'd like to get my clothes. Where are they? You can tell me now." And she spoke to him as if he were a child, she realized, with a parent's calm, but it didn't sound right, he wasn't stupid, she knew, and the condescension was unmistakable.

"Go look out that window," he told her evenly with his strange new voice.

"Which window?"

"That one in front of you. Tell me what you see."

She got to her feet, wrapping her arms around her breasts, and padded over to the window, bent and covering herself. The final slant of a red sunset touched the trees and for a moment the view comforted her.

"What?" she asked, looking out. "See what?" He came and stood beside her.

"Here, put this on," he said, and she turned to see that he held the sapphire ring. Obediently, she allowed him to slip it on her index finger.

"There we are. My signature," he announced, smiling, and his voice, she decided, was like a trained actor's, a voice that could project or dive into a whisper and that knew exactly its effect.

"You're not from Texas, are you, Boomer?" she asked, and her own voice trembled with the question.

"Sure I am," he told her. "Same as the Bowie knife. Like the drought in summer or the blizzard in winter. A force of nature. Like the tornado. Like the rattlesnake and scorpion. Same as the blinding dust storm. That's exactly who I am and where I'm from."

It seemed like a practiced speech, one delivered by a curious foreigner, and although her mouth twitched involuntarily and although she wanted to bolt away she gazed out the window yet again to see the sun's last rays pick up something metallic in the hillside stand of cottonwoods. A car. It was out there in the woods. She looked more closely and knew this was what he had meant her to see. Somebody's car, green. And then she knew.

"Come on, we'll get your clothes," he told her, leading her away. She embraced his words in hopeless hope, wanting everything to be zany and perfectly all right, wanting Boomer to be the guy at the pinball machine, the big clumsy guy, but she knew better. The ring, she knew, had belonged to some woman before her. His signature. Prayers and memories fell on her, then, like weights.

He led her through the master bedroom to an enormous bathroom covered with the remains of Mary Beth and Luke. In a far corner, smeared with blood and casually tossed aside, was the pinstripe baseball cap, and why, she asked herself, why me? I don't deserve this, nobody does, I'm really a good person, a little lonely, trying hard, and he's not even named Boomer, he used somebody else's name, and I don't even believe he's from Texas, not at all, he's lying, he's not one of us.

ALAN HEATHCOCK

Peacekeeper

FROM *The Virginia Quarterly Review*

Spring, 1993: There were more direct routes to the Oddfellows Hall, on a dry knob north of town, but Helen Farraley could not see below the muddy flood waters, couldn't risk wrecking the boat on a tree, or chimney, or telephone pole; who knew what was just below the surface? The streets of town were lined with ancient oak, the leafy tops of which stuck out from the water like massive shrubs, and Helen steered the boat through the channel between them. The others in the boat sat silent as they passed their neighbors' homes, slate-shingled Victorians underwater to the second-floor windows. Helen trolled high above the town's main street, Old Saints Road, and the treetops dropped away as the land sloped into the valley's low.

They passed the Super America gas station, only the hump and peak of the S/A on its road sign visible. The others stared into the muck water as if they might see the pumps or store below. Afloat in the current was random lumber, tree branches and strips of siding, a pair of trundling bar stools, a long metal box Helen believed was either a school locker or a feed trough. Then came Freely's Diner and Freely's General, three-story brownstones on opposite sides of the road, water up to the white-stone facing, roofs like rectangular docks. They passed within arm's distance of the electric sign that read FREELY'S, which usually shone bright red, but was now dark and hung just above the water line. Freda Lawson, who wore a chambray dress over yellow waders and sat beside Helen, ran a finger along the sign's second *E*. Helen yanked down the woman's arm.

"They's wires," she snapped. Then she gently held Freda's elbow and softened. "Please be careful, hon."

They passed high above the converted boxcar that was the old Fox Tavern, and the First Baptist Church, its steeple jutting crooked from the water like the mast of a sunken ship.

"They'll steal everything we got," Jake Tiernen said from the bow, his wife beneath his arm. "They'll take what all they want."

Freda twisted the hem of her dress around her fist. "I wet myself," she whispered to Helen, crying.

"Ain't nobody stealing nothing," Helen said, and leaned a shoulder into Freda to let her know she'd been heard.

"To hell," Jake said. "To hell they won't."

Christmas Eve, 1992: Light from Freely's Diner spilled over the snowy walkway and into the cruiser. Helen checked her face in the rearview mirror. Her left eye was badly swollen, and she tried to hide it by tilting her cap over her brow. She considered driving on. But then Freely stood in the diner's window, the old man thin and hunched and his hands cupped against the glass. Helen climbed out into the cold. She walked around the car and Freely moved to the door and opened it a crack.

"I got pecan pie," the old man said through the crack, then Helen was at the door and he opened it wide.

Helen stepped in and Freely had his arms around her in a hug. Ten years she'd worked in Freely's General before becoming Krafton's first and only law officer. It'd been Freely, longtime mayor of Krafton, who decided any real town had a sheriff, and raised funds to buy an old cruiser from the Boonville force, and called a town meeting in the First Baptist Church. It'd been a joke that Helen, a middle-aged grocery store manager, had been nominated and then elected, and when protests arose — *I thought it'd be a goof to vote for her, didn't think she'd win* — it was Freely who declared civilized democracies stuck by a vote.

The dinner crowd had just left. Ham and potatoes fragranced the air. "I ain't hungry," Helen said. "Just saw the lights on."

"No, no," the old man said, hustling behind a glass counter. He pulled one of two pies from the dessert case and put the pie in a box. "You coming for Christmas supper? Marilyn said you might."

Helen studied the front window. Jocey Dempsy's photo was in all the shop windows: her middle-school portrait, a ponytail tied with red ribbon, braces, a blemish on her hawk nose. MISSING across the top. REWARD across the bottom. "Don't know," Helen said.

The old man was in front of her again. He held the box with the pie inside and wore a fur-lined coat that was much too large for him. "What you done to your eye?"

Helen turned toward the door. "Slipped on some ice."

"Clumsy girl," and he took her arm. "Walk me home?"

They left out onto the walkway. Freely's hand quivered and he struggled to put the key in the lock. His house was down the road and up a small hill. Warm light shone from the windows, colored lights twined around two large spruce by the porch steps. "Looky there," he said, pointing across the road. Over the dark field colored sparks burst, rained, faded in the night sky. They sounded far away, maybe miles, the pop of fireworks like a puff of breath in Helen's ear.

December 19, 1992: The cruiser's headlights caught the shadows of footprints across the road's new snow, and Helen pulled to the shoulder. The gravel sky looked heavy, the woods flanking Pentland Road lost in a fog of flurries. The footprints disappeared through a gap in the brambles. The girl, Jocey Dempsy, hadn't come home from school, had been gone over a day. Nobody in town had seen or heard from her. Her folks said she often took walks in these woods. Helen retrieved the holster and pistol from the seat beside her. She turned the cruiser's spotlight on the tree line but could not see through the falling snow. She shut off the engine. The motor ticked in the dark quiet, wet snow piling upon the windshield.

Christmas Eve, 1992: In the glass of the door Helen's swollen eye looked as if a stone had risen onto her face. Snow curled up the porch steps and over her boots. The door opened. There stood Connie Dempsy wearing a red sweater with snowflakes embroidered in silver thread. She did not say hello but stepped aside for Helen to pass.

The front hall smelled of popcorn, of cinnamon. A little girl in pajamas, a smiling bear on her belly, hid behind Connie's leg. She was Jocey's baby sister and looked like her. Warm light fell into the hall from the kitchen, and then David was in the light, wiping his hands on an apron. Helen did not know where to stand. There was no doormat and she did not want to track snow into their house.

"Merry Christmas," she said.

Connie lifted the girl into her arms, would not look at Helen.

"Would you like something to eat?" David asked, still down the hall in the kitchen doorway.

A puddle had formed on the tiles beneath her boots. "I don't have any news," Helen said. They did not move. They said nothing. Helen held out the pie box and another package wrapped in green paper with a white ribbon. "Here's one of Freely's pies," she said. "And I got something for the girl. It ain't much of anything, but it's something."

They went into the family room, an upright piano in the corner, the tree beside it, tiny colored lights flashing. Helen had removed her boots and was afraid her feet stunk; she'd worn the same wool socks five straight days. But she smelled only popcorn and cinnamon. The family sat on a sofa, the girl in the middle. Helen faced them in a high-backed wooden chair, her gun belt awkward against the armrest.

The little girl did not tear the paper like most kids. She picked at the tape, her mother helping, and carefully unfolded the wrapping to reveal a box. Inside was a tiny pink shirt. Across the front was a golden star and the words JUNIOR DEPUTY; KRAFTON, INDIANA. Connie and David glanced at each other. Light glimmered off the silver thread in Connie's sweater. The apron hung down between David's legs. The little girl wrinkled her nose and stared at Helen's face, and Helen was sure she'd ask about her swollen eye.

Helen crossed one socked foot over the other. She looked at Connie. "It ain't much," she said. "I didn't know what to give a child."

December 19, 1992: Helen crossed Pentland Road and pushed through brambles and into the woods. Her flashlight created a tunnel of light, inside of which were the arms of catbrier and low-slung limbs and the occasional shallows of footprints. She pulled her stocking cap to her brow. She felt the immense silence. Helen trudged on, and deeper in, where gray dusk lit the bench above her, she saw tracks of black soil where the snow had been tramped.

Helen climbed, her feet slipping as she scaled the slope and stopped on the ridge to examine a scuttle of boot prints.

Slivers of pink broached the flurries in the western sky. She paused, breathing heavily, and stared down over the valley. A black stream cut the mottled white, powdered trees hunched on their hummocks. In one distant corner of the prairie the last of daylight glinted off a tin roof.

Some gentle movement in her periphery made her notice the near trees. Far below, a large white oak still held its autumn leaves, its branches gently waving. Through a gap in its canopy she glimpsed a flash of pale skin. Her breath drew away, and then she was shuffling down the bench, and she slipped and fell hard on her back, sliding in the new snow to the base of the slope.

The oak towered above her. She shone her light up into it, over the girl's exposed ribs, her dangling arms, and between her buds of breasts curved a swag of dried blood, dripped from where the rope had torn the skin of her neck. Helen turned on her side and retched. Vomit steamed in the dirt. She took clean snow into her mouth and caught her breath. She stood and unsnapped the latch over her pistol, and approached the darkness beneath the boughs.

The girl's toes dangled inches from the ground. She wore only shoes. Clunky black shoes with square heels. Her naked skin glowed white against the dusk. Her mouth hung open and what little light came through the saffron boughs gleamed in her braces. Helen took off her coat. She tried throwing the jacket up over the girl's shoulders, but it slid off and fell in a lump on the ground.

It was the girl. Jocelyn Dempsy, who everyone called Jocey. She raced motorbikes on a dirt track by the old mill, played J.V. basketball as an eighth grader. She loved Moon Pies. Loved cherry cola. She'd come to the General and buy them, and Helen would watch her eat alone by the road and return the bottle before riding off.

Brisk wind whistled through the limbs. Helen stumbled to sit against the trunk of the oak, her legs stretched out before her, pistol drawn in her lap. Dusk had settled. The prairie was tinted blue, shocks of blue sedge stiffly swaying.

Spring, 1993: The current took the boat and she shone the spotlight across the black water and onto the house, the flood up to its second-floor sills. She hooked the tow rope around a window box and the prow knocked against the siding. She pressed her forehead to the window's cool glass. The room's red fabric wallpaper had silver stripes that flashed in the spotlight like metal bars. A twin bed lay diagonal in the middle of the room. A cardboard box made a crater in the mattress, a new-looking ball glove atop the box. Alone on a wall above a small dresser hung a poster of three busty women in yellow swimsuits, each suit with two letters that when pressed tightly together spelled YAMAHA.

Helen forced open the window. Careful not to sway the boat, she held her holster and stepped down into the room. It was the first time in hours she'd been out of the boat, and her legs tingled. The carpet glistened in the spotlight, a dark line three feet up the wall marking the flood's highest point.

The room had not been disturbed, was kept like a museum; Helen had been in the room that winter, putting on a play of sorts, searching the girl's drawers and beneath her bed and taking notes on what she passed off as evidence — report cards, a menu from the Boston Connection restaurant in Terre Haute, a ticket stub from a motocross event at the Motorhead in Evanston — she knew would lead nowhere. She wrote it all up in a report for the Staties.

The bedroom door was locked from the inside. Helen opened the lock and door, wiped the knob clean, then walked down the hall. Water splashed with each step. The walls were tiled with Dempsy family photos: Jocey, very young, donning a boy's shag haircut and straddling a small motorbike; the family in matching cream sweaters with David on a hay bale, the baby on his lap, Jocey and Connie each behind one of his shoulders; Jocey's school portrait, a ponytail tied with red ribbon, braces, a blemish on her nose.

At the back of the house Helen entered the master bedroom. A canopy bed filled most of the room. Helen gazed out the bedside window at the flooded world, the dark roofs of houses spread wide like barges on a big river. Everything smelled of soil and fish. So much water, so much washed over, but perhaps when they'd start anew everything could be better, everything forgiven. Perhaps God would allow the girl to be dredged up by the flood and found, her parents granted their closure, yet the unrighteous cause of her death kept a gracious unknown.

Helen walked to a bureau and searched the drawers, one filled with scarves and nylons, the next with panties neatly folded and separated by color. She moved to the closet and shone her light over the clothes: pants at one end, then blouses, then dresses. Sweaters were on a shelf above the hanging clothes. She pulled the red sweater from the middle of a stack, unfolded it to be sure it was the right one. The silver thread of the embroidered snowflakes twinkled in Helen's spotlight. She held the sweater to her face; it smelled faintly of Connie's perfume. It was an impulse, and Helen could not explain why she needed it other than to say it was something clean and lovely in a world of mud. She hugged the sweater to her throat and lay down on the bed, the mattress soft and pulling her in, her boot heels heavy on the waterlogged carpet.

December 19, 1992: Blue smoke trailed from a pipe in the cabin's tin roof. His footprints had frozen like fossils in the snow, and Helen tracked them down through the prairie. The cabin belonged to Robert Joakes, who came into town once a month for supplies and sold beaver and coon pelts to a coatmaker in Jasper. A dim light came from the cabin's only window, a small square high up the wall. Helen stood on her numb toes and peered through the window. A lantern on a rough wood table gave a scant circle of light. A figure hunched beside an iron stove. Helen removed a glove and drew her pistol, felt its weight in her hand, adjusted her finger on the trigger. For a good while she watched the dark figure, embers glowing behind the stove grate. Then Joakes moved off into the shadows.

Helen crouched beneath the window. Whittled gray clouds raced in from the north. The wind tore through her. Her hand on the pistol grew terribly cold. A half-mile away in the tree, Jocey's body was freezing solid, and Helen felt herself at the center of something enormous and urgent, bigger than her mind could hold, and though terrified, and angry, mainly she felt desperately alone. The urge to flee, to hide, was overwhelming. This is how Jocey felt, she thought, and clicked off her pistol's safety.

She eased each step through the crackling snow, past firewood stacked to the roof, on around to the door where a metal bucket gave off the stench of urine. A dog barked inside the door, heavy and loud barking that did not cease.

Christmas Eve, 1992: She followed at a safe distance, as children on inner tubes towed behind a pick-up made wide tracks in the road's snow. More children huddled in the truck's bed, sparklers burning in their mittens and gloves. The truck took the curve of Elm Road, and the inner tubes swung out, the last in line dropping into the ditch before the whip cracked and yanked it back onto the road. Helen switched on the blue and red lights atop the squad car. The truck did not pull to the shoulder but merely slowed and stopped, the inner tubes sliding forward, one knocking into the next. Helen grabbed her flashlight and walked out into the snow, the kids splayed and breathing hard on their tubes.

"We ain't done nothing," said the boy on the last tube, a boy they all called Knight, his chin resting on his gloves.

"Not yet, you ain't," and Helen stayed the flashlight beam on his face just to get him riled.

"You're piss mean even at Christmas," Knight snapped, and all the other kids laughed.

Helen passed the kids in the truck bed, their sparklers hissing glitter and glistening in their eyes. "You kids cold?"

"No'm," said one boy. "I am," said a girl, and the boy told her to shut up.

Then Helen was at the truck's door, and Willie Sharpton grinned at her, the flaps of his hat down over his ears and a cigarette in the slit between his mustache and beard. Helen put a boot up on the truck's running board and leaned in the window.

"Them kids just grabbed hold of my truck," Willie said. "Don't know whose they are."

"They just lassoed your tailgate?"

"That's about right," and Willie blew smoke back into the truck as to not blow it on Helen. He turned and studied her face and closed one of his eyes. "That eye looks like hell."

"Our wedding pictures'll look awful."

It was a play on an old joke, one neither smiled at. Knight yelled for them to come on, that his nuts were freezing. Willie patted Helen's arm and took a drag on the cigarette. He stared ahead where the snow was yet to be tracked by tires.

"Any leads?" he asked.

"No."

Then they were quiet, and Helen stepped down from the truck's runner and looked back at the children. The sparklers had burned out and the bed was dark. Drift snow crawled out of the ditch and sidewound over the road. She shone her flashlight on the line of tubes. The kids had their hoods pulled over their faces.

December 19, 1992: Footsteps and a man's scolding voice came behind the cabin door. The barking ceased. Flat against the weatherboards, Helen tried keeping her frozen fingers from gripping the gun too tight. The door unlatched and swung open, its shadow covering her. A large yellow-haired dog ran into the prairie, stopped, raised its head, sniffed at a briar. Joakes walked out into the snow, shirtless, thick hair covering his shoulders and back. He watched the dog in the prairie. Helen stepped out. She pressed the gun against the dark beard of his cheek and yelled at him to get on the ground.

Joakes whirled and hit Helen with an elbow, and she slipped to one knee. He paused and glanced over his shoulder, maybe looking for the dog, maybe checking to see if there were others. Helen drove into his legs and took him to the ground. Forearm under his chin, she pulled mace from her belt and doused his eyes. He flailed his fists. She scrambled out of his reach, then stepped forward and sprayed him again. He covered his face, mace dripping down his fingers and chin. The dog charged in, sniffing at the man and barking. Helen approached, both pistol and mace drawn, the dog baring its teeth, yapping, pouncing. She sprayed the dog and it recoiled, pawing its snout, then came at her again, viciously snapping at her legs. She fired the gun. The dog fell in a lump, a hole bore through its neck, hot blood leaching into the snow.

A knee in Joakes's back, Helen pressed the gun to his ear and said she figured to kill him for what he'd done. His eyes were shut tight. He sniveled like a child. He did not move.

Spring, 1993: Helen stared at the canopy's sheer fabric and heard it again; hissing and what sounded like a gunshot. She rose from the Dempsys' bed and stepped to the window. Again came the hissing. In the northern sky the pop unleashed golden sparks that willowed down. On what she knew was Macey Goff's roof stood a silhouette, another whining flare rising from its arm and exploding high above, green sparks shimmering, falling.

Helen held the Christmas sweater to her breast, like a child with her blanket. She stuffed it into her jacket, zipped up, and hustled down the damp hall to her boat. She hooked in the oars and began rowing around the Dempsys' house, making for the Goffs'. The current was strong. To keep the boat straight Helen pulled twice on the right oar for each on the left. Across the bay a silver bass boat hitched to a second-floor window thudded against the house. The man on the roof wore jeans tucked into his boots and a sleeveless flannel shirt unbuttoned to show a mural of tattoos across his chest and abdomen. He dropped a Roman candle into the guttering, drew a fresh wand from his boot. He was Danny Martin, a young strip miner who'd been a great ball player, even had offers to play in college, but then he beat up a girl and it all went to hell.

Blue sparks fell directly above. Helen brought in the oars and the boat glided. A flashlight beam waggled inside the house. She drew her pistol and switched on the boat's spotlight. Inside the room a large long-haired man in black waders spun around. The spotlight threw his shadow on the back wall and when he shielded his eyes the shadow took the appearance of a hunchback, then grew larger as he ran to the window. He clanged out into the bass boat, the hull rocking and sliding away from the house.

"Danny," the man hollered, furiously yanking the motor's cord.

"Stay where you're at," Helen yelled.

A candle shot whistled low overhead. Helen ducked, trained the spotlight on the roof. Danny toed the gutter, the wand aimed down at her. She spun off the bench and onto the wet floor. A shot hissed into the water beside the boat "This is the police," Helen yelled. The other boat's outboard turned over and raised an octave speeding away. Then another pop, and Helen looked to the sky. Golden sparks rained down. Held in an eddy, her boat slowly turning, red sparks fell, and moments later the sky bled green. Then the candle was done and Danny gazed into the whitecaps thrashing the house. He teetered, raised his arms. He leapt from the roof, his legs scissoring as he hit the water.

December 20, 1992: Robert Joakes sat tied to a chair in the lantern's pitiful light; Helen had torn bed sheets and bound his ankles, his thighs, wrists, chest, waist, and gagged his mouth so he could not scream.

She'd found Jocey's clothes atop a mound of salted venison in the root cellar and sat thinking on the cellar steps with the girl's jeans across her lap. Laws on killing, even God's demands, didn't allow for peace. Not always. There'd still be pain; missing that child would break her parents' hearts. But what Helen knew, what she'd seen in those woods, would be too much for them, for everybody.

She made a plan to hide it all and knew she'd have to be careful. She'd be ruined if Joakes got loose, or if someone found him like this, or if he died too soon. Those in town, and especially those from outside Krafton, might not see grace in her methods; what she'd begun to call in her mind *the Big Peace*.

Spring, 1993: Danny emerged far downcurrent, pummeling the churning spate, flopping, thrashing. Helen gave chase, but the current was unpredictable and, afraid she'd brain him with the boat's hull or outboard's blades, she dare not get close. His body went slack, and he was swept toward the ropey tops of willow trees, disappearing through the curtain of their branches.

Helen cut the motor and scrambled to the bow. She grabbed several branches as they whisked past and was jerked backwards into the stern. The rush of water was amplified in the blackness. She held the ropes and took her feet and balanced herself, and with her free hand drew around the boat's spotlight.

The canopy was a crewelwork of limbs, the water topped with brown froth and swirling as if over a drain. Danny draped one arm over a thick branch, his cheek against the trunk, his shoulders beneath the water. Helen pulled the boat deeper through the mess. Danny lifted his head, managed to tilt his chin into the tree's crotch. "We was looking for my dog," he said, gasping.

The branch forked into the water and Helen could not get to him. She leaned over the branch and reached as far as she could. Danny stared blankly at her hand. His head lolled, his elbow unhooking from the branch, and he held on with just his hand, his body dragging in the current. Helen lunged her entire body onto the branch and grabbed his wrist. She centered her weight and pulled until his elbow was hooked back safely, then dropped her feet down into what she thought would be the boat, but instead was the rush of freezing water. The boat had drifted from beneath her, the spotlight a trailing beacon as the hull curled into the rope branches, was held briefly, then the limbs parted and fell back into place and the boat was gone. Helen hugged the branch and held

Danny, the flood whirling darkly around them, Connie Dempsey's Christmas sweater a lump in the gathers of her jacket.

December 22, 1992: Helen scanned the frozen prairie, worried someone had seen her sneak through the dawn-tinged woods and into the cabin. Behind her, bound to the chair, Joakes stank of urine and shit. She carefully untied his ankles, then his legs, his waist.

Three days in the chair and his legs had atrophied; they buckled as he stood, and he staggered as she walked him to a snowy swale in the river's bend. There she took down his soiled pants and told him to relieve himself. He stood shivering, loins exposed, mouth and upper body still bound, head drooped. He fell to his knees, then onto his side, and began to weep. Sunrise washed full over the eastern hills and burned through shreds of fog in the near woods. Someone'll see him, Helen thought, and she rushed to him, trying to pull up his pants and get him to stand. But he just wept and shook, and Helen could do nothing with him.

She dragged him by his armpits, inch by inch, his pants at his ankles, bare legs wet and red with cold, heels leaving ruts in the snow. She dragged him past the pump frozen over with icicles, and past a stack of vegetable crates covered in snow, in which lived brown chickens that did not move and might be dead. The dog's stiff body lay at the side of the stoop; it would look right that way, Helen figured; a man who kills his dog is a man who's lost all hope.

It took half an hour to get him back in the chair. She removed his pants and covered his lower half with a heavy blanket. She carried the pants to the river, stomped a hole through the ice, and dangled the crotch in the water below. She returned and lay the pants over half the stove, and on the other half heated oats in a pot. A square blazon of sunlight flooded the window and covered his face. His eyes, scorched by the mace, were a deep watery red, the skin not covered by beard the color of tin.

She unbound his mouth and pushed oatmeal on a wooden spoon between his lips. He took the oats into his cheeks and she pushed in another spoonful. He stared through her, his red eyes narrowed in the sunlight, and for a moment Helen remembered what he'd done and stood frozen before him.

Joakes spat the oats into her face. He licked his lips. "I'm a Christian man," he said, hoarsely, oats in the beard beneath his mouth. "I'm forgiven."

Christmas Day, 1992: Freely sat in a lounger by the fireplace, a blanket over his lap, his eyelids batting, closing. Helen sat on the hearth, the fire warming her back. She'd not worn her uniform for the first time in a long while, and found her old jeans to be loose in a way she greatly missed. On the floor by the tree a circle of children played a game where they rolled dice and moved tiny farm animals around a board. The adults sat around a long table, drinking hazelnut coffee and discussing a foundry opening in Jasper. Helen's feet prickled with pain, and she worried they were frostbitten. Her swollen eye gave a headache aspirin could not help.

The front bell rang. Freely's wife, Marilyn, walked to the foyer, wiping her hands on the back of her dress. She opened the door and in rushed the cold and the children sat upright to see who was there. Pastor Hamby, a bear of a man in a black overcoat, filled the doorway. Marilyn stepped aside to let him in, but he stayed where he was. He leaned down and talked quietly to Marilyn and glanced into the house at the same time. Then Marilyn turned, and they both looked at Helen, and Pastor Hamby waved her over with a gloved hand.

Helen stepped gingerly out on the porch and closed the door behind her. Four men in parkas, the First Baptist Deacons, stood at different levels on the steps, colored lights in the spruce reflecting in tracks of ice on the porch. Helen did not have her coat, and hugged herself with one arm and sipped her coffee.

Pastor Hamby's cheeks were flushed, his thin lips drawn tightly over his teeth. "We were delivering care baskets out in the knobs like we always do," he said, and looked back at the deacons.

They'd found Joakes's body, this Helen knew by their faces. She tried to still her own face, her heart, to quiet the guilty part of her that wanted to confess and be forgiven. Frank Barker, a squat man in glasses, stepped a boot on the porch and leaned over his leg. "The holidays is hard on some," he said. "It ain't joy and cranberries for everyone. For some it's only lonesome pain."

Spring, 1993: Willow limbs hung limply in the brightening morn, the current's froth filling with light and bending prisms where black branches emerged. All night Helen had listened in darkness to the flood's drone, and in a waking dream she'd seen the girl's body float up from the quarry depths, drift and drift in the murky current to be caught in the high branches of one of the town's ancient oaks, and as the water receded, her neck wedged in a crook, there the girl dangled above Old Saints Road for all to see.

Now Helen sat high in the willow and tore away limbs until she could see out over the water. A single ridge humped out in the east. Her boat was nowhere to be seen. Danny was in a sort of sleep. She'd given him Connie Dempsy's Christmas sweater and handcuffed his wrists to a branch overhead so he would not fall. His head hung in the hammock of his arms, the sweater too small and the sleeves far up his wrists.

To the north sunlight winked off the hull of a bass boat. Helen screamed and screamed, but with the rushing water she knew she would not be heard. She drew her pistol and fired into the gap of sky. She fired twice more before the boat veered their way, then fired again to keep the boat on track. Once it was close enough, she began to holler. She glanced below at Danny, who picked up his head and stared up at her, the sweater stretched tight across his chest. He too began to scream, and Helen could see the boat was steered by the long-haired man from the night before. He cut the motor, the hull piled high with bodies of dogs, and shaded his eyes to see into the tree.

The prow parted the canopy, and Helen stared down between her legs, the long-haired man watching her as he passed below. Danny called out to his friend, and the boat bumped against the trunk. The long-haired man held the tree with one hand, and with the other lifted a shotgun and aimed it up at Helen.

"No, Ray," Danny said. "She's all right," and Danny stared up at her. "You all right, ain't you?"

Helen nodded, held her hands out where he could see them.

"She's all right, Ray," Danny said again, and the man in the boat let the gun fall to his side.

Helen uncuffed Danny and they both climbed carefully into the boat and had to sit on the same tiny bench to avoid the dogs. Dogs filled the hull; a collie atop a German shepherd, and several hunting dogs, blueticks and grays. Stacked in an orderly way, heads at one end, tails the other, stacked like firewood. The boat drifted from beneath the tree, willow branches washing over them, and then the sun was warm.

Wisps of clouds feathered out above. Ray stuffed his lip with chaw and stared Helen down. "I found a body," he said, then turned away and wrapped a cord around the outboard flywheel.

Christmas Eve, 1992: Joakes quietly sobbed, lips smacking as if from thirst, and asked to smoke just one cigarette. Helen considered it a moment, then untied his right arm. She carried the lantern to the cupboard and pushed aside a jar of pickled eggs, and there was the thin wooden box. The smell of tobacco came out strong. She kept the lid open, hoping the smell would overtake the odors of Joakes himself. She even held it beneath Joakes's nose. He shut his eyes and seemed to take solemn pleasure from the scent. Then he opened his lids and his red eyes drew onto her.

Like trap jaws sprung, he snatched the lantern from her and Helen was struck in the face and fell hard to the floor. The lantern light was gone. Moonlight through the tiny window lit a back wall where skinning tools hung on metal pegs. Sharp pain pierced Helen's eye, shot deep into her skull. Chair legs thumped as Joakes rocked and fumbled with his free hand to untie his bindings. Helen's eye swelled quickly; within seconds the eye was closed to sight. Dizzily she took her feet and drew her pistol. She stayed still until she found the pale skin of his bald spot in the moonlight, then Helen struck him and Joakes shrieked. With all her weight she struck him once more. Joakes's head bobbed violently, and he made no sound.

Helen staggered into the yard, clutching her gun, and broke an icicle off the pump's handle. She lay back in the snow, dim stars turning in fractured tracks, the frozen ground beneath her seeming to turn, and though she meant to hold the ice to her eye, she brought up the pistol, and it was cold and soothed her just the same.

December 20, 1992: Parked on the quarry's service road, the cruiser growing cold with the motor off, Helen sipped peppermint schnapps and considered the world made of her design. My religion is keeping peace, she thought. It hadn't begun that way, was nothing she'd planned, but now she saw that's how it was. I just ran a grocery, she thought. I don't want this. I ain't the one to make the world right. She swallowed more schnapps, then capped the bottle and put it away in the glove box.

Helen stepped out onto the road and popped the trunk. The air had warmed, the boreal wind stilled. Like ashes from a furnace, thick and gentle snow began to fall. She'd taken the clothes from Joakes's root cellar, washed them in the river, dressed the girl, and wrapped the girl in a green canvas tarp. Helen struggled lifting the body from the trunk. But she tugged the torso out over the fender and the rest followed and flopped down to the road. Helen had needed a sled, and without knowing its use Freely sold her one at half-price, and now she turned the canvas parcel onto the sheet of red plastic tethered with rope.

She dragged Jocelyn Dempsy on the sled, the girl's weight breaking the undercrust of old snow and new snow collecting in wet mounds about her head. Helen pressed onward, eyes closed to the cold, legs plodding into drifts.

At the quarry's rim she paused to unfasten the tarp. She did not look at the girl. She moved behind the sled and shoved it all over. From her knees she watched the sled and tarp flutter and the body turn and break through the film of ice with barely a sound.

Flakes fused to flakes and piled on her thighs and gloves. The quarry would soon be thick with ice, and what was below would be held for a time. In spring the body would rise through the gray slush and be found. The town told stories of children who'd fallen to their deaths in this quarry. Teenagers were drawn to its danger. They would all believe Jocey had just drowned, and it would be over. Helen gazed into the quarry. This is how I'll be, she thought. I'll be this icy hole, this season, this falling snow. I'll just freeze myself over.

Spring, 1993: In the flume between hillocks the floodwaters converged, dammed by logs and mud, a kitchen chair, a section of roof, a child's plastic slide, refuse thick and high and brown water sluicing through random gaps. A riot of gulls hovered, filling the sky, the refuse wall alive with white birds. Ray ran the boat onto the grassy hillside and hopped out and stomped the anchor into the earth. Helen climbed cautiously over the mound of dogs, a glove to her nose. Scum-water churned at the dam's base. The torrent on the other side, the swollen Little Squirrel River, charged madly east. Helen feverishly scanned the refuse. The tan face of a mare, what looked like a carousel pony, stuck out from beneath what might be a green tarp. Helen's hands trembled; she'd lost control of her hands. She stuffed them in her pockets and clenched them into fists, thinking of Jocey's school portrait on the Evansville news, remembering Freely, only weeks ago, taking down the same picture from his diner window.

They climbed the hill where rail tracks split the ridge and stood on the wooden ties. Down by the river lay swine, black-faced sheep, more dogs. Helen thought of Haley Winters's cattle. Where'd all those cattle gone?

Ray pointed at an outcropping of rock. A body lay on a slab of limestone, fully clothed, feet spread apart. A gull roosted on the body's shoulder, and Helen could not see the face. "I seen that boy some in the Old Fox," Ray said. "Don't know his name. Never said so much as hey to me."

Helen rushed down the hillside, her momentum carrying her in a reckless sort of run. Wind blew the long grass flat. She followed the grass down with her eyes and then she was falling and landed hard on her side. The gull on the body raised its wings and glided downshore. It was Keller Lankford, a hay and bean farmer who lived south of town, nearly three miles from the river. His face was the blue of his overalls, his blackened fingers clawed into a fence slat clutched to his chest. Then Danny was over Helen pleading, *don't do that, oh come on now,* and pulled her into his arms.

Helen shoved him away. She tried taking her feet, only to crumble. Her ankle was badly hurt. She wiped sweat from her eyes and face, and noticed small cuts had brought blood to her palms. "Take off that sweater," Helen screamed at Danny, blood streaked across her cheeks. "Throw it in the river. It ain't yours to be wearing."

Ray was at the water's edge breaking twigs and tossing them into the current. "Get rid of them dogs," she screamed at Ray. "Nobody wants to see them dogs. Just let 'em be gone. You hear what I say?" Ray snapped a twig and brought it to his mouth. He waved up his middle finger.

Danny ran past Ray, and thigh-deep into the raging flood he tore the red sweater off over his head and hurled it into a rush of gulls.

Christmas Morning, 1992: Helen held the lantern to Robert Joakes's swollen face. Faint plumes of breath trickled from his lips.

With a wooden spoon she pried opened his mouth, then pushed the spoon and his head tipped backwards. She considered, as she had many times before, to ask him *why*. Instead, she inserted the barrel of a shotgun into his mouth. He made noises, not words, gagging on the metal. She sat the lantern on the cold stove and closed tight her eyes.

The explosion in the small room made the pots in the cupboard rattle. A ringing pulsed in her ears. Joakes had toppled in his chair and lay in the dark of the floor. She worked fast, looking only when she had to, untying his legs and thighs, his hands and chest, blood pooling blackly over the uneven planks. She worried momentarily as to which hand was his shooting hand, then chose his right, and worked his thumb onto the trigger.

She piled the bindings into a garbage bag and left the lantern burning on the table. She hurried outside, careful with her footprints, stepping sideways into drifts so the snow would collapse, then on the exposed rocks behind his house, up the hill, breaking the ice and splashing through a tiny brook, then down the bluff to the frozen stream, where she paused atop a granite boulder.

The moon was in its descent, the stars fading. She'd wait for dawn, for pale light to arise and cover her. She thought of Freely's grandchildren tearing pretty paper from gifts, and singing "Away in a Manger" in church. She thought of families gathered around tables thick with holly. In her mind she tasted honey-glazed ham, scalloped potatoes, macaroon cookies. But she could not wait for dawn. Her feet were wet and the night was bitterly cold. She clutched her collar and limped along the stony banks, and stepping up to enter the prairie she slipped and fell onto the garbage bag of rags and slid until she was out on the frozen stream. The ice popped, but held. Thistles of pain stabbed her toes. She lay on the brittle black ice and could hear water flowing beneath her.

Spring, 1993: The men had come down the hill from the shelter and gathered around the boat. They were solemn, unshaven, shirts rumpled, the pits of Pastor Hamby's white shirt stained with sweat. The farmer's body lay in the hull where once had been dogs, Helen's jacket shrouding his face. The sun was high, the air damp. A new wall of thunderheads and the fur of rain bulged forth in the west.

"You'll tell the others?" Helen said.

Pastor Hamby nodded. "What can we do for *you*?"

"I need rest," Helen said, wilting, and almost began to cry from tiredness. "Let me rest a while."

Suddenly came the wind, full and strong, and Helen's coat blew off Keller Lankford and tumbled onto the hillside, exposing his blue bloated face. Helen lunged after her coat. Her ankle gave and she caught herself as she fell. A deacon, Jerry Timlinson, clambered into the boat and covered the dead man's face with his own jacket, then squinted up at the approach of weather. Spatterings of rain fell sideways in wind and sunshine. Pastor Hamby and Frank Barker lifted Helen, each with a hand beneath her thigh and another at her back. Slate clouds rowed forward over the sun, its light dappling the hill and then the sun shower was a storm.

The men entered the lightless hall, shirts transparent with rain, Helen riding their arms. "Put me down," she said, clutching their sleeves. Pale faces emerged from the darkness: Walt Freely and Marilyn, Connie and David Dempsy, the little girl held to his shoulder, everyone she knew, grimly nodding, touching her pant legs, stroking her wrists, some speaking her name with quiet reverence. "Let me down," she repeated, but they did not, and Helen began to cry. Rain drummed the masonry. Light from the storm lay a greenish glow in the hall. She could not stop herself from crying. They huddled around Helen, silent in the gloom, then the pastor raised his pulpit voice and called for them all to just clear out and leave her be.

EMORY HOLMES II

A.k.a., Moises Rockafella

FROM *The Cocaine Chronicles*

1.

"You said I could have water. I want some water," Fat Tommy asked again.

"You can have water, Moises, after you tell us how it went down. Understand? That's our deal," Vargas reminded him.

Fat Tommy's big shoulders slumped. He was having a really bad day. His business was gone. His money was gone. His high was gone. And the cops weren't buying his story. He laid his arms tenderly across his knees. He tried to sleep, but the cops kept butting in. He narrowed his eyes in the harsh light and squinted down at his arms. Still, he had to admit . . . he certainly was well dressed.

"Don't give those white folks no excuses, Tommy," his wife, Bea, had advised. "We ain't gonna get kilt over this asshole."

Bea had borrowed her mother's credit card and bought him two brand-new white, long-sleeve business shirts from Sears for his interrogations and, regrettably, for the trial. That was such a sweet thing for Bea to do. Buy him new shirts that the cops would like. He loved his Queen Bea — she had been his sweetheart since grade school, way back when he was skinny and pretty. Bea was sexy, street-smart and loyal to him. After he'd knocked her up, twice, he had started to hang with her, help her with his sons, and had grown to love her.

Gradually, she had helped him develop his posh sartorial style: his dazzling Jheri curl (forty bucks a pop at Hellacious Cuts on Crenshaw); his multiple ropes of gold, bedecked with dangling golden razors, crucifixes, naked chicks, powerfists and coke spoons; his rainbow collection of jogging suits and fourteen pairs of top-of-the-line Air Jordan sneakers (and a pair of vintage Connies for layin' around their new pad). He had restricted himself to only five or six affairs after they got married. The affairs were mostly "strawberries" — amateur whores who turned tricks for dope.

Getting your johnson swabbed by a 'hood rat for a couple of crumbs of low-grade rock — not even a nickel's worth — wasn't like being unfaithful, he figured. It was medicinal; therapeutic; a salutary necessity — more like a business expense. Like buying aspirins or getting a massage on a high-stress job. But that was all past — the whores, the dealing, the violence, the stress. He had resolutely turned his back on "thug life" six months ago, when he realized that a brother, even an old-time G like him, was vulnerable to jail time or a hit — after he had experienced the deadly grotesqueries in which Pemberton was capable of entangling him.

So, hours after that goddamn murder, months before he knew the cops were onto him, he'd flushed the bulk of his street stash down the toilet — 1,800 bindles — and threw away most of his thug-life paraphernalia, even his jack-off books, *Players* and *Hustlers* mostly, and his cherished *Big Black Titty* magazines and, faithfully (except when the Lakers were on TV, or *Fear Factor,* or *The Sopranos*), got down on his knees and read the Bible with Bea and promised to her on his daddy's life, and on his *granddaddy's* soul even, he wasn't going to disappoint her anymore. No more druggin', no more whores, no more hangin' out. No more street. Swear to Jesus . . .

"White folks like white stuff," Bea had explained in the wee morning hours before he surrendered himself. They were in the bedroom of their new Woodland Hills bungalow, and Bea was standing behind him on her tiptoes and pressing her breasts against his back as they faced the dresser mirror. "They like white houses, white picket fences, white bread, and white shirts," she added grimly, peeking over his shoulder to admire her husband and herself in the mirror.

They both looked so sad; so pitiful and wronged, Bea thought. And all because of that shit-for-brains Pemberton. Fat Tommy thought so, too. Recalling those poignant scenes on that morning, he remembered that they'd both cried a little bit, standing there perusing their innocent, sad, sexy selves in the mirror. Little Bea had slipped from view a moment as she helped Tommy struggle out of his nightshirt and unfastened for the final time the nine golden ropes of braid that festooned his massive neck, and then his diamond ear stud. Bea tearfully placed them in a shopping bag of things they would have to hock. She slid the voluminous dress-shirt sleeves over his backswept arms. Then her beautiful, manicured hands appeared, fluttering along his shoulders, smoothing out the wrinkles in his new shirt.

When Bea was satisfied with her effort, she slipped around in front of him and unloosed his lucky nose ring, letting him view her voluptuous little self in the lace teddy he'd bought her for Mother's Day, but which she had seldom worn. Then, while he was distracted ogling her melons, she had seized his right pinkie finger, whose stylish claw he had allowed to flourish there as a scoop for sampling virgin powder on the fly and which he had rakishly polished jet black, and before he could stop her, she deftly clipped it off. Fat Tommy shrieked like a waif.

"It's better this way, Tommy," Bea assured him. She carefully placed the shorn talon in a plastic baggie. It resembled a shiny black roach; but for Fat Tommy, it was like witnessing the burial of a child.

"I'm keeping this for good luck, Tommy," she told him, and stowed it in the change purse of her Gucci bag.

She patted his lumpy belly, which protruded out of the break in the shirt like a fifty-pound sack of muffins. She buttoned up the shirt and put on the new hand-painted Martin Luther King Jr. tie she had especially made for him by a Cuban chick she had met in rehab. She cupped his big pumpkin head in her hands. She had paid her little sister, Karesha, fifteen bucks to touch up his Jheri curl, and the handsome, thick, mane of oily black locks cascaded sensuously, if greasily, down his forehead and neck.

"Try to stay where it's cool, so the Jheri-curl juice don't drip on your brand-new shirt, baby," Bea said in a sweetly admonishing tone.

"This new ProSoft Sport Curl Gel don't drip like that cheap shit, baby," Fat Tommy explained. "It's deluxe. I gave your sister two more dollars so she would use the top-drawer shit. I want to make a good impression."

"I know you do, baby. But you're gonna have a hard time keeping it up in the joint . . . I don't think you —"

Her husband had stopped listening and Bea stared once more into Fat Tommy's eyes. He was such a big baby. Standing there he had reminded her of a holy card she had cherished the two years she went to Catholic school before she met him. St. Sebastian, sad and pitiful, mortally wounded, innocent and wronged, pierced with arrows. She kissed him lightly on his shirt front and pushed him backward onto the edge of the bed.

"Pull yourself together, Tommy. I've got to go drop off the kids," she said.

Fat Tommy was still crying, sitting dejectedly on the side of the bed, long after she had dressed and gone out to drop their boys at her sister's new hideout in Topanga Canyon.

2.

It was still dark when Bea went out. The sun soon poked up. She hardly even noticed. She sped along the freeways, and the awakening valley skies unfurled before her in desolate pink banners of light. She raced over the back roads, hurtling through space along the crests of the canyons. Again and again she skidded in a cloud of dust against the shoulders of the abyss. Again and again she slowed down a moment then, thinking better of it, sped back up. She couldn't stop looking at her boys, couldn't stop cursing Pemberton under her breath and sadly reflecting on how that asshole had put them all up to their eyeballs in shit. The boys woke up during the forty-minute drive over to Karesha's, with Bea the whole time vainly scanning the radio for news of Pemberton's arrest.

Bea's mother was standing at the window when she drove up. Her mother would drive the boys up to Santa Barbara and they would take a cross-country bus to Texas that night. The three women and the two infant boys cried until Bea's mother drove off in Karesha's pink Lexus, fleeing in plain sight, with Little Tommy and baby Kobe waving bye-bye from their car seats.

After their mother and the boys were safely away, Karesha, a cold, deadly customer in most circumstances, confided to Bea that she was a little nervous about the possibility of her own capture or of the jailing — and inevitable execution — of her notorious former squeeze, Cut Pemberton, and what it could all mean for her Hollywood plans, and for her high-toned, social-climbing crew.

"You heard from him?" Bea had asked, as she backed out of the dirt driveway in Karesha's rented, brush-covered hideaway.

"I hear the Columbian's got him," Karesha said quietly. "The cops don't know much about him yet. I'm sure he wants to keep it that way. Anyway, I trashed the cell phone." They were quiet for a moment, then Karesha said, "But if that sick motherfucker come 'round here I'm gonna send him to Jesus." She lifted her T-shirt and showed Bea the pearl-handled .22 Pemberton had bought her as an engagement gift. It was stuffed in the waistband of her jeans.

When Bea arrived back home, the neighbors were out, watering their lawns, pretending they didn't know Fat Tommy was a prime suspect in a vicious murder.

"How do, Miss O'Rourke?" Pearl Stenis, the boldest of her nosy neighbors greeted her.

"I'm blessed, Mrs. Stenis," Bea said flatly.

She pulled into the garage and closed the door. She gathered herself a moment before she got out. She turned on all the lights in the garage and found a flashlight, and took a good twenty minutes making sure the Mercedes was clean of diapers and weapons and works and blow and any incriminating evidence. When she was done, she poked her head into the house and called out, "We're late, Tommy. We're supposed to be there at eight o'clock sharp — it's already eight forty. I'll be in the car. Come on, baby. We got to be on time this time." She waited in the car and honked the horn a half-dozen times but had to come back inside and get Fat Tommy. She found him back in bed, fully dressed, sobbing, with the covers pulled over his head.

"Where the hell you been, baby?" Fat Tommy said. "I thought Cut got you."

"That niggah better be layin' low," Bea said. "These Hollywood cops would love to catch a fuck-up like that and Rodney King his ass to death for the savage shit he done."

"It just ain't fair," Fat Tommy complained.

"Listen here, Tommy," Bea said sternly. "You don't deserve this beef. You don't know nothin'. You didn't see nothin'. You got a wife and family to protect. It was that goddamn Cut that fount Simpson. You didn't even know he was a cop. It was all Cut's idea. We wouldn't be mixed up in none of this if Cut hadn't . . ."

Fat Tommy began sobbing again. After a few minutes, he confessed that he had raided the emergency stash in the bathroom and had done a couple of lines to calm his nerves. He suggested that they do what was left. There was only a half-bindle left anyway. He never did crack; the high felt like a suicide jump. Crack was for kids; toxic, cheap-ass shit meant to sell, not do. Fat Tommy was old school — White Girl all the way. Powder, he believed, was classier, mellower than rock cocaine.

Bea retrieved the emergency bindle out of the bottom of a box of sanitary napkins where she and Fat Tommy stored it. There was only a portion of an eight ball — an eighth of an ounce — left from the half-pound Fat Tommy liked to keep around the pad for Laker games and birthdays and other special occasions. Bea used her mother's Sears card to line out six hefty tracks of the white powder on the dresser top. Rolling their last hundred-dollar bill into a straw, the couple snorted quickly, sucking the lines of blow into their flared nostrils like shotgun blasts fired straight to the back of their brains.

Quickly, the drug began to take effect: it eased its frigid tendrils down the back lanes of their breathing passages, deadening the superior nasal concha, the frontal and sphenoid sinuses, creeping along their soft palates like a snotty glacier before it slid down the interiors of their throats, chilling the lingual nerves and flowing over the rough, bitter fields of papilla at the back of their tongues and ascending, like a stream of arctic ghosts up through their pituitary glands, their spinal walls and veins, and into the uppermost regions of their brains. The pupils of their dark brown eyes became dilated and sparkling.

"Damn, that's good shit," Fat Tommy said, feeling the cold drip of the snow, liquefied and suffused with snot, glazing the commodious interiors of his head and throat.

Fat Tommy shut his eyes tight. The darkness inside his mind began to fill with amorphous, floating colors. His big body seemed to be shapeless and floating, too. He looked down at the drifts of sugary dust remaining on the dresser. Almost four hundred bucks' worth of Girl — gone in six vigorous snorts. As Fat Tommy admired the smeared patterns of residue on the dresser top, Bea leaned down and broadly licked the last thin traces of powder.

Then she swept her lovely, manicured, forefinger across the dresser top, along the trail of spittle her tongue had left, sopping up the final mists of blow. She dabbed this viscous salve along her teeth and gums. Normally Fat Tommy prided himself in always managing to lick up the leftovers before Bea got to them. But he was immobilized with grief; and too, he was froze from his nose to his toes. Now Bea was froze numb, too. The coke was ninety percent pure. It'd only been stepped on once. Chilean. Cream of the Andes. Bea blinked hard and looked up at her husband.

"I'm straight now," Bea said, noting a half moon of white powder showing around the alar grooves of Fat Tommy's right nostril. "Your slip is showin', baby," she said, and pointed to his reflection in the mirror. Fat Tommy pinched his nostrils closed, shut his eyes, and took a sharp snort. The lumps of powder were swept from the grooves in his face, shooting brilliantly past his nasal vestibules and septum in white-hot pellets of snot. His heart began to race. Neither one of them said a word for a few minutes. They closed their eyes and surrendered to the high. When Fat Tommy finally opened his eyes, Bea was staring at him with a beatific look on her face.

"You look nice," Bea said. "Innocent... Don't let 'em punk you, Tommy. Just wear the shit outta this shirt and tie. Dr. King'll bring you through. All business. You know how to talk to white folks. Don't go in there like no G... talking all bad and shit, like you was that goddamn Cut. That's what they want. Give them your A game, and you'll be all right. Remember. You wasn't there. You didn't see nothing. You don't know nobody. *We ain't gonna get kilt over some asshole.*"

Fat Tommy got in the car, gripping his Bible, sobbing and praying and assuring Bea and the Lord he loved them. He promised — between his sobs — he would savor her instructions and repeat them like a mantra: Don't say nothing that's gonna get us kilt *over some asshole.* She reminded him that his stupid-ass Uncle Bunny had done a nickel at Folsom on a break-in after Bunny talked too much. So — don't talk too much. Don't do nothing that will make you look guilty. They got nothing, Bea reminded Fat Tommy. That was the bottom line. They agreed if he was cool and smooth he had a chance to ease his way out of the beef with short time.

3.

The cops were nice to him at first; they said he was a stand-up guy for turning himself in and helping out with the investigation.

They interviewed him all day. Fat Tommy told them he didn't "need no lawyer." He wasn't guilty. The cops didn't seem to be concerned about his coke business so much as they wanted to find out what he knew about the recent murder of the undercover cop — Simpson — right in the middle of the projects on Fat Tommy's home turf, La Caja. Fat Tommy assured him he didn't "have no 'turf,' not anymore, not in La Caja, not nowhere." Moreover, he didn't know anything about a cop killing.

"We know you ain't no killer, Moises," Vargas told him a few minutes into the interrogation. "But you grew up in La Caja, where this murder went down. We figure you might know something. Point us to the bad guys. We know you're in bed with the Columbians. They're all over La Caja these days. One of them called you by name . . . called you Moises. We got him on tape. He's quite fond of you. Says you're a big shot. You're looking at some serious time if you don't play ball, Moises . . . Play along and help us catch this killer . . . you'll be all right . . ."

Vargas offered him a jumbo cup of lemonade and four jelly doughnuts. Vargas said that the pretty cop who had processed him that morning had asked to make the lemonade especially for him.

Fat Tommy said, "That was sure nice of her."

"Yeah. Officer Ospina is a sweetie. Drink up. That's the last of it . . . we need to get started," Vargas said, and smiled at him.

Braddock took the empty cup, crushing it, and banked it into the wastebasket in the back of the interrogation room.

"Great shot," Fat Tommy said. "Three-pointer."

Braddock and Vargas said nothing. Braddock walked to a chair somewhere behind him and Vargas turned on a tape recorder and intoned: "This is Detective Manny Vargas of the Homicide Detail, Criminal Investigation Division of the Van Nuys Police Department. I am joined with Detective Will Dockery and DEA special agent Roland Braddock. This is a tape-recorded interview of Thomas Martin O'Rourke, a.k.a., 'Fat Tommy' O'Rourke, a.k.a., Tommy Martin, a.k.a., Pretty Tommy Banes, a.k.a., Slo Jerry-T, a.k.a., Big Jerry Jay, a.k.a., T-Moose, a.k.a., Moises Rockafella . . ."

"Uh, my name ain't Moises," Fat Tommy protested, interrupting as politely as he could. "Some bad people started calling me that.

But I don't let nobody call me that no more." He tried his sexiest grin.

Vargas looked at him blankly and continued: "This a homicide investigation under Police Report number A-55503. Today's date is March 28, 2005, and the time is now 1349 hours." Then Vargas looked at Fat Tommy and said, "Could you state your name once more for the record?"

"I'm Thomas Martin O'Rourke."

"Address?"

Tommy gave them his parent's address. That's where he got his mail now.

"How old are you?"

"Thirty-four, officer," Fat Tommy said.

"Employed?"

"I was assistant manager at the Swing Shop . . ."

"Was . . . ?"

"I got laid off."

"When was that?"

"1992."

Dockery and Braddock rolled their eyes, then Vargas said, "What were you doing after you got . . . laid off?"

Fat Tommy fingered his Martin Luther King Jr. tie. "Odd jobs, here and there . . ."

"What kind of odd jobs?"

"Church stuff."

"Church stuff?"

Fat Tommy sat up straight in his chair. "I'm a Christian, sir. And I try to help in the Lord's work whenever —"

"You get that fancy Mercedes doing this church work?"

"Naw." Fat Tommy laughed out loud.

"The street tells us you're a big-time coke man — that true, Moises? You a big time coke dealer, Moises?"

"Oh no, sir. Not no more. All that shit is dead . . . I mean, all that *stuff* is dead . . . I don't do no drugs no more. I don't sling coke no more. I got a wife and family . . ."

"You high now?"

"What was that?"

"You under the influence of drugs or alcohol at this time?"

"No. Oh Jesus, no."

Fat Tommy wished to Christ he was.

4.

At many points during the long, arduous interrogation, the men drew in so close on the hulking gangster that the tips of all four men's shoes seemed to be touching. He couldn't make the cops believe him. They wouldn't give him any more lemonade, even though the girl cop made it 'specially for him. They wouldn't give him any more doughnuts — they said they were all out. Cops out of doughnuts! Now, they wouldn't even give him water — and he was dry as shit. That Chilean coke had sucked all of the good spit out of his mouth. If only he could get a glass of water, or maybe some lemonade.

"I'm drying out inside," Fat Tommy pleaded.

Bea's admonitions echoed in his head and gradually, and without realizing it, Fat Tommy allowed a luxuriant smile to creep across the corners of his mouth. Still smiling, he opened his eyes into a narrow slit and gazed down at his handsome shirt sleeves, admiring the shiny contours, like little snow-covered mountains really, that the polyester fabric traced along his massive arms as they lay across his knees.

Christ, he loved this shirt!

"Somethin' I said funny, Fatboy? Somethin' funny?" Braddock yelled, momentarily breaking through his reverie.

He blinked and looked down again at his arms and knees. They were such good arms; good, kind arms; and great knees — great great knees. After a while, he decided, with a hot white tear leaking out of a crack in his right eye, finally, that he loved his knees as much as he loved his dick or his ass — better, probably, now that he had found the Lord again. His regard for his ass and dick now seemed so misguided, so . . . heathen. And these knees were so much more representative of him, innocent, God-fearing, above reproach.

They had taken him all over — all over L.A., the Valley, even to Oak Town once on a church picnic. There was plenty of water there, beer and red pop and lemonade and swine barbeque, too. He was thin then, and pretty. Just a baby boy — so innocent, such a good young brother. The picnic was on the Oakland Bay, and they'd all rode the bus up there, singing gospel songs all the way. There must have been a hundred buses, the whole California

Youth Baptist Convention, someone said. And it was his knees that helped him get through it, basketball, softball, the three-legged race with pretty Althea Jackson. They were nine years old! Those were some of the best times in his life. And he was such a good guy, a regular brother, everyone said so, and now this lunatic murder, and this fucked-up Pemberton, that devil, poking his bloody self like a shitty nightmare in the midst of all his plans.

Fat Tommy ached at beholding all these tender scenes — Bea, the picnic, the tears — all the images like flashing detritus in a river streaming across his upturned hands. It was just too much. He closed his eyes, but the river of images burst inside them, flooding the darkness in his head even more vividly than before: his first day at Teddy Roosevelt Junior High; the time he and Bea won third place at the La Caja Boys and Girls Club Teen Dance-Off; and his best pal . . . not that goddamn Pemberton . . . but Trey-Boy, Trey-Boy Middleton *(rest his soul)*. That was his best friend. It was cool Trey-Boy who befriended him even after he got fat and everyone started treating him like a jerk, and it was Trey-Boy who'd taken pity on him and helped him pimp up his style.

It was Trey-Boy. Not a murderer. A hip brother. True-blue. Trey-Boy showed him how to affect a gangster's scowl, and helped him adopt a slow, hulking walk that could frighten just about anyone he encountered on the street. He'd showed him how to smoke a cigarette, load a gat, roll a blunt, and cop pussy, weed, and blow. He had even showed him how to shoot up once.

And Trey-Boy never got mad, even when that faggot Stick Jenkins bumped him on purpose and made him spill a good portion of the spoon of heroin Trey-Boy had carefully prepared. Trey-Boy had pimp-slapped the faggot — he called him "my sissy" and Stick had just smiled like a bitch and turned red as a yella niggah could get — and everyone laughed.

He remembered how Trey-Boy had cooked up what was left of the little amber drops of Boy they could scrape from the toilet seat and floor and showed him how to tie off and find the vein and shoot the junk even if he only got a little whacked — it was whacked enough to know he wouldn't do that anymore. It wasn't fun at all. He couldn't stop puking. It felt like now — in this hot room with no water, under this white light. But he wasn't no goddamn junkie. None of that puking and noddin' and drooling shit was for him. He was strictly weed and blow, strictly weed and blow. He wasn't no goddamn junkie. Let them try to pin that on him. They'd come up zero. Just like this murder. He wasn't there; he didn't do it. He didn't see nobody; he didn't know nobody.

Trey-Boy had given him his favorite street moniker — Fat Tommy. When Trey-Boy said it, it didn't feel like a put-down. It was a term of war and affection. Fat Tommy was a lumpy 370 pounds but he didn't feel fat when Trey-Boy called him Fat Tommy — he felt big, as in big man, big trouble, big fun — there's a difference, really, when you think about it. A street handle like Fat Tommy made him feel like one of the hoods in *The Sopranos* — his favorite story. He'd made a small fortune with that name — not like he made with Cut Pemberton, when the margins and risks got scary and huge, and the fuckin' Columbians got involved, and people feared him and only knew him by the name Pemberton hung on him, Moises — Moises Rockafella, the King of Rock Cocaine. He didn't make big cake like that with Trey-Boy — but at least he didn't have to worry about a murder beef, and the living was decent.

5.

At one point, Vargas cut on the lights in the interrogation room so brightly that when Fat Tommy looked up he beheld, not a pea-green interrogation room with a trio of sad sack cops trying to sweat him for a cop murder he didn't commit — the whole room seemed to him as a single white spotlight, a moon's eyeball inspecting him on a disc of light. He was so damn dry and tired. He could not see Vargas, but could hear his footfalls pacing back and forth somewhere behind him. He closed his eyes a moment and tried to catch a wink.

"Steady, sweetheart. Just a few more questions and you're home free," Vargas said.

Tommy waited for the next question with the same despairing apprehension with which he had endured all the last. Why these other questions? Why this Moises shit? He wasn't goddamn Moises anymore. That shit was dead; done. Why didn't these pigs believe him? Tommy felt so sorry for himself. None of it was his fault. It was the Columbians and that goddamn Pemberton. He was the bad guy. If they want their devil, there he is. But don't expect Fat Tommy to commit suicide and snitch. That shit was dead.

"I need some lemonade!" he screamed.

Braddock began to mock him. Fat Tommy burrowed himself deeper into his thoughts. The cops kept hammering away at his story. He shut his eyes. He was only pretending to listen, nodding yes, yes, goddamn it, yes, or gazing up at them with a mournful, wounded look in his eyes.

Vargas turned off the tape. Dockery and Braddock pushed their chairs back from the cone of white light that made Fat Tommy look like a Vegas lounge fly sobbing under a microscope. The scraping of their chairs was like an utterance of disgust, and they meant it to be that. It sent shivers up their own backs, and sent a chilling thunderbolt of fear down the back of Fat Tommy O'Rourke. Vargas cut a rebuking glance at Dockery and Braddock.

"It's late," Vargas said, looking around for a clock. They had started this session just before two P.M.

Braddock pulled out his watch bob and flicked it open. To view the dial, he swept his hand through the cone of light that seemed to enclose Fat Tommy in a brilliant Tinker Bell glow and the watch flashed like a little arc of buttery neon framed in white.

"Almost six A.M. Sixteen goddamn hours and not a peep from this shithead," Braddock said. He smacked the back of Fat Tommy's chair.

Dockery felt around in his pant leg for his pack of butts and stood up. "Just a little longer, sport, and you'll be home free, beatin' off in yer cell," Dockery said.

"Yeah, beatin' off in yer cell . . ." Braddock repeated.

"I need a piss break," Fat Tommy said as politely as he could, then added with a smile, "and a big glass of lemonade."

"Good idea, asshole. Think I'll go drain the lizard," Dockery said and looked at Vargas. Vargas nodded and Braddock and Dockery went out.

Fat Tommy sobbed on. He was still crying when Braddock and Dockery came back in laughing. They both held huge cups of lemonade and they were eating fresh Krispy Kreme doughnuts. Braddock tossed a half-eaten doughnut in the trash.

"I'm starvin', officer. I'm sleepy. I don't know about no murder," Fat Tommy tried again. He shut his eyes tight.

"Pale-ass pussy," Braddock muttered. "Yer gonna fry for this. Why don't ya quit yer lying?"

"You said I could have water. I need some water," Fat Tommy asked again.

"You know the game, Fatboy," Detective Dockery broke in, from somewhere behind him. "Yer startin' to piss me off."

"You can have water, Moises, after you tell us how it went down. Understand?" Vargas said. "That's our deal." Vargas turned on the tape.

Fat Tommy didn't understand. The sharp questions droned on like wasps attacking just above his head. He was sleepy. He wanted water. He closed his eyes and took a breath and asked again for the thousandth time, "Please, officer, can I have some water or some lemonade?"

"It's detective," Dockery said.

"Listen here, detective," Tommy assented, his big voice gravelly and frail, "I don't deserve this beef. I don't know nothin'. I didn't see nothin'. Got a wife an' family to protect. Was goddamn Cut who fount Simpson. Didn't even know he was a cop. Ya gotta believe me. I wouldn't be mixed up in none of this if . . ."

The room went dead quiet.

Fat Tommy eased his eyes open and peered sharply down along the tear-dappled lids. He strained to see or hear the shuffling shoes of the cops pacing in front or behind him. He could see nothing and could only hear what seemed to be his own heart galloping away down in the pit of his stomach, *thu-thump, thu-thump*.

"Cut? You never mentioned any Cut," Dockery said after a while.

Fat Tommy could feel the life draining from his chest. He slowly opened his eyes. He began to hyperventilate and for the first time he could feel the Jheri curl gel deluxe begin to drip against his collar.

"Tell us about this Cut," Vargas said. "He got a last name?"

Fat Tommy felt his mouth moving. He couldn't make it stop. "Cut . . . um . . . Cut Pemberton . . . I think," his voice said.

"And . . . ?"

He tried to think of innocent words. He tried to stall and think of what Bea would want him to say. "I didn't know him that good," he said finally.

"Go on," Vargas said. "What's he look like?"

Tommy tried to think of other faces, but all he could see before him was that goddamn Cut. "Gots a cut 'cross his ear, go straight 'cross his lip, like he was wearing a veil on one side of his face."

"Yes . . ."

"Said he got it in a fight with a cracker when he was in the marines. But I heard he got it in prison."

He held his breath and tried to stop his voice from speaking again. He couldn't believe what it was saying, betraying him, snitching on him.

"OK . . . go on."

His mouth burst open again.

"He can talk Spanish," Fat Tommy's voice said, gasping.

"Go on," Dockery said. "Cut . . ."

Tommy's whole body seemed to slump. Special Agent Braddock smacked his chair hard and Tommy sat bolt upright. "Well, Cut was the onliest one that did it," he said.

"Go on," Braddock prodded. "Cut was?"

"What?"

"*He said:* Cut was . . . ?" Vargas said.

"Um . . . Cut was . . . one of them red, freckly niggahs from Georgia . . ."

"Yes."

No one spoke for a moment, then Fat Tommy's voice said, "Spotted like a African cat. I didn't even know him good . . ."

"Um-hum."

"Wore plaits standing all over his head."

"Plaits? Really?"

Fat Tommy grinned, he couldn't help himself. "My Bea used to call him BuckBeet, 'cause he looked like a red pickaninny. That used to piss him off, 'cause of Buckwheat, you know?"

"Yes . . . Cut . . ."

"Yeah, Cut. First I knew of him . . . two years ago . . . when I was staying on Glen Oaks off Paxton . . . him and Karesha — my wife's sister — and my Uncle Bunny banged on my duplex at 'bout two in the morning looking for some crack."

"You mean Bunny Hobart — the second-story man?" Dockery broke in again.

The detectives had two tape recorders going now, but Dockery never trusted electronic equipment and was transcribing everything Fat Tommy said on a yellow legal pad.

"Yeah, that be him," Fat Tommy said with a deep sigh. He

slumped back in the hard metal chair, trembling as he recalled the scene. "Uncle Bunny knew Cut from the joint. Cut had just got out and was chillin' with Karesha . . . Cut was already dressin' like a Crip, all blue, talking shit. I could tell he was trouble. He used to strong-arm young Gs and take their stuff."

"And Bunny told him you were the big-time coke man," Braddock said. It was not a question.

Such a wave of woe swept over Fat Tommy as he contemplated all of this that, softly, he began to weep. His whole bright life was passing before his sad eyes: there were pinwheels of light; a whole series of birthdays; his stint as a fabulous dancer; his wife, Bea, again, his kids — Little Tommy and infant Kobe — cuties! cuties! He didn't deserve this. And too, there was his old job as assistant manager at the Swing Shop — twelve years ago now — all those great records: Tupac, NWA, Biggie, KRS-One, Salt 'N' Pepa, shit, even Marvin Gaye. He knew them like the lines in these hands that now stared up at him, glazed and dotted with sweat.

"I was getting out of the business. I was getting out," Fat Tommy explained. "It was Cut that fucked up all my plans. He wanted to impress the big-time talent . . . I was only staying in 'til he could get on his feets."

"What big-time talent?"

"Columbians? La Caja Crips?" Vargas pressed him.

"It was them goddamn Columbians that tolt Cut about Simpson," Tommy confessed. "Cut came up with the idea of setting the guy up. He told us he was a snitch — not no cop! I tried to talk him out of it; I tried to reason with him . . ."

"A regular Dr. Phil," Braddock said.

"Yes, sir," Fat Tommy said quietly.

Tommy closed his eyes. He felt himself crashing. He flopped his big grease-spangled head down into his hands. From the top of his Jheri curl to the soles of his size 17 Air Jordans, everything about him was huge, extroverted, and showy. Now, he sat hulking and exhausted in the metal chair, hot sweat and gel streaming down his face and neck, trying in vain to make himself smaller, hoping that the willful diminishment of his great size would in turn minimize in the minds of the cops the appalling grandeur of his recent crimes. He sat there in his bright white tent of a shirt with his Martin Luther King Jr. tie strung round his bulging neck like a garrote.

"Catch your breath, son," Vargas said. He turned off the tape.

"Get our boy King Moises some lemonade, will ya, Detective Dockery?"

Dockery went out and Tommy's mind went blank, then black, then pale gray. Now when he squinted into the interrogation room light it didn't even seem like light anymore but a kind of shiny darkness. He felt as though he was falling through the brightness like a brother pitched off a hundred-story building. All the bright scenes of his life seemed to be fading, all of them diminishing like faces in the fog. Even the fabulous good shit that was coming, close on the horizon, that seemed to be diminishing, too. Vargas switched the lights back to a single hot light again. To Fat Tommy the trembling ocean of darkness beyond the spotlight seemed like fathomless midnight. And from the utter depths of its darkness Fat Tommy O'Rourke — a.k.a., Moises Rockafella, the King of Rock Cocaine — could hear a plaintive, high-pitched wail, a shrill, sad voice, strangely resembling his own. He prayed to Christ it was someone else.

WENDY HORNSBY

Dust Up

FROM *Murder in Vegas*

10:00 A.M., April 20
Red Rock Canyon, Nevada

PANSY REYNARD LAY on her belly inside a camouflaged bird blind, high-power Zeiss binoculars to her eyes, a digital sound amplifier hooked over her right ear, charting every movement and sound made by her observation target, an Aplomado falcon hatchling. As Pansy watched, the hatchling stretched his wings to their full thirty-inch span and gave them a few tentative flaps as if gathering courage to make his first foray out of the nest. He would need some courage to venture out, she thought. The ragged, abandoned nest his mother had appropriated for her use sat on a narrow rock ledge 450 vertical feet above the desert floor.

"Go, baby," Pansy whispered when the chick craned back his neck and flapped his wings again. This was hour fourteen of her assigned nest watch. She felt stiff and cramped and excited, all at once. There had been no reported Aplomado falcon sightings in Nevada since 1910. For a mated Aplomado falcon pair to appear in the Red Rock Canyon area less than twenty miles west of the tawdry glitz and endless noise of Las Vegas was singular, newsworthy even. But for the pair to claim a nest and successfully hatch an egg was an event so unexpected as to be considered a miracle by any committed raptor watcher, as Pansy Reynard considered herself to be.

The hatchling watch was uncomfortable, perhaps dangerous, because of the ruggedness of the desert canyons, the precariousness of Pansy's rocky perch in a narrow clifftop saddle opposite the nest, and the wild extremes of the weather. But the watch was very likely essential to the survival of this wonder child. It had been an honor, Pansy felt, to be assigned a shift to watch the nest. And then to have the great good fortune to be on site when the hatchling first emerged over the top of the nest was, well, nearly overwhelming.

Pansy lowered her binocs to wipe moisture from her eyes, but quickly raised them again so as not to miss one single moment in the life of this sleek-winged avian infant. She had been wakened inside her camouflage shelter at dawn by the insistent chittering of the hatchling as he demanded to be fed. From seemingly nowhere, as Pansy watched, the mother had soared down to tend him, the forty-inch span of her black-and-white wings as artful and graceful as a beautiful Japanese silk-print kite. The sight of the mother made Pansy almost forgive Lyle for standing her up the night before.

Almost forgive Lyle: this was supposed to be a two-man shift. Lyle, a pathologist with the Department of Fish and Game, was a fine bird watcher and seemed to be in darned good physical shape. But he was new to the Las Vegas office and unsure about his readiness to face the desert overnight. And he was busy. Or so he said.

Pansy had done her best to assure Lyle that he would be safe in her hands. As preparation, she had packed two entire survival kits, one for herself and one for him, and had tucked in a very good bottle of red wine to make the long chilly night pass more gently. But he hadn't come. Hadn't even called.

Pansy sighed, curious to know which he had shunned, an evening in her company or the potential perils of the place. She had to admit there were actual, natural challenges to be addressed. It was only mid-April, but already the desert temperatures reached the century mark before noon. When the sun was overhead, the sheer vertical faces of the red sandstone bluffs reflected and intensified the heat until everything glowed like — and felt like — the inside of an oven. There was no shade other than the feathery shadows of spindly yucca and folds in the rock formations.

To make conditions yet more uncomfortable, it was sandstorm season. Winds typically began to pick up around noon and could drive an impenetrable cloud of sand at speeds surpassing eighty miles an hour until sunset. When the winds blew, there was nearly no way to escape both the heat and the pervasive, intrusive blast of sand. Even cars were useless as shelter. With windows rolled up and without the AC turned on you'd fry in a hurry. With the AC turned on, both you and the car's engine would be breathing grit. If you could somehow navigate blind and drive like hell, you might drive clear of the storm before sand fouled the engine. But only if you could navigate blind.

People like Pansy who knew the area well might find shelter in random hollows among the rocks, such as the niche where the hatchling sat in his nest. Or the well prepared, for instance Pansy, might hunker down inside a zip-up shelter made to military specs for desert troops, like the one that was tucked inside her survival pack. Or navigate using digital GPS via satellite — Global Positioning System.

Not an environment for neophytes, Pansy conceded, but she'd had high hopes for Lyle, and had looked forward to an evening alone with him and the falcons under the vast blackness of the desert sky, getting acquainted.

Pansy knew she could be a bit off-putting at first meeting. But in that place, during that season, Pansy was in her métier and at her best. Her preparations for the nest watch, she believed, were elegant in their simplicity, completeness, and flexibility: a pair of lightweight one-man camouflage all-weather shelters, plenty of water, a basic all-purpose tool, meals-ready-to-eat, a bodacious slingshot in case snakes or vultures came to visit the nest, good binocs, a two-channel sound amplifier to eavesdrop on the nest, a handheld GPS locator, and a digital palm-sized video recorder. Except for the water, each kit weighed a meager twenty-seven pounds and fit into compact, waterproof, dust-proof saddlebags she carried on her all-terrain motorcycle. The bottle of wine and two nice glasses were tucked into a quick-release pocket attached to the cycle frame. She had everything: shelter, food, water, tools, the falcon, a little wine. But no Lyle.

Indeed, Lyle's entire kit was still attached to the motorcycle she had stashed in a niche in the abandoned sandstone quarry below her perch.

A disturbing possibility occurred to Pansy as she watched the hatchling: maybe Lyle was a little bit afraid of her. A champion triathlete and two-time Ironman medalist, Lieutenant Pansy Reynard, desert survival instructor with the Army's SFOD-D, Special Forces Operational Detachment — Delta Force, out of the Barstow military training center, admitted that she could be just a little bit intimidating.

10:00 A.M., April 20
Downtown Las Vegas

Mickey Togs felt like a million bucks because he knew he looked like a million bucks. New custom-made, silver-gray suit with enough silk in the fabric to give it a little sheen. Not flashy-shiny, but sharp — expensively sharp, Vegas player sharp. His shirt and tie were of the same silver-gray color, as were the butter-soft handmade shoes on his size eight, EEE feet. Checking his reflection in the shiny surface of the black Lincoln Navigator he had acquired for the day's job, Mickey shot his cuffs, adjusted the fat Windsor knot in his silver-gray necktie, dusted some sand kicked up from yesterday's storm off his shoes, and grinned.

Yep, he decided as he climbed up into the driver's seat of the massive SUV, he looked every penny like a million bucks, exactly the sort of guy who had the *cojones* to carry off a million-dollar job. Sure, he had to split the paycheck a few ways because he couldn't do this particular job alone, but the splits wouldn't be equal, meaning he would be well paid. One hundred K to Big Mango the triggerman, one hundred to Otto the Bump for driving, another hundred to bribe a cooperative Federal squint, and then various payments for various spotters and informants. Altogether, after the split, Mickey personally would take home six hundred large; damn good jack for a morning's work.

Mickey Togs felt deservedly cocky. Do a little morning job for the Big Guys, be back on the Vegas Strip before lunch, get a nice bite to eat, then hit the baccarat salon at the Mirage with a fat stake in his pocket. Mickey took out a silk handkerchief and dabbed some sweat from his forehead; Mickey had trained half his life for jobs like this one. Nothing to it, he said to himself, confident that all necessary preparations had been made and all contingencies covered. A simple, elegant plan.

Mickey pulled the big Navigator into the lot of the Flower of the Desert Wedding Chapel on South Las Vegas Boulevard, parked, and slid over into the front passenger seat, the shotgun position. The chapel was in a neighborhood of cheap old motels and auto shops, not the sort of place where Mickey and his hired help would be noticed. In a town where one can choose to be married by

Captain Kirk, Elvis Presley, or Marilyn Monroe, where brides and grooms might dress accordingly, wedding chapels are good places not to be noticed. Even Big Mango, an almost seven-foot-tall Samoan wearing a turquoise Hawaiian shirt and flip-flops, drew hardly a glance as he crossed the lot and climbed into the back seat of the Navigator.

Otto the Bump, a one-time welterweight boxer with cauliflower ears and a nose as gnarled as a bag full of marbles, ordinarily might draw a glance or two, except that he wore Vegas-style camouflage: black suit, starched white shirt, black tie, spit-shined black brogans, a clean shave, and a stiff comb-over. He could be taken for a maitre d', a pit boss, a father of the bride, a conventioneer, or the invisible man just by choosing where and how he stood. As he hoisted himself up into the driver's seat of the Navigator, Otto looked every inch like a liveried chauffeur.

"What's the job?" Otto asked as he turned out of the lot and into traffic.

"The Feds flipped Harry Coelho," Mickey said. "He's gonna spill everything to the grand jury this morning, and then he's going into witness protection. We got one shot to stop him. Job is to grab him before he gets to the courthouse, then take him for a drive and lose him as deep as Jimmy Hoffa."

"A snitch is the worst kind of rat there is," Otto groused. "Sonovabitch deserves whatever he gets."

"Absolutely," Mickey agreed. Big Mango, as usual, said nothing, but Mickey could hear him assembling the tools for his part of the job.

"How's it going down?" Otto asked.

"Federal marshals are gonna drive Harry from the jail over to the courthouse in a plain Crown Victoria with one follow car."

"Feds." Otto shook his head. "I don't like dealing with the Feds."

"Don't worry, the fix is in," Mickey said, sounding smug. "I'll get a call when the cars leave the jail. The route is down Main to Bonneville, where the courthouse is. You get us to the intersection, park us on Bonneville at the corner. We'll get a call when the cars are approaching the intersection. When they make the turn, you get us between the two cars and that's when we grab Harry."

"Whatever you say." Otto checked the rearview mirror. "But what's the fix?"

Mickey chuckled. "You know how federal squints are, doughnut-eating civil servants with an itch to use their guns; they get off playing cops and robbers. A simple, good follow plan just doesn't do it for them, so they gotta throw in some complication. This is it: Harry leaves the jail in the front car. Somewhere on the route, the cars are going to switch their order so when they get to the courthouse Harry will be in the second car."

"How do you know they'll make the switch?"

"I know my business," Mickey said, straightening his tie to show he had no worries. "I got spotters out there. If the switch doesn't happen or the Feds decide to take a different route or slip in a decoy, I'll know it." He snapped his manicured fingers. "Like that."

Otto's face was full of doubt. "How will you know?"

"The phone calls?" Mickey said. "They're coming from inside the perp car. I bought us a marshal."

"Yeah?" Otto grinned, obviously impressed. "You got it covered, inside and outside."

"Like I say, I know my business," Mickey said, shrugging. "Here's the plan: Otto, you get us into position on Bonneville, and we wait for the call saying they're approaching. When the first car makes the turn off Main, you pull in tight behind it and stop fast. From then till we leave, you need to cover the first car; don't let anyone get out. Mango, you take care of the marshals in the second car any way you want to, but if you gack the marshal riding shotgun, you can have the rest of the bribe payment I owe him."

"Appreciate it," Mango said. "You want me to take out Harry, too?"

"Not there. I'll go in myself and get him. Otto, you stay ready to beat us the hell out when I say we're taking Harry for a little drive and getting him lost. Are we clear?"

"Candy from a little baby," Otto said. Mango, in the back seat, grunted. Could be gas, could be agreement, Mickey thought. Didn't much matter. Mango got paid to do what he did and not for conversation. With a grace that belied his huge size, Mango rolled into the back deck of the vast SUV and began to set up his firing position at the back window. Quiet and efficient, Mickey thought, a true pro.

The first call came. Harry Coelho left the Clark County jail riding in the back seat of a midnight blue Crown Victoria. The follow car was the same make, model, color. After two blocks, as planned, the cars switched positions, so that the follow car became the lead, and Harry Coelho's ass was hanging out in the wind with no rear cover.

When the second call came, the Navigator was in position on Bonneville, a half-block from the courthouse, waiting.

The snatch went smooth, by the book exactly the way Mickey Togs wrote it, the three of them moving with synchronicity as honed as a line of chorus girls all high-kicking at the same time. The first Crown Vic made the turn. Otto slipped the massive Navigator in behind it and stopped so fast that the second Crown Vic rear-ended him; the Crown Vic's hood pleated up under the Navigator's rear bumper like so much paper, didn't leave a mark on the SUV. Before the Crown Vic came to a final stop, Mango, positioned in the back deck, flipped up the rear hatch window and popped the two marshals in the front seat — fwoof, fwoof, that breezy sound the silencer makes — just as Mickey snapped open the back door and yanked out Harry Coelho, grabbing him by the oh-so-convenient handcuffs. They were back in the Navigator and speeding away before the first carload of Feds figured out that they had a problem on their hands.

No question, Otto was the best driver money could buy. A smooth turn onto Martin Luther King, then a hop up onto the 95 freeway going west into the posh new suburbs where a behemoth of an SUV like the Navigator became as anonymous and invisible as a dark-haired nanny pushing a blond-haired baby in a stroller.

After some maneuvers to make sure there was no tail, Otto exited the interstate and headed up into Red Rock Canyon.

10:50 A.M.
Red Rock Canyon

The hatchling was calling out for a feeding again when Pansy Reynard heard the rumble of a powerful engine approaching. Annoyed that the racket might frighten her falcons, she peered over the edge of her perch.

The sheer walls of the abandoned sandstone quarry below her were a natural amplifier that made the vehicle sound larger than it actually was, but it was still huge, the biggest, blackest pile of personal civilian transport ever manufactured. Lost, she thought when she saw the Navigator, and all of its computer-driven gadgets couldn't help it get back to the freeway where it belonged.

For a moment, Pansy considered climbing out of her camouflaged blind and offering some help. But she sensed there was something just a little hinky about the situation. Trained to listen to that quiet inner warning system, Pansy held back, focused her binoculars on the SUV, and waited.

The front, middle, and back hatch doors opened at once and four men spilled out: two soft old guys wearing suits and dress shoes, a Pacific Islander dressed for a beach party, and a skinny little man with a hood over his head and his hands cuffed behind his back. The hood muffled the little man's voice so that Pansy couldn't understand his words, but she certainly understood his body language. Nothing good was happening down there. She set the lens of her palm-sized digital video recorder to zoom and started taping the scene as it unfolded below.

The hooded man was marched to the rim over a deep quarried pit. His handlers stood him facing forward, then stepped aside. With a cool and steady hand, Beach Boy let off two silenced shots. A sudden burst of red opened out of the center of the hood, but before the man had time to crumple to the sandstone under him, a second blast hit him squarely in the chest and lifted him enough to push him straight over the precipice and out of sight.

"*Kek, kek, kek.*" The mother Aplomado falcon, alarmed perhaps by the eerie sound of the silencer or maybe by the burst of energy it released, screeched as she swooped down between the canyon walls as if to dive-bomb the intruders and distract them away from her nest. The two suits, who peered down into the abyss whence their victim had fallen, snapped to attention. Beach Boy, in a clean, fluid motion, pivoted the extended gun arm, spotted the mother and — fwoof, fwoof — she plunged into a mortal dive.

The hatchling, as if he saw and understood what had happened, set up his chittering again. Pansy saw that gun arm pivot again, this time toward the nest.

"No!" Pansy screamed as she rose, revealing herself to draw fire away from the precious, now orphaned hatchling. Binoculars and camera held aloft where they could be seen, she called down, "I have it all on tape, you assholes. Come and get it."

Pansy kept up her screaming rant as she climbed out of the blind and rappelled down the backside of the cliff, out of view of the miscreants but certainly within earshot. She needed them to come after her, needed to draw them away from the nest.

When she reached the canyon floor, Pansy pulled her all-terrain motorcycle out of its shelter among the rocks, gunned its powerful motor, and raced toward the access road where the men could see her. The survival kit she had packed for Lyle — damn him, anyway — was still attached to the cycle's frame.

Otto the Bump scrambled back into the Navigator while Mickey and Mango pushed and pulled each other in their haste to climb inside lest they get left behind.

"Feds," Otto growled between clenched teeth as he started the big V-8 engine. "I told you, I don't like messing with Feds."

"She ain't the freaking Feds," Mickey snapped. His face red with anger, he turned on Mango. "You want to shoot off that piece of yours, you freaking idiot, shoot that damn girl. Otto, go get her."

The old quarry made a box canyon. Its dead-end access road was too narrow for the Navigator to turn around, so it had to back out the way it came in. Pansy was impressed by the driver's skill as he made a fast exit, but she still beat the Navigator to the mouth of quarry. For a moment, she stopped her bike crosswise to the road, blocking them. There was no way, she knew, that she could hold them until the authorities might arrive. Her entire purpose in stopping was to announce herself and to lure them after her, away from the nest. She hoped that they would think that size and firepower were enough to take her out.

Pansy'd had enough time to get a good look at her opponents, to make some assessments. The two little guys were casino rats with a whole lot of starched cuff showing, fusspot city shoes, jackets buttoned up when it was a hundred freaking degrees out there. Beach Boy would be fine in a cabana, but dressed as he was and without provisions . . . Vegas rats, she thought; the desert would turn them into carrion.

Rule one when outmanned and outgunned is to let the enemy defeat himself. Pansy figured that there was enough macho inside the car that once a little-bitty girl on a little-bitty bike challenged them to a chase, they wouldn't have the courage to quit until she was down or they were dead. Pansy sniffed as she lowered her helmet's face guard; overconfidence and geographic naiveté had brought down empires. Ask Napoleon.

Pansy didn't hear the burst of gunfire, but twice she felt the air wiffle past her head in that particular way that makes the hair of an experienced soldier stand up on end. As she bobbed and wove, creating an erratic target, she also kept herself just outside the range of the big handgun she had seen. Still, she knew all about random luck and reminded herself not be too cocky herself, or too reliant on the law of averages.

Because she was in the lead, Pansy set the course. Her program involved stages of commitment: draw them in, give them a little reward as encouragement, then draw them in further until their training and equipment were overmatched by the environment and her experience. Play them.

The contest began on the decently paved road that headed out of Lee Canyon. Before the road met the freeway, Pansy veered onto a gravel by-road that took them due north, bisecting the canyons. When the road became a dry creek bed, Pansy disregarded the dead-end marker and continued to speed along; the Navigator followed. The canyons had been cut by eons of desert water runoff. The bottoms, except during the rainy season, were as hard-packed as fired clay and generally as wide as a two-lane road, though there were irregular patches of bone-jarring embedded rocks and small boulders and some narrows. The bike could go around obstacles; the four-wheel-drive Navigator barreled over them.

Pansy picked up a bit of pavement in a flood control culvert where the creek passed under the freeway, and slowed slightly to give the Navigator some hope of overtaking her. But before they could quite catch her, she turned sharply again, this time onto an abandoned service road, pulling the Navigator behind as she continued north.

At any time, Pansy knew she could dash up into any of the narrow canyons that opened on either side of the road, and that the big car couldn't follow her. She held on to that possibility as an emergency contingency as she did her best to keep her pursuers intrigued.

The canyons became smaller and broader, the terrain flatter, and Pansy more exposed. Sun bore down on her back and she cursed the wusses behind her in their air-conditioned beast. At eleven o'clock, right on schedule, the winds began to pick up. Whorls of sand quickly escalated to flurries and then to blinding bursts. Pansy pulled down the sand screen that was attached to her face guard, but she still choked on grit, felt fine sand grind in her teeth. None of this, as miserable as it made her feel, was unfamiliar or anything she could not handle.

Always, Pansy was impressed by the skill of the driver following her and by his determination. He pushed the big vehicle through places where she thought he ought to bog down. And then there were times that, if he had taken more risk, he could have overcome her. That he had refrained clued Pansy to the strategy: the men in the car thought they were driving her to ground. They were waiting for her to fall or falter in some way. She used this assumption, feigning, teasing, pretending now and then to weaken, always picking up her speed or maneuvering out of range just before they could get her, to keep them engaged. Some birds used a similar ploy, pretending to be wounded or vulnerable as a feint to lure predators away from their nests.

The canyons ended abruptly and the terrain became flat, barren desert bottom. There was no shelter, no respite, only endless heat and great blasts of wind-whipped sand. Pansy could no longer see potholes or boulders, nor could any of them see roadside markers. Though Pansy could not see the road and regularly hit bone jarring dips and bumps, she was not navigating blind. Three times a year she ran a survival course through the very same area. She had drawn her pursuers into the hollow between Little Skull and Skull Mountains, headed toward Jackass Flats, a no man's land square in the middle of the Nellis Air Force Base gunnery range.

"Get her," Mickey growled. The silk handkerchief he held against his nose muffled his words. "I have things to do in town. Take her out. Now."

Mango's only response was to reload.

Otto swore as he switched off the AC and shut down the vents. Sand so fine he could not see it ground under his eyelids, filled his nose and throat, choked him. Within minutes the air inside the car was so hot that sweat ran in his eyes, made his shirt stick to his chest and his back, riffled down his shins. There was no water, of course, because this was supposed to be a quick job, out of Vegas and back in an hour. He had plenty besides heat and thirst to make him feel miserable. First, he thought he could hear the effects of grit on the car's engine, a heaviness in its response. Next, he had a pretty good idea what Mickey would do to him if he let the girl get away.

How could they have gotten so far into this particular hell? Otto wondered. In the beginning, it had seemed real simple. Follow the girl until they were out of the range of any potential witnesses, then run over the girl and her pissant bike like so much road kill. But every time he started to make his move, she'd pull some damn maneuver and get away: she'd side-slip him or head down a wash so narrow that he had to give the road — such as it was — his undivided attention. The SUV was powerful, but it had its limitations, the first of which was maneuverability: it had none.

And then there was Mickey and his constant nudging, like he could do any better. By the time they came out of the canyons and onto the flats, Otto was so sick and tired of listening to Mickey, contending with the heat, the sand, and the damn girl and her stunts that he didn't care much how things ended, only that they ended immediately. He knew desperation and danger could be found on the same page in the dictionary, but he was so desperate to be out of that place that he was ready to take some risks; take out the girl and get back up on the freeway and out of the sand, immediately.

Between gusts Otto caught glimpses of the girl, so he knew more or less where she was. Fed up, he put a heavy foot on the accelerator and waited for the crunch of girl and bike under his thirty-two-inch wheels.

Pansy heard the SUV's motor rev, heard also the big engine begin to miss as it became befouled by sand. With the Navigator accelerating toward her, Pansy snapped the bottle of wine out of its breakaway pouch, grasped it by the neck, gave it a wind up swing as she spun her bike in a tight one-eighty, and let the bottle fly in a trajectory calculated to collide dead center with the rapidly approaching windshield.

As she headed off across the desert at a right angle to the road, she heard the bottle hit its target and pop, heard the windshield give way, heard the men swear, smelled the brakes. The massive SUV decelerated from about fifty MPH to a dead, mired stop in the space of a mere sixty feet. Its huge, heavy-tread tires sliced through the hard desert crust and found beneath it sand as fine as talcum powder and as deep as an ocean. Forget four-wheel drive; every spin of the wheels merely kicked up a shower of sand and dug them in deeper. The behemoth SUV was going nowhere without a tow.

When she heard the rear deck hatch pop open, Pansy careened to a stop and dove behind a waist-high boulder for cover. As Beach Boy, leaning out the back hatch, unloaded a clip in her general direction, Pansy, lying on her belly, pulled out her slingshot, strapped it to her wrist, reached into the pouch of three-eighths-inch steel balls hanging from her belt, and, aiming at the dull red flashes coming from the end of Beach Boy's automatic, fired back. She heard random pings as her shot hit the side of the Navigator.

"She's packing heat," Otto yelled. Pansy continued to ping the side of the car with shot; sounded enough like bullet strikes.

Mango finally spoke. More exactly, Mango let out an ugly liquid-filled scream when Pansy's steel balls pierced his throat and his cheek. Mortally hit, he grabbed his neck as he fell forward, tumbling out of the SUV. With the big back window hanging open, the SUV quickly filled with fire-hot, swirling yellow sand.

"She got Mango!" Otto yelled in Mickey's direction. "We try to run for it, she'll get us, too."

Mickey Togs, feeling faint from the heat, barely able to breathe, pulled his beautiful silver-gray suit coat over his head, being careful not to wrinkle it or get sweat on it, and tried, in vain, to get a signal on his cell phone. He didn't know who to call for help in this particularly humiliating situation, or, if he should be able to get a call out — and he could not — just where he happened to be for purposes of directing some sort of rescue.

Otto the Bump heard Mickey swear at his dead phone and nearly got hit with it when Mickey, in a rage, threw the thing toward the cracked and leaking windshield. Not knowing what else to do, Otto reached for the little piece strapped to his left ankle.

"I'm making a run for it," Otto said.

"Idiot, what are your chances?" Mickey asked. "You got thirty, forty miles of desert, no water, can't see through that damn sand, and a lunatic out there trying to kill you."

"If I stay in this damn car or I make a run for it, I figure it's eighty-twenty against me either way," Otto said. "I prefer to take it on the run than sitting here waiting."

"Ninety-five to five." Mickey straightened the knot in his tie. "You do what you think you gotta do. I'm staying put."

"Your choice, but you still owe me a hundred K," Otto said. He chambered a round as he opened the car door, brought his arm against his nose, and dropped three feet down to the desert floor.

5:00 P.M., April 20
Downtown Las Vegas, Nevada

Without pausing for so much as a perfunctory hello to the clerk on duty, Pansy Reynard strode past the reception desk of the regional office of the Department of Fish and Game and straight back to the pathology lab. Pansy had showered and changed from her dirty desert camouflage BDUs — battle-dress utilities — into sandals, a short khaki skirt, and a crisp, sleeveless linen blouse; adaptability, she knew well, is the key to survival.

She opened the lab door and walked in. When Lyle, the so recently absent Lyle, looked up, she placed a large bundle wrapped in a camouflage tarp onto his desk, right on top of the second half of a tuna sandwich he happened to be eating, and then she flipped her sleek fall of hair over her shoulder for effect.

Eyes wide, thoroughly nonplused, Lyle managed to swallow his mouthful of sandwich and to speak. "What's this?"

"I went back to the nest this afternoon after the sandstorm blew out." Pansy unfastened the bundle and two long, graceful wings opened out of the tarp chrysalis. "I found her in the canyon."

"Oh, damn." Lyle stood, ashen-faced now, tenderly lifted the mother Aplomado falcon and carried her to a lab bench. He examined her, discovered the deep crimson wound in her black chest. Through gritted teeth he said, "Poachers?"

"Looks like it," Pansy said.

"What about the hatchling?"

"He's okay but he has to be hungry." With reverent sadness, Pansy stroked the mother falcon's smooth head. "Another week or two and the baby will be ready to fend for himself. But in the meantime, someone needs to get food to him. Or he needs to be brought in to a shelter."

Lyle sighed heavily. He was obviously deeply moved by this tragedy, a quality that Pansy found to be highly attractive.

"What are you going to do, Lyle?"

"I'll ask for a wildlife team to come out," he said. "Someone will get up there tomorrow to rescue the hatchling. Too bad, though. We've lost a chance to reestablish a nesting pattern."

"Tomorrow?" There was a flash of indignation in her tone.

"He'll be okay overnight."

"What if the poachers come back tonight?"

Again he sighed, looked around at the cluttered lab and the stacks of unfinished paperwork. Then he turned and looked directly into Pansy's big brown eyes.

"Pansy, I need help," he said. "Will you watch the nest tonight?"

"Me?" She touched her breastbone demurely, her freshly scrubbed hand small and delicate-looking. "Alone? Lyle, there are people with guns out there."

"You're right," he said, chagrined. "Sorry. Of course you shouldn't be alone. You shouldn't have been alone last night and this morning, either. It's just I got jammed up here in the office with a possible plague case in a ground squirrel, Chamber of Commerce all in a lather that word would get out. I couldn't break away."

"Ground squirrels aren't in danger of extinction," she said.

"I am sorry, very sorry," Lyle said, truly sounding sorry. "Look, Pansy, I really need you. If I join you, will you be willing to go back to the nest tonight?"

She took a long breath before responding, not wanting to sound eager. After a full ten count, during which he watched her with apparent interest, she nodded.

"The two of us should be able to handle just about anything that comes up," she said. "I'll meet you out front in five minutes."

"In five," he said as he peeled off his lab coat. "In five."

ANDREW KLAVAN

Her Lord and Master

FROM *Dangerous Women*

IT WAS OBVIOUS she'd killed him, but only I knew why. I'd been Jim's friend, and he'd told me everything. It was a shocking story in its way. I found it shocking, at any rate. More than once, when he confided in me, I'd felt the sweat gathering under my collar, on my chest. Goose bumps, and what in a more decorous age we would have called a "stirring in the loins." Nowadays, of course, we're supposed to be able to talk about these things, about anything, in fact. There are so many books and movies and television shows claiming to shatter "the last taboo" that you'd think we were in danger of running out of them.

Well, let's see. Let's just see.

Jim and Susan knew each other at work, and began a relationship after an office party, standard stuff. Jim was Vice President in charge of Entertainment at one of the larger radio networks. "I don't know what my job is," he used to say, "but by gum I must be doing it." Susan was an Assistant Manager in Personnel, which meant she was the secretary in charge of scheduling.

Jim was a tallish, elegant Harvard grad, thirty-five. On the job, he had a slow, thoughtful manner, a way of appearing to consider every word he spoke. Plus a way of boring into your eyes when you spoke, as if every neuron he had was engaged in whatever tedious matter you'd brought before him. After hours, thankfully, he became more satirical, more sardonic. To be honest, I think he considered most people little better than idiots. Which makes him a cockeyed optimist, if you ask me.

Susan was sharp, dark, energetic, in her twenties. A little thin and beaky in the face for my taste, but pretty enough with long, straight, black, black hair. Plus she had a fine figure, small and compact and gracefully, meltingly round at breast and hip. Her attitude was aggressive, funny, challenging: You gonna take me as I am, pal, or what? Which I think disguised a certain defensiveness about her Queens background, her education, maybe even her intelligence. In any case, she could put a charge in your morning, striding by in a short skirt, or drawing her hair from her mouth with one long nail. A Watercooler Fuck, was the general male consensus. In those sociological debates in which gentlemen are prone to discuss how their various female colleagues and acquaintances should be coupled with, Susan was usually voted the girl you'd like to shove against the watercooler and take standing up with the overnight cleaning crew vacuuming down the hall.

So at a party one February at which we celebrated the launch and certain failure of some new moronic management scheme or other, we watched with glee and envy as Jim and Susan stood together, talked together, and eventually left together. And eventually slept together. We didn't watch that part, but I heard all about it later.

I'm a news editor, thirty-eight, once divorced, seven years, two months, and sixteen days ago. Sexually, I think I've pretty much been around the block. But we've all pretty much been around the block these days. They probably ought to widen the lanes around the block to ease the traffic. So, at first, what Jim was telling me brought no more than a mild glaze of lust to my eyes, not to mention the thin line of drool running unattended from the corner of my mouth.

She liked it rough. That's the story. Now it can be told. Our Susan enjoyed the occasional smack with her rumpty-tumpty. Jim, God love him, seemed somewhat disconcerted by this at first. He'd been around the block too, of course, but it was a block in a more sedate neighborhood. And I guess maybe he'd missed that particular address.

Apparently, when they went back to his apartment, Susan had presented Jim with the belt to his terrycloth bathrobe and said, "Tie me." Jim managed to follow these simple instructions and also the ones about grabbing her black, black hair in his fist and forcing her mouth down on what I will politely assume to be his throbbing tumescence. The smacking part came later, after he'd hurled her bellyward onto his bed and was ramming into her from behind. This, too, at her specific request.

"It was kind of kinky," Jim told me.

"Hey, I sympathize," I said. "What does this make you, only the second or third luckiest man on the face of the earth?"

Well, it was a turn-on, Jim admitted that. And it wasn't that he'd never done anything like it before. It was just that, in Jim's experience, you had to get to know a girl a little before you started clobbering her. It was intimate, fantasy stuff, not the sort of thing you did on a first date.

Plus, Jim genuinely liked Susan, He liked the tough, working-stiff jazz of her and the chip-on-the-shoulder wisecracks with the vulnerability underneath. He wanted to get to know her, be with her a while, maybe a long while. And if this was where they started, he wondered, where exactly were they going to go?

But any awkwardness, it turned out, was all on Jim's side. Susan seemed perfectly comfortable when she woke in his arms the next morning. "It was nice last night," she whispered, stretching up to kiss his stubble. And she held his hand as they hailed a cab to take her home for a change of clothes. And she wowed and charmed him with her office etiquette, giving not a clue to the world of their altered state, giving even him only a single token of it when they passed each other, nodding, in the hall, and she murmured, "God, we are *so* professional."

And they had dinner together up on Columbus at the Moroccan and she went on, hilarious, about the management types in her department. And Jim, who usually expressed amusement by narrowing his eyes and smiling thinly, fell back in his chair and laughed with his teeth showing, and had to wipe tears out of his crow's feet with the four fingers of one hand.

That night, she wanted him to thrash her with his leather belt. Jim demurred. "Don't we ever get to do it just the regular way?" he asked.

But she leaned in close and smoldered at him. "Do it. I want you to."

"You know, I'm a little concerned about the noise. The neighbors and everything."

Well, he had a point there. Susan went into the kitchen and returned with a wooden spoon. They don't make quite the crack, apparently. Jim, always the gentleman, proceeded to tie her to the bedposts.

"The woman's killing me, I'm exhausted," he told me a couple of weeks later.

I put my hand under my shirt and moved it up and down so he could see my heart beating for him.

"I mean it," he said. "I mean, I'm up for this stuff sometimes. It's sexy, it's fun. But Jesus. I'd like to see her face from time to time."

"She'll calm down. You're just getting started," I said. "So she digs this stuff. Later, you can gently instruct her in the joys of the missionary position."

We had this conversation at a table in McCord's, the last unspoiled Irish bar on the gentrified West Side. The news team does tend to drift down here of an evening, so we were already speaking in undertones. Now, Jim leaned in toward me even closer. Our foreheads were almost touching and he glanced side to side before he went on.

"The thing is," he said, "I think she's serious."

"What do you mean?"

"I mean, I'm all for fantasy stuff and all that. But I don't think she's kidding around."

"What do you mean?" I said again, more hoarsely and with a bead of sweat forming behind my ear.

It turned out their relationship had now progressed to the point where they were divvying up the household chores. Susan had doled out the assignments and it fell to her to clean Jim's apartment, cook his dinner, and wash the dishes. Naked. Jim's job was to force her to do these things and whip, spank, or rape her if she showed reluctance or made, or pretended to make, some kind of mistake.

Now there's always an element of braggadocio when men complain about their sex lives, but Jim really did seem troubled by this. "I'm not saying it doesn't turn me on. I admit, it's a turn-on. It's just getting kind of . . . ugly at this point. Isn't it?" he said.

I wiped my lips dry and dropped back in my seat. When I could finally stop panting and move my mouth, I said, "I don't know. To each his own. I mean, look, if you don't like it, eject. You know? If it doesn't work for you, hit the button."

Obviously, this thought had occurred to him before. He nodded slowly, as if considering it.

But he didn't eject. In fact, another week or so, and for all intents and purposes Susan was living with him.

At this point, my information becomes less detailed. Obviously, a guy's living with someone, he doesn't go on too much about their sex life. Everyone at the net knew the affair was a happening thing by now, but Susan and Jim remained entirely professional and detached on the job. They'd walk to work together holding hands. They'd kiss once outside the building. And after that, it was business as usual. No low tones in the hallway, no closed office doors. The few times we all went out drinking together after work, they didn't even sit next to each other. Through the bar window, when they left, we'd see Jim put his arm around her. That was all.

The last time Jim and I talked about it before he died was in McCord's again. I came in there one night and there he was sitting at a corner table alone. I knew by the way he was sitting — bolt upright with his eyes half open, staring, glazed — that he was drunk as God on Sunday. I sat down across from him and he made a sloppy gesture with his hand and said, "Drinks are on me." I ordered a Scotch.

If I'd been smart, I would've stuck to sports. The Knicks were getting murdered, the Yanks, after a championship season, were struggling to keep pace with Baltimore as the new season got under way. I could've talked about all of that. I should've. But I was curious. If curious is the word I want. "Prurient," maybe, is the *mot juste*.

And I said, "So how are things going with Susan?"

And he said, as you will when you're serious about someone, "Fine. Things with Susan are fine." But then he added, "I'm her Lord and Master." Sitting bolt upright. Waving slightly like a lamppost in a gale.

Susan had scripted their routines, but he knew them by heart now and ran through them without prompting. This was apparently more efficient because it left her free to beg him to stop. He would tie her and she would beg him and he would beat her while she begged. He would sodomize her and grab her hair, force her head around so she had to watch him while he did it. "Who's your Lord and Master?" he would say. And she would answer, "You're my Lord and Master. You are." Later she would do the chores, naked or in this lace-and-suspender outfit she'd bought. Usually she'd fumble something or spill something, and he would beat her, which got him ready to take her again.

After he told me this, his eyes sank closed, his lips parted. He seemed to sleep for a few minutes, then woke up with a slight start. But bolt upright always, always straight up and down. Even when he got up to leave, his posture was stiff and perfect. He wafted to the door as if he were one of those old deportment instructors. He was a funny kind of a drunk that way, even more dignified than when he was sober, a sort of exaggerated, comic version of his reserved, dignifed sober self.

I watched him leave with a half-smile on my face. I miss him.

Susan stabbed him with a kitchen knife, one of those big ones. Just a single convulsive jab but it went straight in, severed the vena cava. He bled out lying on the kitchen floor, staring up at the ceiling while she screamed into the phone for an ambulance.

Jim being a bit of a muck-a-muck, it made the news. Then the feminists got ahold of it, the real bully girls who consider murdering your boyfriend a form of self-expression. They wanted the case dismissed out of hand. And a lot of people agreed they had a point this time. Susan, it was found, had bruises all over her torso, was bleeding from various orifices. And Jim had pretty clearly been wielding a nasty-looking sex store paddle when she went for the knife. According to the political dicta of the day, it was an obvious case of long-term abuse and long-delayed self-defense.

But the cops, for some reason, were not immediately convinced. In general, cops spend enough time in the depths of human depravity to keep a spare suit in the closet there. They know that even the most obvious political axioms don't always cut it when you're dealing with true romance.

So the Manhattan DA's office was caught between the devil and the deep blue sea. Susan had gotten a good lawyer fast and had said nothing to anyone. The police suspected they'd find evidence of consensual rough sex in Susan's life but so far hadn't produced the goods. The press, meanwhile, was starting to link Susan's name with the word "ordeal" a lot, and were running her story next to sidebars on sexual abuse, which was their way of being "objective" while taking Susan's side entirely, Anyway, the last thing the DA wanted was to jail the woman and then release her. So he waffled. Withheld charges for a day or two, pending further investigation. And, in the meantime, the prime suspect was set free.

As for me, all was depression and confusion. Jim wasn't my brother or anything, but he was a good buddy. And I knew I was probably the best friend he had at the network, maybe even in the city, maybe in the world. Still there were moments, watching the feminists on TV, watching Susan's lawyer, when I thought: How do I know? The guy says one thing, the girl says something else. How do I know everything Jim told me wasn't some kind of crazy lie, some sort of justification for the bad stuff he was doing to her?

Of course, all that aside, I called the police the day after the murder, Friday, the first I heard. I phoned a contact of mine in Homicide and told him I had solid information on the case. I think I half-expected to hear the whining sirens of the squad coming for me even as I hung up the phone. Instead, I was given a Monday morning appointment and asked to wander on by the station house to talk to the detectives in charge.

Which gave me the weekend free. I spent it anchored to the sofa by a leaden nausea. Gazing at the ceiling, arm flung across my brow. Trying to force tears, trying to blame myself, trying not to. The phone rang and rang, but I never answered it. It was just friends — I could hear them on the answering machine — wanting to get in on it: the sympathy, the grief, the gossip. Everybody craving a piece of a murder. I didn't have the energy to play.

Sunday evening, finally, there was a knock at my door. I'm on the top floor of a brownstone so you expect the street buzzer, but this was a knock. I figured it must be one of my neighbors who'd seen the story on TV. I called out as I put my shoes on. Tucked in my shirt as I went to the door. Pulled it open without even looking through the peephole.

And there was Susan.

A lot of things went through my mind in the second I saw her. As she stood there, combative and uncomfortable at once. Chin raised, belligerent; glance sidelong, shy. I thought: Who am I supposed to be here? What am I supposed to be like? Angry? Vengeful?

Chilly? Just? Lofty? Compassionate? Christ, it was paralyzing. In the end, I just stood back and let her enter. She walked into the middle of the room and faced me as I closed the door.

Then she shrugged at me. One bare shoulder lifted, one lifted corner of her mouth, a wise-guy smile. She was wearing a pale spring dress, the thin strings tied round her neck in a bow. It showed a lot of her dark flesh. I noticed a crescent of discolor on her thigh beneath the hem.

"I'm not too sure about the etiquette here," I said.

"Yeah. Maybe you could look under 'Entertaining the Girl Who Killed Your Best Friend.'"

I gave her back her wise-guy smile. "Don't say too much, Susan, okay? I gotta go in to see the cops on Monday."

She stopped smiling, nodded, turned away. "So — what? Like, Jim told you everything? About us?" She toyed with the pad on my phone table.

I watched her. My reactions were subtle but intense. It was the way she turned, it was that thing she said. It made me think about what Jim had told me. It made me look, long and slow, down the line of her back. It made my skin feel hot, my stomach cold. An interesting combination.

I moistened my lips and tried to think about my dead friend. "Yeah, that's right," I said gruffly. "He told me pretty much everything."

Susan laughed over her shoulder at me. "Well, that's embarrassing, anyway."

"Hey, don't flirt with me, okay? Don't kill my friend and come over here and flirt with me."

She turned round again, hands primly folded in front of her. I looked so steadily at her face she must've known I was thinking about her breasts. "I'm not flirting with you," she said. "I just want to tell you."

"Tell me what?"

"What he did, that he beat me, that he humiliated me. He was twice my size. Think how you'd like it, think what you would've done if someone was doing that to you."

"Susan!" I spread my hands at her. "You asked him to!"

"Oh, yeah, like, 'She was asking for it,' right? Like you automatically believe that. Your buddy says it so it must be true."

I snorted. I thought about it. I looked at her. I thought about Jim. "Yeah," I said finally. "I do believe it. It was true."

She didn't argue the point. She went right on. "Yeah, well, if it is true, it doesn't make it any better. You know? I mean, you should've seen the way it turned him on. I mean, he could've stopped it. I'd've stopped. He could've changed everything any time, if he wanted to. But he liked it so much... And then there he is, hurting me like that, and all turned on by it. How do you think that makes a person feel?"

I am not too proud to admit that I actually scratched my head, dumb as a monkey.

Susan ran one long nail over the phone table pad. She looked down at it. So did I. "Are you really going to the cops?"

"Yeah. Hell, yeah," I said. Then, as if I needed an excuse, "It's not like they won't find someone else. Some other guy you did this stuff with. He'll tell them the same thing."

She shook her head once. "No. There's only you. You're the only one who knows." Which left nothing to say. We stood there silent. She thinking, me just watching her, just watching the lines and colors of her.

Then, finally, she raised her eyes to me, tilted her head. She didn't slink toward me, or tiptoe her fingers up my chest. She didn't nestle under me so I could feel the heat of her breath or smell her perfume. She left that for the movies, for the femme fatales. All she did was stand there like that and give me that Susan look, chin out, dukes up, her soul in the offing, almost trembling in your hand.

"It gives you a lot of power over me, doesn't it?" she said.

"So what?" I said back.

She shrugged again. "You know what I like."

"Get out," I said. I didn't give myself time to start sweating. "Christ. Get the fuck out of here, Susan."

She walked to the door. I watched her go. Yeah, right, I thought. I have power over her. As if. I have power over her until they decide not to charge her, until the headlines disappear. Then where am I? Then I'm her Lord and Master. Just like Jim was.

She passed close to me. Close enough to hear my thoughts. She glanced up, surprised. She laughed at me. "What. You think I'd kill you too?"

"I'd always have to wonder, wouldn't I?" I said.

Still smiling, she jogged her eyebrows comically. "Whatever turns you on," she said.

It was the comedy that did it. I couldn't resist the impulse to wipe that smile off her murdering face. I reached out and grabbed her hair in my fist. Her black, black hair.

It was even softer than I thought it would be.

ELMORE LEONARD

Louly and Pretty Boy

FROM *Dangerous Women*

HERE ARE SOME DATES in Louly Ring's life from 1912, the year she was born in Tulsa, Oklahoma, to 1931, when she ran away from home to meet Joe Young, following his release from the Missouri State Penitentiary.

In 1918 her daddy, a Tulsa stockyard hand, joined the U.S. Marines and was killed at Bois de Belleau during the World War. Her mom, sniffling as she held the letter, told Louly it was a woods over in France.

In 1920 her mom married a hard-shell Baptist by the name of Otis Bender and they went to live on his cotton farm near Sallisaw, south of Tulsa on the edge of the Cookson Hills. By the time Louly was twelve, her mom had two sons by Otis and Otis had Louly out in the fields picking cotton. He was the only person in the world who called her by her Christian name, Louise. She hated picking cotton but her mom wouldn't say anything to Otis. Otis believed that when you were old enough to do a day's work, you worked. It meant Louly was finished with school by the sixth grade.

In 1924, that summer, they attended her cousin Ruby's wedding in Bixby. Ruby was seventeen, the boy she married, Charley Floyd, twenty. Ruby was dark but pretty, showing Cherokee blood from her mama's side. Because of their age difference Louly and Ruby had nothing to say to each other. Charley called her kiddo and would lay his hand on her head and muss her bobbed hair that was sort of reddish from her mom. He told her she had the biggest brown eyes he had ever seen on a little girl.

In 1925 she began reading about Charles Arthur Floyd in the paper: how he and two others went up to St. Louis and robbed the

Kroger Food payroll office of $11,500. They were caught in Sallisaw driving around in a brand-new Studebaker they bought in Ft. Smith, Arkansas. The Kroger Food paymaster identified Charley, saying, "That's him, the pretty boy with apple cheeks." The newspapers ate it up and referred to Charley from then on as Pretty Boy Floyd.

Louly remembered him from the wedding as cute with wavy hair, but kind of scary the way he grinned at you — not being sure what he was thinking. She bet he hated being called Pretty Boy. Looking at his picture she cut out of the paper Louly felt herself getting a crush on him.

In 1929, while he was still in the penitentiary, Ruby divorced him on the grounds of neglect and married a man from Kansas. Louly thought it was terrible, Ruby betraying Charley like that. "Ruby don't see him ever again going straight," her mom said. "She needs a husband the same as I did to ease the burdens of life, have a father for her little boy, Dempsey." Born in December of '24 and named for the world's heavyweight boxing champ.

Now that Charley was divorced Louly wanted to write and sympathize but didn't know which of his names to use. She had heard his friends called him Choc, after his fondness for Choctaw Beer, his favorite beverage when he was in his teens and roamed Oklahoma and Kansas with harvest crews. Her mom said it was where he first took up with bad companions, "those drifters he met at harvest time," and later on working oil patches.

Louly opened her letter "Dear Charley," and said she thought it was a shame Ruby divorcing him while he was still in prison, not having the nerve to wait till he was out. What she most wanted to know: "Do you remember me from your wedding?" She stuck a picture of herself in a bathing suit, standing sideways and smiling over her shoulder at the camera. This way her fourteen-year-old breasts, coming along, were seen in profile.

Charley wrote back saying sure he remembered her, "the little girl with the big brown eyes." Saying, "I'm getting out in March and going to Kansas City to see what's doing. I have given your address to an inmate here by the name of Joe Young who we call Booger, being funny. He is from Okmulgee but has to do another year or so in this garbage can and would like to have a pen pal as pretty as you are."

Nuts. But then Joe Young wrote her a letter with a picture of himself taken in the yard with his shirt off, a fairly good-looking bozo with big ears and blondish hair. He said he kept her bathing-suit picture on the wall next to his rack so he'd look at it before going to sleep and dream of her all night. He never signed his letters Booger, always, "With love, your Joe Young."

Once they were exchanging letters she told him how much she hated picking cotton, dragging that duck sack along the rows all day in the heat and dust, her hands raw from pulling the bolls off the stalks, gloves after a while not doing a bit of good. Joe said in his letter, "What are you a nigger slave? You don't like picking cotton leave there and run away. It is what I done."

Pretty soon he said in a letter, "I am getting my release sometime next summer. Why don't you plan on meeting me so we can get together." Louly said she was dying to visit Kansas City and St. Louis, wondering if she would ever see Charley Floyd again. She asked Joe why he was in prison and he wrote back to say, "Honey, I'm a bank robber, same as Choc."

She had been reading more stories about Pretty Boy Floyd. He had returned to Akins, his hometown, for his daddy's funeral — *Akins only seven miles from Sallisaw* — his dad shot by a neighbor during an argument over a pile of lumber. When the neighbor disappeared there were people who said Pretty Boy had killed him. Seven miles away and she didn't know it till after.

There was his picture again. PRETTY BOY FLOYD ARRESTED IN AKRON for bank robbery. Sentenced to fifteen years in the Ohio State Penitentiary. Now she'd never see him but at least could start writing again.

A few weeks later another picture. PRETTY BOY FLOYD ESCAPES ON WAY TO PRISON. Broke a window in the toilet and jumped off the train and by the time they got it stopped he was gone.

It was exciting just trying to keep track of him, Louly getting chills and thrills knowing everybody in the world was reading about this famous outlaw she was related to — by marriage but not blood — this desperado who liked her brown eyes and had mussed her hair when she was a kid.

Now another picture. PRETTY BOY FLOYD IN SHOOTOUT WITH POLICE. Outside a barbershop in Bowling Green, Ohio, and got away. There with a woman named Juanita — Louly not liking the sound of that.

Louly and Pretty Boy

Joe Young wrote to say, "I bet Choc is threw with Ohio and will never go back there." But the main reason he wrote was to tell her, "I am getting my release the end of August. I will let you know soon where to meet me."

Louly had been working winters at Harkrider's grocery store in Sallisaw for six dollars a week part-time. She had to give five of it to Otis, the man never once thanking her, leaving a dollar to put in her running-away kitty. From winter to the next fall, working at the store most of six months a year, she hadn't saved a whole lot but she was going. She might have her timid-soul mom's looks, the reddish hair, but had the nerve and get-up-and-go of her daddy, killed in action charging a German machine-gun nest in that woods in France.

Late in October, who walked in the grocery store but Joe Young. Louly knew him even wearing a suit, and he knew her, grinning as he came up to the counter, his shirt wide open at the neck. He said, "Well, I'm out."

She said, "You been out two months, haven't you?"

He said, "I been robbing banks. Me and Choc."

She thought she had to go to the bathroom, the urge coming over her in her groin and then gone. Louly gave herself a few moments to compose herself and act like the mention of Choc didn't mean anything special, Joe Young staring in her face with his grin, giving her the feeling he was dumb as dirt. Some other convict must've wrote his letters for him. She said in a casual way, "Oh, is Charley here with you?"

"He's around," Joe Young said, looking toward the door. "You ready? We gotta go."

She said, "I like that suit on you," giving herself time to think. The points of his shirt collar spread open to his shoulders, his hair long on top but skinned on the sides, his ears sticking out, Joe Young grinning like it was his usual dopey expression. "I'm not ready just yet," Louly said. "I don't have my running-away money with me."

"How much you save?"

"Thirty-eight dollars."

"Jesus, working here two years?"

"I told you, Otis takes most of my wages."

"You want, I'll crack his head for him."

"I wouldn't mind. The thing is, I'm not leaving without my money."

Joe Young looked at the door as he put his hand in his pocket saying, "Little girl, I'm paying your way. You won't need the thirty-eight dollars."

Little girl — she stood a good two inches taller than he was, even in his run-down cowboy boots. She was shaking her head now. "Otis bought a Model A Roadster with my money, paying it off twenty a month."

"You want to steal his car?"

"It's mine, ain't it, if he's using my money?"

Louly had made up her mind and Joe Young was anxious to get out of here. She had pay coming, so they'd meet November first — no, the second — at the Georgian Hotel in Henryetta, in the coffee shop around noon.

The day before she was to leave Louly told her mom she was sick. Instead of going to work she got her things ready and used the curling iron on her hair. The next day, while her mom was hanging wash, the two boys at school, and Otis was out in the field, Louly rolled the Ford Roadster out of the shed and drove into Sallisaw to get a pack of Lucky Strikes for the trip. She loved to smoke and had been doing it with boys but never had to buy the cigarettes. When boys wanted to take her in the woods she'd ask, "You have Luckies? A whole pack?"

The druggist's son, one of her boyfriends, gave her a pack free of charge and asked where she was yesterday, acting sly, saying, "You're always talking about Pretty Boy Floyd, I wonder if he stopped by your house."

They liked to kid her about Pretty Boy. Louly, not paying close attention, said, "I'll let you know when he does." But then saw the boy about to spring something on her.

"The reason I ask, he was here in town yesterday, Pretty Boy Floyd was."

She said, "Oh?" careful now. The boy took his time and it was hard not to grab him by the front of his shirt.

"Yeah, he brought his family down from Akins, his mama, two of his sisters, some others, so they could watch him rob the bank. His grampa watched from the field across the street. Bob Riggs, the bank assistant, said Pretty Boy had a Tommy gun, but did not shoot anybody. He come out of the bank with two thousand five-hundred and thirty-one dollars, him and two other fellas. He gave some of the money to his people and they say to anybody he thought hadn't et in a while, everybody grinning at him. Pretty Boy had Bob Riggs ride on the running board to the end of town and let him go."

This was the second time now he had been close by: first when his daddy was killed only seven miles away and now right here in Sallisaw, all kinds of people seeing him, damn it, but her. Just yesterday...

He knew she lived in Sallisaw. She wondered if he'd looked for her in the crowd watching.

She had to wonder, too, if she *had* been here would he of recognized her, and bet he would've.

She said to her boyfriend in the drugstore, "Charley ever hears you called him Pretty Boy, he'll come in for a pack of Luckies, what he always smokes, and then kill you."

The Georgian was the biggest hotel Louly had ever seen. Coming up on it in the Model A she was thinking these bank robbers knew how to live high on the hog. She pulled in front and a colored man in a green uniform coat with gold buttons and a peaked cap came around to open her door — and saw Joe Young on the sidewalk waving the doorman away, saying as he got in the car, "Jesus Christ, you stole it, didn't you. Jesus, how old are you, going around stealing cars?"

Louly said, "How old you have to be?"

He told her to keep straight ahead.

She said, "You aren't staying at the hotel?"

"I'm at a tourist court."

"Charley there?"

"He's around someplace."

"Well, he was in Sallisaw yesterday," Louly sounding mad now, "if that's what you call *around*," seeing by Joe Young's expression she was telling him something he didn't know. "I thought you were in his gang."

"He's got an old boy name of Birdwell with him. I hook up with Choc when I feel like it."

She was almost positive Joe Young was lying to her.

"Am I gonna see Charley or not?"

"He'll be back, don't worry your head about it." He said, "We got this car, I won't have to steal one." Joe Young in a good mood now.

"What we need Choc for?" Grinning at her close by the car. "We got each other."

It told her what to expect.

Once they got to the tourist court and were in No. 7, like a little one-room frame house that needed paint, Joe Young took off his coat and she saw the Colt automatic with a pearl grip stuck in his pants. He laid it on the dresser by a full quart of whiskey and two glasses and poured them each a drink, his bigger than hers. She stood watching till he told her to take off her coat and when she did told her to take off her dress. Now she was in her white brassiere and panties. Joe Young looked her over before handing the smaller drink to her and clinking glasses.

"To our future."

Louly said, "Doing what?" Seeing the fun in his eyes.

He put his glass on the dresser, brought two .38 revolvers from the drawer and offered her one. She took it, big and heavy in her hand and said, "Yeah . . . ?"

"You know how to steal a car," Joe Young said, "and I admire that. But I bet you never held up a place with a gun."

"That's what we're gonna do?"

"Start with a filling station and work you up to a bank." He said, "I bet you never been to bed with a grown man, either."

Louly felt like telling him she was bigger than he was, taller, anyway, but didn't. This was a new experience, different than with boys her age in the woods, and she wanted to see what it was like.

Well, he grunted a lot and was rough, breathed hard through his nose, and smelled of Lucky Tiger hair tonic, but it wasn't that much different than with boys. She got to liking it before he was finished and patted his back with her rough, cotton-picking fingers till he began to breathe easy again. Once he rolled off her she got her douche bag out of Otis's grip she'd taken and went in the bathroom, Joe Young's voice following her with, "Whooooee . . ."

Then saying, "You know what you are now, little girl? You're what's called a gun moll."

Joe Young slept a while, woke up still snookered, and wanted to get something to eat. So they went to Purity, Joe said was the best place in Henryetta.

Louly said at the table, "Charley Floyd came in here one time. People found out he was in town and everybody stayed in their house."

"How you know that?"

"I know everything about him was ever written, some things only told."

"Where'd he stay in Kansas City?"

"Mother Ash's boarding house on Holmes Street."

"Who'd he go to Ohio with?"

"The Jim Bradley gang."

Joe Young picked up his coffee he'd poured a shot into. He said, "You're gonna start reading about me, chile."

It reminded her she didn't know how old Joe Young was and took this opportunity to ask him.

"I'm thirty next month, born on Christmas Day, same as Baby Jesus."

Louly smiled. She couldn't help it, seeing Joe Young lying in a manger with Baby Jesus, the three Wise Men looking at him funny. She asked Joe how many times he'd had his picture in the paper.

"When I got sent to Jeff City they's all kinds of pictures of me was in there."

"I mean how many different times, for other stickups?"

She watched him sit back as the waitress came with their supper and he gave her a pat on the butt as she turned from the table. The waitress said, "Fresh," and acted surprised in a cute way. Louly was ready to tell how Charley Floyd had his picture in the Sallisaw paper fifty-one times in the past year, once for each of the fifty-one banks robbed in Oklahoma, all of them claiming Charley as the bank robber. But if she told him, Joe Young would say Charley couldn't of robbed that many since he was in Ohio part of '31. Which was true. An estimate said he might've robbed thirty-eight banks, but even that might cause Joe Young to be jealous and get cranky, so she let it drop and they ate their chicken-fried steaks.

Joe Young told her to pay the bill, a buck-sixty for everything including rhubarb pie for dessert, out of her running-away money. They got back to the tourist court and he screwed her again on her full stomach, breathing through his nose, and she saw how this being a gun moll wasn't all a bed of roses.

In the morning they set out east on Highway 40 for the Cookson Hills, Joe Young driving the Model A with his elbow out the window, Louly holding her coat close to her, the collar up against the wind, Joe Young talking a lot, saying he knew where Choc liked to hide. They'd go on up to Muskogee, cross the Arkansas, and head down along the river to Braggs. "I know the boy likes that country around Braggs." Along the way he could hold up a filling station, show Louly how it was done.

Heading out of Henryetta she said, "There's one."

He said, "Too many cars."

Thirty miles later leaving Checotah, turning north toward Muskogee, Louly looked back and said, "What's wrong with that Texaco station?"

"Something about it I don't like," Joe Young said. "You have to have a feel for this work."

Louly said, "You pick it." She had the .38 he gave her in a black and pink bag her mom had crocheted for her.

They came up on Summit and crept through town, both of them looking, Louly waiting for him to choose a place to rob. She was getting excited. They came to the other side of town and Joe Young said, "There's our place. We can fill up, get a cup of coffee."

Louly said, "Hold it up?"

"Look it over."

"It's sure a dump."

Two gas pumps in front of a rickety place, paint peeling, a sign that said EATS and told that soup was a dime and a hamburg five cents.

They went in while a bent-over old man filled their tank, Joe Young bringing his whiskey bottle with him, almost drained, and put it on the counter. The woman behind it was skin and bones, worn out, brushing strands of hair from her face. She placed cups in front of them and Joe Young poured what was left in the bottle into his.

Louly did not want to rob this woman.

The woman saying, "I think she's dry."

Joe Young was concentrating on dripping the last drops from his bottle. He said, "Can you help me out?"

Now the woman was pouring their coffee. "You want shine? Or I can give you Kentucky for three dollars."

"Gimme a couple," Joe Young said, drawing his Colt, laying it on the counter, "and what's in the till."

Louly did not want to rob this woman. She was thinking you

didn't *have* to rob a person just 'cause the person had money, did you?

The woman said, "Goddamn you, mister."

Joe Young picked up his gun and went around to open the cash register at the end of the counter. Taking out bills he said to the woman, "Where you keep the whiskey money?"

She said, "In there," despair in her voice.

He said, "Fourteen dollars?" holding it up, and turned to Louly. "Put your gun on her so she don't move. The geezer come in, put it on him, too." Joe Young went through a doorway to what looked like an office.

The woman said to Louly, pointing the gun from the crocheted bag at her now, "How come you're with that trash? You seem like a girl from a nice family, have a pretty bag . . . There something wrong with you? My Lord, you can't do better 'n him?"

Louly said, "You know who's a good friend of mine? Charley Floyd, if you know who I mean. He married my cousin Ruby." The woman shook her head and Louly said, "Pretty Boy Floyd" and wanted to bite her tongue.

Now the woman seemed to smile, showing black lines between the teeth she had. "He come in here one time. I fixed him breakfast and he paid me two dollars for it. You ever hear of that? I charge twenty-five cents for two eggs, four strips of bacon, toast, and all you want of coffee, and he give me two dollars."

"When was this?" Louly said.

The woman looked past Louly trying to see when it was and said, "Twenty-nine, after his daddy was killed that time."

They got the fourteen from the till and fifty-seven dollars in whiskey money from the back, Joe Young talking again about heading for Muskogee, telling Louly it was his instinct told him to go in there. How was this place doing business, two big service stations only a few blocks away? So he'd brought the bottle in, see what it would get him. "You hear what she said? 'Goddamn you,' but called me 'Mister.'"

"Charley had breakfast in there one time," Louly said, "and paid her two dollars for it."

"Showing off," Joe Young said.

He decided they'd stay in Muskogee instead of going down to Braggs and rest up here.

Louly said, "Yeah, we must've come a good fifty miles today."

Joe Young told her not to get smart with him, "I'm gonna put you in a tourist cabin and see some boys I know. Find out where Choc's at."

She didn't believe him, but what was the sense of arguing?

It was early evening now, the sun going down.

The man who knocked on the door — she could see him through the glass part — was tall and slim in a dark suit, a young guy dressed up, holding his hat at his leg. She believed he was the police, but had no reason, standing here looking at him, not to open the door.

He said, "Miss," and showed her his I.D. and a star in a circle in a wallet he held open. "I'm Deputy U.S. Marshal Carl Webster. Who am I speaking to?"

She said, "I'm Louly Ring?"

He smiled straight teeth at her and said, "You're a cousin of Pretty Boy Floyd's wife, Ruby, aren't you?"

Like getting ice-cold water thrown in her face she was so surprised. "How'd you know that?"

"We been making a book on Pretty Boy, noting down connections, everybody he knows. You recall the last time you saw him?"

"At their wedding, eight years ago."

"No time since? How about the other day in Sallisaw?"

"I never saw him. But listen, him and Ruby are divorced."

The marshal, Carl Webster, shook his head. "He went up to Coffeyville and got her back. But aren't you missing a automobile, a Model A Ford?"

She had not heard a *word* about Charley and Ruby being back together. None of the papers ever mentioned her, just the woman named Juanita. Louly said, "The car isn't missing, a friend of mine's using it."

He said, "The car's in your name?" and recited the Oklahoma license number.

"I paid for it out of my wages. It just happens to be in my stepfather's name, Otis Bender."

"I guess there's some kind of misunderstanding," Carl Webster said. "Otis claims it was stolen off his property in Sequoyah County. Who's your friend borrowed it?"

She did hesitate before saying his name.

Louly and Pretty Boy

"When's Joe coming back?"

"Later on. 'Cept he'll stay with his friends if he gets too drunk."

Carl Webster said, "I wouldn't mind talking to him," and gave Louly a business card from his pocket with a star on it and letters she could feel. "Ask Joe to give me a call later on, or sometime tomorrow if he don't come home. Y'all just driving around?"

"Seeing the sights."

Every time she kept looking at him he'd start to smile. Carl Webster. She could feel his name under her thumb. She said, "You're writing a book on Charley Floyd?"

"Not a real one. We're collecting the names of anybody he ever knew that might want to put him up."

"You gonna ask me if I would?"

There was the smile.

"I already know."

She liked the way he shook her hand and thanked her, and the way he put on his hat, nothing to it, knowing how to cock it just right.

Joe Young returned about 9:00 A.M. making awful faces working his mouth, trying to get a taste out of it. He came in the room and took a good pull on the whiskey bottle, then another, sucked in his breath and let it out and seemed better. He said, "I don't believe what we got into with those chickens last night."

"Wait," Louly said. She told him about the marshal stopping by, and Joe Young became jittery and couldn't stand still, saying, "I ain't going back. I done ten years and swore to Jesus I ain't ever going back." Now he was looking out the window.

Louly wanted to know what Joe and his buddies did to the chickens but knew they had to get out of here. She tried to tell him they had to leave, *right now*.

He was still drunk or starting over, saying now, "They come after me they's gonna be a shoot-out. I'm taking some of the scudders with me." Maybe not even knowing he was playing Jimmy Cagney now.

Louly said, "You only stole seventy-one dollars."

"I done other things in the state of Oklahoma," Joe Young said. "They take me alive I'm facing fifteen years to life. I swear I ain't going back."

What was going *on* here? They're driving around looking for

Charley Floyd — the next thing this dumbbell wants to shoot it out with the law and here she was in this room with him. "They don't want *me*," Louly said. Knowing she couldn't talk to him, the state he was in. She had to get out of here, open the door and run. She got her crocheted bag from the dresser, started for the door, and was stopped by the bullhorn.

The electrified voice loud, saying, "JOE YOUNG, COME OUT WITH YOUR HANDS IN THE AIR."

What Joe Young did — he held his Colt straight out in front of him and started firing through the glass pane in the door. People outside returned fire, blew out the window, gouged the door with gunfire, Louly dropping to the floor with her bag, until she heard a voice on the bullhorn call out, "HOLD YOUR FIRE."

Louly looked up to see Joe Young standing by the bed with a gun in each hand now, the Colt and a .38. She said, "Joe, you have to give yourself up. They're gonna kill both of us you keep shooting."

He didn't even look at her. He yelled out, "Come and get me!" and started shooting again, both guns at the same time.

Louly's hand went in the crocheted bag and came out with the .38 he'd given her to help him rob places. From the floor, up on her elbows, she aimed the revolver at Joe Young, cocked it, and *bam*, shot him through the chest.

Louly stepped away from the door and the marshal, Carl Webster, came in holding a revolver. She saw men standing out in the road, some with rifles. Carl Webster was looking at Joe Young curled up on the floor. He holstered his revolver, took the .38 from Louly, and sniffed the end of the barrel and stared at her without saying anything before going to one knee to see if Joe Young had a pulse. He got up saying, "The Oklahoma Bankers Association wants people like Joe dead, and that's what he is. They're gonna give you a five-hundred-dollar reward for killing your friend."

"He wasn't a friend."

"He was yesterday. Make up your mind."

"He stole the car and made me go with him."

"Against your will," Carl Webster said. "Stay with that, you won't go to jail."

"It's true, Carl," Louly said, showing him her big brown eyes. "Really."

*

The headline in the Muskogee paper, over a small photo of Louise Ring, said SALLISAW GIRL SHOOTS ABDUCTOR.

According to Louise, she had to stop Joe Young or be killed in the exchange of gunfire. She also said her name was Louly, not Louise. The marshal on the scene said it was a courageous act, the girl shooting her abductor. "We considered Joe Young a mad-dog felon with nothing to lose." The marshal said that Joe Young was suspected of being a member of Pretty Boy Floyd's gang. He also mentioned that Louly Ring was related to Floyd's wife and acquainted with the desperado.

The headline in the Tulsa paper, over a larger photo of Louly, said GIRL SHOOTS MEMBER OF PRETTY BOY FLOYD GANG. The story told that Louly Ring was a friend of Pretty Boy's and had been abducted by the former gang member, who, according to Louly, "was jealous of Pretty Boy and kidnapped me to get back at him."

By the time the story had appeared everywhere from Ft. Smith, Arkansas, to Toledo, Ohio, the favorite headline was GIRLFRIEND OF PRETTY BOY FLOYD GUNS DOWN MAD-DOG FELON.

The marshal, Carl Webster, came to Sallisaw on business and stopped in Harkrider's for a sack of Beech-Nut scrap. He was surprised to see Louly.

"You're still working here?"

"I'm shopping for my mom. No, Carl, I got my reward money and I'll be leaving here pretty soon. Otis hasn't said a word to me since I got home. He's afraid I might shoot him."

"Where you going?"

"This writer for *True Detective* wants me to come to Tulsa. They'll put me up at the Mayo Hotel and pay a hundred dollars for my story. Reporters from Kansas City and St. Louis, Missouri, have already been to the house."

"You're sure getting a lot of mileage out of knowing Pretty Boy, aren't you?"

"They start out asking about my shooting that dumbbell Joe Young, but what they want to know if I'm Charley Floyd's girlfriend. I say, 'Where'd you get that idea?'"

"But you don't deny it."

"I say, 'Believe what you want, since I can't change your mind.' What I wonder, you think Charley's read about it and seen my picture?"

"Sure he has," Carl said. "I imagine he'd even like to see you again, in person."

Louly said, "Wow," like she hadn't thought of that before this moment. "You're kidding. Really?"

LAURA LIPPMAN

The Crack Cocaine Diet
(Or: How to Lose a Lot of Weight and Change
Your Life in Just One Weekend)

FROM *The Cocaine Chronicles*

I HAD JUST BROKEN UP with Brandon and Molly had just broken up with Keith, so we needed new dresses to go to this party where we knew they were going to be. But before we could buy the dresses, we needed to lose weight because we had to look fabulous, kiss-my-ass-fuck-you fabulous. Kiss-my-ass-fuck-you-and-your-dick-is-really-tiny fabulous. Because, after all, Brandon and Keith were going to be at this party and if we couldn't get new boyfriends in less than eight days, we could at least go down a dress size and look so good that Brandon and Keith and everybody else in the immediate vicinity would wonder how they ever let us go. I mean, yes, technically, *they* broke up with *us*, but we had been thinking about it, weighing the pros and cons. (Pro: They spent money on us. Con: They were childish. Pro: We had them. Con: Tiny dicks, see above.) See, we were being methodical and they were just all impulsive, the way guys are. That would be another con — poor impulse control. Me, I never do anything without thinking it through very carefully. Anyway, I'm not sure what went down with Molly and Keith, but Brandon said if he wanted to be nagged all the time, he'd move back in with his mother, and I said, "Well, given that she still does your laundry and makes you food, it's not as if you really moved out," and that was that. No big loss.

Still, we had to look so great that other guys would be punching our exes in the arms and saying, "What, are you crazy?" Everything is about spin, even dating. It's always better to be the dumper instead of the dumpee, and if you have to be the loser, then you need to find a way to be superior. And that was going to take about seven pounds for me, as many as ten for Molly, who doesn't have my discipline and had been doing some serious break-up eating for the past three weeks. She went face down in the Ding Dongs, danced with the Devil Dogs, became a Ho Ho ho. As for myself, I'm a salty girl, and I admit I had the Pringles Light can upended in my mouth for a couple of days.

So anyway, Molly said Atkins and I said not fast enough, and then I said a fast-fast and Molly said she saw little lights in front of her eyes the last time she tried to go no food, and she said cabbage soup and I said it gives me gas, and then she said pills and I said all the doctors we knew were too tight with their 'scrips, even her dentist boss since she stopped blowing him. Finally, Molly had a good idea and said: "Cocaine!"

This merited consideration. Molly and I had never done more than a little recreational coke, always provided by boyfriends who were trying to impress us, but even my short-term experience indicated it would probably do the trick. The tiniest bit revved you up for hours and you raced around and around, and it wasn't that you weren't hungry, more like you had never even heard of food; it was just some quaint custom from the olden days, like square dancing.

"Okay," I said. "Only, where do we get it?" After all, we're girls, *girly* girls. I had been drinking and smoking pot since I was sixteen, but I certainly didn't buy it. That's what boyfriends were for. Pro: Brandon bought my drinks, and if you don't have to lay out cash for alcohol, you can buy a lot more shoes.

Molly thought hard, and Molly thinking was like a fat guy running — there was a lot of visible effort.

"Well, like, the city."

"But where in the city?"

"On, like, a corner."

"Right, Molly. I watch HBO, too. But I mean, what corner? It's not like they list them in that crap Weekender Guide in the paper — movies, music, clubs, where to buy drugs."

So Molly asked a guy who asked a guy who talked to a guy, and it turned out there was a place just inside the city line, not too far from the interstate. Easy on, easy off, then easy off again. Get it? After a quick consultation on what to wear — jeans and T-shirts and sandals, although I changed into running shoes after I saw the condition of my pedicure — we were off. Very hush-hush because, as I explained to Molly, that was part of the adventure. I phoned my mom and said I was going for a run. Molly told her mom she was going into the city to shop for a dress.

The friend of Molly's friend's friend had given us directions to what turned out to be an apartment complex, which was kind of disappointing. I mean, we were expecting row houses, slumping picturesquely next to each other, but this was just a dirtier, more run-down version of where we lived — little clusters of two-story townhouses built around an interior courtyard. We drove around and around and around, trying to seem very savvy and willing, and it looked like any apartment complex on a hot July afternoon. Finally, on our third turn around the complex, a guy ambled over to the car.

"What you want?"

"What you got?" I asked, which I thought was pretty good. I mean, I sounded casual but kind of hip, and if he turned out to be a cop, I hadn't implicated myself. See, I was always thinking, unlike some people I could name.

"Got American Idol and Survivor. The first one will make you sing so pretty that Simon will be speechless. The second one will make you feel as if you've got immunity for life."

"*O-kay.*" Molly reached over me with a fistful of bills, but the guy backed away from the car.

"Pay the guy up there. Then someone will bring you your package."

"Shouldn't you give us the, um, stuff first and then get paid?"

The guy gave Molly the kind of look that a schoolteacher gives you when you say something exceptionally stupid. We drove up to the next guy, gave him forty dollars, then drove to a spot he pointed out to wait.

"It's like McDonald's!" Molly said. "Drive through!"

"Shit, don't say McDonald's. I haven't eaten all day. I would kill for a Big Mac."

"Have you ever had the Big 'N' Tasty? It totally rocks."

"What is it?"

"It's a cheeseburger, but with, like, a special sauce."

"Like a Big Mac."

"Only the sauce is different."

"I liked the fries better when they made them in beef fat."

A third boy — it's okay to say boy, because he was, like, thirteen, so I'm not being racist or anything — handed us a package, and we drove away. But Molly immediately pulled into a convenience store parking lot. It wasn't a real convenience store, though, not a 7-Eleven or a Royal Farm.

"What are you doing?"

"Pre-diet binge," Molly said. "If I'm not going to eat for the next week, I want to enjoy myself now."

I had planned to be pure starting that morning, but it sounded like a good idea. I did a little math. An ounce of Pringles has, like, 120 calories, so I could eat an entire can and not gain even half a pound, and a half pound doesn't even register on a scale, so it wouldn't count. Molly bought a pound of Peanut M&Ms, and let me tell you, the girl was not overachieving. I'd seen her eat that much on many an occasion. Molly has big appetites. We had a picnic right there in the parking lot, washing down our food with diet cream soda. Then Molly began to open our "package."

"Not here!" I warned her, looking around.

"What if it's no good? What if they cut it with, like, something, so it's weak?"

Molly was beginning to piss me off a little, but maybe it was just all the salt, which was making my fingers swell and my head pound a little. "How are you going to know if it's any good?"

"You put it on your gums." She opened the package. It didn't look quite right. It was more off-white than I remembered, not as finely cut. But Molly dove right in, licking her finger, sticking it in, and then spreading it around her gum line.

"Shit," she said. "I don't feel a thing."

"Well, you don't feel it right away."

"No, they, like, totally robbed us. It's bullshit. I'm going back."

"Molly, I don't think they do exchanges. It's not like Nordstrom, where you can con them into taking the shoes back even after you wore them once. You stuck your wet finger in it."

"We were ripped off. They think just because we're white suburban girls they can sell us this weak-ass shit." She was beginning to sound more and more like someone on HBO, although I'd have to

The Crack Cocaine Diet

say the effect was closer to *Ali G* than *Sopranos*. "I'm going to demand a refund."

This was my first inkling that things might go a little wrong.

So Molly went storming back to the parking lot and found our guy, and she began bitching and moaning, but he didn't seem that upset. He seemed kind of, I don't know, amused by her. He let her rant and rave, just nodding his head, and when she finally ran out of steam, he said, "Honey, darling, you bought heroin. Not cocaine. That's why you didn't get a jolt. It's not supposed to jolt you. It's supposed to slow you down, not that it seems to be doing that, either."

Molly had worked up so much outrage that she still saw herself as the wronged party. "Well, how was I supposed to know that?"

"Because we sell cocaine by vial color. Red tops, blue tops, yellow tops. I just had you girls figured for heroin girls. You looked like you knew your way around, got tired of OxyContin, wanted the real thing."

Molly preened a little, as if she had been complimented. It's interesting about Molly. Objectively, I'm prettier, but she has always done better with guys. I think it's because she has this kind of sexy vibe, by which I mean she manages to communicate that she'll pretty much do anyone.

"Two pretty girls like you, just this once, I'll make an exception. You go hand that package back to my man Gordy, and he'll give you some nice blue tops."

We did, and he did, but this time Molly made a big show of driving only a few feet away and inspecting our purchase, holding the blue-capped vial up to the light.

"It's, like, rock candy."

It did look like a piece of rock candy, which made me think of the divinity my grandmother used to make, which made me think of all the other treats from childhood that I couldn't imagine eating now — Pixy Stix and Now and Laters and Mary Janes and Dots and Black Crows and Necco Wafers and those pastel buttons that came on sheets of wax paper. Chocolate never did it for me, but I loved sugary treats when I was young.

And now Molly was out of the car and on her feet, steaming toward our guy, who looked around, very nervous, as if this five-foot-five, size-ten dental hygienist — size eight when she's being good

— could do some serious damage. And I wanted to say, "Dude, don't worry! All she can do is scrape your gums until they bleed." (I go to Molly's dentist and Molly cleans my teeth, and she is seriously rough. I think she gets a little kick out of it, truthfully.)

"What the fuck is this?" she yelled, getting all gangster on his ass — I think I'm saying that right — holding the vial up to the guy's face, while he looked around nervously. Finally, he grabbed her wrist and said: "Look, just shut up or you're going to bring some serious trouble to bear. You smoke it. I'll show you how . . . Don't you know anything? Trust me, you'll like it."

Molly motioned to me and I got out of the car, although a little reluctantly. It was, like, you know, that scene in *Star Wars* where the little red eyes are watching from the caves and suddenly those weird sand people just up and attack. I'm not being racist, just saying we were outsiders and I definitely had a feeling all sorts of eyes were on us, taking note.

"We'll go to my place," the guy said, all super suave, like he was some international man of mystery inviting us to see his etchings.

"A shooting gallery?" Molly squealed, all excited. "Ohmigod!"

He seemed a little offended. "I don't let dope fiends in my house."

He led us to one of the townhouses, and I don't know what I expected, but certainly not some place with doilies and old overstuffed furniture and pictures of Jesus and some black guy on the wall. (Dr. Martin Luther King Jr., I figured out later, but I was really distracted at the time, and thought it was the guy's dad or something.) But the most surprising thing was this little old lady sitting in the middle of the sofa, hands folded in her lap. She had a short, all-white Afro, and wore a pink T-shirt and flowery ski pants, which bagged on her stick-thin legs. Ski pants. I hadn't seen them in, like, forever.

"Antone?" she said. "Did you come to fix my lunch?"

"In a minute, Grandma. I have guests."

"Are they nice people, Antone?"

"Very nice people," he said, winking at us, and it was only then that I realized the old lady was blind. You see, her eyes weren't milky or odd in any way, they were brown and clear, as if she was staring right at us. You had to look closely to realize that she couldn't really see, that the gaze, steady as it was, didn't focus on anything.

Antone went to the kitchen, an alcove off the dining room, and fixed a tray with a sandwich, some potato chips, a glass of soda, and an array of medications. How could you not like a guy like that? So sweet, with broad shoulders and close-cropped hair like his granny's, only dark. Then, very quietly, with another wink, he showed us how to smoke.

"Antone, are you smoking in here? You know I don't approve of tobacco."

"Just clove cigarettes, Grandma. Clove never hurt anybody."

He helped each of us with the pipe, getting closer than was strictly necessary. He smelled like clove, like clove and ginger and cinnamon. Antone the spice cookie. When he took the pipe from Molly's mouth, he replaced it with his lips. I didn't really want him to kiss me, but I'm so much prettier than Molly. Not to mention thinner. But then, I hear black guys like girls with big behinds, and Molly certainly qualified. You could put a can of beer on her ass and have her walk around the room and it wouldn't fall off. Not being catty, just telling the literal truth. I did it once, at a party, when I was bored, and then Molly swished around with a can of Bud Light on her ass, showing off, like she was proud to have so much baggage.

Weird, but I was hungrier than ever after smoking, which was so not the point. I mean, I wasn't hungry in my stomach, I was hungry in my mouth. And what I wanted, more than anything in the world, were those potato chips on the blind lady's tray, They were Utz Salt 'n' Vinegar; I had seen Antone take them out of the green-and-yellow bag. I looooooooooooooooooooooooove Utz Salt 'n' Vinegar, but they don't come in a light version, so I almost never let myself have any. So I snagged one, just one, quiet as a cat. But, like they say, you can't eat just one. Okay, so they say that about Lays, but it's even more true about Utz, in my personal opinion. I kept stealing them, one at a time.

"Antone? Are you taking food off my tray?"

I looked to Antone for backup, but Molly's tongue was so far in his mouth that she might have been flossing him. When he finally managed to detach himself, he said: "Um, Grandma? I'm going to take a little lie-down."

"What about your guests?"

"They're going," he said, walking over to the door with a heavy tread and closing it.

"It's time for *Judge Judy*!" his granny said, which made me wonder, because how does a blind person know what time it is? Antone used the remote control to turn on the television. It was a black-and-white, total Smithsonian. After all, she was blind, so I guess it didn't matter.

Next thing I knew, I was alone in the room with the blind woman, who was fixated on *Judge Judy* as if she was going to be tested on the outcome, and I was eyeing her potato chips, while Antone and Molly started making the kind of noises that you make when you're trying so hard not to make noise that you can't help making noise.

"Antone?" the old lady called out. "Is the dishwasher running? Because I think a piece of cutlery might have gotten caught in the machinery."

I was so knocked out that she knew the word *cutlery*. How cool is that?

But I couldn't answer, of course. I wasn't supposed to be there.

"It's — okay — Granny," Antone grunted from the other room. "It's — all — going — to — be — *Jesus Christ* — okay."

The noises started up again. Granny was right. It did sound like a piece of cutlery caught in the dishwasher. But then it stopped — Antone's breathing, the mattress springs, Molly's little muffled grunts — they just stopped, and they didn't stop naturally, if you know what I mean. I'm not trying to be cruel, but Molly's a bit of a slut, and I've listened to her have sex more times than I can count, and I know how it ends, even when she's faking it, even when she has to be quiet, and it just didn't sound like the usual Molly finish at all. Antone yelped, but she was silent as a grave.

"Antone, what are you doing?" his granny asked. Antone didn't answer. Several minutes went by, and then there was a hoarse whisper from the bedroom.

"Um, Kelley? Could you come here a minute?"

"What was that?" his granny asked.

I used the remote to turn up the volume on *Judge Judy*, "DO I LOOK STUPID TO YOU?" the judge was yelling. "REMEMBER THAT PRETTY FADES BUT STUPID IS FOREVER. I ASKED IF YOU HAD IT IN WRITING, I DON'T WANT TO HEAR ALL THIS FOLDEROL ABOUT ORAL AGREEMENTS."

When I went into the bedroom, Molly was under Antone, and

The Crack Cocaine Diet

I remember thinking — I was a little high, remember — that he made her look really thin because he covered up her torso, and Molly does have good legs and decent arms. He had a handsome back, too, broad and muscled, and a great ass. Brandon had no ass (con), but he had nice legs (pro).

It took me a moment to notice that Antone had a pair of scissors stuck in the middle of his beautiful back.

"I told him no," Molly whispered, although the volume on the television was so loud that the entire apartment was practically reverberating. "No means no."

There was a lot of blood, I noticed. A lot.

"I didn't hear you," I said. "I mean, I didn't hear you say any *words*."

"I mouthed it. He told me to keep silent because his grandmother is here. Still, I mouthed it. 'No.' 'No.'" She made this incredibly unattractive fish mouth to show me.

"Is he dead?"

"I mean, I was totally up for giving him a blow job, especially after he said he'd give me a little extra, but he was, like, uncircumcised. I just couldn't, Kelley, I couldn't. I've never been with a guy like that. I offered him a hand job instead, but he got totally peeved and tried to force me."

The story wasn't tracking. High as I was, I could see there were some holes. *How did you get naked?* I wanted to ask. *Why didn't you shout? If Granny knew you were here, Antone wouldn't have dared misbehaved.* He had clearly been more scared of Granny than he was into Molly.

"This is the stash house," Molly said. "Antone showed me."

"What?"

"The drugs. They're here. All of it. We could just help ourselves. I mean, he's a rapist, Kelley. He's a criminal. He sells drugs to people. Help me, Kelley. Get him off me."

But when I rolled him off, I saw there was a condom. Molly saw it, too.

"We should, like, so get rid of that. It would only complicate things. When I saw he was going to rape me, I told him he should at least be courteous."

I nodded, as if agreeing. I flushed the condom down the toilet, helped Molly clean the blood off her, and then used my purse to pack up what we could find, as she was carrying this little bitty Kate Spade knockoff that wasn't much good for anything. We found some cash, too, about $2,000, and helped ourselves to that, on the rationale that it would be more suspicious if we didn't. On the way out, I shook a few more potato chips on Granny's plate.

"Antone?" she said. "Are you going out again?"

Molly grunted low, and that seemed to appease Granny. We walked out slowly, as if we had all the time in the world, but again I had that feeling of a thousand pairs of eyes on us. We were in some serious trouble. There would have to be some sort of retribution for what we had done. What Molly had done. All I did was steal a few potato chips.

"Take Quarry Road home instead of the interstate," I told Molly.

"Why?" she asked. "It takes so much longer."

"But we know it, know all the ins and outs. If someone follows us, we can give them the slip."

About two miles from home, I told her I had to pee so bad that I couldn't wait and asked her to stand watch for me, a longtime practice with us. We were at that point, high above the old limestone quarry, where we had parked a thousand times as teenagers. A place where Molly had never said "No" to my knowledge.

"Finished?" she asked, when I emerged from behind the screen of trees.

"Almost," I said, pushing her hard, sending her tumbling over the precipice. She wouldn't be the first kid in our class to break her neck at the highest point on Quarry Road. My high school boyfriend did, in fact, right after we broke up. It was a horrible accident. I didn't eat for weeks and got down to a size four. Everyone felt bad for me — breaking up with Eddie only to have him commit suicide that way. There didn't seem to be any reason for me to explain that Eddie was the one who wanted to break up. Unnecessary information.

I crossed the hillside to the highway, a distance of about a mile, then jogged the rest of the way. After all, as my mother would be the first to tell you, I went for a run that afternoon, while Molly was off shopping, according to her mom. I assumed the police would tie Antone's dead body to Molly's murder and figure it for a revenge killing, but I was giving the cops too much credit. Antone rated a paragraph in the morning paper. Molly, who turned out to be pregnant, although not even she knew it — probably wouldn't even have known who the father was — is still on the front page all these weeks later. (The fact that they didn't find her for three days heightened the interest, I guess. I mean, she was just an overweight dental hygienist from the suburbs — and a bit of a slut, as I told you, But the media got all excited about it.) The general consensus seems to be that Keith did it, and I don't see any reason to let him off the hook, not yet. He's an asshole. Plus, almost no one in this state gets the death penalty.

Meanwhile, he's telling people just how many men Molly had sex with in the past month, including Brandon, and police are still trying to figure out who had sex with her right before she died. (That's why you're supposed to get the condom on as early as possible, girls. Penises *drip.* Just fyi.) I pretended to be shocked, but I already knew about Brandon, having seen Molly's car outside his apartment when I cruised his place at 2 A.M. a few nights after Brandon told me he wanted to see other people. My ex-boyfriend and my best friend, running around behind my back. Everyone feels so bad for me, but I'm being brave, although I eat so little that I'm down to a size two. I just bought a Versace dress and Manolos for a date this weekend with my new boyfriend, Robert. I've never spent so much money on an outfit before. But then, I've never had $2,000 in cash to spend as I please.

ED MCBAIN

Improvisation

FROM *Dangerous Women*

"WHY DON'T WE kill somebody?" she suggested.

She was a blond, of course, tall and willowy and wearing a sleek black cocktail dress cut high on the leg and low at the neckline.

"Been there," Will told her. "Done that."

Her eyes opened wide, a sharp blue in startling contrast to the black of the dress.

"The Gulf War," he explained.

"Not the same thing at all," she said, and plucked the olive from her martini and popped it into her mouth. "I'm talking about murder."

"Murder, uh-huh," Will said. "Who'd you have in mind?"

"How about the girl sitting across the bar there?"

"Ah, a random victim," he said. "But how's that any different from combat?"

"A *specific* random victim," she said. "Shall we kill her or not?"

"Why?" he asked.

"Why not?" she said.

Will had known the woman for perhaps twenty minutes at most. In fact, he didn't even know her name. Her suggestion that they kill someone had come in response to a standard pickup line he'd used to good effect many times before, to wit: "So what do we do for a little excitement tonight?"

To which the blond had replied, "Why don't we kill somebody?"

Hadn't whispered the words, hadn't even lowered her voice. Just smiled over the rim of her martini glass and said in her normal speaking voice, "Why don't we kill somebody?"

The *specific* random victim she had in mind was a plain-looking woman wearing a plain brown jacket over a brown silk blouse and a darker brown skirt. There was about her the look of a harried file clerk or lower-level secretary, the mousy brown hair, the unblinking eyes behind what one had to call spectacles rather than eyeglasses, the thin-lipped mouth and slight overbite. A totally unremarkable woman. Small wonder she was sitting alone nursing a glass of white wine.

"Let's say we *do* actually kill her," Will said. "What'll we do for a little excitement afterward?"

The blond smiled.

And crossed her legs.

"My name is Jessica," she said.

She extended her hand.

He took it.

"I'm Will," he said.

He assumed her palm was cold from the iced drink she'd been holding.

On this chilly December evening three days before Christmas, Will had no intention whatever of killing the mousy little file clerk at the end of the bar, or anyone else for that matter. He had killed his fair share of people a long time ago, thank you, all of them *specific* random victims in that they had been wearing the uniform of the Iraqi Army, which made them the enemy. That was as specific as you could get in wartime, he supposed. That was what made it okay to bulldoze them in their trenches. That was what made it okay to *murder* them, whatever fine distinction Jessica was now making between murder and combat.

Anyway, Will knew this was merely a game, a variation on the mating ritual that took place in every singles bar in Manhattan on any given night of the year. You came up with a clever approach, you got a response that indicated interest, and you took it from there. In fact, he wondered how many times, in how many bars before tonight, Jessica had used her "Why don't we kill somebody?" line. The approach was admittedly an adventurous one, possibly even a dangerous one — suppose she flashed those splendid legs at someone who turned out to be Jack the Ripper? Suppose she picked up a guy who really *believed* it might be fun to kill that girl sitting alone at the other end of the bar? Hey, great idea, Jess, let's do it! Which, in effect, was what he'd tacitly indicated, but of course she knew they were just playing a game here, didn't she? She certainly had to realize they weren't planning an actual murder here.

"Who'll make the approach?" she asked.

"I suppose I should," Will said.

"Please don't use your 'What'll we do for a little excitement tonight?' line."

"Gee, I thought you liked that."

"Yes, the first time I heard it. Five or six years ago."

"I thought I was being entirely original."

"Try to be more original with little Alice there, okay?"

"Is that what you think her name is?"

"What do you think it is?"

"Patricia."

"Okay, I'll be Patricia," she said. "Let me hear it."

"Excuse me, Miss," Will said.

"Great start," Jessica said.

"My friend and I happened to notice you sitting all alone here, and we thought you might care to join us."

Jessica looked around as if trying to locate the friend he was telling Patricia about.

"Who do you mean?" she asked, all wide-eyed and wondering.

"The beautiful blond sitting right there," Will said. "Her name is Jessica."

Jessica smiled.

"Beautiful blond, huh?" she said.

"*Gorgeous* blond," he said.

"Sweet talker," she said, and covered his hand with her own on the bar top. "So let's say little Patty Cake decides to join us. Then what?"

"We ply her with compliments and alcohol."

"And then what?"

"We take her to some dark alley and bludgeon her to death."

"I have a small bottle of poison in my handbag," Jessica said. "Wouldn't that be better?"

Will narrowed his eyes like a gangster.

"Perfect," he said. "We'll take her to some dark alley and poison her to death."

"Wouldn't an apartment someplace be a better venue?" Jessica asked.

And it suddenly occurred to him that perhaps they weren't discussing murder at all, jokingly or otherwise. Was it possible that what Jessica had in mind was a three-way?

"Go talk to the lady," she said. "After that, we'll improvise."

Will wasn't very good at picking up girls in bars.

In fact, aside from his "What'll we do for a little excitement tonight?" line, he didn't have many other approaches in his repertoire. He was emboldened somewhat by Jessica's encouraging nod from where she sat at the opposite end of the bar, but he still felt somewhat timid about taking the empty stool alongside Alice or Patricia or whatever her name was.

It had been his experience that plain girls were less responsive to flattery than were truly knockout beauties. He guessed that was because they were expecting to be lied to, and were wary of being duped and disappointed yet another time. Alice or Patricia or Whoever proved to be no exception to this general Plain-Jane observation. Will took the stool next to hers, turned to her, and said, "Excuse me, Miss," exactly as he'd rehearsed it with Jessica, but before he could utter another word, she recoiled as if he'd slapped her. Eyes wide, seemingly surprised, she said, "What? What is it?"

"I'm sorry if I startled you . . ."

"No, that's all right," she said. "What is it?"

Her voice was high and whiny, with an accent he couldn't quite place. Her eyes behind their thick round lenses were a very dark brown, still wide now with either fright or suspicion, or both. Staring at him unblinkingly, she waited.

"I don't want to bother you," he said, "but . . ."

"That's all right, really," she said. "What is it?"

"My friend and I couldn't help noticing . . ."

"Your friend?"

"The lady sitting just opposite us. The blond lady at the other end of the bar?" Will said, and pointed to Jessica, who obligingly raised her hand in greeting.

"Oh. Yes," she said. "I see."

"We couldn't help notice that you were sitting here, drinking alone," he said. "We thought you might care to join us."

"Oh," she said.

"Do you think you might care to? Join us?"

There was a moment's hesitation. The brown eyes blinked, softened. The slightest smile formed on her thin-lipped mouth.

"I think I would like to, yes," she said. "I'd like to."

They sat at a small table some distance from the bar, in a dimly lighted corner of the room. Susan — and not Patricia or Alice, as it turned out — ordered another Chardonnay. Jessica stuck to her martinis. Will ordered another bourbon on the rocks.

"No one should sit drinking alone three days before Christmas," Jessica said.

"Oh, I agree, I agree," Susan said.

She had an annoying habit of saying everything twice. Made it sound as if there were an echo in the place.

"But this bar is on my way home," she said, "and I thought I'd stop in for a quick glass of wine."

"Take the chill off," Jessica agreed, nodding.

"Yes, exactly. Take the chill off."

She also repeated *other* people's words, Will noticed.

"Do you live near here?" Jessica asked.

"Yes. Just around the corner."

"Where are you from originally?"

"Oh dear, can you still tell?"

"Tell what?" Will asked.

"The accent. Oh dear, does it still show? After all those lessons? Oh my."

"What accent would that be?" Jessica asked.

"Alabama. Montgomery, Alabama," she said, making it sound like "Mun'gummy, Alabama."

"I don't hear any accent at all," Jessica said. "Do you detect an accent, Will?"

"Well, it's a regional dialect, actually," Susan said.

"You sound like you were born right here in New York," Will said, lying in his teeth.

"That's so kind of you, really," she said. "Really, it's so very kind."

"How long have you been up here?" Jessica asked.

"Six months now. I came up at the end of June. I'm an actress."

An actress, Will thought.

"I'm a nurse," Jessica said.

An actress and a nurse, Will thought.

Improvisation

"No kidding?" Susan said. "Do you work at some hospital?"

"Beth Israel," Jessica said.

"I thought that was a synagogue," Will said.

"A hospital, too," Jessica said, nodding, and turned back to Susan again. "Would we have seen you in anything?" she asked.

"Well, not unless you've been to Montgomery," Susan said, and smiled. "*The Glass Menagerie*? Do you know *The Glass Menagerie*? Tennessee Williams? The play by Tennessee Williams? I played Laura Wingate in the Paper Players' production down there. I haven't been in anything up here yet. I've been waitressing, in fact."

A waitress, Will thought.

The nurse and I are about to kill the plainest waitress in the city of New York.

Or worse, we're going to take her to bed.

Afterward, he thought it might have been Jessica who suggested that they buy a bottle of Moët Chandon and take it up to Susan's apartment for a nightcap, the apartment being so close and all, just around the corner, in fact, as Susan herself had earlier pointed out. Or perhaps it was Will himself who'd made the suggestion, having consumed by then four hefty shots of Jack Daniels, and being somewhat bolder than he might ordinarily have been. Or perhaps it was Susan who invited them up to her place, which was in the heart of the theatrical district, right around the corner from Flanagan's, where she herself had consumed three or four glasses of Chardonnay and had begun performing for them the entire scene in which the Gentleman Caller breaks the little glass unicorn and Laura pretends it's no great tragedy, acting both parts for them, which Will felt certain caused the bartender to announce last call a full ten minutes earlier than he should have.

She was some terrible actress.

But oh so inspired!

The minute they hit the street outside, she raised her arms to the heavens above, her fingers widespread, and shouted in her dreadful Southern accent, "Just look at it! Broadway! The Great White Way!" and then did a little sort of pirouette, twirling and dancing up the street, her arms still high over her head.

"My God, let's kill her *quick*!" *Jessica* whispered to Will.

They both burst out laughing.

Susan must have thought they were sharing her exuberance.

Will guessed she didn't know what lay just ahead.

Or maybe she did.

At this hour of the night, the hookers had already begun their stroll up Eighth Avenue, but none of them so much as lifted an eyebrow to Will, probably figuring he was a John already occupied twice over, one on each arm. In an open liquor store, he bought a bottle of not Moët Chandon but Veuve Clicquot, and they went walking up the avenue together again, arm in arm.

Susan's apartment was a studio flat on the third floor of a walkup on Forty-ninth and Ninth. They climbed the steps behind her, and she stopped outside apartment 3A, fiddled for her keys in her handbag, found them at last, and unlocked the door. The place was furnished in what Will called Struggling Young Actress Thrift. A tiny kitchen to the left of the entrance. A double bed against the far wall, a door alongside it leading to what Will supposed was a bathroom. A sofa and two easy chairs and a dresser with a mirror over it. There was a door on the entrance wall, and it opened onto a closet. Susan took their coats and hung them up.

"Mind if I make myself comfortable?" she asked, and went into the bathroom.

Jessica waggled her eyebrows.

Will went into the kitchen, opened the refrigerator, and emptied two of the ice cube trays into a bowl he found in the overhead cabinets. He also found three juice glasses he supposed would have to serve. Jessica sat on the sofa watching him while he started opening the champagne. A loud pop exploded just as another blond stepped out of the bathroom.

It took him a moment to realize this was Susan.

"Makeup and costume go a long way toward realizing a character," she said.

She was now a slender young woman with short straight blond hair, a nice set of jugs showing in the swooping neckline of a red blouse, a short tight black skirt, good legs in very high-heeled black pumps. She held dangling from her right hand the mousy brown wig she'd been wearing in the bar, and when she opened her left hand and held it out to him, palm flat, he saw the dental prosthesis

Improvisation

that had given her the overbite. Through the open bathroom door, he could see her frowzy brown suit hanging on the shower rod. Her spectacles were resting on the bathroom sink.

"Little padding around the waist thickened me out," she said. "We have all these useful props in class."

No Southern accent anymore, he noticed. No brown eyes, either.

"But your eyes . . ." he said.

"Contact lenses," Susan said.

Her *real* eyes were as blue as . . . well, Jessica's.

In fact, they could pass for sisters.

He said this out loud.

"You could pass for sisters," he said.

"Maybe 'cause we are," Jessica said. "Sure had you going, though, didn't we?"

"I'll be damned," he said.

"Let's try that champagne," Susan said, and swiveled into the kitchen where the bottle was now resting in the bowl of ice. She lifted it, poured into the juice glasses, and carried back into the other room the three glasses in a cradle of fingers and thumbs. Jessica plucked one of the glasses free. Susan handed one to Will.

"Here's to the three of us," Jessica toasted.

"And improvisation," Susan added.

They all drank.

Will figured this was going to turn into one hell of a night.

"We're in the same acting class," Jessica told him.

She was still sitting on the sofa, legs crossed. Splendid legs. Will was in one of the easy chairs. Susan was in the easy chair opposite him, her legs also crossed, also splendid.

"We both want to be actors," Jessica explained.

"I thought you were a nurse," Will said.

"Oh, sure. Same way Sue is a waitress. But our ambition is to act."

"We're gonna be stars one day."

"Our names up in lights on Broadway."

"The Carter Sisters," Jessica said.

"Susan and Jessica!" her sister said.

"I'll drink to that," Will said.

They all drank again.

"We're not really from Montgomery, you know," Jessica said.

"Well, I realize that now. But that certainly was a good accent, Susan."

"Regional dialect," she corrected.

"We're from Seattle."

"Where it rains all the time," Will said.

"Oh, that's not true at all," Susan said. "Actually it rains less in Seattle than it does in New York, that's a fact."

"A statistically proven fact," Jessica said, nodding in agreement and draining her glass. "Is there any more bubbly out there?"

"Oh, lots," Susan said, and shoved herself out of the easy chair, exposing a fair amount of thigh as she got to her feet. Will handed her his empty glass, too. He sure hoped the ladies wouldn't be drinking too much here. There was some serious business to take care of here tonight, some serious improvisation to do.

"So how long have you been living here in New York?" he asked. "Was it true what you said in the bar? Is it really only six months?"

"That's right," Jessica said. "Since the end of June."

"We've been taking acting classes since then."

"Were you really in *The Glass Menagerie?* The Paper Players? Is there such a thing as the Paper Players?"

"Oh yes," Susan said, coming back with their replenished glasses. "But in Seattle."

"We've never been to Montgomery."

"That was part of my character" Susan said. "The character I was assuming in the bar. Little Suzie Sad Ass."

Both girls laughed.

Will laughed along with them.

"I played *Amanda* Wingate," Jessica said.

"In *The Glass Menagerie,*" Susan explained. "When we did it in Seattle. Laura's mother. Amanda Wingate."

"Actually I am the older one," Jessica said. "In real life."

"She's thirty," Susan said. "I'm twenty-eight."

"Here all alone in the big bad city," Will said.

"Yep, here all alone," Jessica said.

"Is that where you girls sleep?" Will asked. "The bed across the room there? The two of you all alone in that big bad bed?"

"Uh-oh," Jessica said. "He wants to know where we sleep, Sue."

"Better be careful," Susan said.

Will figured he ought to back off a little, play it a bit more slowly here.

Improvisation

"So where's this acting school you go to?" he asked.

"Right on Eighth Avenue."

"Near the Biltmore," Susan said. "Do you know the Biltmore Theater?"

"No, I don't," Will said. "I'm sorry."

"Well, near there," Jessica said. "Madame D'Arbousse, do you know her work?"

"No, I'm sorry, I don't."

"Well, she's only famous," Susan said.

"I'm sorry, I'm just not familiar with . . ."

"The D'Arbousse School? You've never heard of the D'Arbousse School of Acting?"

"I'm sorry, no."

"It's only world-famous," Susan said.

She seemed to be pouting now, almost petulant. Will figured he was losing ground here. Fast.

"So . . . uh . . . what was the idea of putting on the costume tonight?" he asked. "Going to that bar as a . . . well . . . I hope you'll me . . . a frumpy little file clerk, was what I thought you were."

"It was that good, huh?" Susan said, smiling. Her smile, without the fake overbite, was actually quite lovely. Her mouth didn't look as thin-lipped anymore, either. Amazing what a little lipstick could do to plump up a girl's lips. He imagined those lips on his own lips, in the bed across the room there. He imagined her sister's lips on his, too. Imagine all their lips entangled, intertwined . . .

"That was part of the exercise," Susan said.

"The exercise?"

"Finding the place," Jessica said.

"The *character's* place," Susan said.

"For a private moment," Jessica explained.

"Finding the place for a character's private moment."

"We thought it might be the bar."

"But now we think it might be here."

"Well, it *will* be here," Jessica said. "Once we create it."

They were losing Will. More important, he felt he was losing them. That bed, maybe fifteen feet away across the room, seemed to be receding into an unreachable distance. He had to get this thing back on track. But he didn't know how quite yet. Not while they were rattling on about . . . what were they saying, anyway?

"I'm sorry," he said, "but *what* exactly is it you're trying to create?"

"A character's private moment," Jessica said.

"Is this the place we're going to use?" Susan asked.

"I think so, yes. Don't you think so? Our own apartment. A real place. It feels very real to me. Doesn't it feel real to you, Sue?"

"Oh, yes. Yes, it does. It feels *very* real. But I don't feel private yet. Do you feel private?"

"No, not yet."

"Excuse me, ladies . . ." Will said.

"Ladies, ooo hoo," Susan said, and rolled her eyes.

". . . but we can get a lot *more* private here, if that's what you ladies are looking for here."

"We're talking about a private *moment*," Jessica explained. "The way we behave when no one's watching."

"No one's watching us right now," Will said encouragingly. "We can do whatever we wish to do here, and no one will ever . . ."

"I don't think you understand," Susan said. "A *character's* private feelings and emotions are what we're trying to create here tonight."

"So let's *start* creating all these feelings and emotions," Will suggested.

"These feelings have to be *real*," Jessica said.

"They have to be *absolutely* real," Susan said.

"So that we can apply them to the scene we're doing."

"Ah-ha!" Will said.

"I think he's got it," Jessica said.

"By George, he's got it."

"You're rehearsing a scene together."

"Bravo!"

"What scene?" Will asked.

"A scene in Macbeth," Susan said.

"Where she tells him to screw his courage to the sticking point," Jessica said.

"Lady Macbeth."

"Tells Macbeth. When he's beginning to waver about killing Duncan."

"Screw your courage to the sticking point," Jessica said again, with conviction this time. "And we shall not fail."

Improvisation

She looked at her sister.

"That was very good," Susan said.

Will figured maybe they were back on track again.

"Screw your courage, huh?" he said, and smiled knowingly, and took another sip of champagne.

"She's telling him not to be such a wuss," Susan said.

"The thing is they're plotting to kill the king, you see," Jessica said.

"This is a private moment for both of them."

"Where they're both examining what they're about to do."

"They're planning a *murder*, you see."

"What does that *feel* like?" Susan asked.

"What is that like inside your *head*?" Jessica said.

"That private moment inside your *head*."

"When you're actually contemplating someone's death."

The room went silent for an instant.

The sisters looked at each other.

"Would anyone like some more champagne?" Susan asked.

"I'd love some," Jessica said.

"I'll get it," Will said, and started to rise.

"No, no, let me," Susan said, and took his glass and carried all three empty glasses into the kitchen. Jessica crossed her legs. Behind him, in the kitchen, Will could hear Susan refilling their glasses. He watched Jessica's jiggling foot, her pump half-on, half-off, held only by her toes.

"So that stuff in the bar was all part of the exercise, right?" Will said. "Your suggesting we kill somebody? And then choosing your sister as the victim?"

"Well, sort of," Jessica said.

Her pump fell off. She bent over to retrieve it, spreading her legs, the black dress high on her thighs. She crossed one leg over the other, put the pump back on, smiled at Will. Susan was back with the full glasses.

"Still some more out there," she said, and passed the glasses around. Jessica held hers up in a toast.

"From this time such," she said, "I account thy love."

"Cheers," Susan said, and drank.

"Meaning?" Will said, but he drank, too.

"That's in the scene," Jessica said. "Actually, it's at the start of the scene. Where he's beginning to waver. By the end of the scene, she's convinced him the king must die."

"False face must hide what the false heart doth show," Susan said, and nodded.

"That's Macbeth's exit line. At the end of the scene."

"Is that why you were dressed as a file clerk? False face must hide . . . whatever it was you just said?"

"What the false heart doth show," Susan repeated. "But no, that's not why I was in costume."

"Then why?"

"It was my way of trying to create a character."

"Maybe he hasn't got it, after all," Jessica said.

"A character who could kill," Susan said.

"You had to become a *frump?*"

"Well, I had to become someone *else,* yes. Someone not like myself at all. But it turned out that wasn't enough. I had to find the right place, too."

"The place is *here,*" Jessica said.

"And *now,*" Will said. "So, ladies, if no one minds . . ."

"Ooo hoo, ladies again," Susan said, and again rolled her eyes.

". . . can we get off all this acting stuff for a moment . . . ?"

"How about *your* private moment?" Susan said.

"I don't have any private moments."

"Don't you ever fart alone in the dark?" Jessica asked.

"Don't you ever jack off alone in the dark?" Susan asked.

Will's mouth fell open.

"Those are private moments," Jessica said.

For some reason, he could not close his mouth again.

"I think it's beginning to work," Susan said.

"Take the glass from his hand before he drops it," Jessica said.

Will watched them with his eyes and his mouth wide open.

"I'll bet he thinks it's curare," Jessica said.

"Where on earth would we get curare?"

"The jungles of Brazil?"

"Venezuela?"

Both girls laughed.

Will didn't know if it was curare or not. All he knew was he couldn't speak and he couldn't move.

Improvisation

"Well, he *knows* we didn't go all the way down to the Amazon for any poison," Jessica said.

"That's right, he knows you're a nurse," Susan said.

"Beth Israel, you bet," Jessica said.

"Access to lots of drugs there."

"Even *synthetic* curare drugs."

"Plenty of those around."

"List them for him, Jess."

"Don't want to bore him, Sue."

"You have to *inject* curare, Will, did you know that?"

"The natives dip their darts in it."

"Shoot the darts from blowpipes."

"The victims are paralyzed."

"Helpless."

"Death comes from asphyxia."

"That means you can't breathe."

"Because the respiratory nerve muscles get paralyzed."

"Are you having trouble breathing yet, Will?"

He did not think he was having trouble breathing. But what were they saying? Were they saying they'd poisoned him?

"The synthetics come in tablet form," Susan told him.

"Easy to pulverize."

"Easy to dissolve."

"Lots of legitimate uses for synthetic curare drugs," Jessica said.

"Provided you're careful with the dosage."

"We weren't particularly careful with the dosage, Will."

"Did your champagne taste a little bitter?"

He wanted to shake his head no. His champagne had tasted just fine. Or had he been too drunk to know just *how* it had tasted? But he couldn't shake his head, and he couldn't talk.

"Let's watch him," Susan said. "Study his reactions."

"Why?" Jessica asked.

"Well, it could be helpful."

"Not for the scene we're doing."

"Killing someone."

"Killing someone, yes. Duh, Susan."

Killing *me*, Will thought.

They are actually killing me here.

But, no . . .

Girls, he thought, you're making a mistake here. This is not the way to go about this. Let's go back to the original plan, girls. The original plan was to pop a bottle of bubbly and hop into the sack together. The original plan was to share this lovely night three days before . . . actually only two days now, it was already well past midnight . . . *two* days before Christmas, share this sweet uncomplicated night together, a sister act with a willing third partner is all this was supposed to be here. So how'd it get so serious all of a sudden? There was no reason for you girls to get all serious about acting lessons and private moments, really, this was just supposed to be fun and games here tonight. So why'd you have to go drop poison in my champagne? I mean, *Jesus,* girls, why'd you have to go do that when we were getting along so fine here?

"Are you feeling anything?" Susan asked.

"No" Jessica said. "Are you?"

"I thought I'd feel . . ."

"Me, too."

"I don't know . . . sinister or something."

"Me, too."

"I mean, *killing* somebody! I thought it would be something special. Instead . . ."

"I know what you mean. It's just like watching somebody, I don't know, getting a *haircut* or something."

"Maybe we should have tried something else."

"Not poison, you mean?"

"Something more dramatic."

"Something scarier, I know what you mean."

"Get some kind of reaction out of him."

"Instead of him just *sitting* there."

"Sitting there like a dope and dying."

The girls leaned over Will and peered into his face. Their faces looked distorted, so close to his face and all. Their blue eyes looked as if they were popping out of their heads.

"Do something," Jessica told him.

"Do something, asshole," Susan said.

They kept watching him.

"It's not too late to stab him, I suppose," Jessica said.

"You think?" Susan said.

Please don't stab me, Will thought. I'm afraid of knives. Please don't stab me.

"Let's see what's in the kitchen," Jessica said.

Improvisation

He was suddenly alone.
The girls were suddenly gone.
Behind him . . .
He could not turn his head to see them.
. . . behind him he could hear them rummaging through what he guessed was one of the kitchen drawers, could hear the rattle of utensils . . .
Please don't stab me, he thought.
"How about this one?" Jessica asked.
"Looks awfully big for the job," Susan said.
"Slit his fuckin' throat good," Jessica said, and laughed.
"See if he sits there like a dope then," Susan said.
"Get some kind of *reaction* out of him."
"Help us to *feel* something."
"Now you've got it, Sue. That's the whole point."
Will's chest was beginning to feel tight. He was beginning to have difficulty breathing.
In the kitchen, the girls laughed again.
Why were they laughing?
Had they just said something he couldn't hear? Were they going to do something *else* with that knife, other than slit his throat? He wished he could take a deep breath. He knew he would feel so much better if he could just take a deep breath. But he . . . he . . . he didn't seem to be . . . to be able to . . .
"Hey!" Jessica said. "You! Don't poop out on us!"
Susan looked at her.
"I think he's gone," she said.
"Shit!" Jessica said.
"What are you doing?"
"Taking his pulse."
Susan waited.
"Nothing," Jessica said, and dropped his wrist.
The sisters kept looking at Will where he sat slumped in the easy chair, his mouth still hanging open, his eyes wide.
"He sure as hell *looks* dead," Jessica said.
"We'd better get him out of here."
"Be a good exercise," Jessica said. "Getting rid of the body."
"I'll say. I'll bet he weighs at least a hun' ninety."
"I didn't say good *exercise,* Sue. I said *a* good exercise. A good *acting* exercise."

"Oh. Right. What it feels like to get rid of a dead body. Right."

"So let's do it," Jessica said.

They started lifting him out of the chair. He was, in fact, very heavy. They half-carried him, half-dragged him to the front door.

"Tell me something" Susan said. "Do you . . . you know . . . *feel* anything yet?"

"Nothing," Jessica said.

MIKE MACLEAN

McHenry's Gift

FROM *Thuglit*

THERE WAS A KNOCK at the door. Dillon Leary grabbed the .45 from underneath his mattress and pressed himself flat against the wall. He thumbed the safety off then racked the pistol's slide, jacking a round into the chamber. It was a big sound in the little apartment.

"Who is it?" Dillon called out.

"UPS. Got a package out here."

"Leave it."

"I need a signature, sir."

Dillon glanced through the peephole. The man outside was dressed from head to toe in brown. Brown shorts. Brown shirt. Brown cap. Standard issue UPS uniform. He even had one of those electronic clipboards to sign. The kind that looked like an Etch A Sketch toy but that recorded names into a vast computer database. From all appearances, the guy seemed like the real thing. But appearances could be deceiving.

Taking a deep breath, Dillon caught a whiff of the mildew and grime that permeated his little apartment. On Saturday nights the elevators smelled like vomit, the halls like piss. Dillon snuck another look out the peephole. The UPS guy stood motionless, head down, cap low over his eyes.

Screw it, thought Dillon. He held the .45 low behind his back and opened the door an inch. "Pass me the board."

The guy did as he was told, slipping the Etch A Sketch toy through the crack of the door. Dillon scrawled his name on the monitor screen and handed it back. "Take off," he said.

Shaking his head, the UPS guy disappeared down the hall. Dillon waited two and a half minutes. Then he quickly swung the door open and swept the package up from the floor. It was lighter than he thought it would be. He shook it gently. It made no noise.

Who could've sent such a thing?

Great lengths had been gone to conceal Dillon's whereabouts. His dingy little hideaway sat surrounded by government housing projects, pawnshops, and liquor stores. It was a place where people minded their business and kept their mouths shut. Dillon had grown up in a neighborhood like this. He knew how to blend in, how to disappear, becoming another face in the crowd. No one had a clue Dillon was here.

So how did the UPS find him?

As he turned the dead bolts behind him, Dillon scanned the box's surface, reading the return address. Printed clearly in the upper left-hand corner was the name Wilson McHenry.

Dillon's blood went cold, chilling his veins. The box nearly slipped from his grasp.

He had just received a package from a dead man.

Wilson McHenry didn't look like a drug runner. He was tall and thin with stooped shoulders and a salt-and-pepper beard, a little more salt these days than pepper. Sometime in his late thirties he'd gone bald. Now at sixty, he was rarely seen without his trademark black fedora. It wasn't a look many men could pull off, but it seemed to suit McHenry fine.

It was the hat that Dillon first recognized as he trudged over a hill at Cedarbrook park. He spotted McHenry on a bench facing the lake, feeding ducks from a brown paper bag. Along with the fedora, the old guy wore a pair of khakis and a tattered tweed jacket. More like a college professor than a career criminal. Dillon took a seat next to him and stretched out his legs. The lake smelled like wet grass.

"You ever eat one of those things?" asked Dillon, nodding toward the ducks.

"Every Christmas when I was a boy," said McHenry. He pulled a handful of bread crumbs from his bag and threw them into the pond. A pair of silky green mallards plucked them from the water and quacked for more.

"What'd they taste like?"

"Like a greasy turkey. But greasy in a good way. Maybe I'll make one next holiday. You can come over and try it for yourself."

"I'd like that."

McHenry finished with the bread crumbs, crumpled the bag, and sky-hooked it into a trash can a few feet away. There was a simple grace to his movements. McHenry was no athlete, not anymore. But he was comfortable in his skin, comfortable in his aging bones. He propped the fedora high on his head and squinted in the sun. "So why am I here?"

"Estaban sent me. He wanted us to talk."

"Estaban, huh? You on his clock now?"

Dillon went silent.

"I have to admit," said McHenry, "never saw that one coming."

"Writing's on the wall," said Dillon. "You've had a good run, Mac. Longer than anyone I know. But Estaban is a Colombian. And this is a Colombian's game."

McHenry smiled sadly. "And it's a young man's game too, is that it?"

Dillon peered out at the water. Gray clouds reflected off its glimmering surface, a bit of sunlight fighting through. "He wants thirty percent. And you have to chip in to pay off the *federales*. Maybe an extra five a month."

"That sound like a fair deal to you?"

Dillon shrugged. "It's what he's offering."

"And if I say no?"

"This is Estaban Gomez we're talking about. A Mexican judge said *no* to him once. They still haven't found the body."

The old man leaned back against the bench, letting out a long sigh. "You know, I was only nineteen when I started in this business. I'd fly a little Piper cub back and forth to Mexico a few times a month. It was pot back then, a little cocaine here and there. God, I was a cocky little shit. Did it more for the thrills than anything else. Now it's all about the money. Been that way for some time."

"It was always about the money, Mac. You just never noticed."

"Maybe so."

"So why not get out?" said Dillon. "You've got enough put away. And Estaban won't bother you as long as you're not competition."

"Sorry, kid," said McHenry. "Not ready to give up the reins yet."

Dillon closed his eyes, listened to the ducks as they drifted away on the water. "Is that your answer then?"

"I'll talk to the boys. Let them decide for themselves. But I'm still in it."

Dillon stood, brushed off the seat of his jeans, and rolled the kinks out of his shoulders. He looked down at the old man, seeing his steel-blue eyes, dark in the shade of the fedora's brim. "I wish you'd change your mind."

McHenry shook his head. "You know me better than that."

Dillon nodded and headed back up the hill. Just as he was about to disappear over its edge, McHenry called out to him.

"Hey," said the old man, "you still flying?"

"No. Too busy on the ground."

"That's a shame. You always were pretty good at the controls. Had some real talent up there."

"It wasn't talent," said Dillon. "I had a good teacher."

Night fell and the apartment filled with gray shadows. Dillon barely noticed. He sat in a dark corner, silent and unmoving, staring at the package on his kitchen counter. He'd been sitting that way for over an hour.

When the package first arrived, Dillon almost opened it. Then he noticed the overnight sticker. The parcel had been sent within the last twenty-four hours, sometime after McHenry's death. Which meant someone had sent it on the old man's behalf, possibly someone looking for revenge. If that was the case, maybe opening the package wasn't such a good idea. It wasn't ticking, but that didn't mean anything. Digital timers didn't make noise, Dillon told himself. And neither did trip wires.

Now, sitting in the dark corner, Dillon finally willed himself to move. He went to the kitchen and pulled a Budweiser from the fridge. Taking a drink, he circled the package a few times, trying to guess what could be inside.

A small block of C-4 would do the trick, he thought. *Or maybe a stick of good old-fashioned dynamite.*

No, the old man wasn't like that. McHenry saw killing as a necessary evil, but one to be avoided at all cost. Pure and simple, he didn't like to hurt people. And he certainly didn't have the heart to order Dillon's death. Did he?

Dillon thought back to their last moment together. He had seen a father's love in the old man's eyes. Even in the end.

Setting his bottle down, Dillon found a box cutter in a cabinet over the range top. He just had to know. Carefully, he steadied the package and gripped the box cutter tightly. He was sweating and the plastic handle felt slick in his hand. Once he made his first cut, there was no going back.

He placed the blade lightly against the box top, about to slice into the tape. Then the phone rang. Dillon let out a heavy breath and went to answer it.

"Yeah?"

The voice on the other end was frantic, speaking rapid-fire English with a thick Colombian accent. "Leary, is that you? I have bad news. Very bad. *Dios mio,* you not going to believe it."

Dillon recognized the voice instantly. It belonged to Miguel Ortiz, one of Estaban's L.A. lieutenants.

"Miguel, slow down," said Dillon. "What're you talking about?"

"It's Señor Gomez. He's dead."

"What?"

"Estaban is dead," said Miguel, this time louder. "Someone blew up his Mercedes. Right in front of that house he bought in Brentwood. You hear me, Leary? You there?"

Dillon didn't answer. In a daze, he set the phone back on the receiver and looked once again at the package.

Maybe he was wrong about Wilson McHenry. Maybe the old man was as cutthroat as Dillon himself had been.

Dillon had put McHenry's prize Dobermans to sleep with a pair of drugged T-bones, then scaled the south wall of the old man's estate. The wall's razor wire cut into Dillon's work gloves, but left his skin unmarked. He would leave no blood at the scene, no DNA, no fingerprints.

Once inside the walls, Dillon carefully made his way across the grounds, sticking to the shadows and avoiding security cameras. He moved very slowly, very patiently. When he finally reached the main house, he saw McHenry sitting alone outside on the deck, drinking a margarita. The old man looked strange there for some reason. Dillon couldn't put a finger on what it was. Then it occurred to him that McHenry wasn't wearing his fedora. He looked unnatural without it, like he was missing a limb.

"You didn't kill my dogs, did you?" asked the old man.

Dillon stepped into the glare of a flood lamp, his shadow stretching across the lawn. "They're just napping."

"I appreciate that." McHenry took a sip of his margarita and eyed Dillon from head to toe, pausing briefly at the .45 automatic in Dillon's hand. "I've let the boys go for the evening," he said, "so you won't have any trouble."

"I'm sorry about this."

"Don't be. In a way, I'm glad it's you and not some punk kid. So how much is Estaban paying anyway?"

"Not enough. But I've got family. A sister out in Pasadena. Estaban knows where she lives."

"I understand. And, believe it or not, I don't hold a grudge. This is all just part of the deal."

A cool breeze swept across the old man's back yard, rustling leaves in the tree branches. McHenry shifted in his chair, set his drink down on the deck floor. "Hey," he said with a smile, "you remember your first run? Down in Colombia?"

"It was Peru. Eight years ago."

"That's right, Peru. We landed that old twin-engine prop on some godforsaken airfield up in the mountains. In high wind too. You were what, twenty-three, twenty-four maybe? Christ, I don't know what scared you more, the landing or them guys waiting for us."

"Bunch of mountain men with automatic weapons," said Dillon, chuckling. "Almost wet my pants when I saw them. Kept seeing scenes from *Deliverance* run through my head."

"But how did you feel after it was through?"

"Like I'd won the lottery," said Dillon.

McHenry's smile faded. "I miss that feeling. Miss the rush. I guess it was over for me a while ago."

The old man stared blankly into the night sky, not looking at anything in particular. All the life seemed to drain from his eyes. "I've made some arrangements," he said.

"We're not talking about a will, are we?"

"Estaban's a snake, always has been. Play with a snake, sooner or later you'll get bit. But I'm not going down alone. I've seen to that."

"What're you saying, Mac?"

McHenry faced him. For the first time, Dillon noticed the deep lines of age etched into the old man's brow, like time had run a razor across his skin. "In this game, every move is a risk," he said. "Everything you do has repercussions. I want you to remember that."

Dillon nodded. "I'll remember."

"Good," said McHenry. "Now let's get this over with."

The old man rested back in his chair and closed his eyes, as if he was about to take an afternoon nap. His face held an eerie calm.

Slowly, Dillon raised the .45 and took careful aim. Never in his life had a gun felt so heavy.

McHenry's boys had been busy. Within an hour, Miguel had phoned Dillon's apartment three more times, the panic in the Colombian's voice growing with each call. Three of Estaban's former lieutenants were dead. One went by bomb. Two others were shot. Then the phone calls stopped all together, and Dillon began to wonder if Miguel himself had gotten hit.

Silence hung in the apartment like a poisonous gas. Walking to the fridge, Dillon dug out another beer and tilted the bottle back. Four empties sat on the kitchen counter.

What the hell was he still doing here? He should've taken off by now. Yet something kept him. Dillon tried to tell himself he was just biding his time, waiting for things to cool down before he made his run. But that was a lie, and he knew it. It was the package. He had to know what was inside.

Dillon took one last swig of beer then set the bottle next to its empty brothers. He grabbed hold of the package with both hands, carefully lifting it off the counter, testing its weight. It felt light. He shook it a little, hearing no hint at what was inside.

If it was a bomb, it would've gone off by now, thought Dillon. He picked the box cutter up and repeated the words in his head, over and over. *It would've gone off. It would've gone off. It would've gone off.*

Hand shaking, Dillon ran the cutter's blade along the box top, slitting the tape wide. Nothing happened. He closed his eyes and quickly ripped open the package's flaps.

There were no explosives, no wires, no timers. Instead, the package was filled with paper shavings cut from the *L.A. Times.* Nestled among the shavings was Wilson McHenry's old black fedora.

Dillon let himself breathe again. He lifted the fedora out by its brim and looked at it hard. He recalled his last conversation with McHenry — the old man sitting on the deck, talking about "arrangements" and "consequences." Dillon had thought it was some sort of threat, a last-ditch effort by the old man to stay alive. He should've known better. McHenry didn't play that way.

So what was McHenry's game? The answer came to Dillon as he pulled the hat on over his brow.

McHenry was tired of the business; he had said so himself. But he'd held on so long, he didn't know how to let go anymore. He needed Dillon's help. That was why he said he didn't hold a grudge. McHenry wanted out, and he understood that Dillon was just protecting himself and his family.

The fedora then was a symbol. McHenry was passing the baton. By having Estaban and his men killed, he was clearing a path so Dillon could take over. Run things the way the old man would have.

Dillon couldn't help but smile. Christ, McHenry was crazy. He wished he could see him now, have a drink together, tell a few jokes maybe. But all Dillon had left of the old man was the hat.

Tossing the empty package in the trash, Dillon smoothed out the brim of his new fedora. He wouldn't be anyone's muscle anymore, or a pilot running product. He was going to make something of himself, he decided. He'd make a deal with McHenry's boys and reorganize what was left of Estaban's crew. March right out and take control. After all, that's what the old man would've wanted.

Two of McHenry's boys sat in a Plymouth parked under a dead street lamp, waiting. They were both big men with square jaws and shoulders cut from stone. A sawed-off shotgun rested in the passenger's lap, out of sight below the window.

"Someone's coming," said the driver, nodding in the direction of the apartments across the street.

The passenger peered through the front windshield, catching sight of a figure stepping out the front entrance. "That's him."

"You a hundred percent?"

"Trust me, it's him."

"We don't got a picture or nothing. How can you be so sure?"

The passenger pumped the shotgun. A twelve-gauge slug cranked into the chamber, ready for business. "The old man left clear instructions," said the passenger. "Told us to look for a guy wearing a funny old hat."

WALTER MOSLEY

Karma

FROM *Dangerous Women*

LEONID MCGILL SAT at his desk, on the sixty-seventh floor of the Empire State Building, filing his nails and gazing at New Jersey. It was three-fifteen. Leonid had promised himself that he'd exercise that afternoon but now that the time had come he felt lethargic.

It was that pastrami sandwich, he thought. *Tomorrow I'll have something light like fish and then I can go to Gordo's and work out.*

Gordo's was a third-floor boxer's gym on Thirty-first Street. When Leonid was thirty years younger, and sixty pounds lighter, he went to Gordo's every day. For a while Gordo Packer wanted the private detective to go pro.

"You'll make more money in the ring than you ever will panty sniffin'," the seemingly ageless trainer said. McGill liked the idea but he also loved Lucky Strikes and beer.

"I can't bring myself to run unless I'm being chased," he'd tell Gordo. "And whenever somebody hurts me I wanna do him some serious harm. You know if a guy knocked me out in the ring I'd probably lay for him with a tire iron out back'a Madison Square when the night was through."

The years went by and Leonid kept working out on the heavy bag two or three times a week. But a boxing career was out of the question. Gordo lost interest in Leonid as a prospect but they remained friends.

"How'd a Negro ever get a name like Leonid McGill?" Gordo once asked the P.I.

"Daddy was a communist and Great-Great-Granddaddy was a slave master from Scotland," Leo answered easily. "You know the black man's family tree is mostly root. Whatever you see aboveground is only a hint at the real story."

Leo got up from his chair and made a stab at touching his toes. His fingers made it to about midshins but his stomach blocked any further progress.

"Shit," the P.I. said. Then he returned to his chair and went back to filing his nails.

He did that until the broad-faced clock on the wall said 4:07. Then the buzzer sounded. One long, loud blare. Leonid cursed the fact that he hadn't hooked up the view-cam to see who it was at the door. With a ring like that it could have been anyone. He owed over forty-six hundred dollars to the Wyant brothers. The nut was due and Leonid had yet to collect on his windfall. The Wyants wouldn't pay any attention to his cash flow problems.

It might have been a prospective client at the door. A real client. Someone with an employee stealing from him. Or maybe a daughter being influenced by a bad crowd. Then again it could be one of thirty or forty angry husbands wanting revenge for being found out at their extramarital pastimes. And then there was Joe Haller — the poor schnook. But Leonid had never even met Joe Haller. There was no way that that loser could have found his door.

The buzzer sounded again.

Leonid got up from his chair and walked into the long hall that led to his reception room. Then he came to the front door.

The buzzer blared a third time.

"Who is it?" McGill shouted in a southern accent that he used sometimes.

"Mr. McGill?" a woman said.

"He's not here."

"Oh. Do you expect him back today?"

"No," Leonid said. "No. He's away on a case. Down in Florida. If you tell me what it is you want I'll leave him a note."

"Can I come in?" She sounded young and innocent but Leonid wasn't about to be fooled.

"I'm just the building janitor, honey," he said. "I'm not allowed to let anybody in any office in this here building. But I'll write down your name and number and leave it on his desk if you want."

Leonid had used that line before. There was no argument against it. The janitor couldn't be held responsible.

There was silence from the other side of the door. If the girl had an accomplice they'd be whispering about how to get around his ploy. Leonid put his ear against the wall but couldn't hear a thing.

"Karmen Brown," the woman said. She added a number with the new 646 prefix. Probably a cell phone, Leonid thought.

"Hold on. Let me get a pencil," he complained. "Brown, you say?"

"Karmen Brown," she repeated. "Karmen with a *K*." Then she gave the number again.

"I'll put it on his desk," Leonid promised. "He'll get it the minute he gets back to town."

"Thank you," the young woman said. There was hesitation in her voice. If she was a thinking girl she might have wondered how a janitor would know the whereabouts of the private detective. But after a moment or two he could hear her heels clicking down the hall. He returned to his office to stay a while just in case the girl, and her possible accomplice, decided to wait until he came out.

He didn't mind hanging around in the office. His sublet apartment wasn't nearly as nice, or quiet, and at least he could be alone. Commercial rents took a nosedive after 9-11. He picked up the ESB workspace for a song.

Not that he'd paid the rent in three months.

But Leonid Trotter McGill didn't worry about money that much. He knew that he could pull a hat trick if he had to. Too many people had too many secrets. And secrets were the most valuable commodity in New York City.

At 5:39 the buzzer sounded again. But this time it was two long blasts followed by three short. Leonid made his way down the hall and opened the front door without asking who it was.

The man standing there was short and white, balding and slim. He wore an expensive suit with real cufflinks on a white shirt that had some starch in the collar and cuffs.

"Leon," the small white man said.

"Lieutenant. Come on in."

Leonid led the dapper little man through the reception area, along the hallway (that had three doors down its length), and finally into his office.

"Sit down, Lieutenant."

"Nice office. Where's everybody else?" the visitor asked.

"It's just me right now. I'm in a transition phase. You know, trying to develop a new business plan."

"I see."

The slender white man took the chair in front of Leonid's desk. From there he could see the long shadows across New Jersey. He shifted his gaze from the window to his host. L. T. McGill, P.I.

Leonid was short, no taller than five seven, with a protruding gut and heavy jowls. His skin was the color of dirty bronze and covered with dark freckles. There was a toothpick jutting out from the right side of his mouth. He wore a tan suit that had been stained over time. His shirt was lime green and the thick gold band on his left pinky weighed two or three ounces.

Leonid McGill had powerful hands and strong breath. His eyes were suspicious and he would always appear to be a decade over his actual age.

"What can I do for you, Carson?" the detective asked the cop.

"Joe Haller," Carson Kitteridge said.

"Come again?" Leonid let his face wrinkle up, feigning ignorance if not innocence.

"Joe Haller."

"Never heard that name before. Who is he?"

"He's a gigolo and a batterer. Now they're trying to tell me he's a thief."

"You wanna hire me to find something on him?"

"No," the cop said. "No. He's in the Tombs right now. We caught him red-handed. He had thirty thousand right there in his closet. In the briefcase that he carried to work every day."

"That makes it easy," Leonid said. He concentrated on his breathing, something he had learned to do whenever he was being questioned by the law.

"You'd think so, wouldn't you?" Carson asked.

"Is there a problem with the case?"

"You were seen speaking to Nestor Bendix on January four."

"I was?"

"Yeah. I know that because Nestor's name came up in the robbery of a company called Amberson's Financials two months ago."

"Really?" Leonid said. "What does all that have to do with Joe whatever?"

"Haller," Lieutenant Kitteridge said. "Joe Haller. The money he had in the bag was from the armored car that had just made a drop at Amberson's."

"An armored car dropped thirty thousand dollars at the place?"

"More like three hundred thousand," Kitteridge said. "It was for their ATM machines. Seems like Amberson's had got heavy into the ATM business in that neighborhood. They run sixty machines around midtown."

"I'll be damned. And you think Joe Haller and Nestor Bendix robbed them?"

Lieutenant Carson Kitteridge stayed silent for a moment, his gray eyes taking in the rough-hewn detective.

"What did you and Nestor have to say to each other?" the cop asked.

"Nothing," Leonid said, giving a one-shoulder shrug. "It was a pizza place down near the Seaport, if I remember right. I ducked in there for a calzone and saw Nestor. We used to be friends back when Hell's Kitchen was still Hell's Kitchen."

"What did he have to say?"

"Not a thing. Really. It was just a chance meeting. I sat down long enough to eat too much and find out that he's got two kids in college and two in jail."

"You talk about the heist?"

"I never even heard about it until you just said."

"This Joe Haller," the policeman said. "He practices what you call an alternative lifestyle. He likes married women. It's what you might call his thing. He finds straight ladies and bends them. They say he's hung like a horse."

"Yeah?"

"Yeah. What he does is gets the ladies to meet him at hotels near where he works and goes in to teach them about how the other eight inches live."

"You've lost me, Lieutenant," Leonid said. "I mean unless one of the she-guards at Amberson's is Haller's chicken."

The elegant policeman shook his head slightly.

"No. No. This is how I see it, Leon," the policeman said. He sat forward in his chair and laced his fingers. "Nestor pulled off the robbery but somebody let it slip and me and my crew got on his ass. So he calls on you to find him a pigeon and you give him Haller. Don't ask me how. I don't know. But you set up the Romeo and now he's looking at twenty years in Attica."

"Me?" Leonid said, pressing all ten fingers against his breast. "How the hell you think I could do something like that?"

"You could pluck an egg out from under a nesting eagle and

she'd never even know it was gone," Kitteridge said. "I got a man in jail and his alibi girlfriend saying that she never even heard his name. I got an armed robber laughing at me and a P.I. more crooked than any crook I ever arrested lyin' in my face."

"Carson," Leonid said. "Brother, you got me wrong. I did see Nestor for a few minutes. But that's all, man. I've never been to this Amberson's place and I never heard of Joe Haller or his girlfriend."

"Chris," Kitteridge said. "Chris Small. Her husband has already left her. That's what our investigation has accomplished so far."

"I wish I could help you, man, but you got me wrong, I wouldn't even know how to set up some patsy for a crime after it was committed."

Carson Kitteridge stared mildly at the detective and the darkening neighbor state. He smiled and said, "You can't get away with it, Leon. You can't break the law like that and win."

"I don't know nuthin' about nuthin', Lieutenant. Maybe the man you caught really is the thief."

Katrina McGill was a beauty in her day. Svelte and raven-haired, from Latvia or Lithuania — Leonid was never sure which one. They had three kids, of which at least two were not Leonid's. He'd never had them tested. Why bother? The East European beauty had left him early on for a finance lion. But she got fat and the sugar daddy went broke so now the whole crowd (minus the sugar daddy) lived on Leonid's dime.

"What's for dinner, Kat?" he asked, breathing hard after scaling the five flights to their apartment door.

"Mr. Barch called," she answered. "He said that either you pay up by Friday or he's going to start eviction."

It was the square shape of her face and the heaviness around her eyes that made her ugly. When she was young gravity was in suspense but he should have seen the curtain coming down.

The kids were in the living room. The TV was on but no one was watching. The oldest boy, the redheaded Dimitri, was reading a book. He had ocher skin and green eyes. But he had Leonid's mouth. Shelly, the girl, looked more Chinese than anything else. They used to have a Chinese neighbor when they lived on Staten Island. He worked at an Indian jewelers' center in Queens. Shelly was sewing one of Leonid's jackets. She loved her father and never questioned her mother or the face in the mirror.

Shelly and Dimitri were eighteen and nineteen. They went to City College and lived at home. Katrina would not hear of them moving out. And Leonid liked having them around. He felt that they were keeping him anchored to something, keeping him from floating away down Forty-second Street and into the Hudson.

Twill was the youngest boy. Sixteen and self-named. He'd just come home after a three-month stay at a youth detention center near Wingdale, New York. The only reason he was still in high school was that that was part of his release agreement.

Twill was the only one who smiled when Leonid entered the room.

"Hey, Pop," he said. "Guess what? Mr. Tortolli wants to hire me at his store."

"Hey. Good." Leonid would have to call the hardware man and tell him that Twill would open his back door and empty out the storeroom in three weeks' time.

Leonid loved him but Twill was a thief.

"What about Mr. Barch?" Katrina said.

"What about my dinner?"

Katrina knew how to cook. She served chicken with white wine sauce and the flakiest dumplings he had ever eaten. There was also broccoli and almond bread, grilled pineapples, and a dark fish sauce that you could eat with a spoon.

Cooking was difficult for Katrina since her left hand had become partially paralyzed. The specialist said that it was probably due to a slight stroke. She worried all the time. Her boyfriends had stopped calling years before.

But Leonid took care of her and her kids. He even asked to have sex with her now and then because he knew how much she hated it.

"Did anybody else call?" he asked when the college kids were in their rooms and Twill was back out in the street.

"A man called Arman."

"What he say?"

"There's a little French diner on Tenth and Seventeenth. He wants to see you there at ten. I told him I didn't know if you could make it."

When Leonid moved to kiss Katrina she leaned away and he laughed.

"Why don't you leave me?" he asked.
"Who would raise our children if I did that?"
This caused Leonid to laugh even harder.

He reached Babette's Feast at nine-fifteen. He ordered a double espresso and stared at the legs of a mature woman seated at the bar. She was at least forty but dressed as if she were fifteen. Leonid felt the stirrings of the first erection he'd had in over a week.

Maybe that's why he called Karmen Brown on his cell phone. Her voice had sounded as if it should be clad in a dress like that.

When the call was answered Leonid could tell that she was outside.

"Hello?"

"Miss Brown?"

"Yes."

"This is Leo McGill. You left a message for me?"

"Mr. McGill. I thought you were in Florida." The roar of an engine almost drowned out her words.

"I'm sorry if it's hard to hear me," she said. "There was a motorcycle going down the street."

"That's okay. How can I help you?"

"I'm having a problem and, and — well, it's rather personal."

"I'm a detective, Miss Brown. I hear personal stuff all the time. If you want me to meet with you then you'll have to tell me what it's about."

"Richard," she said, "Mallory. He's my fiancé and I think he's cheating on me."

"And you want me to prove it?"

"Yes," she said. "I don't want to marry a man who will treat me like that."

"How did you get my name, Miss Brown?"

"I looked you up in the book. When I saw where your office was I thought that you must be good."

"I can meet you sometime tomorrow."

"I'd rather meet tonight. I don't think I'll get any sleep until this thing is settled."

"Well," the detective hesitated. "I have a meeting at ten and then I'm going to see my girlfriend." It was a private joke, one that the young Miss Brown would never understand.

"Maybe I can meet you before you see your girlfriend," Karmen suggested. "It should only take a few minutes."

They agreed on a pub on Houston two blocks east of Elizabeth Street, where Gert Longman lived.

Just as Leonid was removing the hooked earphone from his ear Craig Arman entered the bistro. He was a large white man with a broad, kind face. Even the broken nose made him seem more vulnerable than dangerous. He wore faded blue jeans and a T-shirt under a large loose-knit sweater. There was a pistol hidden somewhere in all that fabric, Leonid knew that. Nestor Bendix's *street accountant* never went unarmed.

"Leo," Arman said.

"Craig."

The small table that Leonid had chosen was behind a pillar, removed from the rest of the crowd in the popular bistro.

"Cops got their package," Arman said. "Our guy was in and out of his place in ten minutes. A quick call downtown and now he's in the Tombs. Just like you said."

"That means I can pay the rent," Leonid replied.

Arman smiled and Leonid felt a few ounces being placed on his thigh under the table.

"Well, I got to go," Arman said then. "Early to bed, you know."

"Yeah," Leonid agreed.

Most of Nestor's boys didn't have much truck with the darker races. The only reason Nestor ever called was that Leonid was the best at his trade.

Leonid caught a cab on Seventh Avenue that took him to Barney's Clover on Houston.

The girl sitting at the far end of the bar was everything Katrina had once been except she was blond and her looks would never fade. She had a porcelain face with small, lovely features. No makeup except for a hint of pale lip gloss.

"Mr. McGill?"

"Leo."

"I'm so relieved that you came to meet me," she said.

She was wearing tan riding pants and a coral blouse. There was a white raincoat folded over her lap. Her eyes were the kind of brown that some artist might call red. Her hair was cut short —

boyish but sexy. Her tinted lips were ready to kiss babies' butts and laugh.

Leonid took a deep breath and said, "I charge five hundred a day — plus expenses. That's mileage, equipment rentals, and food after eight hours on the job."

He had just received twelve thousand dollars from Craig Arman but business was business.

The girl handed him a large manila envelope.

"This is his full name and address. I have also included a photograph and the address of the office where he works. There's also eight hundred dollars in it. You probably won't need more than that because I'm almost sure that he'll be seeing her tomorrow evening."

"What you drinkin', guy?" the bartender, a lovely-faced Asian boy, asked.

"Seltzer," the detective asked. "Hold the rocks."

The bartender smiled or sneered, Leonid wasn't sure which. He wanted a scotch with his fizzy water but the ulcer in his stomach would keep him up half the night if he had it.

"Why?" Leonid asked the beautiful girl.

"Why do I want to know?"

"No. Why do you think he's going to see her tomorrow night?"

"Because he told me that he had to go with his boss to see *The Magic Flute* at Carnegie Hall. But there is no opera scheduled."

"You seem to have it all worked out yourself. Why would you need a detective?"

"Because of Dick's mother," Karmen Brown said. "She told me that I wasn't worthy of her son. She said that I was common and coarse and that I was just using him."

The anger twisted Karmen's face until even her ethereal beauty turned into something ugly.

"And you want to rub her face in it?" Leonid asked. "Why wouldn't she be happy that her boy found another girl?"

"I think that the woman he's seeing is married and older, way older. If I could get pictures of them then when I leave at least she won't be so smug."

Leonid wondered if that would be enough to hurt Dick's mother. He also wondered why Karmen suspected that Dick was seeing an older married woman. He had a lot of questions but didn't ask them. Why question a cash cow? After all, he had two rents to pay.

The detective looked over the information and glanced at the cash, held together by an oversized paper clip, while the young bartender placed the water by his elbow.

The photograph was of a man whom he took to be Richard Mallory. He was a young white man whose face seemed unfinished. There was a mustache that wasn't quite thick enough and a mop of brown hair that would always defy a comb. He seemed uncomfortable standing there in front of the Rockefeller Center skating rink.

"Okay, Miss Brown," Leonid said. "I'll take it on. Maybe we'll both get lucky and it'll be over by tomorrow night."

"Karma," she said. "Call me Karma. Everybody does."

Leonid got down to Elizabeth Street a little after ten thirty. He rang Gert's bell and shouted his name into the security microphone. He had to raise his voice to be heard over the roar of a passing motorcycle.

Gert Longman lived in a small studio on the third floor of a stucco building put up in the fifties. The ceiling was low but the room was pretty big and Gert had set it up nicely. There was a red sofa and a mahogany coffee table with cherry wood cabinets that had glass doors along the far wall. She had no kitchen but there was a miniature refrigerator in one corner with a coffee percolator and a toaster on top. Gert also had a CD player. When Leonid got there she was playing Ella Fitzgerald singing Cole Porter tunes.

Leonid appreciated the music and said so.

"I like it," Gert said, somehow managing to negate Leonid's compliment.

She was a dark-skinned woman whose mother had come from the Spanish side of Hispaniola. Gert didn't speak with an accent, though. She didn't even know the Spanish tongue. Actually Gert knew nothing about her history. She was proud to say of herself that she was just as much an American as any Daughter of the American Revolution.

She sat on the southern end of the sofa.

"Did Nestor pay you yet?" Gert asked.

"You know I been missing you, Gertie," Leonid said, thinking about her satin skin and the fortyish woman in the teeny-bopper dress from the French bistro.

"That's done, Leo," Gert said. "That was over a long time ago."

"You must still have needs."

"Not for you."

"One time you told me you loved me," Leonid replied.

"That was after you told me that you weren't married."

Leonid sat down a few inches away from her. He touched her knuckle with two fingers.

"No," Gert said.

"Come on, baby. It's hard as a boil down there."

"And I'm dry to the bone."

. . . but to a woman a man is life, Ella sang.

Leonid sat back and shoved his right hand into his pants pocket.

After Karmen Brown had left him at Barney's Clover Leonid ducked into the john and counted out Gert's three thousand from the twelve Craig Arman had laid on his lap. He took the wad from his pocket.

"You could at least give me a little kiss on my boil for all this," he said.

"I could lance it too."

Leonid chuckled and Gert grinned. They'd never be lovers again but she liked his ways. He could see that in her eyes.

Maybe he should have left Katrina.

He handed her the roll of hundred-dollar bills and asked, "Could anybody find a trail from you to Joe Haller?"

"Uh-uh, no. I worked in a whole 'nother office from him."

"How did you find out about his record?"

"Ran off a list of likely employees for the company and did a background search on about twenty."

"From your desk?"

"From the public library computer terminal."

"Can't they trace you back on that?" Leonid asked.

"No. I bought an account with a Visa number I got from Jackie P. It's some poor slob from St. Louis. There's no tracing that. What's wrong, Leo?"

"Nuthin'," the detective said. "I just want to be careful."

"Haller's a dog," Gert added. "He'd been doin' them girls around there for months. And when Cynthia Athol's husband found out and came after him Joe beat him so bad that he had to go to the hospital. Broke his collarbone. He beat Chris Small with a strap just two weeks ago."

When Nestor asked Leonid to find him a patsy for a midday crime Leonid came to Gert and she went to work as a temp for Amberson's Financials. All she had to do was come up with a guy with a record who might have been part of the heist; a guy who no one could connect with Nestor.

She did him one better. She came up with a guy that no one liked.

Haller had robbed a convenience store twelve years before, when he was eighteen. And now he was a gigolo with some kind of black belt in something. He liked to overwhelm the silly office secretaries with his muscles and his big thing. He didn't mind if their significant others found out because he believed he could take on almost any man one on one.

Gert had been told that he once said, "Any woman with a real man wouldn't let me take her like that."

"Don't worry," Gert said. "He deserves whatever happens to him and they'll never follow it back to me."

"Okay," Leonid said.

He touched her knuckle again.

"Don't."

He let his fingers trail up toward her wrist.

"Please, Leo. I don't want to wrestle with you."

Leonid's breath was shallow and the erection was pressing against his pants. But he moved away.

"I better be going," he said.

"Yeah," Gert agreed. "Go home to your wife."

It didn't take long to get past security at the Empire State Building. Leonid worked late at least three nights a week.

He didn't want to go home after Gert had turned him down.

He never knew why he took Katrina back in.

He never knew why he did anything except if it had to do with the job.

Leonid became a P.I. because he was too short to qualify for the NYPD when he was eligible. They changed the requirements soon after that but by then he'd already been busted for unlawful entry.

He didn't care. The private sector was more lucrative and he could work his own hours.

He found a Richard Mallory in the phone book that had the same address that Karmen Brown had typed out on her fiancé's fact sheet. Leonid dialed the number. Someone answered on the third ring.

"Hello?" a tremulous man's voice asked.

"Bobbi Anne there?" Leonid asked in one of his dozen accents.

"What?"

"Bobbi Anne. She there?"

"You have the wrong number."

"Oh. All right," Leonid said and then he hung up.

For a dozen minutes by the big clock on the wall Leonid thought about the voice of the man who might have been Richard Mallory. Leonid thought that he could tell the nature of anyone if he could talk to him just when he was roused out of a deep sleep.

It was 2:34 A.M. And Richard, if that was Richard, sounded like a straightforward guy, a working stiff, somebody who didn't cross the line over into the Life.

This was important to Leonid. He didn't want to get involved following some guy who might turn around and blow his head off.

At half past three he called Gert.

"Six-two-oh-nine," the recording of her voice said after five rings. "I'm not available right now but if you leave a message I'll be sure to call you back."

"Gertie, it's Leon. I'm sorry about before. I miss you, honey. Maybe we can have dinner tomorrow night. You know — I'll make it up to you."

He didn't hang up for a few seconds more, hoping that Gert was listening and would decide to pick up.

The buzzer woke him. The clock had it just past nine. The window was filled with cloud — just a pillowy white gauze that didn't give three inches' visibility.

The buzzer jangled his dull mind again. Another long ring. But this time Leonid wasn't awake enough to have fear. He stumbled down the hall in the same suit he'd been wearing for over twenty-four hours.

When he opened the front door the two thugs pushed in.

One was black with a bald head and golden-rimmed glasses while the other was white with thick greasy hair.

They each had five inches on Leonid.

"The Wyants want forty-nine hundred," the black man said. His mouth on the inside was the color of gingivitis. His eyes behind the lenses had a yellowy tint.

"Forty-six," Leonid corrected groggily.

"That was yesterday, Leo. That interest is a motherfucker." The black man closed the door and the white one moved to Leonid's left.

The white hooligan grinned and Leonid felt a hatred in his heart that was older than his communist father's father.

The white man had coarse chestnut hair that had been hacked rather than cut. His eyes were bisected between blue and brown and his lips were ragged, as if he had spent a portion of his earlier life soul-kissing a toothy leopard.

"We wake you up?" the black collector asked, just now remembering his manners.

"Li'l bit," Leonid said, stifling a yawn. "How you been, Bilko?"

"Okay, Leon. I hope you got the money, 'cause if you don't they told us to bust you up."

The white man snickered in anticipation.

Leonid reached into his breast pocket and came out with the thick brown envelope he'd received the night before.

While counting out the forty-nine hundred-dollar bills Leonid had a familiar sensation: the feeling of never having as much money as he thought he did. After his debt and interest to the Wyants, this month's rent and last on his apartment, after his wife's household expenses and his own bills, he would be broke and still three months behind on his office rent.

This made him even angrier. He'd need Karmen Brown's money and more if he was going to keep his head above water. And that white fool just kept on grinning, his head like a wobbling tenpin begging to fall down.

Leonid handed the money to Bilko, who counted it slowly while the white goon licked his ragged lips.

"I think you should tip us for havin' to come all the way up here to collect, Leon," the white man said.

Bilko looked up and grinned. "Leon don't tip the help, Norman. He's got his pride."

"I knock that outta him right quick," Norman said.

"I'd like to see you try it, white boy," Leonid dared. Then he looked at Bilko to see if he had to take on two at once.

"It's between you two," the black capo said, holding up one empty hand and one filled with Leonid's green.

Norman was faster than he looked. He laid a beefy fist against Leonid's jaw, knocking the middle-aged detective back two steps.

"Whoa!" Bilko cried.

Norman's frayed lips curved into a smile. He stood there looking at Leonid, expecting him to fall down.

That was the mistake all of Leonid's sparring partners had made at Gordo's gym. They thought the fat man couldn't take a punch. Leonid came in low and hard, hitting the big white man three times at the belt line. The third punch bent Norman over enough to be a sucker for a one-two uppercut combination. The only thing that kept Norman from falling was the wall. He hit it hard, putting his hands up reflexively to ward off the attack he knew was coming.

Leonid got three good blows to Norman's head before Bilko pushed him away.

"That's enough now, boy," Bilko said. "That's enough. I need him on his feet to get back out on the street."

"Take the asshole outta here then, Bilko! Take him outta here before I kill his ass!"

Dutifully Bilko helped the half-conscious, bleeding white man away from the wall. He pointed him at the door and then turned to Leonid.

"See you next month, Leon," he said.

"No," Leonid replied, breathing hard from the exertion. "You won't be seeing me again."

Bilko laughed as he led Norman toward the elevators.

Leonid slammed the door behind them. He was still in a rage. After all his pay he was still broke and hard-pressed by fools like Bilko and Norman. Gert wouldn't take his calls and he didn't even have a bed that he could sleep in alone. He would have killed that ugly fool if it wasn't for Bilko.

Leonid Trotter McGill let out a roar and kicked a hole in the paneled veneer of his nonexistent receptionist's cubicle wall. Then he picked up the phone, called Lenny's Delicatessen on Thirty-fifth Street and ordered three jelly doughnuts and a large cup of coffee with cream.

He called Gert again but she still wasn't answering.

It was a small office on the third floor above a two-story Japanese restaurant called Gai. There was no elevator so Leonid took the stairs. Just those twenty-eight steps winded him. If Norman had fought back at all, Leonid realized, he would be broken and broke.

The receptionist weighed less than ninety-eight pounds fully dressed and she was nowhere near fully dressed. All she had on was a black slip trying to pass as a dress and flat paper sandals. Her arms had no muscle. Everything about the girl was preadolescent except her eyes, which regarded the bulky P.I. with deep suspicion.

"Richard Mallory," Leonid said to the brunette.

"And you are?"

"Looking for Richard Mallory," Leonid stated.

"What business do you have with Mr. Mallory?"

"No business of yours, honey. It's man-talk."

The young woman's four-ounce jaw hardened as she stared at Leonid.

He didn't mind. He didn't like the girl; dressed so sexy and talking to him as if they were peers.

She picked up a phone and whispered a few angry words, then she walked away from her post into a doorway behind her chair, leaving Leonid to stand there at the waist-high barrier-desk. In the mirror on the wall Leonid could see through the window behind his back and out onto Madison Avenue. He could also see the swelling on the right side of his head where Norman had hit him.

A few moments later the tall man with a sparse mustache strode out. He wore black trousers and a tan linen jacket and the same uncomfortable expression he had on the photograph in Leonid's pocket.

Leonid hated him too.

"Yes?" Richard Mallory said to Leonid.

"I'm looking for Richard Mallory," Leonid said.

"That's me."

The P.I. took a deep breath through his nostrils. He knew that he had to calm down if he wanted to do his job right. He took another, deeper breath.

"What happened to your jaw?" the handsome young man asked the amateur boxer.

"Edema," Leonid said easily. "Runs on my father's side of the family."

Richard Mallory was stymied by this. Leonid thought that he probably didn't know the definition of the word.

"I want to talk business with you, Mr. Mallory. Something we can both make money on."

"I don't see what you mean," Mallory said with the blandest of bland expressions on his face.

Leonid produced a card from his breast pocket. It read:

> Van Der Zee Domestics and In-Home Service Aides
> Arnold DuBois, Agent

"I don't understand, Mr. DuBois," Mallory said, using the French pronunciation of McGill's alias.

"Du *boys*," Leonid said. "I represent the Van Der Zee firm. We're just establishing ourselves here in New York. We're from Cleveland originally. What we want is to get our people in as domestics, care for the aged, dog walkers, and nannies in the upper-crust buildings. All of our people are highly presentable and professional. They're bonded too."

"And you want me to help you get in?" Mallory asked, still a little leery.

"We'll pay fifteen hundred dollars for every exclusive presentation you get us in for," Leonid said. By now he had forgotten his dislike of the receptionist and Mallory. He wasn't even mad at Norman anymore.

The mention of fifteen hundred per presentation (whatever that meant) moved Dick Mallory to action.

"Come with me, Mr. DuBois," he said, pronouncing the name the way Leonid preferred.

The real estate agent led the fake employment agent down a hall of cubicles inhabited by various other agents.

Mallory took Leonid to a small conference room and closed the door behind them. There was a round pine table that had three matching chairs. Mallory gestured and they both sat down.

"Now what is it exactly that you're saying, Mr. DuBois?"

"We have a young girl," Leonid said. "A pretty thing. She sets up a small table in the entry hall of any building you say. She talks to the tenants about all the various types of in-home labor they might need. Somebody might want an assistant twice a week to help with filing and shopping. They might already have an assistant but still need somebody to walk their pets when they're away. Once somebody hires one of our people we're confident that they will hire others as needs arise. All we want is your okay to install the young lady and we pay you fifteen hundred dollars."

"For every building I get you into?"

"Cash."

"Cash?"

Leonid nodded.

The young man actually licked his lips.

"If you can guarantee us a lobby in an upscale building, I can pay you as early as tonight," Leonid said.

"Does it have to be that soon?"

"I'm an agent on commission for Van Der Zee Enterprises, Mr. Mallory. In order to make a profit I have to produce. I'm not the only one out here trying to make contacts. I mean, you can call me whenever you want, but if you can't promise me a lobby by the end of today then I will have to go farther down my list of contacts."

"But —"

"Listen," Leonid said, cutting off any logic that Richard Mallory might have brought to bear. He reached into his pocket and brought out three one-hundred-dollar bills. These he placed on the table between them. "That's one-fifth up front. Three hundred dollars against you finding me one lobby that I can send Arlene to tomorrow morning."

"Tomorrow —"

"That's right, Richard. Van Der Zee Enterprises will give me control over the whole Manhattan operation if I'm the first one to bring in a lobby."

"So I get to keep the money?"

"With twelve hundred more coming to you at eight this evening if you have the lobby set for me."

"Eight? Why eight?"

"You think you're the only guy I'm talking to, Richard? I have four other meetings set up this afternoon. Whoever gets to me when it's all done, at eight o'clock, will get at least part of the prize. Maybe he'll get the whole thing."

"But I have a date tonight —"

"Just call me on the phone, Richard. Tell me where you are and I'll bring you the money and the letter confirming to the super that Arlene can set up her table."

"What letter?"

"I hope you don't think I'm going to be handing you fifteen hundred dollars a week in cash without getting a letter for the super to show my boss," Leonid said blandly. "Don't worry, we won't mention the money, just that Van Der Zee Enterprises can set up in the lobby offering our services."

"But what if somebody complains?"

"You can always tell your bosses that you were thinking on your own, trying to offer a service. They won't know about the money changing hands. At the very least we'll be thrown out, but that'll take a coupla days, and Arlene is very good at handing out those brochures."

"That's fifteen hundred in cash a week?"

"Twice that if we can find another Arlene and you can hook us up like I been told."

"But I'm going to be out tonight," Mallory complained.

"So? Just call me. Give me the address. And I'll drop by with the form. We're talkin' ten minutes for twelve hundred dollars."

Richard fingered the money. Then he tentatively picked it up.

"I can just take this?"

"Take it. And take the rest tonight and then that much again once a week for the next four or five months." Leonid grinned.

Richard folded the money and put it in his pocket.

"What's your phone number, Mr. DuBois?"

Leonid called his wife and told her to have his brown suit ready and pressed by the time he got home.

"Am I your maid now?" she asked.

"I got the rent and the expenses here in my pocket," Leonid growled. "All I'm asking from you is a little cooperation."

The private eye then called his cell phone service. When the voice on the line said to record a new message, Leonid said, "Hello.

This is Arnold DuBois, employment agent for Van Der Zee Enterprises. At the tone leave me what you got."

When he got home he found the suit folded on the bed and Katrina gone. Alone in the house, he drew a bath and poured himself a glass of ice water. He wanted a cigarette but the doctors had told him his lungs could barely take New York air.

He sat back in the old-fashioned tub, turning the hot water on and off with his toes. His jaw ached and he was almost broke again. But still he had a line on Richard Mallory and that made the detective happy.

"At least I'm good at what I do," he said to no one. "At least that."

After the bath Leonid called Gert again. This time the phone rang and rang with no interruption. That was very odd. Gert had it set up so that her service picked up when she was on the line.

Sometimes he didn't talk to Gert for months at a time. She had made it clear that they could never be intimate again. But he still felt something for her. And he wanted to make sure that she was okay.

When Leonid got to Gert's near four he found the downstairs door had been wedged open.

Her front door was crisscrossed with yellow police ribbon.

"You know her?" a voice asked.

It was a small woman standing at a doorway down the hall. She was old and gray and wore gray clothes. She had watery eyes and mismatched slippers. There was a low-grade emerald ring on the index finger of her right hand and the left side of her mouth lagged just a bit.

Leonid noticed all of this in a vain attempt to work away from the fear growing in his stomach.

"What happened?"

"They say he musta come in last night," the woman said. "It was past midnight, the super says. He just killed her. Didn't steal anything. Just shot her with a gun no louder than a cap pistol, that's what they said. You know you're not safe in your own bed anymore. People out here just get some crazy idea in their head and you find yourself dead with no rhyme or reason."

Leonid's tongue went dry. He stared at the woman so intensely that she stopped rambling, backed into her apartment, and closed the door. He leaned against the doorjamb, dry-eyed but stunned.

Leonid had never cried. Not when his father left home for the revolution. Not when his mother went to bed and never came out again. Never.

There was a different bartender serving drinks at Barney's Clover that afternoon. A woman with faded blue-green tattoos on her wrists. She was thin and brown-eyed, white, and past forty.

"What you have, mister?"

"Rye whiskey. Keep 'em comin'."

He was on the sixth shot when his cell phone sounded. The ring had been programmed by his son Twill. It started with the sound of a lion's roar.

"'lo?"

"Mr. DuBois? Is that you?"

"Who is this?"

"Richard Mallory. Are you sick, Mr. DuBois?"

"Hey, Dick. Sorry I didn't recognize you. I got some bad news today. An old friend of mine died."

"I'm so sorry. What happened?"

"It was a long illness," Leonid said, finishing one shot and gesturing for another.

"Should I call you later?"

"You got me a lobby, Dick?"

"Um, well yes. A fairly large building on Sutton Place South. The super is a friend of mine and I promised him five hundred."

"That's the way to do business, Dick. Share the wealth. That's what I've always done. Where are you?"

"It's a Brazilian place on West Twenty-six. Umberto's. On the second floor, between Sixth and Broadway. I don't know the exact address."

"That's okay. I'll get it from information. See you about nine. Looks like we're gonna be doing some business, you and me."

"Okay, um, all right. I'm sorry about your loss, Mr. DuBois. But please don't call me Dick. I hate that name."

*

Umberto's was an upscale restaurant on a street filled with wholesalers of Indian trinkets, foods, and clothing. Leonid sat across the street in his 1963 Peugeot.

It was after ten and the fat detective was drinking from a pint bottle of bourbon in the front seat. He was thinking about the first time he had met Gert, about how she knew just what to say.

"You're not such a bad man," the sultry New Yorker had said. "It's just that you been making your own rules for so long that you got a little confused."

They spent that night together. He really didn't know that she'd be upset about Katrina. Katrina was his wife but there was no juice there. He remembered the hurt look on Gert's face when she finally found out. After that came the cold anger she treated him with from then on.

They'd remained friends but she would never kiss him again. She would never let him into her heart.

But they worked well together. Gert had been in private security for a dozen years before they met. She enjoyed her *shady cases,* as she called them. Gert didn't believe that the law was fair and she didn't mind getting around the system if that was the right thing to do.

Maybe Joe Haller didn't rob Amberson's, but he'd beaten and humiliated both men and women pursuing his perverse sexual appetites.

Leonid wondered if Nestor Bendix could have had something to do with Gert's killing. But he'd never told anyone her name. Maybe Haller got out and somehow traced his problem back to her. Maybe.

A lion roared in his pocket.

"Yeah?"

"Mr. McGill? This is Karma."

"Hey. I'm on the case. He *is* on a date but I haven't seen her yet. I'll have the pictures for you by tomorrow afternoon. By the way, I had to lay out three hundred to get this address."

"That's all right, I guess," she said. "I'll pay for it if you can bring me proof about his girlfriend."

"All right. Let me off now. I'll call you when I have something for sure."

When Leonid folded the phone a colony of monkeys began chattering.

"Yeah?"

"You knew Gert Longman, didn't you?" Carson Kitteridge asked.

Ice water formed in Leonid's lower intestine. His rectum clenched.

"Yeah."

"What's that supposed to mean?"

"You asked me if I knew someone and I told you. Yeah. We were close there for a while."

"She's dead."

Leonid remained silent for a quarter face sweep of his Timex's second hand. That was long enough to seem as if he was shocked by the news.

"How did it happen?"

"Shot."

"By who?"

"A man wielding a long-barreled .22 pistol."

"Do you have a suspect?"

"That's the kinda pistol you like to use, isn't it, Leon?"

For a moment Leonid thought that the lieutenant was just blowing smoke, trying to get under his skin. But then he remembered a gun that he'd lost. It was seventeen years before. Nora Parsons had come to him scared to death that her husband, who was out on bail before sentencing in his embezzlement trial, was going to come kill her. Leonid had given her his pistol, and after her husband, Anton, was sentenced, she'd told him that she was afraid to have the pistol in the house so she threw it into a lake.

It was a cold piece. Nothing to it.

"Well?" Detective Kitteridge asked.

"I haven't owned a gun in twenty years, man. And even you can't think that I'd use my own piece if I wanted to kill somebody."

But still he thought he might give Nora Parsons a call. Maybe.

"I'd like you to come in for voluntary questioning, Leon."

"I'm busy right now. Call me later," Leonid said, and then he disconnected the call.

He didn't want to be so rude to a member of New York's finest but Richard was coming out of the front door of Umberto's Brazilian Food. He was accompanied by the haughty receptionist from the real estate company. Now she was wearing a red slip and black pumps with a gossamer pink shawl around her bare shoulders. Her limp brown hair was up.

Richard glanced around the street, probably looking for Mr. DuBois, then hailed a cab.

Leonid turned over the engine. He watched as a cab swooped down to pick them up. The driver wore a Sikh turban.

They went up to Thirty-second Street, headed east over to Park, and then up to the Seventies.

They got out at a building with big glass doors and two uniformed doormen.

Almost as if they were posing, the two stopped on the street and entwined their lips in a long soul kiss. Leonid had been taking photographs since he'd hung up on the cop. He had shots of the taxi's numbers, the driver, the front of the building, and the couple talking, holding hands, dueling tongues, and grasping at skin.

They reminded Leonid of Gert, of how much he wanted her. And now she was dead. He put down his camera and bowed his head for a moment. When he raised it again Richard Mallory and the receptionist were gone.

"You awake?" Leonid whispered in bed next to Katrina.

It was early for him, only one thirty. But she had been asleep for hours. He knew that.

In the old days she was always out past three and four. Sometimes she wouldn't come in till the sun was up — smelling of vodka, cigarettes, and men.

Maybe if he had left her and gone to Gert. Maybe Gert would still be alive.

"What?" Katrina said.

"You wanna talk?"

"It's almost two."

"Somebody I been working with the last ten years died tonight," Leonid said.

"Are you in trouble?"

"I'm sad."

For a few moments Leonid listened to her hard breath.

"Will you hold hands with me?" the detective asked his wife.

"My hands hurt," she said.

For a long time after that he lay on his back staring at the darkness before the ceiling. There was nothing he could think that did not damn him. There was nothing he had done that he could remember with pride.

Maybe an hour later Katrina said, "Are you still up?"

"Yeah."

"Do you have a life insurance policy? I'm just worried for the kids."

"I got better than that. I got a life insurance philosophy."

"What's that?" Katrina asked.

"As long as I'm worth more alive than dead I won't have to worry about banana peels and bad broth."

Katrina sighed and Leonid climbed out of the bed.

Just as he got to the small TV room Twill came in the front door.

"It's three in the morning, Twill," Leonid said.

"Sorry, Dad, But I got into this thing with the Torcelli sisters and Bingham. It was their parents' car so I had to wait until they were ready to go home. I told them that I was on probation but they didn't care —"

"You don't have to lie to me, boy. Come on, let's sit."

They sat across from each other over a low coffee table. Twill lit up a menthol cigarette and Leonid enjoyed the smoke secondhand.

Twill was thin and on the short side but he carried himself with understated self-importance. The bigger kids left him alone and the girls were always calling. His father, whoever he was, had some Negro in him. Leonid was grateful for that. Twill was the son he felt closest to.

"Somethin' wrong, Dad?"

"Why you ask that?"

"'Cause you're not ridin' me. Somethin' happen?"

"An old friend died today."

"A guy?"

"No. A woman named Gert Longman."

"When's the funeral?"

"I — I don't know," Leonid said, realizing that he never wondered who would bury his ex-lover. Her parents were dead. Her two brothers were in prison.

"I'll go with you, Dad. Just tell me when it is and I'll cut school."

With that Twill got up and headed for his bedroom. At the door he stopped and turned.

"Hey, Dad."

"What?"

"What happened to the guy slammed you in the jaw?"

"They had to carry him out."

Twill gave the father of his heart a thumbs-up and then moved into the darkness of the doorway.

Leonid was at work at five. It was dark in Manhattan and in New Jersey across the river. He'd put twenty-five hundred dollars in Katrina's wallet, dropped the film off at Krome Addict Four-Hour Developing Service, and bought an egg sandwich with Bermuda onions and American cheese. He didn't turn on the lights. As the morning wore on the dawn slowly invaded his room. The sky cleared and then opened — after a while it turned blue.

Carson Kitteridge came to the door a little before seven.

Leonid ushered him to the back office where they took their regular seats.

"Did you and Gertie have a fight, Leo?" the cop asked.

"No. Not really. I mean I mighta got a little fresh and she had to show me the door but I was sorry. I wanted to take her out to dinner. You're not dumb enough to think that I would have killed Gert?"

"If somebody gave me information that you were involved with John Wilkes Booth I'd take the time to check it out, Leon. That's just the kind of guy I think you are."

"Listen, man. I have never killed anybody. Never pulled a trigger, never ordered a job done. I didn't kill Gert."

"You called her," Kitteridge said. "You called her from that phone on your desk just about when she was getting killed. It speaks to your innocence but one wonders what you had to talk to her about at that hour, on that night? What were you apologizing for?"

"I told you — I got a little fresh."

"And here I thought you had a wife."

"Listen. She was my friend. I liked her — a lot. I don't know who did that to her but if I find out you can be sure that I'll let you know."

Kitteridge made a silent clapping gesture.

"Get the fuck out of my office," Leonid said.

"I have a few more questions."

"Ask 'em out in the hall." Leonid stood up from his chair. "I'm through with you."

The policeman waited a moment. Maybe he thought that Leonid would sit back down. But as the seconds ticked by on the wall clock it began to dawn on him that Leonid's feelings were actually hurt.

"You're serious?" he asked.

"As a heart attack. Now get your ass outta here and come back with a warrant if you expect to talk to me again."

Kitteridge stood.

"I don't know what you're playing here, Leon," he said. "But you can't put out the law."

"But I can put out an asshole who doesn't have a warrant."

The lieutenant delayed another moment and then began to move.

Leonid followed him down the hall and to the door, which he slammed behind the lawman. He kicked another hole in the wall and marched back to his office, where his gut began to ache from whiskey and bile.

"Yes, Ms. Brown," Leonid was saying to his client on the telephone later that afternoon. "I have the photographs right here. It wasn't an older woman like you suspected."

"But it was a woman?"

"More like a girl."

"Is there any question about their, um . . . their relationship?"

"No. There's no doubt of the intimate nature of their relationship. What do you want me to do with these pictures and how will we settle accounts?"

"Can you bring them to me? To my apartment? I'll have the money you put out and there's one more thing that I'd like you to do."

"Sure I'll come by to you if that's what you want. What's the address?"

Karmen Brown lived on the sixth floor. He pressed the number she gave him, sixty-two, and found her waiting at the door.

The demure young thing had on a dark brown leather skirt that wouldn't keep her modest if she sat without crossing her legs. Her blouse had the top three buttons undone. She wasn't a large-breasted girl but what she had was mostly visible.

Her delicate features were serious but Leonid wouldn't have called her brokenhearted.

"Come in, Mr. McGill."

The apartment was small — like Gert's.

There was a table in the middle with a brown manila folder on it. Leonid held a similar folder in his right hand.

"Sit down," Karmen said, gesturing toward a blue sofa.

In front of the couch was a small table holding up a decanter half-filled with an amber fluid and flanked by two squat glasses.

Leonid opened the folder and reached for the photographs he'd taken.

She held up a hand to stop him.

"Will you join me in a drink first?" the young siren asked.

"I think I will."

She poured and they both slugged back hard.

She poured again.

After three stiff drinks and with a new one in her glass Karmen said, "I loved him more than anything, you know."

"Really?" Leonid said, his eyes drifting between her cleavage and her crossed legs. "He seemed like kind of a loser to me."

"I would die for him," she said, gazing steadily into Leonid's eyes.

He brought out the dozen or so pictures.

"For this louse? He doesn't even respect you or her." Leonid felt the whiskey behind his eyes and under his tongue. "Look at him with his hand under her dress like that."

"Look at this," she replied.

Leonid looked up to see her ample mound of pubic hair. Karmen had pulled up her skirt, revealing that she wore nothing underneath.

"This is my revenge," she said. "You want it?"

"Yes, ma'am," Leonid answered, thinking that this was the other *thing* she wanted him to take care of.

He had been half-aroused since the last night he saw Gert. Not sexy but prey to a sexual hunger. The whiskey set that hunger free.

She got down on her knees on the blue sofa and Leonid dropped his pants. He didn't remember the last time he'd been that eager for sex. He felt like a teenager. But push as he would he couldn't press into her.

Finally she said, "Wait a minute, Daddy," and reached around to lubricate his erection with her own saliva.

After his first full thrust he knew he was going to come. He couldn't do anything about it.

"Do it, Daddy! Do it!" she cried.

Leonid thought about Gert, realizing at that moment that he had always loved her, and about Katrina who he was never good enough for. He thought about that poor child so much in love with her man that she had to have revenge on him by giving her love away to an overweight, middle-aged gumshoe. All of that went through his mind but nothing could stand in the way of the pulsing rhythm. He was slamming against Karmen Brown's slender backside. She was yelling. He was yelling.

And then it was over — just like that. Leonid didn't even feel the ejaculation. It all blended into his violent, spasmodic attack.

Karmen had been thrown to the floor. She was crying.

He reached to help her up but she pulled away.

"Leave me alone," she said. "Let me go."

She was in a heap with her skirt up around her waist and the slick sheen of spit on her thighs.

Leonid pulled up his pants. He felt something like guilt about having had sex with the girl. She was only just a few years older than his wife's girl, the daughter of the Chinese jeweler.

"You owe me three hundred dollars," he said.

Maybe sometime in the future he'd tell someone that the best tail he ever had paid him three hundred dollars for the privilege.

"It's in the envelope on the table. There's a thousand dollars there. That and the ring and the bracelet he gave me. I want you to give them back to him. Take it and go. Go."

Leonid tore open the envelope. There he found the money, a ring with a large ruby in it, and a tennis bracelet lined with quarter-karat diamonds.

"What do you want me to tell him?" Leonid asked.

"You won't have to say a word."

Leonid wanted to say something but he didn't.

He went out the door, deciding to take the stairs rather than wait for the elevator.

On the first flight down he thought about Karmen Brown begging for sex and then crying so bitterly. On the third flight he started thinking about Gert. He wanted to reach out and touch her but she was gone.

On the first floor he passed a tattooed young man waiting at the elevator doors.

When Leonid glanced at the young man he looked away.
He was wearing leather gloves.
Leonid went out the door and turned westward.
He took four steps, five.
He made it all the way to the end of the block and it was then, when he had the urge to take off his jacket, because of the heat, that he wondered why somebody would be wearing leather gloves on a hot day. He thought about the tattoos and the image of a motorcycle came into his mind.
It had been parked right outside Karmen Brown's front door.

He pressed every buzzer on the wall until someone let him in. He was even ready to run up the stairs but the elevator was there and open.
On the ride he was trying to make sense out of it.
The doors slid open and he lurched toward Karmen's apartment.
The young man with the tattooed arms was coming out. He jumped back and reached for his pocket but Leonid leaped and hit him. The young man took the punch hard but he held on to the pistol. Leonid grabbed his hand and they embraced, performing an intricate dance that revolved around their strengths and that gun. When the kid wrenched the pistol from Leonid's hand the heavier man let his weight go dead and they fell to the floor. The gun went off.
Leonid felt a sharp pain at just about the place that his liver was situated. He leaped back from the motorcycle man, grabbing at his belly. There was blood on the lower half of his shirt.
"Shit!" he cried.
His mind went to November 1963. He was fifteen and devastated at the assassination of Kennedy. Then Oswald was shot by Ruby. Shot in the liver and in excruciating pain.
That's when Leo realized that his pain had passed. He turned toward his opponent and saw that he was lying on his back, gasping for air. And then, mid-gasp, he stopped breathing.
Realizing that the blood on him was the kid's, Leo stood up.
Karmen lay on the floor in the corner, naked. Her eyes were open and very, very bloodshot. Her throat was dark from strangulation.

But she wasn't dead.

When Leonid leaned over her those destroyed eyes recognized him. A deep gurgling went off in her throat and she tried to hit him. She croaked a loud inarticulate curse and actually sat up. The exertion was too much. She died in a sitting position, her head bowed over her knees.

There was no blood under her nails.

Why was she naked? Leonid wondered.

He went into the bathroom to check the tub — but it was dry.

He thought about calling the hospital but . . .

The kid had used a .22 caliber long-barrel pistol. Leonid was sure that it was the pistol Nora Parsons said that she lost seventeen years before.

In her wallet the dead girl's license had the name Lana Parsons.

It was then that Leonid felt the heat from her jewelry and cash in his own pocket.

The killer had a backpack. It contained two stamped envelopes. One was addressed to a lawyer named Mazer and the other to Nora Parsons in Montclair, New Jersey.

The letter to her mother included one of the photographs that Leonid had taken of Richard Mallory and his girlfriend.

Dear Mom,

While you were in the Bahamas with Richard last year I went to your house looking for anything that might have belonged to dad. You know that I loved him so much. I just thought you might have something I could remember him by.

I found a rusty old metal box in the garage. You still had the key in the hardware drawer. I guess it shouldn't surprise me that you hired a detective to prove that daddy was stealing from his company. He must have told you and you figured you could keep his money and your boyfriends while he was dying in prison.

I waited for a long time to figure out what to do about it. Finally I decided to use the man you used to kill daddy to break your heart. Here's a picture of your precious Richard and his real girlfriend. The boy you say you love. The boy you sent through college. What do you think about that?

And I took the report Leonid McGill made about daddy. I'm sending it to my lawyer. Maybe he can prove some kind of conspiracy. I'm sure you framed daddy and if the lawyer can prove it then maybe they'll send both of you to prison. Maybe even Mr. McGill would testify against you.

See you in court.
Your loving daughter,
Lana

To the lawyer she sent a yellowing and frayed report that Leonid had made many years before. It detailed how Nora's husband kept a secret account with money that he'd embezzled from a discretionary fund he controlled. Leonid remembered the meeting with Mrs. Parsons. She'd said that she couldn't trust a man who was a thief. Leo didn't argue. He was just there to collect his check.

Lana had included a copy of the letter to her mother in the lawyer's envelope. She asked him to help her get justice for her father.

Leonid washed his hands carefully and then removed any sign that he had been in the girl's apartment. He rubbed down every surface and the glass he drank from. He gathered the evidence he'd brought and the unmailed letters, then buttoned his coat over the bloody shirt and hurried away from the crime scene.

Twill was wearing a dark blue suit with a pale yellow shirt and maroon tie that had a wavering blue line orbiting its center. Leonid wondered where his son got such a fine suit but he didn't ask.

They were the only two in the small funeral parlor chapel where Gert Longman lay in an open pine coffin. She looked smaller than she had in life. Her stiff face seemed to be fashioned from wax.

The Wyant brothers fronted him fifty-five hundred dollars for the funeral. They gave him their preferential rate of two points a week.

Leonid lingered at the casket while Twill stood to the side — half a step behind him.

Behind the pair two rows of folding chairs sat like a mute crowd of spectators. The director had set the room for a service but Leonid didn't know if Gert was religious. Neither did he know any of her friends.

After the forty-five minutes they were allotted Twill and Leonid left the Little Italy funeral home. They came out onto the bright sun shining on Mott Street.

"Hey, Leon," a voice called from behind them.

Twill turned but Leonid did not.

Carson Kitteridge, dressed in a dark gold suit, walked up.

"Lieutenant. You met my son Twill."

"Isn't it a school day, son?" the cop asked.

"Grief leave, Officer," Twill said easily. "Even prison lets up in cases like that."

"What you want, Carson?" Leonid said.

He looked up over the policeman's head. The sky was what Gert used to call blue-gorgeous. That was back in the days when they were still lovers.

"I thought that you might want to know about Mick Bright."

"Who?"

"We got an anonymous call five days ago," Carson said. "It was about a disturbance in an apartment building on the Upper East Side."

"Yeah?"

"When the officers got there they found a dead girl named Lana Parsons and this Mick Bright — also dead."

"Who killed 'em?" Leonid asked, measuring his breath.

"Looks like a rape and robbery. The kid was an addict. He knew the girl from the Performing Arts high school."

"But you said that he was dead too?"

"I did, didn't I? Best the detectives could tell the kid was high and fell on his own gun. It went off and nicked his heart."

While saying this Carson stared deeply into McGill's eyes.

Twill glanced at his father and then looked away.

"Stranger things have happened," Leonid said.

Leonid had long since realized that Lana found the pistol in her mother's metal box too. He knew why she'd killed Gert and had Bright kill her. She wanted to hurt him and then send him off to prison like he'd done to her father.

It was as good a frame as he would have thought up himself. The lawyer would make the letters available to the cops. Once they suspected Leonid they'd match his semen inside her. She would expect him to have kept the expensive jewelry. Robbery, rape, and murder and he would have been as innocent as Joe Haller.

I'd die for him, she'd said. She was talking about her father.

"I been knowing about the case for days," Kitteridge said. "The girl's name stuck in my head and then I remembered. Lana Parsons was the daughter of Nora Parsons. You ever hear of her?"

"Yeah. I brought her information about her husband. She was considering a divorce."

"That's right," Kitteridge said. "But he wasn't fooling around. He was embezzling money from their own company. They sent him to jail on the dirt you dug up."

"Yeah."
"He died in prison, didn't he?"
"I wouldn't know."

Leonid burned the letters Lana had intended to incriminate him.

His work for Lana's mother had driven the girl to murder and suicide. For a while he considered sending the photograph of Richard and his girlfriend to Lana's mother. At least he could accomplish one thing that she intended to do. But he decided against it. Why hurt Nora when he was just as guilty?

He kept the picture, though, in the top drawer of his desk. The shot of Richard with his hand up under the receptionist's red dress, out on Park Avenue after a spicy Brazilian feast. Next to that he had placed an item from the *New York Post*. It was a thumbnail article about a prisoner on Ryker's Island named Joe Haller. He'd been arrested for robbery. While waiting to stand trial he hung himself in his cell.

JOYCE CAROL OATES

So Help Me God

FROM *The Virginia Quarterly Review*

PHONE RINGS. My cousin Andrea answers.

It's a pelting-rain weekday evening last April, just past 7 P.M. and dark as midnight.

Without so much as glancing toward me Andrea picks up the receiver as if she's in her own home and not mine, shifting her infant daughter onto her left hip in a way to make you think of a migrant farm wife in a classic Walker Evans photograph of the 1930s.

Phone rings! I will wish I'd snatched the receiver from her hand, slammed it down before any words were exchanged.

But Andrea is answering in her wishing-to-be-surprised high school voice, not taking time to squint at the caller ID my husband, a St. Lawrence County law enforcement officer, has had installed for precisely these evenings when he's on the night shift and his young wife is alone in this house in the country except for the accident of Andrea dropping by with the baby and interfering with my life.

"Yes? *Who* is this?"

Andrea laughs, blinking and staring past me. Whoever is on the other end of the line is intriguing to her, I can see.

I'm checking the digital code which has come up UNAVAILABLE. Sometimes it reads NO DATA GIVEN which is the same as UNAVAILABLE and a signal you don't want to pick up. At least, I don't. In Au Sable Forks, which is the center and circumference of my world, everyone is acquainted with everyone else and has been so since grade school. It's rare that an unknown name comes up for on the fingers of one hand I can count the people likely to be calling me at this or any hour which is why ordinarily I'd have let UN-

AVAILABLE leave a message on the machine figuring it must be for my husband.

UNAVAILABLE could be *anyone*. Like seeing on your doorstep a hulking individual wearing a paper bag over his head, or a ski mask. Do you throw open the door?

I could wring Andrea's neck the way she's smiling, shaking her head, "*Which* one? *Who?*" opening the damn door wide. Wish I'd never called her this afternoon hinting I was lonely.

This pelting rain! The kind of rain that hammers at your head like unwanted thoughts.

Andrea hands over the phone saying in a low thrilled voice, "It's this person won't identify himself but I think it's Pitman."

Pitman! My husband. His first name is Luke but everyone calls him Pitman.

Andrea shivers giving me the receiver. There has been this shivery thing between her and Pitman dating back to before Pitman and I were married. When I'm in a suspicious mood I think it might predate my meeting Pitman when I was fourteen, an honors student vowing to remain a virgin all my life. I've never confronted either of them.

Pitman says my Daddy injected my vertebrae with Rayburn family pride, why I walk like there's a broomstick up my rear. Why I'm so stiff (Pitman is just teasing!) in bed.

"Yes? Who is this please?" I'm determined to remain cool and poised for Pitman and I parted early this morning with some harsh words flung about on both our sides like gravel. My husband is known as a man who flares up quickly in anger but, flaring down, which can be just a few minutes later, he expects me to laugh, forgive and forget as if nothing hurtful passed between us. Pitman is a longtime joker and this wouldn't be the first time he has played phone games with me so I'm primed to hear his voice in this deep-gravelly male voice so suddenly intimate in my ear asking: "Are you Ms. Pitman, the lady of the house?" Quick as Ping Pong I say, "Mister, who are you? I don't talk to strangers."

You'd think that after living with a man for more than five years and being crazy in love with him for six years preceding you'd at least recognize his phone voice, but damned if Pitman hasn't disguised it with something like pebbles in his mouth (?) or a layer of some fabric over the phone receiver, and speaking with the broad A's of a Canadian! Also he's making me nervous so I am not thinking as clearly as usual. The voice is chiding, "Ms. Pitman! You sound like some stiff-back old Rayburn," which convinces me that this is Pitman, who else. My face is hot and eyes tearing up as they do with any strong emotion, sweat breaking out on my body, I hate how Pitman has this effect upon me, and my cousin a witness. The voice is inquiring, "Is this 'Pitman' an individual of some size and reputation?" — a strange thing to ask, I'm thinking.

So I say, "'Pitman' is a law enforcement officer of dubious reputation, a cruel tease I am considering reporting to authorities." My teasing with Pitman is never so inspired or easy as his with me, it's like wrestling with Pitman on our bed: I'm a scrawny ninety-seven pounds, half his size. The voice responds quick as if alarmed, "Hang on, now, *baby:* what authorities?" and I hear *baby*, this has got to be Pitman, *baby* in his mouth and it's like he has touched me between the legs and any ice-scrim that has built up between us begins rapidly to melt. I'm saying, my voice rising, "He knows who! So he'd better stop playing games," and the voice says in mock alarm, or maybe, genuine alarm, "What authorities? Sheriff? Police?" and I say, "Pitman, damn! Stop this," but the voice persists, "Is this 'Pitman' armed and dangerous at all times, baby?" and there's something about this question, a strangeness of diction, the sick sensation washes over me, *This isn't Pitman* and my throat shuts up, and the voice continues to tease, husky and breathy in my ear, "Fuck Pitman, baby — what are you wearing?" and I slam down the receiver.

Andrea takes my hands, says they are like ice.

"Oh, Lucretia! Wasn't it Pitman, I thought for sure it was."

Andrea thinks that I should report the call and I tell her yes, I will tell Pitman and he can report it. He's a law enforcement officer, he will know best how to proceed.

Things you do when you're crazy in love, you'll look back upon with astonishment. Maybe a kind of pride. Thinking *That could not have been me. I am not that person.*

When I married Pitman, my Daddy disowned me. Daddy had come to believe that Pitman had cast some sort of spell over me. I was not his daughter any longer. I had not been his daughter for some time.

My father was a stubborn man but I was stubborn, too.

Eighteen when I married Lucas Pitman, old enough to be legally married in New York State, but not old enough to be so coldly discarded by my father whom I loved. I'd come to believe that I hated Daddy and this was so, but I loved Daddy, too. I would never forgive him!

My mother disapproved of Pitman, of course. But knew better than to forbid me marrying him. She'd seen how Pitman had worked his way under my skin, cast his "spell" over me. She'd known long before Daddy had. Back when I was fourteen, in fact. Skinny pale-blond girl with sly eyes given to believe that, because she's conceded to be the smartest student in the sophomore class at Au Sable High, she can't mess up her life like any trailer-trash Adirondack girl.

I never did get pregnant, though. Pitman saw to that.

Luke Pitman was the youngest deputy in the St. Lawrence County sheriffs department when we first met: twenty-three. He'd been hired out of the police academy at Potsdam and before that he'd served in the navy. There were Pitmans scattered through the county, most of them with reputations. To have a "reputation" means nothing good except when it's made clear what the reputation is for: integrity, honesty, business ethics, and Christian morals. For instance, Everett Rayburn, my father, had a reputation in St. Lawrence County and beyond as an "honest" contractor and builder. Everett Rayburn was "reliable" — "good-as-his-word" — "decent." Only the well-to-do could afford to hire him and in turn Daddy could afford to hire only the best carpenters, painters, electricians, plumbers. Daddy wasn't an architect but he'd designed our house which was the most impressive in Au Sable Forks, a split-level "contemporary-traditional" on Algonquin Drive. In school I hated how I had to be friends with the few "rich" kids. I got along with the trailer-trash kids a lot better.

There were Pitmans who lived in trailers as well as in dilapidated old farmhouses in the area. Pitman himself was from Star Lake in the Adirondacks but he'd moved out of his parents' house at the age of fifteen. He told me he had a hard time living in any kind of close quarters with other people and if our marriage was going to endure I would have to grant him "space."

Right away I asked Pitman would he grant me "space" too and Pitman said, tugging my ponytail so it hurt: "That depends, baby."

"Like there's a law for you, but a different law for me?"

"Damn right, baby."

You couldn't argue with Pitman. He'd stop your mouth with his mouth. You tried to speak and he'd suck out your breath. You tried to get serious with him and he'd laugh at you.

How I met Pitman was quite a story I never told it to anyone except Andrea.

I was bicycling back home from Andrea's house in the country. She lived about a mile and a half outside Au Sable Forks which is not an actual town but a "village." Summers, Andrea and I bicycled back and forth to see each other all the time; it was something to do. Andrea had more household chores than I did and my bicycle was newer and faster than hers and I was the one who got restless and bored so it was usually me on my bicycle slow and dreamy and coasting when I could and not paying much attention to cars and pickups that swung out to pass me. It was late August and boring-hot and I was wearing white shorts, a little green Gap T-shirt, flip-flops on my feet; I wasn't so young as I looked. My ash-blond ponytail swept halfway down my back and my toenails were painted this bright sparkly green Daddy insisted I had to cover up, wear socks or actual shoes at mealtimes. I was maybe smiling thinking of how Daddy got upset, or pretended to, at the least "infraction" of household rules on my part, when Pitman came cruising in the car marked ST. LAWRENCE CO. SHERIFF. I wasn't paying too much attention to this vehicle coming up behind me until a male voice came out of nowhere: "You, girl — got a license for that bike?"

I didn't know Pitman, then. Didn't know what you'd call Pitman-teasing. Almost crashed my bicycle, I was so scared. For there was this police officer glaring out his car window at me. He wasn't smiling. His aviator sunglasses were tinted so dark I couldn't see his eyes except they were not friendly eyes. His hair was tarry-black and shaved at the sides and back of his head but grew long and tufted on top like a rock musician's. How old he was, I couldn't have guessed. I was so scared I could hardly focus my eyes.

What followed next, Pitman would recount with laughter, in the years to come. I guess it was funny! Him demanding to see my "bike license" and me stammering I didn't have one, didn't know you had to have a license to ride a bicycle . . . Fourteen years old and scared as a little kid, calling Pitman "sir" and "officer" and Pitman had all he could do to keep from laughing. He'd say afterward he

So Help Me God

had seen me riding my bike on the Hunter Road more than once, looked like I was in this dream-world pedaling along on an expensive bicycle oblivious of other vehicles even when they passed close to me. He'd had a thought that here was a little blond princess needed a shaking-up for once.

I just didn't get it was a joke. The way Pitman grilled me asking my name, my Daddy's name, and what did my Daddy do for a living, what was my address and telephone number. These facts he seemed to be taking down on a notepad. (He was.) I was straddling my bike by the roadside trying not to cry staring at Pitman who so captivated my attention it was like the earth had opened up, I was slipping and falling inside. Pitman must've seen my knobby knees shaking but he kept on his interrogation with no mercy.

Daddy would say Pitman had cast a spell on his only daughter, when Daddy was being nasty he'd call it a sex-spell and I concede that this was so, Pitman's power over girls and women was sexual but it was more than only this, I swear. For there was this Pitman-soul you saw in the man's eyes when he was in one of his moods, or you felt in the heat of his skin, a soul that was pure flame: a weird wild happiness like electricity coursing through him. Just to touch it was dangerous, but you had to touch!

Can't take your eyes off him, he's beautiful.

"Well, now. 'Lucretia Rayburn.' Seeing as how you are a minor, maybe I won't run you into headquarters. Maybe just a ticket."

By this time most of the blood had drained out of my face, my lips must have been stark-white. Trembling, and fighting tears. I was so grateful, Pitman was taking pity on me. But before I could thank him, he said, as if the thought had only just occurred to him: how old was that bicycle, where had it been purchased and how much did it cost? "Looks like a pretty expensive bicycle, Lucretia, One of them 'mountain bikes.' You got the bill of sale for that bike, girl, to prove it ain't stolen property?"

I did just about break down, at this. Had to say I didn't have any bill of sale but my father might have it, at home. Please could I go home? Pitman shakes his head gravely saying he has no choice but to "confiscate" the bike and run me into headquarters after all — "See! they got to take your prints, Lucretia Rayburn, and run 'em into the computer. See if they match up with known felons. For all I know, you ain't even 'Lucretia Rayburn,' you're just impersonating her" And I'm stammering *no please, officer, please.* But Pitman has climbed out of the cruiser to loom above me frowning and severe-seeming. He's six foot two or three, a hard-muscled youngish man in a uniform made of a silvery-blue material and I'm seeing that he's wearing a gold-glinting badge and a leather belt and holster and in the holster there's a gun, and a roaring comes up in my ears like I'm going to faint. Pitman takes my arm, not hard, but firm, and Pitman leads me around to the passenger's side of the cruiser, sits me down in the seat like I was a little girl and not this skinny-leggy girl of fourteen with a glamour ponytail halfway down her back. He notes the sparkly green toenail polish but refrains from comment. Takes from his belt a pair of metal handcuffs that are these adult-sized cuffs and says, still not cracking a smile, "Got to cuff you, Lucretia. It's for your own protection, too." By this time I'm sick with shame. I can't think how this nightmare will end. Pitman takes my arms that are covered in goose pimples from fear of him, gently draws them behind my back and slips on the cuffs and snaps them shut. These cuffs twice the size of my wrists! Yet I still didn't catch on that Pitman was teasing. There wasn't much teasing in the Rayburn household where I was the only child, born late to my parents and so prized by them you'd think I was sickly or handicapped in some secret way. Pitman would say afterward he was beginning to be worried, I was some poor retarded girl, only looked like a normal blond-princess type with the most beautiful brown doe-eyes he'd ever seen.

"You having trouble with them cuffs, Lucretia? Not resisting arrest, are you?"

This comical sight: I'm so scared of this uniformed man looming over me, I am actually trying to keep the damn handcuffs from sliding off my wrists behind my back.

Finally Pitman laughs aloud. And I realize he isn't serious, none of this is serious. Pitman's laughter isn't cruel like you'd expect from boys my age but a tender kind of male laughter that enters my heart with such suddenness and warmth, I think I began to love Pitman right then. This St. Lawrence County deputy sheriff who has scared the hell out of me has become my rescuer, hauling me up from drowning. Saying, "If the damn cuffs don't fit how'm I gonna arrest you, girl? Might as well let you go."

For a moment I just sit there, dazed. It's like a bad dream ending, I can't believe that I am free.

The smell of the man (hair oil, tobacco, spearmint chewing gum) is close and pungent in my nostrils. The feel of the man (a stranger, touching my bare arms!) will remain with me for a long time.

Last thing Pitman tells me, deadpan, he won't be writing up his report — "Best keep it a secret between us, Lucretia."

Pitman climbs back into the police cruiser and drives off. But I know he's watching me in his rearview mirror as I get back onto my bike and pedal behind him, shaky and self-conscious. I can feel how my little Gap T-shirt is damp with sweat. I can feel the muscles straining in my bare legs as I pedal the bike, and I can feel the thrill of my quickened heartbeat.

Something has happened to me! I have become someone special.

Three years, two months and eleven days after the handcuffs, Pitman and I were married.

Daddy disowned me and good riddance! — I disowned *him.*

A wife cleaves to her husband and forsakes all else. I think so. Mom was hurt, heartbroken, wet-hen-furious, but couldn't stay away from her only daughter's wedding. (In secret) she harbored a liking for Sheriff's Deputy Lucas Pitman herself.

It was hard to resist Pitman when he wished to make you like him. A man that size deferring to Mom, calling her "Mrs. Rayburn" like she was the most gracious lady he'd ever met. (Probably, Mom was.) Called her "ma'am" with such courtesy, like her own son, she'd forget objections she was trying to make.

Till finally Mom hugged me one day, conceding, "Your husband certainly adores you, Lucretia. Maybe that's all that matters."

"All that matters to me, Mom."

I spoke a little stiffly. In this matter of allegiance a wife cleaves to her husband. She is reticent with her mother. Anything else is betrayal.

We had our honeymoon house. A rented, winterized bungalow outside town. Pitman whistled painting the outside robin's-egg blue that dried a brighter and sharper color than the paint sample indicated, and I made a mess painting the rooms inside: pale yellow, ivory. The little bedroom was hardly big enough for our jangly brass bed we'd bought at a farm sale. This bed for one oversized man and one undersized girl, I took pride outfitting with the nicest sheets, goose-feather pillows, and a beautiful old handmade quilt in purple and lavender. This bed Pitman and I would end up in, or on, more times a day than just nighttime.

Only a coincidence: our honeymoon house was close by the Hunter Road. In the foothills east of Au Sable Forks. Mt. Hammer in the distance. Our bedroom overlooked a branch of the Au Sable Creek that sounded like rushing wind when the water level was high and like a faint teasing trickle by late summer when the water level was low. Our house was exactly 2.6 miles from my parents' house in town.

Some months after we came to live here, Pitman was assigned to a new shift. Later hours, farther away. Now he and his partner patrolled little crossroads mountain towns like Malvern, North Fork, Chapprondale, Stony Point, and Star Lake. From his miffed attitude I had to conclude that Pitman wasn't happy with this assignment but he'd only joke: "That's where a cop can expect to get it. Up in the hills."

It's cruel for a law enforcement officer to joke in this way with his wife but that was Pitman for you. Seeing tears in my eyes he'd turn repentant, brushing them away with his big thumbs and kissing me hard on the mouth. Saying, "Never mind, baby. Nobody's gonna get me."

This seemed likely. Pitman was fearless. But Pitman was also shrewd and knew to watch his back.

This night. It was a turn, I'd come to see later.

Pitman came home late from his night shift smelling of beer, fell into our bed only partly undressed, hugging me so tight my ribs were in danger of cracking. He hadn't wakened me from any actual sleep but I was pretending so. Pitman disliked me to be waiting up for him and worrying so I had a way of feigning sleep, even with the bedside lamp and the TV on. In those early months I was grateful my husband came home at all, wasn't shot down or run off the highway by some maniac, I'd forgive him anything, or almost.

Pitman hid his hot face in my neck. Said, shuddering like a horse tormented by flies: "This thing over in Star Lake, baby. It's ugly."

Star Lake. Pitman's old hometown. He had family there he kept his distance from. There'd been a murder/suicide in a cabin above Star Lake, detectives from the sheriff's office were investigating. Not from Pitman but from other sources I knew that a Star Lake man had strangled his wife and killed himself with some kind of firearm. I had not heard that any Pitmans were involved and was hoping this was so. Pitman had many blood relatives with names not known to me including some living on the Tuscarora Indian reservation.

I had learned not to press Pitman on certain matters having to do with his job or any of his personal life in fact. He'd promised he would always tell me what I was required to know. He would not upset me with the things he saw that upset him. Or things a woman would not wish to know. Law enforcement officers have this way about them: they don't answer questions, they ask. If you ask you see a steely light come into their eyes warning you to back off.

Pitman was asking did I know what a garrote was, and I right away said no, no I did not know what a garrote was, though in fact I did, but I knew that Pitman would not wish his eighteen-year-old wife who had only graduated from high school a few months before to know such a thing. Pitman raised himself above me on his elbows peering into my face. He had horse-eyes that seemed just a little too large for his face, beautiful dark staring eyes showing a rim of white above the iris. They were eyes to express mirth, wonderment, rage. They were not eyes to make you feel comfortable. Pitman said, "A garrote is a thing used to strangle. It's two things. It's a thing like a cord or a scarf you wrap around somebody's throat, and it's a thing like a tick or a rod you twist that with. So you don't have to touch the throat with your actual hands."

Pitman was touching my throat with his hands, though. His hands that were strong, and big. Circling my throat with his fingers and thumbs and squeezing. Not hard but hard enough.

I laughed and pushed at him. I wasn't going to be frightened by Pitman-teasing.

I asked if that was how the woman at Star Lake was strangled, and Pitman ignored my question as if it had not been asked. He was leaning above me staring at me. I remembered how at the wedding ceremony he'd been watching me sidelong, and when he caught my eye he winked. Just between the two of us, a flame-flash of understanding. Like Pitman was thinking of that first secret between us, how he'd handcuffed me in the police cruiser on Hunter Road.

How reckless Pitman had been! Risking all hell playing such a trick on a fourteen-year-old girl. Misusing his authority. *Sexual harassment* it would have been called if given a name. Except we'd been fated to meet, Pitman believed. That day or some other, in a town small as Au Sable Forks, we'd have met and fallen in love.

Of course I'd never told my parents. It was the great secret of my girlhood as it marked the end of my girlhood. Never told anyone except my cousin Andrea but by that time I was seventeen, a senior in high school confounding my parents and teachers by deciding not to apply for college as I'd been planning and everyone was expecting of me.

(Secretly) engaged to Pitman by then. (Secretly) making love with Pitman every chance I had.

He was saying now, stumbling out the words as they came to him: "A garrote takes time. A garrote takes planning. Anybody who garrotes his victim, it's 'premeditated.' There's a sick purpose to it, Lucretia. You wouldn't know."

Damn right, I wouldn't know! I was trying not to panic pushing at Pitman's hands, easing them from my throat. His big thumbs I grasped in both my hands as a child might. It wasn't the first time Pitman had put his hands on me in a way to frighten me but it was the first time when we hadn't been making love and it hadn't seemed like an accident.

Pitman said, "See, if you garrote somebody you can strangle her till she passes out, then you can revive her. You can strangle her till she passes out again, then you can revive her. You don't exert any pressure with your own hands. Your own hands are spared. It's a cruel method but effective. It's the way Spaniards used to execute condemned prisoners. It's rare, in the United States."

This was a long speech for Pitman. He was drunker than he'd seemed at first, and very tired. I knew not to let on any uneasiness I felt for that would offend Pitman who deemed himself my protector. I only laughed now, pulled his hands more firmly away from my throat and leaned up awkwardly to kiss him.

"Mmmm, Pitman, come to bed. We both need to sleep."

I helped Pitman pull off more of his clothes. He was big and floppy like a fish. By the time I leaned over to switch out the lamp Pitman was asleep and snoring.

It was that night the thought came to me for the first time: *It's a garrote I am in.*

"Such an ugly story! Those people."

My mother spoke with repugnance, disdain. *Those people* referred

So Help Me God

to people who got themselves killed, written up in local papers. People of a kind the Rayburns didn't know.

I was in my mother's kitchen reading the *Au Sable Weekly*. For some reason our paper hadn't been delivered. On the front page was an article about the murder/suicide in Star Lake fifteen miles to the east. The name was Burdock not Pitman. I resolved that I would not make inquiries whether the two might be related. It was my reasoning that mountain towns like Star Lake are so small and remote, inhabitants are likely to be related to one another more frequently than they are elsewhere. If Pitman was related to the wife-murderer/suicide Amos Burdock it wouldn't be helpful for me to know.

"I didn't actually finish reading it." Mom sat across from me, pushing a plate of something in my direction. It is a mother's destiny always to seduce with home-baked cookies evocative of someone's lost childhood but I would not eat, I would save my appetite for my own mealtimes with Pitman. "I suppose Pitman knows all about it. Is he 'investigating'?"

No mention of a garrote in the article. Only just the coroner ruled death of the female victim, the wife, by strangulation. It was secret information, evidently. Known to only a few individuals.

"Pitman isn't a detective, Mom. You know that. So, no."

Strangle, revive. Strangle, revive. The way Pitman had teased me on the Hunter Road. Scaring me, then seeming to relent. Then scaring me again. Really scaring me. And then relenting. *Best keep it a secret between us, Lucretia.*

Daddy's favorite music is opera. His favorite opera, *Don Giovanni*. Which I came to know by heart, listening to it all my life. The way Daddy took us to any production of any Shakespeare play within a fifty-mile radius and each summer for years to the Shakespeare Festival over in Stratford, Ontario.

For Daddy, *Don Giovanni* and Shakespeare were rewards for the time he spent in the world "out there." Dealing with men, customers, and employees. Dealing with building materials. Making money. Pitman seemed to think a lot of money. *Your old man's a millionaire, baby. Why you're so stuck up. Hell, you got a right.*

When I'd wanted to rile Daddy up I would say the world isn't Mozart and Shakespeare, the world is country-and-western music. The world is cable TV, Wal-Mart, *People*. I knew that I was right, Daddy's face would redden. I was the bright schoolgirl, Daddy's little girl, also something of a smart aleck, like Daddy himself. He's a handsome man for an old guy in his fifties with a high, hard little belly that looks like a soccer ball under his shirt that's usually a white starched cotton shirt. Prematurely white hair, trimmed by a barber every third Friday. Daddy would no more miss a Friday in the barber's chair than he would miss his daily morning shower.

I knew that I was right but Daddy never gave in.

"Not so, Lucretia. The world is *Don Giovanni*, and the world is Shakespeare. Minus the beauty."

Not so, Daddy. The world is plenty beautiful. If you're lucky in love.

For a long time, I believed this. I think I did.

Soon as I married Lucas Pitman, I had to know the man was *vigilant*.

Through the day he'd call on his cell phone. Mostly from the cruiser. In his lowered sexy voice saying, "My little princess is never off my radar." Asking where was I, what was I doing. What was I wearing. What was I thinking. Was I touching myself? Where?

Pitman was proud of his little blond princess-wife. A rich man's spoiled daughter he'd seduced, slept with while she was in high school, and married soon as she turned eighteen, thumbing her nose at her old man. Pitman was proud of how she adored him but he didn't like other guys staring at her. Well, he did, sure he did, but not too obviously. It had to be a subtle thing. It could not be crude. Pitman had a temper, his own friends backed off from him when he'd been drinking and was quick to take offense.

In these country places in the mountains where Pitman was known. Weekends he'd take me dancing, for a while after we were married as we'd done before we were married, and Pitman would dance like some stoned MTV kid, long legs, arms, feet as fast as my own, grabbing me and leaning me back in my high-heeled shoes, little T-shirt, and jeans tight so that the crease pinched me between the legs and Pitman could run his fingers along that crease quick and sly not minding who might be watching. Pitman the law enforcement officer out of uniform, wild to have a good time. Desperate to have a good time. He had a few cop friends, younger guys like himself. I was too young to realize that Pitman and his friends were not likely to be promoted very far up police ranks; I was too adoring of Pitman to guess that his superiors — even that Pitman had "superiors" — might not admire his brashness the way I did. His scorn was for desk work, computers, "investigating teams" that depended upon forensics lab reports and not action. He liked being in uniform, in the cruiser, and in perpetual motion. He liked the .45-caliber police service revolver visibly gleaming on his hip.

Pitman was an Adirondack boy, he'd grown up with guns. In our honeymoon bungalow he kept his "arsenal": two rifles, a Springfield double-barreled twelve-gauge shotgun, several handguns. He'd wanted to teach me to shoot so that we could go hunting (white-tailed deer, pheasant) together, but I refused — "Why'd I want to kill some beautiful blameless creature?" Pitman winked, "Well hell, baby, somebody's got to." I had to love how Pitman took boyish pride in his Smith & Wesson .45-caliber revolver with "zebra wood" gun grip he'd acquired in a poker game. He took pride in his Winchester .30-caliber deer rifle with its long sleek blue-black barrel and maplewood handle he was obsessive about keeping polished the way, at our house, my Mom kept the good silverware polished; this was the firearm Pitman kept *loaded and ready* at all times, in case of intruders, break-ins. He'd showed me where the rifle was positioned on the closet shelf, how I was to take it up and hold it, how I was to shift the safety *off* in any time of danger but I was nervous backing off, laughing and fluttering my hands. No, no! Anybody was going to protect me, it had to be my husband.

At our kitchen table while I prepared a sizzling frying-pan meal Pitman would drink Coors and listen to Neil Young, sometimes Dee Dee Ramone turned up high as he dismantled, cleaned, and oiled his long-barreled police service revolver with the tenderness you'd hope to see in a man bathing an infant. Pitman interpreted my fear of firearms as respect for him, and he liked that. Of all things Pitman required respect. The Pitmans and their numerous kin were not generally respected. They were feared and scorned in about equal measure. Pitman wished to be feared and respected in equal measure. Sure, he liked to laugh and have a good time but respect was more important. He knew of my father's disdain for fishing, hunting, guns of any kind and had a way of alluding to "your esteemed father Mr. Everett who pays other guys to do his shooting for him" that was startling to me, like for an instant Pitman's brain was sliced open and you could see the shrewdness inside, the class-hatred, anger. The next instant it was gone, Pitman liked to tease-taunt me in a way that was like sex, the prelude to sex. Telling me of the times he'd had to use his weapon. Drew his gun and aimed it as he'd been trained — and called out a warning — "Put your hands where I can see them! Put your hands where I can see them! Come forward slowly! Come forward slowly!" — but he'd had no choice except to fire. Since being sworn in as a deputy sheriff he'd had to shoot and kill two men, and he'd wounded others. Not always alone but with his partner, or others. It was rare for a law enforcement officer to use his weapon alone. Did he have any regrets, hell no. He'd never been reprimanded for excessive force. The shootings had been investigated and cleared. On one occasion, Pitman was credited for saving the life of another deputy. He'd received citations. He never dreamt about these actual shootings but he dreamt about shooting. A lot.

Pitman smiled his slow easy smile, telling me this. I felt my breath come short.

It was a requirement of the St. Lawrence County sheriff that deputies were required to fire no less than two bullets at their target if they fired one.

"Why is that? What if you change your mind?"

"You don't."

"But, if you've made a mistake..."

"You don't make a mistake."

"A deputy never makes a mistake?"

Pitman laughed at me. Those days, I never knew if I was pretending to be shocked by him or truly shocked. I saw that steely light come into his eyes. He leaned over and drew the revolver barrel along the side of my thigh, slowly. In a way that made me know he was quoting somebody he revered he said "A forty-five is not an equal opportunity employer."

The last time Pitman took me dancing.

This hillbilly tavern out on Hammer Lake. We'd been married about three years. We'd go out with other couples, the guys were friends of Pitman's. (My old high school friends, I rarely saw. They were away at college. When they came home to visit, I made ex-

So Help Me God

cuses not to see them.) Still I was Pitman's blond princess he loved to show off. Still I was in love with Pitman in terror of what it might mean if I was not. Old disco music blared on the jukebox. Music to make you laugh it's so awful yet there's the beat, the tawdry-glamour beat, raw-sex beat, gets you on your feet dancing like the floor beneath you is burning hot, you can't stop. I felt Pitman's strong arms against my ribs and smelled his breath and oiled hair and it came over me like a sickness how I missed Daddy, I missed my mom and the house on Algonquin Avenue so bad.

Sharp-eyed Pitman knew my every shift in mood.

"Where's your mind, baby? You look spaced out."

I was drunk. A few quick drinks made me drunk. And "I Will Survive" pounding on the jukebox.

I laughed and hid my face against Pitman's chest. Slid my arms around him and pressed so close against Pitman I heard his big heart beating like it was my own.

It was after Pitman's partner and close friend Reed Loomis died, Pitman began to drink mornings.

This was early in April. Not long before the anonymous calls began.

Was there some connection, yes I guess there must have been. I tried not to think what it was.

Oh, I'd liked Reed Loomis! Everybody did. The friendliest man, a blunt porky face and buzz-cut hair, more resembled a high school sports coach than a sheriff's deputy. Loomis was six years older than Pitman and even bigger than Pitman; he'd asked him to be his son's godfather and Pitman was deeply moved by the request. "Only time anybody's going to hear 'god' and 'Pitman' in the same breath."

Pitman wasn't the one to tell me, he could not utter these words, but Loomis had died of a fast-spreading pancreatic cancer. Pitman was stunned and distracted. Pitman looked like a man staring into a blinding light unable to shield his eyes. Muttering, "Can't believe it. Reed is gone." He'd been noticing how lately he was doing most of the driving in the cruiser because Loomis had a headache, trouble with his eyes, was feeling "weird," one day Loomis's legs give out in the parking lot and his white blood cell count is crazy, there's a diagnosis, and a few weeks later Loomis is dead.

Abruptly one day Pitman ceased speaking of Loomis. If I brought up the subject, he chilled me out.

Sometimes he tried to hide the morning drinking from me. Sometimes not.

"It won't bring Reed back, honey. What you're doing to yourself." (Did I say these words? These are words you say, believe me.) Pitman sneered like he was just discovering he'd married a mental defective. "This ain't for Reed, baby. This is for me."

Sometimes hearing just the intake of my breath, Pitman reacted quick as an animal defending itself. Shoving me aside, hard. "Get away! Don't touch."

And he's out the door, and gone.

It was a cold season, I wore long sleeves to hide the bruises.

Scarves tied around my neck. Makeup layered on my thin pale face and lipstick so cheery you'd expect me to burst into song.

Never said a word to Andrea. Certainly not to Mom.

Nor to Daddy who it seemed was watching me, waiting.

By this time, four years into the marriage and still living in the four-room bungalow off the Hunter Road, I understood that Daddy had forgiven me. Daddy had not a thing to say about my marriage. So much time had passed, maybe he was impressed I had not once asked him for money. In fact, Daddy had offered Pitman and me money at Christmas to buy a new car replacing the '88 Chevy Malibu but Pitman had his pride just as Daddy did, I knew to say *Oh, thanks, Daddy! But no.*

During the day Mom frequently called. A ringing phone and RAYBURN on caller ID meant my mother. Sometimes I picked up eager as a lonely child. Sometimes I backed off, sneering.

Oh, Mom was cheerful! Though cautious. An intelligent woman aware of mother-in-law jokes. She knew not to press too far with her questions. Asking how is Pitman and I told her Pitman is fine, you know Pitman. And I'm fine, Mom. What about you and Daddy.

Like a tick beneath the skin the idiot word *fine* had snagged in my vocabulary. Itchy as hell, hard to dislodge. There was always a beat, a moment when I might have told Mom more. And maybe Mom knew more. Probably yes she knew more. Au Sable Forks is a small town, word travels fast.

Mornings, afternoons! The slow slide into evening.

It was, as Pitman said, a shitty spring. Pelting rain, so much mud people laid down planks to walk on.

Cloudbursts, and a leaking roof. Like an animated cartoon figure I set out pots, pans, baking trays to catch the drips. Then the sky opened, there came blinding sunbursts. Truly, your brain is sliced open. In rubber boots I went tramping along Hunter Road, along farmers' lanes and into fields. I hiked beside Au Sable Creek where the mud-colored water rushed like a speeding vehicle. This is a part of New York State, where the sky draws your attention. Not the mountains that are mostly covered in trees, but the sky forces your eyes to lift. Always there is the anticipation of seeing something in the sky you can't name except to know you won't see it anywhere else.

This was the season I sent away for catalogues from Cornell, St. Lawrence University, McGill University in Montreal. Hiding them in the closet beneath towels, bed linens where Pitman would never look.

Cornell was where I'd been planning on going. Before I fell in love with Pitman. Except maybe this wasn't so. Maybe I'd fallen in love with him that day on the Hunter Road. The rest was just waiting.

You never think you will get old. Or even your face.

The happiest time of your life. Oh, Lucretia . . .

Mom was weepy, nagging. My senior year at Au Sable Forks High. That year I'd quit most of my "activities." Cut classes. A blur in my memory as if I'd been riding in a drunken speeding vehicle. The landscape is beautiful but moving too swiftly past to be seen.

Think what you are giving up. For that man. It's your body, Lucretia. Wanting to have babies.

I hit her then. I hit my mother. I saw my hand shoot out, I saw my mother wince, I never told anyone not even Pitman.

Didn't want Pitman to know the meanness in my heart. His blond princess.

Daddy had ceased interfering. Daddy kept his distance, a gentlemanly distance, those final months. While I was still his daughter, living at home. Could not trust himself to speak to me.

Goddamn I'd vowed I would not cry. Neither of my parents could make me cry. I wasn't their virgin-daughter, I was Pitman's girl. I would be Pitman's wife. You want to know if he fucks me, yes he fucks me. I fuck him, the way he's taught me. I don't cry for you now, I cry for Pitman. Of all the world only Pitman has that power.

The one thing Mom did, with Pitman in agreement, was arrange for a church wedding. An actual church wedding. Very small, and hurriedly arranged. Daddy threatened to stay away but was finally the gentleman, of course he came. Though stony-faced, force-smiling. Having to see how at the very altar Luke Pitman nudged his daughter in her silken white side and cast her a sidelong winking bad-boy grin.

I was repainting the bathroom, a better quality paint this time.

Smiling. I think I was smiling. Having to concede, when you're in high school you can't wait to get out, it's like a prison you have come to hate, then when you're out you look back, remembering.

I didn't drop out of school, finally. Attended my graduation with the others. My last term was the worst in all my school years, not a single A. If I hadn't broken his heart marrying a man my father considered low-life Adirondack trailer trash I'd have broken his heart getting such rotten grades.

Painting the bathroom ivory. Not hearing the phone ring.

The anonymous calls came in the evening or middle of the night when Pitman was out. Whoever it was knew Pitman's schedule. Or knew from the driveway that Pitman's car was gone.

Or it was Pitman. One of his games.

Sometimes I drifted to the phone waiting for it to ring. And it rang. And I saw UNAVAILABLE on caller ID and I smiled thinking *You can't. You have no power over me. I am not afraid of you.*

I never answered. I erased the answering tape without listening.

Well, maybe I listened. Maybe once, twice. The voice was as I'd remembered it: husky, Canadian-sounding. I had to wonder if it belonged to one of Pitman's fellow deputies. One of Pitman's relatives. Someone Pitman had made an enemy of. Gotten under the skin of. It was no one from my life, I knew.

"Hey, I know you're there, baby! Know you're listening. Whyn't you pick up, baby? Afraid?"

Pause. Breathing wetly into the mouthpiece.

"'Lady of the house, Ms. Pitman.' *Pig*man? Standin' there all alone."

Another pause. (He's trying not to laugh?)

"Maybe not alone enough, eh? Baby?"

It wasn't Pitman's way of speech, I thought. The broad Canadian vowels, the quirky *eh*? Still, this might be a trick. Pitman might be there beside the caller, listening.

After the calls when Pitman came home there was a strangeness between us. I think this was so. I don't think I was imagining it. Pitman was waiting for me to acknowledge the calls. (Was he?) But it was too late now. There had been too many. And if the calls were made by someone else, Pitman would be uncontrollable, so furious. I had to acknowledge, he might blame me.

I'd had boyfriends, a few. In school. But only just boys. And nothing sexual. Pitman knew this but possibly he'd forgotten. He was likely to be jealous. Suspicious. Why hadn't I told him after the first call? I could not tell him *But maybe it was you.*

He'd snag on a word sometimes. A word would snag on him. I wondered was this a thing that happened to drinkers.

Face, for instance.

Baby-face, he'd call me. Angel-face.

Or, "Just don't get in my face, Lucretia."

Or, "Want me to break your fucking face?"

Burdock had been a relative, in fact. He'd garroted his estranged wife, blew himself away with a shotgun. Not from Pitman did I learn this of course. Pitman never spoke of any of his relatives. His mother was still living, I think. He had an older half-brother in Attica serving a sentence of thirty years to life.

Like shrapnel working its way outward through tissue, Pitman's fury was surfacing. *Pitman! Crazy guy.* That admiring way men have of speaking of a friend who's cracking up. Bringing Pitman home falling-down drunk and the Chevy Malibu left behind as far away as Tupper Lake, in the morning I'd have to drive Pitman back to retrieve it. In June, Pitman pursued a drunk driver west out of Malvern on Route 3 resulting in the young man (twenty, from the Tuscarora reservation) crashing his vehicle into a bridge and shearing off part of his skull. The St. Lawrence County sheriff defended his deputy (publicly) but reprimanded him (privately). Pitman spoke of quitting his job. He spoke of reenlisting in the navy. He seemed, in his indignation, unaware that he'd become a man in his mid-thirties and was no longer a brash young kid of eighteen. A ring of flesh around his waist, his tar-colored hair streaking with gray and thinning. No longer could Pitman stay up much of the night drinking and rely upon three or four hours' sleep to restore his strength, his clarity of mind, and his willingness to face the next day.

From the cruiser Pitman would call on his cell: "Hey, baby, this is a fucking long morning. It ain't even noon?"

You could get addicted to it. The anger. The taste of it on his mouth like hot acid. I never believed that Pitman was crazy. He was too shrewd and methodical. Just this fury in him. It was more than Reed Loomis dying. Those little mountain towns dying. Pitman himself dying. He'd sweat through the bedclothes groaning and grinding his teeth after the boy died on Route 3, Pitman insisted he had done nothing wrong. He had followed procedure. He'd used his siren, his lights. The kid had outstanding warrants which was why probably he'd accelerated his speed to almost eighty miles an hour on that sharp-curving highway in the mountains, narrowing to a single-lane bridge. Drunk kid, thumbing his nose at the law. Pitman said fuck, he had no regrets, wasn't going to lose sleep over this one. One Sunday afternoon lying with me on our bed gripping me in his arms as if we were drowning together. Not releasing me for forty-five minutes and only then when I begged him insisting I had to pee, did he want me to wet the bed?

"You would not ever betray me, Lucretia? Would you?"

In the cruiser calling on his cell. These were not UNAVAILABLE but WIRELESS CALLER so I could pick up if I wished. Calling me Baby, saying he loved me he did not ever mean to hurt me, I was the only thing he loved in this shitty life he hoped to Christ I knew that, he'd make it up to me. Saying it was a hard time for him right now, he was begging to be forgiven. Saying I was his princess, I was never off his radar.

Phone rings. Impulsively my hand lifts the receiver, "Yes? Hello?"

It's like striking a match. That quick. UNAVAILABLE isn't prepared for a living voice. I hear him draw breath. I've surprised him. Maybe I've shocked him. It takes him a moment to adjust.

That low, gravelly mock-courteous voice, "The lady of the house, Ms. Pitman?" and I hear myself say, "Who's this?" and he pauses not expecting this, either; doesn't expect a female voice that isn't intimidated.

"Your friend, Lucretia. This is your friend."

There's excitement here. The way he pronounces *Lu-cre-tia*. It's no way I have heard Pitman pronounce my name. These past few months Pitman has not called me by any name at all only *Baby*. Or *you*.

This is the first time I've heard my caller's living voice since that pelting-rain night in April. And it's late August now. And Pitman is away. I've been watching local TV news out of Canton, Watertown. Surfing the channels. It's nearing midnight. Old movies, *Law & Order* reruns. Final ten minutes of a rebroadcast of a performance of *Tosca*, one of Daddy's operas. Lying on the jiggly-jangly brass bed. The handmade quilt, fraying-soft from many washings, is neatly folded at the foot of the bed. I'm in a silky champagne-colored nightgown, also fraying-soft from many washings, Pitman bought me when we were married. Still warm, flushed-feeling from my bath. And still with some makeup on my face. Pitman doesn't care for washed-out female faces, I know from remarks he's made. I try to look good for Pitman, it's a habit. Whether he sees or not. Whether he's here or not. In my hand a juice glass of Parrot Bay Puerto Rican rum I stole out of Daddy's teakwood cabinet last time I visited the house on Algonquin Avenue. The type of liquor Daddy never drinks, the near-full bottle pushed to the back of the cabinet.

I'm not drinking to get drunk, like Pitman. Only to make the sharp edges of things softer.

Saying, in my scratchy voice, "My friend who? Who's my friend? I want a friend, friend. I'm needful of a friend."

This is daring! My toes are twisty, twitchy. Wish I could see this guy's face, the surprise in it like someone has grabbed him between the legs.

Now it begins. Now, like Ping-Pong. He's asking me why I need a friend and I'm saying 'cause I'm lonely, that's why. He's asking why a married woman is lonely and I'm saying that's what I'd like to know, too. He asks what am I wearing, and I say, Ohhh, this outfit with just one button I got for my birthday. So funny, I'm laughing to make the brass headboard jiggle. I'm laughing, the plumy-dark rum near about spills on my belly. My caller, my friend he calls himself, is laughing, too. Saying oh baby he wishes he could see that birthday suit. I say actually I just got out of the bath. I'm all alone here just out of the bath. And he says, D'you need help drying, and I say, Noooo. Maybe. And he says, First things first, honey: your titties. Start with your titties, honey-baby. Your nipples. And I'm feeling my breath come short. And I'm laughing so it hurts, like a knife blade in my side. Being called honey, baby: it's so sweet. It's funny but so sweet, I know that I am making a terrible mistake like accelerating on black ice but I can't stop. He's saying more words, I can't hear for laughing. Throwing your life away, oh Lucretia, your precious life, my mother had wept. It's my life to throw away, God damn my life. It's my life not yours leave me alone. And I'm thinking *This is Pitman, he is testing me. He will murder me.*

Might've said, "Pitman! I know it's you. Damn you, Pitman, come home, I'm lonely."

Instead, I slam down the receiver. I've been staring at my toes. Narrow waxy-white feet. Haven't polished my toenails in years. Last time, Pitman failed to notice. In fact, my feet look like some withered old-woman feet, not a young girl's any longer.

So *help me God* is a way of speaking. You might laugh at such a desperate way of speaking until it becomes your own.

It was to keep him from hurting me. It was to keep him at a distance. Just to frighten him off. I knew that I deserved to be hurt by my husband but I was terrified of the actual hurt. A man's fingers closing around my throat. There is nothing so terrible as strangulation. He would thump my head against the wall. Thump — slam! — my head against the wall. I seemed to be remembering this, it had already happened. Unless it was the brass headboard he'd shoved me against, jangling and creaking.

You would not ever betray me, Lucretia. Would you.

Whimpering to myself like a frightened child, a guilty child fumbling in Pitman's gun closet. Overhead the light bulb swings on a chain. This closet I have avoided, never open. Disliking and fearing Pitman's weapons. Repugnance for Pitman's weapons. But now I need the rifle. Have not seen Pitman's deer rifle in years but I recognize it on the shelf at eye level: the long sleek blue-black barrel, polished wooden handle Pitman so admires. *Loaded and ready.*

Safety lock *off.*

You have been so reckless. You have made a mistake. Drunk reckless mistake. Others can forgive, but not Pitman.

The rifle is much heavier than I expect. You think of a rifle as a graceful weapon unlike a shotgun but this rifle is awkward in my arms, and so heavy. I'm not drunk but I feel faint, sick. My heart is beating like a crazed thing inside my rib cage. My breath comes so fast and ragged, I'm having trouble focusing my eyes.

Trying to see where the trigger is. How my fingers should fit.

He'd wanted to teach me. He'd taunted me, I was Daddy's little princess, content to have others do my shooting for me.

I love him! Want him to forgive me.

I will beg him I didn't mean it, I was only pretending. I knew it was you, my friend on the phone. Pitman, I knew!

Seems like I have already told him this . . . Then my head thump-thumping against the wall.

It's a bad sign, Pitman arrives home early. Lately he's been staying out until the taverns close at 2 A.M., doesn't get home before 2:30 A.M. but tonight his headlights swing into the driveway at just 1 A.M.

So I know. I can't not know.

I am waiting for him, hiding. I think that I am starkly sober as a creature that has been skinned alive but still my hands are shaking and my teeth are chattering and I've been crouched so long my knees are beginning to buckle.

Ask me why I did not run away, I am that man's wife. Nowhere for that man's wife to hide. He would find me if I ran to hide with my parents. He would hurt my parents, too.

Pitman enters the house through the back door, into the kitchen. Making no effort to be quiet. Stumbling, cursing. In the bedroom where I am crouched behind the bureau, amid a smell of spilled rum, animal panic, perfumey steam . . . from the bathroom, the TV is on, muted. The phone receiver is off the hook. Only the bedside lamp is burning. At the foot of the brass bed, the quilt of lavender and purple squares has been neatly folded. In the night Pitman kicks the quilt off, in the morning I haul it up, spread it back over the bed neatly. Pitman has acknowledged, yes, the quilt is "nice." Like other things I've brought into the house. If "nice" things matter.

The heavy deer rifle I've laid across the bureau top, aimed toward the doorway. This could be an intruder, any night a woman is alone in a house in the country is a night of danger, risk. I think it must be a child's desperate strategy. A hope that magic will intervene. I don't know how to shoot a firearm except to aim, shut my eyes, and pull the trigger. Thinking it might be a Pitman trick, what if the rifle isn't loaded?

"Hey, baby. What the fuck."

Pitman stands swaying in the doorway. His face is dark and glowering, but bemused. His jaws are stubbled; he hasn't shaved since 6 A.M. the previous morning. The eyes are Pitman-eyes, horsey eyes, glassy but alert, interested. There's a relief in this, I'm thinking that I will never again have to smell another woman on him. I will never again have to smell the fury leaking through his pores . . . A slow smile breaks over Pitman's face. His big horsey teeth bared, almost happy. You'd say it was a mean taunting smile but mostly it's teasing.

"Baby, you better take careful aim with that fucker. You got one shot before I'm on you."

"What we will do, Lucretia, is . . ."

He's my Daddy come in the night to help me. Ashen-faced and shaken but taking charge. He's in clothes he threw on hurriedly over his pajamas. Saying, licking his lips and repeating as if he's having difficulty articulating such words, "What you will say, Lucretia, is . . ."

I called home at 1:14 A.M. Not 911. Phone records will show. How soon after I called Daddy has arrived I don't know. I was on the floor in the darkened living room where he found me. Through this roaring in my ears I am not able to hear everything Daddy says, he must grip my shoulders, shake me gently. This drawn sickly-white face is not exactly Daddy's handsome face but of course this is Everett Rayburn. I can't recall when his hair has become so thin. He has led me into the bathroom to wash my face. Comb out my matted hair. I rinsed my mouth, that plumy rum-taste. I could not reenter the bedroom, Daddy went inside to bring clothes for me. A pair of sandals, I laughed to see sandals! I have not looked into the bedroom since Daddy arrived. When he first came and went immediately to see Pitman where he'd fallen, I'd been frantic crying, "Is he dead, Daddy? He's dead, isn't he?"

Dial 911. Daddy dials 911. Daddy dials the (memorized) number of his lawyer who lives in Canton.

"Yes, honey. He's dead."

So Help Me God

The rifle that was too heavy for me to lift in my arms and aim is on the floor of the bedroom, where it fell. Daddy has seen but not touched the rifle. Daddy has crouched over the man's body, seen but not touched.

Two bullets. For the first was not enough to stop him.

In the distance, a siren. It's rare to hear a siren in the night in the country. In my skinned-alive state that seems to me a pure and spiritual state I am sitting on the living room sofa, in the way my parents wished their daughter to sit at mealtimes. Perfect posture. Head back. Take pride, don't slump shoulders. Not ever.

Now we're alone in this house Daddy has never visited, Daddy seems clumsy, confused. He's breathing so quickly. Gripping my hands in his. Before he became a builder and a rich man, Daddy was a cabinetmaker, still works with his hands sometimes, and his hands are strong and calloused. I like the feel of Daddy's hands, though the fingers are not warm as I remember. Hands so much larger than my own.

Daddy is swallowing hard and trying to control his breathing hearing the siren approach saying again that I must tell the truth exactly as it happened why I had to fire that rifle to save my life.

And all that led to it. All.

"Just tell the truth, Lucretia."

Which is what I will do, so help me God.

SUE PIKE

A Temporary Crown

FROM *Murder in Vegas*

DOLORES SHUFFLED into the Solarium looking for the paper cups the nurses used to distribute the meds. It was a hobby of hers, collecting the tiny, fluted cups. She liked to put treasures in them and line them up on the windowsill of her hospital room.

Leonard was slouched on the sofa watching TV and scratching his head. Leonard was always scratching his head. It was sort of a hobby of his, Dolores thought. She spotted four abandoned cups on the card table, but just as she was gathering them up her attention was caught by an image on the TV. She sucked in her breath as Bryce and a young woman drove onto the screen riding a huge black motorcycle, the pink sand of the Nevada desert glowing behind them in the evening sun. They skidded to a stop, pulled off their helmets, and waved at the camera. The woman shook her head, catching Bryce full across the face with a sheet of long blond hair. Bryce brushed the hair away, threw his arm around the blond girl's shoulder, and laughed. Then Leonard started laughing and Dolores had to flap her hands to shush him so she could hear the commentary.

"Bryce Campion, best known for his role in *Worlds Apart,* and Marie-France Lapin, of Jazz Hot, the all-girl band from Paris that's been making waves all over the country, announced their upcoming nuptials today in Las Vegas. Bryce is currently headlining a brand-new show at the Three Crowns..."

Her knees wobbled and she dropped into a chair, sending the paper cups skittering to the floor. That made Leonard laugh some more, but when she started to shush him again she caught herself.

His eyes had that glittery look that meant something crazy was going on in his head and she'd better watch out.

She leaned closer to the screen. "The wedding will take place next week in the Little White Wedding Chapel, a Las Vegas landmark."

Dolores began to hum two notes over and over. It was something she did when she could feel her heart beating too fast. She was going to have to decide what to do but she couldn't think in here with the TV and Leonard scratching his head and laughing too loud in all the wrong places. She grunted as she leaned over and picked up the cups from the floor and then she pulled herself to her feet and shuffled away as fast as her swollen legs would carry her.

Back in her room, she tore a sheet from the steno pad Dr. Bradford gave her at their first session. She was supposed to be using it for a journal, writing about all the times she felt angry and all the times she felt sad. But the pages were mostly empty and every time he asked her about it she just hummed a bit and stared at the floor while he gripped the desk so hard his fingers went white.

She reached between the mattress and the box spring and fished out a silver pen she'd found on Dr. Bradford's desk one day when he was looking at something in her file. After scribbling a few words on the paper, she reached into the crevice under the radiator where she'd hidden the blank stamped envelope she'd found a few weeks ago at the nursing station when the matron had gone to the bathroom. She addressed it to Bryce Campion, Three Crowns Hotel, Las Vegas, Nevada, and then tucked it into the zippered compartment of her bag. They were releasing her to the group home tomorrow and she'd be able to slip out and mail it once the social worker was through talking to her. She sat on the edge of the bed for a minute or two and then reached behind the radiator again to check the money hidden in there. She liked to think of it as her nest egg. That's what her grandmother had called the money in the cookie tin she kept high up on the shelf over the icebox. Dolores had stood on a chair and reached for the tin one day when she thought her grandmother was lying down in the next room. It slipped out of her fingers, and the coins had clattered to the floor. Her grandmother had shot into the room and yanked the chair right out from under Dolores, making her crack her head on the table as she fell. The social worker had asked how she'd hurt herself, but she never said. Not that time. Not ever.

Dolores stepped out of the cool of the Greyhound Bus Terminal onto South Main and caught her breath. The noise and heat and brilliant sunshine jumbled together inside her head and made it hard to think clearly. She shuffled a few blocks before she dropped her pack onto the sidewalk and leaned against the wall of an office building. She put both hands behind her and pushed hard against the wall, feeling the stucco bite into her fingers, trying to read the bumps as if they were Braille. She took a deep breath and tried to think about the mantra Dr. Bradford had taught her, but sounds and images were jittering around in her mind so fast she couldn't remember how it began. After a while she rummaged in her bag for a jam jar of water and with a few sips she felt strong enough to push away from the wall and pick up her pack again. She stood for a moment and tried to get her bearings. In her letter she'd described the doughnut shop where he should meet her. It was one she'd discovered last year when she'd come here to be with him. But she didn't want to think about that time and had to hum very loud to keep it out of her head, only the trouble with that was it kept the location of the doughnut shop out of her head as well. But it was on the Strip, that much she could remember, so she set off again humming even louder to take her mind off her heartbeat and her sore ankles.

When she'd gone to the group home the social worker had watched her unpack her bag and fold things into the dresser drawer. Dolores smiled, remembering how easy it had been to push everything back in the bag and drop it from the window the next day. When she walked out the front door she'd called to Stella, who was in the kitchen making lunch, and told her she was just going for a walk and then she'd gone around back, picked up her pack, and walked to the bus terminal. It took most of her nest egg to buy the one-way ticket.

Dolores walked on, stumbling a bit every once in a while, holding onto the walls of buildings when she was afraid she might fall. She thought about Dr. Bradford and how he made everything he said sound like he was talking to a child. "Doris," he'd said, always calling her Doris even though she'd corrected him so many times.

"Doris, sometimes people think they have a connection to people they've never met. Especially celebrities. Some even believe they're married to well-known men like Bryce Campion." He'd looked sad when he said it, like it was one of the big tragedies of the world. "You understand you're not married to him, don't you?" He'd twisted his pencil between his lips, making it squeak and then he'd pulled it out with a wet popping sound and leaned forward, trying to catch her eye. "You can get rid of this obsession, Doris. You have the power to make yourself better." She'd had to hum hard into her pillow that night, remembering the little frown between his eyebrows that made an upside-down V like the pitched roof on her grandmother's hen house. But she didn't really blame Dr. Bradford. He didn't know any better. He hadn't seen the look Bryce had given her that night in the movie theater. He hadn't been there the night Bryce had asked her to marry him. She could still remember it as clear as day. She was sitting in the second row and he was looking down at her from the shiny, pebbly screen. There was a hurt look on his face, as though afraid she'd refuse. "Dolores," he'd said, "Marry me, Dolores. Please." She'd said yes right there, out loud. Some people in the audience laughed, but she didn't care. He'd said the words she'd been waiting to hear all her adult life. After that she'd watched every movie he ever made. And she'd gone to the library and looked through all the movie and entertainment magazines in hopes of finding a photo of him. When they stopped making musical films he'd taken a job in Las Vegas, singing in one of the smaller hotels. And she'd gone along last year to be with him. But it hurt to think about that right now.

She'd managed to make her way to the area known as the Strip with its confusing jumble of moving lights and jangly music that hurt her head. The pack was scraping against her so she put it down on the sidewalk and slumped onto it, splaying out her legs.

"Hey, watch it." A young girl veered around her, her roller blades screeching on the sidewalk just inches from Dolores's worn plastic thongs. The girl flipped her hair and a barrette dropped to the sidewalk.

"Watch it yourself," she shouted back, scooping up the barrette and running her fingers along its surface. It was just the right size to fit into one of the fluted paper cups she had stacked in her bag. She shoved it into a side pocket and struggled to her feet again.

She had to find the doughnut shop fast in case Bryce was waiting for her. She stared along the Strip, humming to keep her heart from pounding. It was packed with people looking in shops and restaurants, but they weren't looking at her so that was okay. She walked on, stumbling a bit with fatigue and confusion and then she spotted it, just a little way down a little side street, nestled between an adult video store and a newspaper shop.

It was wonderfully cool inside. She dropped her bag into a booth and peeled a couple of dollars from what was left of the nest egg in her pocket. A young man with acne and a tattoo of an alligator on his left arm took her order for three chocolate glazed and a large coffee and then, balancing her meal in both hands, she squeezed between the molded chair and table and began the serious business of eating. Dr. Bradford would have a fit if he saw her. He'd handed her some diet sheets at one of their last sessions and made her promise to read them. Easy for him to eat all those fruits and vegetables, half of which she'd never even heard of. He didn't have to live on the little bit of money she got from welfare.

"Mind if I share your table?" A young woman with black hair swept back into a wide red ribbon made Dolores jump. She looked around the restaurant but almost all the other tables were empty.

She shrugged and chocolate crumbs cascaded to the white plastic table.

"Man," the woman giggled. "Is it ever hot today." She tossed a couple of parcels onto the bench beside Dolores's pack and threw her cotton jacket on top.

"Looks like you could use another coffee." The woman was still standing, the smell of perfume wafting about her. "Can I get you anything else?"

Dolores shrugged again without looking up and the woman strode away leaving her jacket and parcels behind. Dolores sneaked a peek at the top one. Neiman Marcus, it said. Well, well. All right for some, she thought, resentment pinching her lips together.

"Here you go. I picked up a couple more doughnuts as well." She giggled again. "I'm Jennifer, by the way. What's your name?"

Dolores pulled the new bag of chocolate glazed toward her and counted four. They would have cost a fortune, she thought, toting up the total in her head. "Dolores."

"Well, *bon appetit*, Dolores!" Jennifer smiled brightly while she dusted the bench and perched gingerly on the edge. She stacked a pile of napkins onto the table and placed a carrot raisin muffin in the exact center. She turned the napkin pile around a couple of times before breaking off a tiny portion from the top and popping it into her mouth. A couple of miniscule crumbs dropped onto the table. "Mm-mm," she said, and giggled again while she touched the corners of her mouth with the longest, pinkest nails Dolores had ever seen. She pushed her own hands with their gnawed nails into her lap while she examined the woman across from her. Jennifer had one of those smiles that made her nose scrunch up, the kind the girls in high school used to try on in front of the restroom mirror until they caught her watching and made her leave. It was definitely the kind of smile for girls who giggled a lot.

"So," Jennifer studied her largely undamaged muffin and then looked up. "Where are you from?"

Dolores hesitated wondering if this was a trap. "Why? What makes you think I'm not from here?"

"Oh, I don't know. Nobody you meet around here is actually from Las Vegas. Most people are tourists." Jennifer leaned toward her conspiratorially. "I'll bet you flew here, right?"

Oh sure. On her budget. "Huh-uh. Bus from Chicago."

Jennifer flapped her hand with its pink nails in front of her mouth indicating it was full, but the muffin sitting on the tidy pile of napkins appeared almost whole. "Chicago?" she said after she swallowed. "I love Chicago!"

"Um . . ." Dolores looked into the doughnut bag and selected another chocolate glazed. She didn't want to talk about Chicago. It made her think of Dr. Bradford and the little roof-shaped frown.

"What did your mother call you, Doris?" he'd asked at their last session.

"I told you, I don't have a mother."

"Grandmother, then. What did she call you?"

"You know," she'd mumbled. She wished she'd never told him about the Doris Doolittle rhyme.

"Huh?" she looked up at Jennifer, realizing she'd missed a question.

"I asked if you had a place to stay."

Dolores shrugged.

"I could help you find a nice motel room and give you a lift, if you'd like."

Dolores scanned the seats in the doughnut shop again. "No, thanks. I'm meeting someone."

"Oh!" Jennifer beamed at her. "A boyfriend, I'll bet." She looked around herself at the mostly empty tables. "Is it a boyfriend, Doris?"

"My name's Dolores." The familiar anger bubbled up, pricking her eyes with tears.

"Oops. Sorry." Jennifer grinned. "I'll bet he's gorgeous. Is he gorgeous?"

Dolores shrugged. "He's not all that young any more."

"A sophisticated older man. They're the best kind. I'll bet he's nice. Is he nice?"

Dolores thought about the last time she saw him. She remembered the restraining orders and the policeman who'd yanked her arms behind her back and bent her over the hood of the squad car. "I dunno. Not nice exactly."

"Men, huh?" Her frown looked a lot like Dr. Bradford's. "Well, he should be here to meet you. That's for sure." She rummaged in her purse and produced a cell phone. "Why don't we call him and tell him to get on over here." The long pink nails hovered over the keypad like butterflies waiting to land. "What's the number?"

"I . . . I don't know the number. It's probably unlisted." Dolores could feel her breathing getting fast again. She wanted to hum but thought she'd better not. "Anyway, he's probably just busy." She wanted to tell Jennifer about Bryce's act at the Three Crowns and that he couldn't just drop everything at a moment's notice but she was afraid, afraid she'd get that look on her face like Dr. Bradford's. She was afraid Jennifer would talk about obsessions and stalking and all those things people said when they didn't understand about Bryce and her.

But Jennifer wasn't even looking at her. She seemed to be looking at something inside her own head and her eyes had gone all glittery, like Leonard's did when he had his scary thoughts. "Men need to be taken down a peg, don't you agree? Think they can walk all over us." Her laugh was a little bit like Leonard's, too. "My own so-called boyfriend tells me the other day he's going to marry someone else. Didn't want me to see it first on TV, can you believe it?" The pink fingernails were drumming the table so hard the tip of the middle one snapped off, but Jennifer didn't seem to notice. "I've been his secretary, his lover, even his laundress." She made a disgusted snort. "I've answered thousands of letters from his retarded fans. And now he tells me he's knocked up some blond bimbo and he's going to marry her. Can you believe it?"

"Um . . ." Dolores wanted to tell her about the fingernail but Jennifer suddenly sniffed and then giggled again. "Well, enough about me. I'm just a teensy bit angry." She crumbled a corner off her muffin, popped it into her mouth, and bit down hard on it. Suddenly her eyes widened and she grabbed her jaw. "Oh shit." She fished around inside her mouth with the thumb and forefinger of her left hand, withdrawing something white.

Dolores was alarmed. It looked like a tooth. She'd had enough teeth yanked out of her head to know how painful it was, but when she looked at Jennifer's face the woman seemed more furious than wounded. She sucked the thing once and then dropped it into the ashtray and got to her feet. Dolores stared at it.

"Is that your tooth?"

"That piece of shit is a temporary crown. I'm not getting the real thing installed until tomorrow." She rolled her tongue around inside her mouth and then turned away. "I'm going to the washroom to rinse out my mouth."

Dolores stared at the thing, tipping it this way and that in the ashtray, amazed at the contours, trying to imagine where it had come from and if this one was temporary what the real crown would look like.

Jennifer reappeared and gathered up her parcels from the bench. The muffin lay abandoned on the table. "Okay. I think we need to take you to your boyfriend's place."

"Um. That's okay. I'll wait here a while."

"He's never going to come." The giggle and the scrunched-up smile had vanished but the eyes were still glittering. "You need to have it out with him, Doris. Once and for all." She grabbed her parcels and the duffle bag and headed for the door. Dolores sat for a moment, humming softly, and when she looked over and saw the woman and her bag disappearing out the door she scooped the temporary crown into a napkin and shoved it in her pants pocket. The tip of the pink nail was harder to find. It had slipped under the pile of napkins holding the scarcely touched muffin. Dolores gathered the whole thing together and put it in the pocket of her shirt.

She pushed through to the heat and confusion of the street and found Jennifer standing beside a black convertible, holding the passenger door open. Dolores sank with difficulty into the seat and then had to pull her swollen legs in after her.

She peered at the console once they were moving. "What is this thing?"

"You're kidding, right?" Jennifer frowned at her. "You've never seen a Jaguar before?"

"Um . . ." Dolores found she could hum under her breath and the sound of the motor masked it.

Within minutes they were pulling up to the shipping entrance to Three Crowns. The woman reached across Dolores's stomach and pushed the passenger door open. "Out you get. I'll go and park this thing and then I'll get the key for you from the front desk." She checked over her shoulder watching for an opportunity to pull out, but then she appeared to change her mind and reached across again, this time to open the glove compartment. Dolores was stunned. Inside was the biggest pile of quarters she'd ever seen. Jennifer scooped up two handfuls and thrust them into her lap.

"You can play the slot machines while you wait." She gave Dolores a little shove. "Off you go. But stay in the lobby, okay? That way I can find you again."

Dolores stumbled out of the car, shoving coins into her pants pockets. Several quarters dropped to the sidewalk and she had to stoop down to retrieve them. When she looked up again the car and the woman and all Dolores's possessions had disappeared.

She stood still for a full minute, trying to make sense of what had happened, feeling the pockets of her yellow knit pants stretch under the weight of the coins. She wanted to sag against the wall and close her eyes but she hadn't liked that glittery look in Jennifer's eyes so she pulled herself together and shuffled around to the front entrance of the hotel.

She gasped. A big poster advertising Bryce's show took up most of the front of the building. He seemed to be looking right into her eyes and she ran her fingers through her hair trying to tidy it. She didn't want him to see her looking like she'd just stepped off the bus. There were little trees in cement boxes lining the drive and she stood behind one for a moment watching the doorman in his red and black uniform. A limousine pulled up to the curved driveway and the man tugged at his tunic and ran over to open the driver's door. Dolores could hardly believe it. Jonathan Finn from *Las Vegas Nights* stepped from the car and handed the doorman the keys. He took the stairs to the entrance two at a time and just before he pushed through he turned and smiled at Dolores. She thought she saw his lips move, saying, "I love you, Dolores." She had to hang onto one of the little trees for a minute and take a deep breath. What would Leonard say about this? It was his favorite TV show. She waited another minute until the doorman got into the limousine and began to drive it off, and then she sidled through the revolving doors and into the lobby of the Three Crowns. Jonathan Finn was nowhere in sight, but she knew what she'd seen. He loved her. She hummed to herself, hugging this new knowledge to her heart.

She wanted to stop and stare at the colors in the carpet and the impossibly soft sofas and chairs but she knew from last year that if the management noticed her they'd ask her to leave. She spotted banks and banks of slot machines lining the walls and found an unoccupied one tucked away behind a huge potted plant. She watched a man put his quarters into the machine next to hers and listened to the jangly sounds. She was astounded. They sounded a lot like the notes she hummed when she tried to get calm.

Dolores had no idea how long she'd been standing there sometimes shoving quarters into the machine and sometimes staring at the flashing lights. Once she was surprised by a shower of coins but was afraid of the noise the machine made when she won, fearing people would be drawn to it and ask her what she thought she was doing in such a fancy place. Hunger pangs and worry about Jennifer and her duffle bag made her eat the muffin in her pocket and now she was hungry again.

Suddenly Jennifer was there, standing beside her, just as she had been in the doughnut shop. Only this time she was wearing a scarf, dark glasses, and black leather gloves, and she was holding out a plastic card with a strip on one side.

"Here's the key to your boyfriend's suite." She pushed her sunglasses onto her head for a moment and her eyes were glittering even more than Leonard's when he was about to do something crazy. "I think you'd better get right up there. Tell him how you feel about things."

Dolores took the card and ran her finger over the surface. It wouldn't fit in the little paper cups but she'd keep it anyway. "My bag . . .?"

"It's still in the car. I'll go and get it while you're going to the room."

"Where do I go?" Dolores was confused about so many things; all she really wanted to do was lean against the wall and close her eyes.

"He's on the top floor where the big suites are. The elevators are over here." She put the sunglasses on and took Dolores's elbow, pushing her across the thick carpet, past the gorgeous sofas and into a marble foyer with elevators along both walls. "It's straight ahead when you get out of the elevator." She seemed to remember something. "You know how to use this key?"

Dolores stared at the floor.

"Okay, you shove it into the slot above the handle with the strip away from you. Bring it out again and when the little light turns green, you can open the door."

"But my bag? Where'd you say my bag was?"

"I'll be waiting right here with your bag." Jennifer was talking very softly now, almost whispering. "When you've told him . . . well, whatever you want to tell him, come back here and I'll give you your bag." She pushed something with her gloved finger and the elevator door slid open.

Dolores hesitated but Jennifer pushed her in and reached behind her to push a button inside the elevator.

When the elevator stopped, Dolores peered out, making sure there was no one in the hall. She held the card that Jennifer had called a key but the door across from the elevator was already ajar. She pushed it farther open and stuck her head in, humming the two notes as loud as she could. When no one stopped her she stepped into a light green vestibule with a huge painting of cactus and desert sand on the right wall. She hesitated and then called out softly, "Bryce?" She wished she'd rehearsed what she'd say to him but there was no answer. She walked into a living room, with another of the scrumptious sofas on a pale beige carpet. Two glasses half full of some kind of liquid and melting ice cubes sat on the coffee table. She glanced at the kitchen but it was empty. There was another half-open door leading off the living room. She walked over and pushed it fully open.

At first she thought they were sleeping, Bryce on his back, his naked torso partly covered by a sheet and the girl with her long blond hair spread out on the pillowcase. But then she saw the blood and the hole in Bryce's forehead where no one should have a hole. And when she leaned over to get a better look, she noticed the girl's hair was covering a section of her cheek that was red and pulpy and leaking blood.

A gun lay on the pillow. She thought for a second about picking it up, but it was much too big for her treasure collection so she left it where it was. She felt sad about Bryce and about the pretty girl too. But she knew in her heart that what Dr. Bradford had said was true. She and Bryce weren't really engaged. It was just a kind of dream of hers.

She heard a siren and then another and when she looked out the window she saw several police cars pulling up to the hotel's entrance. The doorman was tugging on his tunic and flapping his arms around.

Dolores decided to take the stairs down. She could stop at each floor and see if there was any sign of Jonathan Finn. He might be wondering where she'd got to and she didn't like to keep him waiting.

Before she left she looked again at the couple on the bed. She'd like to leave a gift for them, some sort of memorial like people left her when her grandmother died, but all of her treasures were in Jennifer's car. Then she remembered the temporary crown in its little bed of napkins in her pants pocket. She pulled it out and dropped it near Bryce's hand. She noticed the little pink fingernail was caught in the folds, but it looked so pretty against the white sheet she decided to leave that as well.

EMILY RABOTEAU

Smile

FROM *The Gettysburg Review*

"Row!" his père commands but Tee Paul's arms are jelly. His père's back at the prow of the pirogue is a trunk of muscle. "Row you peeshwank capon, row!" Between them on the peeling pirogue floor lies Bowleg's boy, Smile, with a broken head. "Row!" His père's oar slides into the brack like a knife, deeper and darker down bayou they go, until the shore lights extinguish, until even the shadows have shadows. His throat is a knot. The bullfrogs croak, "Oh no, oh no."

Tee Paul can't work his oar for looking into his podna's licorice face in the lantern light. Smile's blood is mixing with the half-inch pool of swamp water down there. Smile's eyes are two dead coins with a hold on him.

"Row!" Instead of sailing straight, the boat wig-wags like a lizard tail through the silent, bearded cypress. And slowly because only his père is doing the work. *"Row!"*

"Can't, Pop," Tee Paul says. He's got those jelly arms. He hasn't the strength to slap at a mosquito.

"What?" his père spits, spinning around. He's got the whiskey smell and the mad dog look.

"I got the mal au coeur!" he says and vomits a slop as thick as the Atchafalaya itself over the side of his père's pirogue.

Tawk! His père reaches his oar across and cracks him one good on the head, same way he did Smile with the doorstop rock for stealing his alligator money. Tee Paul's afraid now. The shock freezes him. The fear moves him. Father and son cut the swamp like lard.

A smell rises. Smile must've shit his pants in a death spasm. "Pooye-ye," says Tee Paul's père. When the flies come he ropes Smile's middle to the anchor and dumps him by the roots of a strangler tree. The swamp swallows Smile up fast, bottom first, head last. The old man tips a bit and says, "Listen, couyon. He was a no-good burglar nigger, him. Dass all. Not of we and us."

On the long way back, he's thinking how the tooloulou must be fiddling over Smile's face already, pinching out his eyes. Or maybe a gator would get him.

Back in their shack on stilts, Hermogine, in her stovepipe hat, squats, skinning a beaver from one of the traps. All Tee Paul meant was to save enough to steal her from harm, to stow away with her on a big river barge. He could have carried her off on his back. She's a little wisp of a thing, sickly. Her nightgown is so thin. There's a blue vein beating in her forehead.

"Why you wake, bebette?" their père grumbles, freeing his bunions from his boots. "Fais do-do." She asks do they want coffee, but the old man's already reaching for the other stuff.

Tuesday is her birthday. They wrap her in a quilt, set her in the buggy, and ride her to town to pick out a gift.

Do she want dat doll? Do she want a yard of dat yellow gingham to make a apron? Do she want dis pop-up picture book from France? No, she want de pair of chartreuse lovebirds in dat cage over de crawdaddy barrel. Can she have dem birds? Weh, she can.

The old man pays with a cut of his rescued money. Tee Paul had stole it one nickel at a time. All winter long he stashed the money in his podna's tackle box, where his père was never meant to look. Smile kept count for him. They'd lay down their fishing poles in the muck to look at all the coins collecting in there. "Soon," Smile would smile then draw his harmonica out from the bib of his overalls. "Mais, I'm gon miss ya podna." When there was enough Tee Paul would run away. He would carry his little sister up the Bayou on his back. He would save her.

The coins clink on the counter now like chains. Hermogine's kissing at the birds through the bars. Un p'tit bec. Their wings are clipped. Their beaks are coming off. They have reptilian eyes. They are not cheap.

"Dôn say I never did nothing nice, Gine-Gine," their père says, not looking at her, but at Tee Paul. The old man's eyes are possum pink.

"Look!" says Hermogine out on the groaning porch of the dry

goods store. The sun is too bright. "Dass Mister Bowleg, de zydeco man! Where his accordion at?"

Bowleg's in the street, dragging his potbelly mule. "Hey-o!" he calls. "Ya'all seen my boug?"

Tee Paul looks at the rusty cage in his sister's arms. His finger twitches, but he knows if he unlatches the cage door to let them go, those birds won't fly away. They'll just drop like turds to the floorboards. He licks his dry lips, and his père grips his shoulder, hard.

"Ya seen my boug, Smile?"

R. T. SMITH

Ina Grove

FROM *The Virginia Quarterly Review*

The Rockbridge County Gazette, June 28, 1904
PAINTER, THE IRISH CREEK DESPERADO, ARRAIGNED
by Reese Prescott

LEXINGTON: After two hours of deliberation, a panel of magistrates today in the circuit court of Rockbridge turned in an indictment in the rape and murder case of Brodie Painter, the so-called Irish Creek Desperado. The crime, which raised a significant stir hereabouts, involved felonious assault on a fourteen-year-old girl named Ina Grove, and the prosecutor, Captain Stansfield, now has plans to petition Judge Armbruster for the gallows in light of both the harm done the girl and the savagery with which her uncle Leaf Pogue was stabbed to his death.

According to testimony, Painter, a robust man of 35 years and uncertain race, has scaped the ministrations of the law on several previous occasions. Something more than a year ago he killed a neighbor, Cash, in a fracas on the headwaters of Pedlar Creek and eluded punishment when arraigned at Amherst Courthouse, due to a dearth of witnesses. His latest crime was committed in South Mountain on Irish Creek in the county. He had been acknowledged a desperate miscreant and was for some time variously reported either to have fled to territories unknown or to be at large in the dense recesses of South Mountain. Commonwealth's Attorney Moore entreated Governor Montague to levy a reward for Painter's capture, and Richmond offered up a replevin of $100.

This turn of events was kept in camera that Sheriff B. R. Sherburne might initiate proceedings without raising general alarm or alerting the fugitive to the actions of his pursuers. Local enforcement had previously been frustrated on learning that Painter had left the settlement, probably by way of the Norfolk and Western Railroad, his one-time employer. To run his man to ground, the sheriff enlisted the services of Constable John Pink of Buffalo District, a man known in these quarters for his taste for the dangerous.

Pink was himself reared in the Blue Ridge on the Amherst side, often called "The Free State" for its hospitality to fugitives, and is familiar with the locals and all the paths through Pedlar River Country. It was Pink who cast a quiet net and finally located Painter in the environs of his brother Darl, and upon his intelligence Sheriff Sherburne convened his posse comitatus and despite wet weather took the White's Gap Road up into the Blue Ridge.

In what will no doubt be acclaimed the model of corpus juris efficiency, the trap was laid and sprung. The lawmen and their deputies rode through rough mountains. After two days traveling against heavy impairment of weather, they reached an abandoned farm in the precincts of the Painter homestead and there without leave or license secreted their horses in the empty stable. After miles of difficult travel through mud and dense brush, the officers spied the brother and several womenfolk of the Painter clan moving about the place and so deployed sentries. The sheriff kept vigil behind the house, while his subordinates took to the laurel and rocks on foot. All caution was exercised with weapons at the ready, as Painter is a veteran of the Spanish war and numerous violent scrapes and disturbances in the region. Shortly, Police Chief Hazelwood of the party surprised Darl Painter, who had surmised the presence of the lawmen, climbing out a window with intentions of signaling his brother.

It was then felt that the house must at once be searched, and though none of the runagate's kit was discovered, it was determined that Pink's intelligence had been essentially correct, so the posse mounted a hushed ambush about the Painter house. Approaching sunset, according to Sheriff Sherburne, Brodie Painter appeared with a Colt Navy dangling from his hand, at which time Hazelwood showed his shotgun, and as the sheriff reported, the arrest was effected without further incident. The party quickly retraced their steps to their concealed horses and obtained some supper at a house in the mountains before making their way back to Lexington.

Throughout the hearing, attorney Spencer argued that his client had been treated with malice and hard measures, but the examiners pressed vigorously for the facts in the case. The prisoner promptly admitted to the likelihood that his blow had killed Leaf Pogue, albeit in defense of his own life and limb, but he contended in unpopular testimony that no rape had taken place.

Before the bench the accused was shouted down until Judge Armbruster ordered the courtroom cleared of all but the principals. Reading of an affidavit submitted by the alleged victim quickly gave the lie to Painter's desperate strategy. Although not present herself, Miss Grove recorded under licit seal that her uncle, who had acted as her guardian since her father's demise, her mother having died in childbirth, was about to serve supper when a man scarcely known to them burst through the door waving a butcher knife. Her account described the accused in many particulars, including the dark hue of his skin and the blue serpent tattoo on his arm, and outlined a bloody scuffle, followed by reference to unspeakable acts. Injured and in shock, the unfortunate received assistance from a passerby, the widow Kate Fell, the next morning, but it is feared she will be forever damaged by the atrocity.

The sitting panel, including one veteran of the Confederacy and others known to be distinguished citizens of our community, indicted Painter on charges of rape and capital murder, and as many of his other actions came to light during the testimony, his conviction is expected, which many surmise will produce a calm on Irish Creek in the aftermath of his little reign of terror.

The trial, which is expected to draw extensive public interest due to longstanding disputes over property rights and livestock among the denizens of Irish Creek, has been scheduled for August tenth. Although no trouble from the Painter kin is expected, Jailer Lisha Jackson says a double guard will be kept posted around the clock, and no chances will be taken with the outlaw.

Sheriff Blaine Sherburne, His Log, Excerpted

1904 April 13

A chilly evening and still raining. I have been struck with the Arkansas travels and could scarce stir from the office this day, but legal business will not desist on sole account of my bowels' inconvenience. This morning I was informed by Bill Brewster of another killing up on Irish Creek. They are a rough bunch up there and prone to scrap, which I understand is common to such woodloafers and rullions as dwell thereabouts, but I wish those bravos would fashion their own law, however perverse, and stick by it. This new instance is dire, as there is rape of a young girl involved, and I am somewhat acquainted with the supposed killer, one Brodie Painter, who slew his neighbor Sink Cash last autumn but was not testified against and walked scot-free. Tomorrow I will be obliged to ride out beyond the pale and snoop into it, as this rash of misdeed must be stomped out.

The events appear to have unfolded yesterday or the day before, and the victims Ina Grove and her uncle Leaf Pogue have little kin up that way, so at least the lynch talk, according to Brewster, is but a whisper so far. I knew Painter in the Spanish war, and he has ever proved to be a blacksnake who could not keep his hands in his own pockets or his Jemison in his trousers. Of late, by what I hear, he has taken to quarrel and plunder whenever he inclines, showing blade or barrel if opposed. As the region is rife with Ramps, Melungeons, and of recent a swarm of Mormon Saints, reports from the place read like news from the cockpit.

This will be the fourth time already I have had to seek copias on one of those Irish Creek rabbit twisters, and I am inclining to fall in with that faction of the Gentleman's Club that says they should be rousted and shot like so many mad dogs, their sorry cabins blazed, and the whole of South Mountain and Whetstone Ridge sowed with salt. It grows more difficult being the officiary voice in light of such widespread evidence of devilment. With each page of the calendar Adair's father's entreaty that I serve out only my current term and relinquish the star to share his livery concern grows more alluring, though to work daily with a man who incessantly recites from Mrs. Browning is not my aim in life, and I suspect his desire for a grandchild is fueling his offer.

If this rain will let off, we will likely get some warming and I will pack angling gear and strive to at least turn the junket into a couple of trout. Now the wick is raising more smudge in the lamp flute than glow, so I will risk another swallow of Tut's Pellets and try not to wake my sweet Adair when I slip into the covers. I must not propose to excurse to Irish Creek without the pump gun and must never think to foray to such treacherous haunts without full vigilance. For the time, God save the Commonwealth of Virginia, and so good night.

April 22

Granny Kate Fell brought the unfortunate orphan by the house this morning when she delivered our butter. We had talked two days previous, at which time she put forth that the child would be less skittish if we could conduct the interview in a sitting parlor, instead of my office. Adair with her usual breakfast radiance poured us coffee and repaired to her sewing nook. The first thing I noticed was that Ina Grove is hardly a girl, though she claims she will not even reach fourteen till August. Her make is full womanly, and she has the sort of green cat's eyes that follow you without moving and hair of raven silk like mourning clothes, though she does comport herself in bashful manner and is slow to answer even the simplest questions. Probably a sense of shame influences this manner, and I briefly feared that she was as well somewhat slow as a result of the in-turning bedlam mating up there on the thicket slopes, but later I came to appreciate that her shyness is not without device.

In the matter of her testimony, told in the minor key voice common to her stripe, she is consistent with what Granny Kate had previously conveyed. The man known as Brodie Painter, whom she had seen on various occasions but never truly met nor heard named, had on the day in question surprised herself and Pogue as they sat to a meal. Miss Grove steadfastly maintains that the accused rushed through the open door with not a word and knocked her uncle to the floor, then slit him twice with a big knife while she sat frozen and voiceless. Once the uncle was disabled, though still breathing and moaning, the intruder threw her onto the floor, raised her skirts, and ripped her undergarment. When I inquired if she did scream, she reckoned not and said she felt as one seeing actions unfold from outside her natural body. This could result, I suppose, from deep shock. What she remembered was Painter's muddy eyes and a blue or green snake drawn onto his dark arm.

This was, she said, her scandalous despoilment and had made her dirty, and she kept staring at a red knot in the floor, scuffing it with her brogan as if she might shove it aside could she only approach it in some yet-undiscovered fashion. I did not press her hard on any details but the man's build (which she puts at over six feet), his clothes and aspect, as well as the tattoo. On various occasions in our conversation, which filled only just more than a quarter of an hour, Miss Grove did interject that the man's skin was unusual in its color, and sometimes when she shut her eyes she saw him blue. Granny Fell then took her away, confiding that she prayed this child would not be called upon to appear in open court.

Though I would not agree that this girl is so much lacking in art nor such a wilder flower as others might perceive her, there is something of the deeply wounded in her look and the quaver of her voice. Her account having no inconsistencies nor inaccuracies according to my eventual search of the scene of those lamentable events, I find her a credible witness and am ready to sue for warrant, despite Adair's conviction the girl has something of the hussy in her comport.

Whether Painter will be susceptible to surprise or not is yet to be uncovered, but I remain suspicious that this situation will not resolve itself without extensive attention and no small expense. An owner of pasture, paddocks, hauling stock, and Surrey carriages would be at liberty to turn a blind eye to such considerations and enjoy an afternoon glass of Goldbrau to the tune of the overzealous weather. In my position, however, no ostrich logic will suffice.

Adair wishes us to attend a performance of *Lovey Mary* at the Buena Vista Opera House tonight, but I am resolved to plead paperwork concerning the recent embezzlement by Mr. Monroe of Jordan's Point, as some theatrical matters are best left unexplored.

May 1

I would like to boast it is time to soak the rope and stitch a new hood, but we are as far from snagging Brodie Painter as from catching a bingbuffer. I would as lief chase the latter, as its nonfactual nature would excuse my empty-handedness, while Painter is as slippery as the painter cat that shares his name. He was ever known to be an able man in the wild, which is why we never hoped to collar him in casual patrol when he was no more than a fractious misdemeanor up there in the Free State stilling splo, playing the cunny hound, and eye-gouging with his ilk. Now all evidence signifies him as the culprit in this dastardly affair of Leaf Pogue and the girl, and he must be delivered before the gavel. Nor will Cash's intimates in the township let that old matter rest.

Warrants aplenty today for nonpayment, assault, and petty pilfery, but they are the reason deputies are born and sworn. This morning's mail brought a sealed dispatch from the capital that reward will be paid out for leads to Painter's arrest. My own fear is that he has absquatulated, feeling things too hot in my bailiwick for his pleasure, but I will follow the creek again and discover what Nettle Mountain and Yankee Horse Ridge have yet to reveal. Last time I ventured up there to the catamount kingdom was pure snipe hunt, all the shiftless hill hawks mouthing out false information on everything from where the creek forks to if Painter did ever abide in the old bark mill said to be anent his brother's freehold. Although I know those people have been left scathed in the wake of the timber boom and bottom-out of the saltpeter wells, you've got to plant the seeds you're given and grind the corn they grow; whereas, these Cashes and Painters, Eisenhowers and Griffins turned to mischief natural and quick as a roused hornet stings. What I require to sweep this arena is a company of Rough Riders.

The sullen nature of the whole district not being enough, I was fair skunked under the lee of the crest and nearly thrown by Sylvester, whose nose took as much offense from the polecat as mine. You might expect the predictable showers to provide some relief from the insult, but that reasoning suffers defects, and back at the office Lish Jackson found it all a great rusty and howled till he near choked. I am now riled personally on this matter of the renegade and will balk at nothing to fetch him before the bar and thus to the gallows, God willing. If I come back empty this time, it will not be before I am assured of his exile to some place not on the charts.

Responsibility being a many-sleeved jacket, I must now ready myself for Preacher Rose and his pullet wife, who come to take a cold bite with us this evening. Adair has been redding up the house all day, and I must make my manners and pretend interest in questions of new pews and robes for the choir. Will we dispatch a mission to the China, and who will mow the glebe? These are matters meant to keep us of sound mind and not over-trained on the Manchurian war and other major key troubles of the world, so I will endure as well another hour about the pianola, which Adair plays with great enthusiasm and virtue but little glory. It is her armor against tidings I bring home from the courthouse and cell block. Bless her knack for conjuring such foils.

May 6

John Pink sauntered in today. A tanner by trade, he has been of use on occasion as a scout and knows the factions up on Irish Creek, where they call him "Constable Pink" in ridicule. Pink is a rough sort but of good and pliant purpose, and I am comforted to think him on the side of order. His tall size and beard shape him just like another tush hog from that neck of the woods, but he has even judgment, a flair for moderation, and eyes the blue of cue chalk. I have come to abide him well, and he is a crack shot and not a man to chew his tobacco twice before moving.

We drank a full pot of coffee just slightly softened from the flask and scanned the survey map, touching on crossroads and granges where we can trust to what gossip he might assemble. I then walked him down to my father-in-law's stable and rented a good horse, a bay belonging to D. D. Moore himself. So many of our highborn neighbors trust their movements to haggard nags and intractable spavins, I was afforded pleasure to see him thus served. Pink has his own lever rifle, but I gave him a sack of cartridges and my good wishes, plus a dollar for grub. He will be up there mixing with the drovers and their feuds longer than I could stomach, but I trust he is the man for it.

Nothing much more to report but an afternoon on a stern courthouse chair giving testimony on civil matters, for which I again give thanks. Drone and drone. The tedious will weary you, but will not shoot from cover.

May 9

All morning at my paperwork, but crows continue to alight and debate on the backhouse roof. Up close they look as silk, but otherwise live in the sky, which on days like this occasions envy. A telephone message relayed from Pink asserts he has found one reliable spy amid the forked tongues. By general assent Painter is moving among his confederates, broguing it back and forth like a lostling, but never too far from a jug of busthead and a wench. It puts me in mind of Cuba again when we led Colonel Monocle, feather in his cap and pistol popping off to no particular effect, up San Juan Hill. It was a botched job with little of the tactical in it, nothing of the gallant, more blood than design. That such action put the subsidy of "soldier" on a no-count like Brodie Painter taints the whole *Maine* affair further, and what do we want from Cuba anyway, as we raise our own effective cigar burley right here on Commonwealth soil?

This black mood is no doubt come of my knowing I will soon have to jaunt back to Irish Creek and drag the grapple for our prey. It is no wonder legends and ballads rise up from that purlieu. The feel of rot and fester is general, the close-breeding mix little aided by the influx of tin miners and other roughs. Knowing that Jackson came to these surrounds as a mine man and Pink as a hide hunter doesn't abridge the stench of bark mills and tanneries, and I have twice heard hushy mention of a second version of the Leaf murder which I am loath to entertain. Either way, Leaf is dead and Painter is the killer, so I had best cease pollyfoxing and gird myself for a campaign. Daily some well-wisher like Turner or Dr. Cravits stops by the office to wish me luck in the matter, but I can read between the words.

Was ever a man less inclined to keep oiling a Webley and waxing the draw leather than me? The star I collect payment for sporting emits little light in such times. But the vote on which joiner will receive commission on the church pews looms heavy this week. Settle for that distraction and hope for the best. May the daily torrent at least rinse something clean. Now to split some nightwood and turn in. God bless and keep and so on.

May 28

Pouring down rain, pouring down rain. The Maury is at flood again and little chance to move about with dispatch. This wilderness business sits heavy on me. Today I have the chivaree of Bob Dove as accompaniment, as I was roused last night to attend his pranks at the Star Diner and subsequently had to take him into custody. He is most often an affable and harmless drunk, but something was stuck in his craw last night concerning the jibes of some cadets from the Institute, and he was busting glass and spreading threats like broadcasting so much wheat seed, though today his sole crime is that tuneless caterwauling.

I must plot this campaign anew, as the Irish Creek inmates seem little inclined to step forward for the reward, and Pink's agent, whom I know of only as Cratis, has turned in a blank book where details of the fugitive's habits and dens might be concerned. If you believe hearsay, the creature is at once everywhere and none, reeling at a party in Brownsburg and pistol-whipping a barber in Amherst ten minutes later. Pink further reports that Painter has posted in one tawing shop a notice of two dollars reward for the governor's own noble pelt. If there is comedy in this, it is too rustic for my appetite.

I cannot strike from my mind today the first visit I made to the Pogue homestead last month. Granny Fell had already taken the assailed under her roof, and I expected to find the place empty but instead came up a draw on the morningside of the mountain, then over the ditch which resembles nothing so much as a siege moat, only to find myself facing a sallow girl sprite perched on the slanted porch of the shotgun house and plucking a white chicken in lazy and distracted fashion. The house was shabby with loose chinking, bullet scars, and scorch marks where somebody had done mischief. It was just touching twilight, and though the ash and dogwood, the judas and earliest blackberries were showing bloom, the big rose oaks were limb-empty and clutching at the sky with many claws. The first night noises were tuning up. The rain djinns were resting a spell.

I tied Vester to a shrub and approached the urchin when she leveled at me the most unnatural and lifeless pink eyes and commenced to sing softly in a nonsense jargon. She was clad in a coarse sacking, and her one hand began to snatch at the feathers with vim, tossing them aside almost in rhythm with her crude lullaby. It is Bob Dove's infernal serenade that puts me in mind of the scene again, and when I made effort to speak to her as one would gentle a jumpy filly, she slung the corpse over her shoulder, sprang up, and dashed through the gap and into the north room, the hen's red-combed head bouncing on her back as she ran, its dead eye squamous.

When I mounted the scaffold steps and entered, the room was near empty, most likely already plundered by those who knew the place uninhabited. Beside the cookstove a plank table was tossed aside and a rent patch quilt on the floor, the windows glassless but for the front one, the place a general shambles. A few bent speckleware cups and pans about, empty cans and windblown woods-debris, a chipped slop bucket. A whet strop hung nailed to the wall with pellets of scuttling creatures here and there, the whole affair shoddy. Seeing no sign of the child and aware I was soaked to the skin, I paused to surmise the unfolding of the drama — the two victims settling toward dinner, early moon hanging, the alleged felon charging in from the rain with a blade in his hand. Here the two men tangled and fell, there the girl sat shaking. Then the girl grabbed by her garment and thrown, mounted, and trod. I turned aside from it and walked through the open door.

The south room was smaller and more peculiar, as it had instead of door a curtain of loose-threaded feathers from various birds stitched to a hide. Two broken bedsteads with shuck sacking and a rocking chair not much bigger than a grown buck's rack were all the appointments, but the one wall where internal pine paneling had been raised was all scarred and painted in goggle-eye faces which appeared to predate the vacant state of the house. Now as I think back, I am sure there are many instances in which you can see what's not there as plain as Jacob's potatoes. Perhaps that was one such, and I have not thought to ask Granny Fell or Pink about the etchings, which no longer carry a stable shape in my mind.

Outside, an equally empty pig sty and backhouse, but no child, no sign or sound of company other than the poor-wills warming up, though I could see on the far peaks opposite thunderheads were mustering for storm. It was clear from first report that the remote location of the house would eliminate any opportunity to glean corroborations from the scene, and it seemed I could not now even keep hold of the one fleeting soul who had appeared and might be able to answer questions on the practices of the deceased. I shouted out a bold how-do to the general surround and raised no answer but the shadow of my own voice and wondered were the portraits inside a child's rendering of shoats and the old brindle boss Pogue was said to have owned. I had no doubt those beasts would be forever forfeit, melted away like spring ice.

Though there was no time to descend the mountain before full dark and hovering rain, I was disinclined to pass the night on the murder grounds, and as the cutthroat was intimate with the place, I preferred we might stumble upon one another under different circumstances and thus stirred with dispatch toward a homestead known to me just under the ridge, where I was offered a good bait of supper and pallet, along with a gill of other refreshment and fine-strand tobacco for my briar. Sleep came easily but brought vexing dreams of the glimpsed child and the queer drawings, and I wished for the warmth of Adair's flank and the comfort of her steady breath. It is tempting enough to remember that another brand of life might proffer more explicit pleasures than quiet affection and trust, but in suchlike haunts and on such occasions, only a fool would fix merit on anything trimmed with risk or steeped in shadows.

My dark reverie, if that be the wordage for it, was brushed aside by the sound of Lish Jackson's voice declaiming an urgent message, which turned out to be no more than reminder from Adair of our invitation to a garden party at the manse. The commotion was enough to stir Bob's voice to new verses.

The fresh editor of the *Rockbridge County Gazette* is eager to announce the reward, so I must supply my consent. Before we are waded deep into June I hope to put this Brodie case behind me, if I have to posse up and send him and all the moonmen up there to Ujinctum. For the present, it is pressing to attire myself for the soiree. Therefore the thinking day is ended and finds me in dry clothes. For that much, thanks be.

June 4

Today as I loafed by the door of Brown's Forge, I saw the Irish Creek girl passing by, slogging through the mud gum, evidently toting milk for Granny Fell. She stopped full still before McCrum Drug on Nelson Street and gave me a hard look with those bitter eyes. I reckoned she was using jimson weed to darken her stare and berries on her mouth. The only sound discernible to me was Muse Brown's hammer ringing the iron for Vester's left hind shoe, and when she caught my gaze, Miss Grove resumed her stroll, swinging the rack of milk bottles till the sound of glass rattling liked to wash out the racket of metal. As she sashayed down the street, I saw the afternoon sky was gone to quicksilver and doubt not we'll see the resumption of the judgment rain that has baptized us all season. Ofttimes, I almost sense connection between her disturbing aspect and the disrupted sky.

Queries from the citizenry persist. I must soon move to tighten the snare about Painter, who we now learn has not been in the county at all but shammicking down in Roanoke, where the spindle side of his clan was once known to squat. As soon as I can trust a sighting in this district, I will convene a committee of riders and make a sweep. No more stealth and half-measures in this, no more doodle-bug-come-out and hard wishing at prayer meeting. If I am to continue boring with a big auger in this town, results must swiftly unfold.

June 15

The train wreck toward Fairfield has brought news from a brakeman well known to Painter that the wanted man is surely now in the area, tidings that must not lie unemployed. An illusion master said to be able to glean thoughts from the air and to snake-shed his own skin unveils in Buena Vista tonight, and would that I could trust such wonders enough to query him about the slippery outlaw.

    On the journey back from Fairfield, I yearned for time to pause by the old church at Gethsemane, where Mother and Father lie at rest, but the current urgencies allowed only a glance from the road. At least the field is well scythed, and the yews shadow the slope with a feeling of peace. I must return with Adair on Decoration Day to set fresh flowers and clear the stones.

June 20

After several days of sog and commotion I am at last able to report the capture of the outlaw Painter, which went not so smoothly as we had hoped, but as he is the most public catch between Roanoke and Staunton, my relief is not paltry.

    Word came the fugitive had phantomed in and out of our jurisdiction at will in the guise of a woman but was now bold enough to call on his brother Darl and move among other kindred, though always by stealth and moonlight, so I gathered a squad of willing men and headed for the steeps with a provisioned jack in tow. John Pink and his cousin Suttock on the latter's apt-named Mud were there, also Drennin, who is claimed able to track at a gallop, and two others. We met Chief Hazelwood aboard a dapple I do not know on the White's Gap and swept watchfully in a long arc toward the Painter place. As per usual, the rain was our constant companion.

    We assayed first the Blood Tavern, where the accused is wont to linger, and not finding him there put out word among the local hog rangers we would retire to Lexington in defeat, then feinted southwest before double-tracking. The first night found us in Turkey Hollow, confident in our ruse, but we kept a cold camp and slept in a tight of laurel to prevent detection, though our tenting provided inadequate comfort. Of all the wildcats I have pursued this man cat was among the cagiest prey, and with all South Mountain's caves and hells offering refuge, we were far from assured of success.

Next noon found us circling slowly — Dark Hollow and Big Dark, easing in on the base of Nettle Mountain, where we were bound. The woods are lively there, glossy, and more than a few rudducks would break from cover flashing their red wings. This in full sunshine, to our amazement. Twice we spied scheming belltails coiled snug behind conchy logs, but we gave them wide berth. I can easily see how those briar hoppers escape accounting and rusticate while running laurel farms and bobcat herds, as the tales have it. This is not yet a tamed tract. Goat's beard and hellebore were common amid the itch ivy, and the footing treacherous over declines of slate waste. Though it was good to be in the saddle, not a soul we rousted could inform us of any events beyond their immediate sight. If the local denizens harbor any respect for the law, they are sworn to secrecy on the matter.

Vester issued his protest nicker and slung his mane about more than once in the hard going, and I hated to push him through such terrain, as he is no hog pony nor slink hound but a good horse for the chase. Still, there was nothing else for it, as we wished to close in on Painter's trail before he might again flee.

Being apprised of the partisan nature of the neighborhood, we were always on alert for bushwhackers, and the nervous result brought Suttock and Richard Travers near to blows over a trifle on one occasion. Not a little wind was spent on the rascality of Painter, his invisible nature and deep schemes, and I again remarked how he seemed a four-legged painter more than human. Not one man jack among us doubted his culpability, so we moved through briar and blowdown with resolve, always single file, often leading our mounts over scabby ground. We also found that region much tangled in suckle vine, and despite the blossom waft, the Irish Creek area had about it some odor of decay and abandon throughout the ivy slick. The ceiling dropped low and threatening again, and the much-washed earth had sprung up every species of noxious toadstools as recompense. In one beat-down I took for bear wallow a great razorback tushed by and startled the entire party to snatch for weapons. The whole district exhales the hospitality of a grave.

There being no real path in the final mile along the bluff, we were obliged to conceal our horses in a barn and pioneer through dense green to achieve a vantage over what Pink claimed to be the seat of the clan. It was slow going, and the day a sweat bath with further showers impending, but we shuckled as best we could and just before dusk found our target. You could see the frames of drying pelts and a lot full of sorry-looking cull hogs. Critter traps, some bee gums, punky cordwood, and divers trash cluttered the demesne, and from various trees hung a kind of bonechime — jaws, ribs, back knuckles, and skulls still slick with gore, whether to lure ghosts or repel angels no man could have ventured. A slight worm of blue smoke rose from the flag chimney, but no soul moving, so we took to the rocks and laurels, deploying in skirmish fashion, waiting for life signs. Last daylight was a rouged edge through the foliage, but I found little of beauty in it. I checked my watch and my revolver over and again, reminding the Lord to keep a sharp eye, as I was entering danger, though ostensibly clothed in the power of the law.

Before twenty minutes had passed, the jar-flies humming up in their seven-year chirr, I could see a window opened in its sheath at the back of the dark house, and a dim figure appeared — Darl, who having somehow surmised the besiegement of the house intended to make for the tree line and apprise his kin.

That was not allowed, as Chief Hazelwood surprised the brother with a Spencer rifle at the level, as he rounded a strawstack. As Haze marched him around to the front, Darl, who has much of the scarecrow about him, made to jackrabbit, and for his efforts received a blow from the gunstock behind his knees.

Sam Watts of our party then rushed into the house, where the distaff kin huddled, and purported he would kill every man, woman, and child if they issued a sound. He was snarling like a coon dog and they wolving back when I entered the fray and found a quartet of females, all with hacked hair and wearing frocks sewn from the same bolt. All were sparrow-eyed and snaggley, the least a mere imp and the eldest a crone of rawky voice, dugs scarce covered by her cloth, and her steady sneer evidenced she bore no respect for my badge or rabbit-eared two-barrel. Everything in the single-room cabin was ashed and scutty with a stink of fish and rancid lard, and I would have been much pleased to be in any other of the world's sculleries but that one. Soon our party were both in the reeking house and beyond it, a picket line of our deputies to let the fugitive pass through, and with lanterns lit inside, we impressed the women to make supper motions and stir the fire.

Before long, the object of our search emerged from a stand of scrub pine, his expression that of a preacher on a spree, an old Colt Navy dangling from his hand but his gait a carefree lope. Although he was much altered since his soldier days, I knew him at once. He is the blackest of the Painters, likely issued from different loins than Darl, and in that twilight one could indeed describe him as damson. At his approach Pink shouted his name, as in turn did we all to announce the full surround. The women, knowing Painter's indisposition to surrender and seeing so many firearms brandished, commenced to plead and keen for their beloved relative's life, and he raised his hands as if to come in peaceably, bringing me to a sigh of relief. Catching his face holding back all feeling, I had to think for one moment he was but little different from myself — worn out and edgy — and hoped he would yield easy.

But that was not to be. Haze strode forth with the irons in his hand, and just at that pass, Painter abandoned his ruse, roostered his hammer, and dropped to his knee to fire a ball at the Chief. We can only assume that the chamber was null or wet, as the sole sound was a dry snap, and by then Suttock feathered into the man with his Winchester, swatting as if he had an axe handle. Even stunned and bleeding from the temple, Painter, who is both stout and tall, was loath to be manacled or handled roughly, and he thrashed about. I finally had to put on the quietus with a blow to his nape from my belt stick. Peeling back the sleeve of his dustcoat and shirt, I saw the viper drawn into his skin, though hardly visible against his own dark surface. He had affected a handlebar moustache and bore scars unknown to me, but this was surely our culprit.

Even after the man was cuffed and revived and I had served the papers, he was no more cooperative than a mad fox, snarling curses at us and kicking till I decided to hobble him as I would a headstrong colt. When he spat my name and called me a pussle-gutted son of Nick, I had heard enough and swatted him out again. All along Sam Watts held his weapon trained on the rest of the family, taunting them as they reined still enough to satisfy any portrait photographer. Darl was so flinchy-eyed I felt certain he was scouting for some edged tool to make an unwise demonstration, so I judged it best to cuff him as well.

Coming to all bound up, Painter heard Hazelwood to say we should best shoot him on the spot and sling him down the shaft of an old tin mine to save the county money and the poor victim much discomfort and trauma. This was laughed off by some of us, though Pink alleged as this was far the best suggestion of the campaign. For my part, I am sorry to say, the proposal seemed not without merit, but I registered at once we were too many eyes and tongues to keep such a course concealed. The banter seemed to have a sobering effect on the accused, however, who was thereafter compliant except on the matter of his army hat, which he insisted in vain we fetch from his camp among the hemlocks. Watching in lantern light his coiled hair as he sat the jack on our descent, I could not but think this was all a tainted business, neither clean nor worthy of our charge.

After the prisoner was delivered to Lexington the next day in sheveled and humbled state, the posse was dismissed, and the cost of this chapter of the manhunt to the county has been in excess of thirty dollars, including rations, grain for the horses, and three dollars bounty for each volunteer. The distance covered in the hunt, much of it through rough mountain, could scarce be less than a hundred miles, though the map reckoning from Lexington to the headwaters of the Pedlar and back is but forty-two miles. I must continue to implore the county to ordain a constable to take jurisdiction in the Irish Creek region, as upheavals there are frequent and the labor and cost of enforcement from town prohibitive. Though yet a somewhat hale specimen, I do not possess the resources for many more such misadventures, and I relish them not at all.

Tonight I will cap my pen with some small satisfaction and truckle off to bed somewhat less burdened. If the trial unfolds as I foresee, I can either stay my current course or option for the stabling enterprise in the autumn with assurance of widespread support, not to mention Adair's delight, which is nearly enough to put the heart back in me.

Final Testament of Brodie Painter, September 7, 1906

She said he would not be about, would be down in the levels to fetch a spool of wire and a rabbet saw. That is the story I opened to lawyer Spencer, but he allowed as how it would not wash in court. There was a prejudice against me among the hatefuls, and I'd have to make shift for myself. This being my last shot to spill the whole tale with noose-day just around the bend, Mr. Prescott, please be kindly to mark it all down, spike to scut.

As I was saying, Ina and me was no strangers one to the other. There's many a time we had spoke previous, and she had showed me her sweetmeats when I first chanced on her up in the orchard. We had enjoyed full congress every occasion afterwards, as I honed for her steady. Though I am an old hand at scamping about, swiving and giving mustache rides to loose gals from here to Christmas, she was the sort that put your sense away from you, made you give up all other donies and train your heart on her. I thought she seen it that way too, and when we twined, I law, it was like a fire on fire. She made my blood to sing.

I had been paying her that fashion of courtship for two months and had already gave her patent slippers and a red frock when Pogue discovered the pretties and wrenched the matter out of her, and what she pleaded to me was he was agreeable to my repeating so long as he reaped a full dollar each time I called, on account of her age. He would make hisself scarce off with the hogs or out after squirrel, except I could oftener hear him blowing that French harp up in the brush. Spook music is what he made, and it was no aid to love dealing and rankled me somewhat. Still and all, we had some merry times, and when I debouched, I would leave my dollar on the keghead.

That was the bargain, and it suited me well enough till she commenced to whisper that himself was rutting at her too, which was by my reckoning full tilt unnatural. A Pogue will do that, you know, will jape even his mother when in a needful state, and there's slathers of them down in southside who show the nasty fruit of it.

She asked would I spirit her off, as she knowed the whereabouts of his money poke and had some kin over to Kentucky we might veil with and farm moon till Pogue turned over a new leaf, which gave her the giggles. You know, his name. Though I had done struck my bargain with him and spit over it, that was in ignorance, and I won't suffer nobody cutting my territory like that, won't tolerate it.

So that afternoon I come up the wash expecting nothing but a couple of gills from the jug and needling her to the bone, which I done fine and fancy. She has all the buck and moan of a Cuban washwoman, you know. It was a mighty tussle. Later, whilst we was laying up in the shucks listening to the quillerees high in the oak woods, she was snuggling while I stroked her slow along the moosey. As she is honey-voiced, she commenced to croon a little infare, and then we fashioned out our plan to make tracks off for blue grass in just a week, when Pogue would be off trading his angel's teat whiskey. I knowed well my brother Darl would help smuggle us out in a freight wagon, then onto a slow train, and no man be the wiser where she was gone. It was a sweet thought, and whilst I savored it, my heed was down. I was a mooncalf in full daze.

I know you have cause to judge me on further accounts, the killing of Cash and more trifling matters. If ever a man needed a view window in him, Cash was it. He had cleaned my brother's plow twice over the matter of one sorry salt lick, and had once slandered my mama to boot, so his calendar was out of pages. He gloried in everybody's miseries. I admit to plugging him with my daddy's pitted old 32.20, but don't be forgetting he had a rifle gun hisself.

There's always those who put the stain on ridgers like me just to even things. I can shoot sharp and ride like a demon and cipher faster than a storm bolt. My whiskey is always silver bead, and I can ringer a horseshoe most every time. I can shear muttons, skin and stalk and witch wells. I have always been a step ahead of others, and the snake-faced bastards didn't savor it.

Much accused meanness I am lamb-innocent of, but I have drawn slurs like a gutted cur draws flies. It is no doubt the Melungeon in my blood that makes me the blame goat for so much, and even in the Spanish war I found charges heaped against me before ever I could kick off the blanket of a morning. If I am guilty of half what they have laid to my door, let my spirit take flame in hell's hottest stall. I have stilled and scrapped and raised my voice against the heel of lily-white men who wish to scoundrelize us of color. I have thumped those who come up against me and swapped rich people's cattle for binge money, but I never raped at that girl or any other, nor needed to, and what Pogue got he requisitioned on his own account. He will be little missed, especially among those who relish real music.

He come stomping up the porch afore I knew he was on the mountain a-tall, and he called out her name like a he-bear roaring. Ina run out the room with the quilt wrapping her while I snatched my trousers up and legged in. He was storming at her, and when the smack of his hand on her face sounded, I run out the feather curtain and into the kitchen room with my boots in my hand. He saw me then, mister, and slung her aside like a poppet. I could see his face was the hue of lean meat, and he shouted out, Painter of the painter cats, you have brought your prides out into the open in my house onct too often. That was when he snapped the twine round his neck and drew the straight razor from his shirt front. I could see it was a nicked and ugly thing, rusty and long unused for shaving, as Pogue's whiskers were end-of-winter.

He started circling and me circling backwards till I spied the meat knife amongst the dishes, so I seized it up and took a crouch to fend him off. He jumped and I jumped, and it was arms and legs a-tangle for a minute there, me not sure where he left off and myself started, but for his teeth in my neck. Then in a quick jab I drew blood from his belly, and when he staggered back, I went slashing random-like and got the throat, I reckon. I was right drunk, but I am not a man to mess with. If you have seen a pig cut, you have seen that much spray, but if not, you can't even speculate, so I must of got him. He went to knees, then face forward, and the girl was screaming like a wildcat till something over her head seemed to catch her voice and bandy it back down. That was when she went dark and dropped to a heap on the floor.

The boards was loose fitted, and I could see young shoots prying green underneath and thought I might be sniffing the tang of new-sprouted mint. When I leant over to stir Ina that we might scape the place together, I slicked on what must have been his blood leak and fell on my backsides hard, for which there was nothing but to laugh it. All the bouts and skirmish I had been through, and never before ripped a man's life out of him, excepting Cuba and also

Cash, but the court quit me on the Cash matter. It takes a part out of you, killing a man. It sucks you down like a water whirl. Now here I was over a crow-haired, scarce-hipped girl-child all trussed up in the kind of trouble that won't rub off with neither words nor worry, and here I am now about to climb my last stairs.

Laying there, she was blue in the face as a possum's cods, and tossing dung and dogwood on the coals in the stove box, I kettled water and thrashed about for some mixings. I was still blurred in my sight with the whiskey and having some trouble sorting things. What I found was a honey jar with a mouse drowned under the comb, but I poured off the top and tippled a dad of blockade in to stiffen it. That and the cooked water I brought to her lips with honest regard, but once I roused her, she right off started to take Pogue's part, weeping and carrying on like I was the varlet, and I couldn't wedge in so much as a word but what she would scrowl out again. I never known the beat of it, and seeing no hope of our traveling plan coming to bloom at that point, I reckoned such as me had best be scarce when the world come to know whatever story she was fixing to tell. Couldn't no good come of it for me, that was a sure fact. It was a red business all around.

Riddle me how you would of acted in such a mangle. I could figure the law would be on me like ducks on a crippled June bug, so I rifled and skeltered the place till I found the wall board warped out from prizing. Back there was the money poke, sure as ramps root neigh creek, and I took half the eagles, thinking Ina would need some her own self. Then I lit out, not giving a back glance.

What come strange to my ears in the court was all these other tales spun concerning my rangering about in the weeks following. What I really done was leg it down to Vesuvius and wait under Orion and the bears on a steep where the train would stop to take on water for steaming up the grade. Once on, I rode all about, hopping off for provender and some loft sleep, but high-tracking it from Green Cove to Damascus, Bansock to Luray, Lithia back up to Second Pigeon, steering clear of Lexington and its ward. I rode the Norfolk and Western back and fro all over the mountains, breathing in the smoke whilst it shadowed laundry on the line by daylight, laying on my back to watch it silvering against black night. All my running mates from the N & W I would surprise at their lunch pails or when they were frying up corn dodgers at railside. They credited the story I have rendered you and gave me forage, but I will not raise their names in this matter, as I know the law's grudges do not die off easy.

This is my honest story of how a misfortunate man come to be painted as desperado. They come after me in their black coats like corpse birds and sneaked up on me asleep by my fire. They beat me and gave me the boot, called me nigger and spat in my face. They shoved and cuffed my whole family, too.

This is how a man with no evidence against him got hunted down by a pack of bounty hounds. Scribe this down right, mister, and you can show it to whosomever might have an eye for justice, 'cause the public needs knowing even too late to save my neck what manner of rascals ran their statutes and how a man can suffer evil though he swore on the preacher book and let only unscutched truth cross his red tongue. I'll sing the devil this same tune tomorrow in his crowded coal hole, Mr. Prescott. A man in the derbies and the scaffold's shadow has no call to throw the lie.

Oral History, Staunton, Virginia: Ina Grove Fell, 1964

When I came to a woman was screaming through the rain. That's what I thought. I didn't rightly understand where I was, the room blurry with a funny smell, but I could hear her voice, all fury. A light was coming through the apple tree and then the window, a green light, and I thought it was going to sift through me like some loose flour. Thirst was what I felt, almost that only. I thought the scream was going to shake me back to darkness, and I was shivering. Then I knew the woman was that blue jay nesting in the north haw. I smelled the hard smell and saw a rough face moving between me and the green light, and then I felt sore all over, a slow ache that went sharp in my fork. My knickers were gone entirely, and all my clothes. I was twisted in a robe like a Bible wife, but it was a quilt. Things started to remember. The face was moving, and something rusty was dried on my legs, and something else. This feeling had been upon me before, but never so severe. I thought I would die and I wanted to die. I wanted that jay woman to cease screaming, but I was crying to match her, and I thought another bird like some sparrow with purling notes should light in the apple tree any minute and trill out so its song might lift me or duck me under for good. I might just drink it and be drunk by it and rise up invisible as a ghost and shed all my troubles. Woe be.

That was a long time back, and I was only a girl who saw blackbirds in her mirror and eyes of a cat. Some things you misremember, and others shimmer and divide up. I think my daddy used to say we tell stories to forget what we need to get behind us, but I have never told this one, since I was spared most of court. What I swore then was what I thought, and though I had been something of a wild girl, nobody had the right to do me like that and go free. Since Uncle Leaf was dead, it was best to forgive him any trespass or unseemly reaching and move on. I did. I moved on. I know that Painter pushed at me before and pushed till I gave in listening to the yellow jackets drilling windfalls, a red color like off the ripe fruit overhead. When he was done I felt different with a hard rank smell on my clothes and salt in my eyes, but he gave no gentleness, saying all woman folk are born with the round heels. Then he galloused up and said he'd see me again, not even looking back. I hoped he'd never.

When I saw Uncle Leaf sprawled in the blood, his eyes were open and baleful, glaring fierce, and I did not know if he was alive or dead. Stop hexing me, I shouted, and the other face was still moving around me, about the house, its voice saying calming things, but I was not calmed.

Some times you don't want to say a thing as it will loose a whole waterspill of words you can't bear to hear, the rushing of every fear you've ever had burning as it crossed your tongue. I was wracked and damaged, and my only close kin looked dead, no matter how angry his eyes, no matter how little pity he'd showed in his life. The other thing in the room was gone then, but I could taste honey. The watchbird had screamed itself from blue to red, and then it fell off. I went swoony again and slid into the dark.

That night the Io moth came to my window like a mask, its buckeye eyes boring into me. I had been often accused of making flirtation and primping, but this was a new thing, and I did not take pleasure from any of it at all.

Those years I worked for Granny Kate with the stain on my name, most people showed kindness, and I learned the ways of her milk cows and how to churn. Flies would light in the cow pies and then on the bucket rim. People drank it anyway. They didn't see. She gave me Chichester's English Pennywort concoction with a paste of her own devising, and what made me swell seeped out one night, but not without pain of the damned. Granny taught me her potions and poisons and how to gather makings off in the forest. Also to read. Four years after the misdeeds I climbed up after a Christmas snow shower with a jug of coal oil and splashed it about inside the rubble of the old place. I set the match and stood back, shivering under a rind moon, watching the boards smoke and catch and blossom. It was time to sear the ghosts out, time to send my girlish wall etchings back to whence they came, though they had once been my only true friends. I knew the hive in the walls was still and the bees sleeping in their wax wouldn't feel a thing.

Only the spy apple tree by the window caught the fire, its limbs spidery against the winter air and then glowing. The house shouted and crashed, black clouds coaxing night to hurry on, and when the roof caved, something inside me lifted, delivered me, and I was no longer so lost.

I became a woodsweed girl with pestle and mill and steam kettles, a whole cellar of concoctions, but when Granny Fell foxed out that my mama had passed over birthing me, she said I could be a thrush witch, named after the bush bird, and that was my main call, blowing the sick color from the throat of a child. I cut bloodroot and pulled sang. I gathered galax. I was a cat keeper and nightwalker, a tender of gold bees, and I could sew and bantle, nurse and drive a nail straight to the heart. I was alone. I got by.

I won't say there was no other. In the doughboy times I slipped off some and had no regrets, but I had already shut my heart and shot the bolt. It was just a letting go here and there, then back to my pets, my own cow barn by then with peafowl strutting. I would lie under the rhododendrons and stare a lady slipper in the eye. I was comrade to orchids and a friend to owls.

It was the year that rain was raining all the time, and I recall Granny wet and cold when she found me, me cold and wet too by then, because the roof was not tight. It was the year the ferro beetles showed up for their seven-year courtship, and what I heard them saying, even in town, was spoiled, spoiled, spoiled. It was a question why my uncle and another with skin so blue he was a dark flower at first would pitch into killing rage over me, as not one seemed to want much to do with me most days. That is the limitation of a man.

It was a hard tramp down South Mountain to a road, but she propped me and kept shushing when I tried to say what all I reckoned had transpired. She named birds in the trees and flower bells by the pathway, keeping my mind from drifting back to that blood scene. It wasn't till I'd had a night sleep and bowls of broth and some dittany tea with hard brandy that she said, let's tell it now, and the whole swirling tussle came back before me, the blades in frailing light, some rutting and laughter, the red tide and apples, jay scream through green light, and the hint of honey. Before long the pieces in my heart had commenced to come together like a puzzle, while the rain was drumming again, shaking me back to that day with its whirlwind and bloodshed, and then I knew what I knew.

The Account of a Baffling Spirit Appearance as
Reported by Sister Sura Sawyer in the *Roanoke
Alternative Magazine,* April 7, 1965

As I was about to release my familiar, Prince Akira, at the conclusion of a successful séance, a voice unknown to me interceded and delivered a mysterious report which bore on none of the present circle but which seemed not of negligible import. As follows is my best recollection of the monologue spoken by a beard-faced essence hovering above the table but never fully in focus, as tormented spirits are wont to appear:

When my sister Sheila passed in childbirth, I swore to help her lawful husband hold the child precious, as the Irish Creek was rife with copperheads of both the crawling and walking kinds. Poor sister, who was smitten hard with Anders Grove and never recovered from lovewit before she met her end. She was fool for a fiddle, and he bowed string music all along the Pedlar at play parties and stump speeches, moving widows, wives, and maids alike to sashay and smile. I took a shine to himself and pleasured at playing reel music to his devil's box. It's true enough he doted on her, but he had more eyes than the one, and they traveled, so even before Sheila was spent, I had concerns for her and the baby that he mightn't stay and provide. When Anders was done in by a broke shaft timber, I knowed the child would get her best raising from me alone. I might be prone to poach and loath to till, but I had my own ways of bringing the specie in.

Why I come back to speak with the white tongue is to say I done her wrong, swapping care for neglect whilst I milked the worm and horsed barrels of apple pomace about when it was too wet for the wheeling barrow. Good shine kept a roof over us and vittles on the table, but she much growed up her own creature till something ugly in me started taking low notice.

In close quarters like ours, you can't miss seeing, and she bloomed like the May apple all creamy and soft. Seems one day she was a doll child herself scolding the rag baby. Next day I was chewing sweetgum sap to cure my breath for her and sprucing my hair, as she was a little woman with fair flesh to taunt the hungry. I was hungry. I partook.

To even talk moonlight with such close kin is a misdeed, I know, and I would wish for a hard brush to curry myself after we cuddled. I would speak to God to stop me before hard harm grew to habit. I said, Lord, I would not wish to tread her, but I do, and nothing ever smote me.

There's another verse to that song. Ina was rambunctious and would always hide where I could find her. We kept up the tease game for a year, never fording the stream, but then Painter commenced skulking and watching. At first, I took him for a still spy and found relief on him ogling the house from out in the rain. I figured him for a half-breed the John Laws kept in corn to scout us, knowing that'd peg him as lazy. He'd be all vine and no taters, and nobody's idle spy will find where I shift my mash nor cut my faggots on Whetstone. By dark, in case he was peering from some windbreak, I'd have Ina strike the wick of a grease lamp and venture out to the crib or muck house. Anybody taking notice would follow her, and I'd slip over the casement and to my works.

But then I seen he had other notions. She come back from the slope orchard with an ill smile and said, when I asked after the lurker, that she'd seen nothing but two yanks nesting in a white oak and a checkervest hammering his mattock, after tree beetles. It was yet too airish for the birds to be stirring so, just Easter or thereabouts, and she had that grin like a doll's face stitched on. Jealousy is as bad to shake you as the preachers say, and if that Injun was to have zip on his stackcakes, it would not come from my ambry.

One morning I claimed to her I'd be off a whole day decanting my usquebaugh but circled back to catch them in the beast act, and sure enough they was raw and blushed when I come in, Eve and Adam, but him dark as the devil. It was rage, all I saw, and after I slapped her a strong one, I pulled the razor, so we went round, thrashing and panting like we was red-tails mating, but he got lucky and cut my breadbasket, which leached much of the fight out of me. Still I had the advantage, as I'd slung Ina about in my temper, and he went to tend her, then started heating up a pot of water, like he was to care for her, and I had forfeit all his attention on account of my weakness.

That was when I reached for my boot gun, as I should of done at the outset. I knowed it was closing in, the deep moment, and what I was fighting for might fall to me forever mine or never, so I stuck my hand down toward the pistol butt. Then it closed over me, something floating dark and silky as night wind, and I felt my throat tearing like a lamb's, the fountain flowing scarlet.

The spray of my own life toward a sway of darkness was the last thing I could ever see, and I am signed to tell it whenever a listener heeds.

The News-Gazette, March 4, 1968
IRISH CREEK PROPERTY SOLD TO
O'MALLEY LUMBER

The property previously known as the Pogue Homestead on Irish Creek has been sold by the County of Rockbridge to the O'Malley Lumber Company of Fairfield. The twenty-four acres of prime hardwoods had been held in trust by the county for three years against unpaid property taxes, and the commission voted last Tuesday night to approve the sale to Michael O'Malley.

The transaction would have proceeded with little notice but for Felton Newday's insistence that a brief history of the property be read into the record, as the Pogue place was the site of a vicious murder and rape of a young girl sixty-four years ago. It was also the known haunt of brigands and poachers, and the murdered Leaf

Pogue himself was long a recognized trafficker in illegal whiskies. The taxes were for a time paid sub rosa by a Ms. Fell every spring from 1954 until 1966 on the supposed anniversary of the crime, for which one Brodie Painter was convicted and hanged. The felon had put the old Pogue home to the torch after the crimes, but the outbuildings persisted as ramshackle reminders until the late fifties, and excursionists and hunters often used them as shelter. Many local residents will also recollect childhood legends of a spectral hen girl haunting the region.

Mr. O'Malley plans to harvest the timber and eventually offer parcels of the land as multiple homesites in a division to be called Kissing Ridge. The area harbors some of the most majestic white oaks, locusts, and hickories in proximity to Lexington, and it will be a shame to see them laid waste, but the council decided unanimously that continued suspension of taxes would be a burden upon the community budget, and as Chair Wheeler Sherburne remarked, "The time of outlaws like Painter and Pogue has passed, and it would be a relief to see a commercial venture usher the infamous Irish Creek region into the twentieth century."

JEFF SOMERS

Ringing the Changes

FROM *Danger City*

HENRY USED TO BE A JOLLY BASTARD and a lot of fun, but he'd taken the pledge and turned out to be dull as dust when he didn't have a drink in his hand. All he could talk about was his salvation, his sobriety. It was boring stuff. A million weak bastards before him had had the same revelation, and a million more were lining up to dry out after him. Nothing special about it, really, yet people always went on and on about it as if God had reached down and waggled a finger at them and no one else.

At least I was still working, and Henry was pretty good cover. Plus, there wasn't much Henry didn't know about what was happening in outline; his moment of clarity had apparently made old Hankie a good listener, so I felt it was a good idea to stay on his good side, in case I ever needed information. We used to be tight, and he used to be a grand time, so I gave him a little ear-time. I bought him a steady stream of club sodas, which he drank exactly as he'd drunk booze: never putting the glass down, using it to gesture his points, and killing it with a million little sips. If you weren't listening to his endless sermon about giving up The Drink, you'd think his glass was a vodka tonic or a gimlet.

It was slow, and I wasn't making much, so I hurried Henry along. I waved my hand at the bartender and looked at Henry, the dry old bastard.

"Want another?"

"Sure. You shouldn't go so hard, buddy. Believe me, I know."

I nodded, glancing at the bartender. "Another bourbon, kiddo."

He looked down at the pile of money on the bar, a crisp fifty right on top, and took my empty glass away. Keeping an eye on him, I inched my hand over and switched the fifty with one of mine from the bottom.

This is what I did. I made people see what I wanted them to see. Even Henry, who didn't notice that my glass was mostly melted ice and watery booze, hardly touched.

The bartender brought my drink and set it in front of me.

"You should charge more for nonalcoholic drinks, buddy," I said, catching his eye. "Discourage the teetotalers, eh?"

He shrugged, plucking the bill off the top, his eyes on me. "Nah. We don't get many in here anyway."

Without glancing at the money, he carried it to the register and rang up my change, bringing back forty-six real dollars and dumping them on the bar. I left them there for a bit, not even looking at them. After a while I'd collect them and put the fifty back on top. For the time being, I studied Henry as if he was the most interesting guy in the world.

"How long'd you do in Rahway?"

Henry nearly lost control of his glass, gesturing. "Three years. Best thing that ever happened to me."

Henry dried out in prison. At first it wasn't voluntary, of course, but then he hooked up with a substance-anonymous crowd and took the pledge. He was going on four years sober now — four sad, desultory, plodding years, but years he was proud of nevertheless.

"Nothing to do but think in prison," he went on. "Not for me, anyway. Some guys found other distractions, but I never had anything except booze."

Henry had no idea how true that was, I suspected, considering his gray, lifeless demeanor post-booze.

"At first all I thought about was booze. You could get some in prison, but I never could do it. I never had anything to pay with, except my ass, and I wasn't that far gone. So I thought a lot. And I realized that I was in jail because of liquor."

I knew this speech pretty well. Henry got pinched because he'd been loaded. It was pure professionalism that drove the man sober. He never wanted to fuck up again and land back in a place as boring as jail. Henry liked his cable TV.

I stopped listening, letting it wash over me.

Mine wasn't a high-rolling life. I made enough to pay the rent and keep things moving. There were no big scores to be had, I knew this, but there were also few chances at getting killed or arrested if I played it straight. Didn't get fancy. Counterfeit money got traced or sometimes spotted, and a lot of time people remembered me as the guy who spent a lot of fifties. I had to go to different places, work different neighborhoods. If I went to the same place twice, I could get pinched.

My man the bartender wasn't the brightest fellow in the bar, but I didn't think I could pass more than one or two more fifties his way anyway, and Henry was only on chapter one of "How I Won the War," just getting warmed up. So, I gathered up my cash, left a good tip, and stood up. Henry didn't care. He didn't even pause for breath, he just barreled on, giving me the background on his conversion from lush to self-satisfied teetotaler. I knew how it ended — with a lecture from him on why I was a fool to keep drinking.

Which was annoying, since I didn't.

I spoke right over him. "All right, Hankie, I gotta roll."

He trailed off and looked away, insulted. "Yeah, okay."

Walking out of the place, I felt sad. It was a good bar: dark and smoky, wood everywhere, and not filled with complainers. Good jukebox.

The Wallace Hotel was hovering between worlds — middle-class decay on the one hand, and people like me on the other. Cheap tourists stayed a few days at a time, or stylish tourists who liked the old-fashioned look of furnishings that hadn't been changed in fifty years.

And then there were people like me. We didn't have jobs or paperwork. We had cash, and an aversion to questions. I've lived there for two years and some weeks, and I've never once spoken with a neighbor. We were all perfect tenants because *we* didn't shit where we lived. We picked our messages up at the front desk, kept to ourselves, and paid our rent on time. The Wallace, no doubt, wanted more criminals to move in.

I had three rooms, a suite. It was cheap and clean, with a strongbox filled with cash hidden under floorboards beneath the bed: thirty-three thousand dollars, socked away a little at a time. It wasn't a fortune, but it was an insurance policy, a bit of scratch to carry me through a rough patch. I'd earned it all through small, safe grifts. I was careful, slow, and steady.

There was a coffee can in the cupboard with two grand in it. To look at the place, you'd think two grand's about the best I could do. I figured if anyone came snooping, they'd find the coffee can in about five minutes and think that was it.

I worked neighborhoods, using color-copy big bills — twenties and fifties. It wasn't very sophisticated, and it wouldn't pass muster with anyone who knew their currency, but it worked with distracted register jockeys untrained in catching counterfeits. I still got caught from time to time, but I found that I could usually bluff my way out by appearing as surprised as they were. Color-copy counterfeits, even on linen paper, didn't feel like real money, or smell like real money, but since I didn't get greedy, I pulled it off. I'd only print $5,100 in fifties, which is thirty-four double-sided copies. That's two bucks each on a self-serve machine unless I could scam free ones. So, for maybe seventy bucks, I had $5,100 in worthless money, which I then cut at home, carefully. Then I went shopping.

Most shop owners won't break a fifty for something small, but I wanted as much good money back for each fake as I could manage. I usually began by trying to buy a soda for a dollar, or a buck fifty. If they refused, I explained that I needed change. Sometimes I made forty-eight bucks, sometimes forty. Even at the low end, I made about four grand in a week if I managed to pass all the bills, but finding a hundred places in a week was hard. Each store took time, too. I had to cast the spell and do a little dance, be indecisive, pick up items and put them back, ask a lot of questions, be in a hurry — anything to keep the bastard from looking closely at my money.

The other half of my game had one simple rule: never pay bills with fakes. First off, my fakes were lame, easily spotted ones — I counted on bored, distracted people to accept them without question. Banks, on the other hand, would trace me.

The dying afternoon sun sifted through my blinds like dust and warmed the stale air in my suite. I stepped up to the bed, a simple twin with a crappy mattress that came with the place. The only thing I'd done was replace the thin gray mattress with a brand new thin gray mattress. I made money by not spending it, but I drew the line at sleeping with a previous tenant's skin conditions. In fact, news about mattress sales was the only real small talk at the Wallace.

I began emptying my pockets.

Sometimes even I was amazed at how much currency I traded in a day. I tossed bills onto the bed, big sweaty wads of them. I pooled the coins separately, for future sorting. Then, I sat down on the bed and sorted the bills, counting as I went. In bills, I managed three hundred and seventy-three dollars, which wasn't bad for an afternoon that had ended with Henry's lecture of sobriety. I piled the money into neat rubber-banded stacks, pulled out the strongbox, and the place filled with the golden light of upward mobility for a moment, improved the furniture, removed the water stains, and filled the cracks in the walls. I added the cash. A few quick adjustments in the ledger to reflect the new money, and I put everything carefully back where it had been, the strongbox chained to a bolt.

The apartment was transformed back into the last stop on the way down — nothing to see.

I went into the middle room to my bar, which was just a bottle of whiskey and a pitcher of dusty water. I poured two fingers of booze and stood by the grimy windows, yellow light illuminating the dust.

I felt tired and heavy. So much effort, just to survive. So I decided on a steak for dinner. I changed into a light suit to go to Andy's around the corner, where all the waiters had a good-natured competition for my big tips. Down in the lobby, I had messages. One was another grifter seeking a loan, but I had better things to do with my money; it never paid to admit I had enough to lend. The second message was from a police contact, an innocuous note signed "Mr. Blue." I pocketed them both and went to dinner.

My entire life was conducted on borrowed phones. A phone in my room, in my name, was irritating and incriminating, not to mention evidence of income, so I avoided it. At Andy's, I ordered a drink and studied the menu, had the phone brought over, and called the cop. He answered on the fifth ring, sounding breathless.

"Yeah?"

"It's your underground friend."

"Where are you?"

"Andy's on third."

"I'll be there, half an hour. Don't leave."

He hung up. Detective Paul Wilson was middle-aged, unhappy, and not averse to making a few bucks on the side. Nothing major: a little inside information, a little security work for nervous crooks. He never lost sleep over it. I'd had a few minor dealings with him, and we got along well.

I went ahead and ordered dinner. Paul showed up when I was halfway through my steak. He sat down quietly at the table and nodded at me by way of hello.

"Your name came up today," he said. Paul was a heavyset guy, and always sounded out of breath.

"Came up how?"

"In an investigation. Old business, but nasty. They're gonna come round you up. Ask a lot of questions. I thought I'd just let you know."

"What old business?" I kept eating. There wasn't any point in being dramatic about it.

"All I know is, the vic was named Murray. It was about fifteen years ago, but the case is still open." He shifted in his seat. "That's all I got. Just felt you should know, as an associate."

I chewed, trying to figure out if that meant he thought he could get more money out of me, or if he was dishing some honor-amongst-thieves bullshit, or if it was just simple human respect. "Okay," I said. "Thanks."

He waited a moment, unsure, and then stood up. "All right. Just thought you should know."

I nodded again and watched him leave. I knew the name Murray, and it was a problem — one I never thought I'd have to deal with. Then again, my associates were criminals. I never knew what they were going to do. Maybe someone gave up my name out of sheer terror, or happened to remember that I'd been in the same room with so-and-so once. I knew I needed to make some calls, but decided to finish my dinner, have some coffee, and relax like a civilized man.

That was a mistake. The cops, moving with unusual speed, were waiting for me at the Wallace. I didn't get a chance to make my calls. As I walked into my building, I acquired two hefty men in bad suits and gun-crowded shoulders who pushed me into one of the ancient plush chairs in the lobby and stood over me, making a scene in front of the concierge at the front desk.

"Walter 'Poppy' Popvitch?" the one on the left said.

The one on the right didn't wait for an answer. "Where you been, Poppy? We've been waiting for you."

I crossed my legs and regarded them, trying to look calm. "Out to dinner."

"Yeah, so he said, so he said," the one on the left nodded, looking around. "You mind we ask you a few questions?"

I shook my head. "Of course not. Can I ask you what this is about?"

I was selling ignorance, innocence, and confusion but the market was soft. They looked at each other. The one on the right shoved me, lightly. "Come on, let's go back to the station, be friendly."

"Am I under arrest?"

Now, I was selling outrage. This got me nothing but another shove, harder, but still short of a brutality complaint. "Not yet, but it's in your interest to keep us happy, Poppy."

That was annoying; no one called me Poppy. "You don't seem too happy *now*," I pointed out.

The one on the right glanced at his partner, as if saying *See? I told you he wasn't going to be friendly,* and slipped a hand under my armpit, pulling me up roughly.

"Come on, tough guy," he growled.

They had no warrant, and I wasn't under arrest, but I went quietly, like a good citizen. They had only two questions, but they got good mileage out of them, asking them over and over again.

"Did you know Andrew Murray?"

"No."

"Did you have anything to do with his murder?"

"No."

Between repeating their two questions, they jabbered on with a few scary details and hints that they had something on me. They didn't, though. If they had, I would have been under arrest. So, after a few hours, they let me go to think about it and put a tail on me. But I didn't care. I had nothing to hide: not much, anyway. I went back to Andy's, borrowed the phone at the bar, and made my few calls. After half a beer and a lot of dial tones, I tracked down Henry and told him I'd buy him dinner if he'd come down and let me pick his brain. Henry never turned down a free meal, and he knew everything about everyone.

When Henry showed up ten minutes later, I wanted to grill him immediately about Murray, but first, there were pleasantries. I'd offended Henry at our last meeting, and he walked in the place with the wounded air of a true martyr — a sober martyr at that, the worst kind. But I couldn't really blame him; since he'd lost the courage booze had given him, Henry made a good part of his living dealing and acquiring information, so it made sense that he'd want to keep things chatty, and I'd walked out on him mid-sentence. It was damned annoying, though, when I needed information and wanted to shake the bastard until his valuable head popped off.

I bought Henry a soda and let him harangue me about the lush Scotch on the rocks I was nursing. I endured him waving the glass under my nose, thick finger outstretched, as he delivered a sermon about the Rules of Polite Society and how you treated people the way you wanted to be treated yourself. Finally, he sighed piteously and bought me a drink, and I jumped in to bring up business before he could gather his energies for the standard higher-power sermon Henry liked to end ail his tirades with these days.

"I've been hearing a lot about an old piece of business, Hankie, but I can't seem to place the details."

"What business would that be?" he asked, sagging slightly until he seemed to be hanging off the bar.

"Somebody named Murray, gone to lavender a few years ago."

He closed his eyes and settled himself on the stool. Watching Henry think was more interesting than expected. He went into a trance and fidgeted, twitching and raising his eyebrows, scanning back through his photographic memory.

"Okay," he said, his eyes popping open. "I think I've heard about this."

"Good. How far back did you have to go?"

"Oh — about ten."

I nodded. A hundred bucks was cheap. And, it meant that he didn't see much value in the information, so was offering it at a discount. "Good number."

He closed his eyes again. "Andrew Murray, pickpocket. Worked the East Side, mostly. Subsistence kind of career, only big scores were accidental, whatever he happened to pinch. Not real smooth, either. Got caught several times, never arrested, beaten up a few times. Found dead in a public lavatory in Grand Central Station seven years ago, apparently beaten to death with a blunt instrument. Police assumed it was a pocketing gone wrong and didn't wind themselves looking into it. Case remains open.

"Word around town is that it was a fellow grifter did it. No names, just rumors. Doubt that some civilian could have whacked him, posed him in the can, and not leave a trace — must have been someone with skills. He had a lot of enemies, could have been anyone that he owed money to, which were plenty. He drank and gambled and liked to have whores on hand. He liked to live a flashy life on a very small income, and got in deep with shylocks, not to mention anyone dumb enough to give him a friendly loan. Drank like a fish and it sank him in the end. Your basic black hole. We've all known this guy and kept our distance. I used to be this guy."

He looked at me meaningfully, trying to communicate, no doubt, that he thought there was a little bit of black hole in *me*. I rattled the ice in my drink as a talisman and nodded, amazed — I wondered briefly what Henry would have been capable of if he hadn't soaked his brain in liquor for thirty years. But I was satisfied. Nothing unexpected.

"As you know," Henry went on after a moment, "your name comes into it."

I froze, careful not to reveal the shock. I took a sip from my drink, nodding.

"Let's talk about that."

Without opening his eyes, he raised both eyebrows, "Indeed. Let's. There's no direct connection, I don't think. It's a case of degrees of separation. The last person the police believe saw Murray was Miles Tucker. Tucker couldn't be tracked down for years; he'd left the city, and efforts to locate him and his various names and pseudonyms — as lackluster as they were — were fruitless until a week ago when Tuck reappeared at some old haunts, cheerful and buying drinks. Scooped up by some bored crushers, he provided your name as a get-out-of-jail-free card."

"Oh shit," I exhaled, draining my glass. I remembered Tuck, vaguely. Hadn't known him well and couldn't remember if he'd been there that night, but it was possible. It was feasible. I spent my whole life spinning the feasible into reality. I knew how it worked.

"Dismayed, Walt? That's either a fabrication or an inconvenience to you. Either way, the police will no doubt haunt you for a bit."

I nodded, signaling the bartender for another round. The fucking cops hadn't mentioned this guy's alibi to me, but that just meant Tuck wasn't very reliable and the cops were shaking the tree, seeing what fell out.

I dug out two more C-notes and slid them over to Henry. He looked at me.

"Tuck's real name," I said, accepting a fresh drink from the bartender gratefully. "And where he might be found."

Henry made the bills disappear. "Indeed," he said, managing to sound aggrieved about earning money.

After leaving Henry, I let the cops watch me go home. I fixed myself a cup of coffee and sat at the kitchen table for an hour, drinking and thinking. No one gave a shit about this clown Murray. The cops were looking for a quick and easy clearance. They wanted names they could take to court, and I doubted they cared much about the truth. And there I was, plain as day, for the cops to turn over and see what crawled out. I intended to remove myself from the equation.

My coffee finished, I changed into an old suit, opened up the bathroom window, and climbed out. From there, I was able to climb up onto the roof of the building next door. It was dangerous, but I'd done it before. I ran across my building and jumped over to another roof. Three more jumps, and I was able to climb down a series of fire escapes and emerge on the street several blocks away. I hailed a cab, gave the driver an address a few blocks away from the one Henry had given me. Then I spent some time looking out the back window for pursuit. I didn't see any, so I relaxed, watching the city go by.

The taxi let me off in a dingy, rundown neighborhood — I knew this one, knew where it was safe to spend my money and where I'd get broken hands for my trouble. I walked briskly to the address Tuck was using, bristling with anger. I remembered this fuck. We had nothing between us, I thought, but here he was, trying to jam me up. It pissed me off.

His brownstone, weathered and chipped, was in the middle of the block. The streetlight was broken, leaving the house in a shadow. This wasn't the sort of work I was used to doing, but I did what I had to do.

I walked up and rang the bell. The rest happened quickly.

The door opened, and an unfamiliar shape filled the space. I didn't pause to be sure, or to be clean. My knife came out, and I leaned in. I pushed it forward and up, pulled it out, then back again, punching him. He leaned backward, trying to climb up off my blade, but he leaned too far, and he toppled over. I stepped in and shut the door behind me. I looked down at Tucker. I was glad he wasn't some poor ass who got in the way, but regardless, this is how it had to be done — fast and thoughtless.

Sometimes, I cut a corner each off of four twenty-dollar bills and pasted the corners onto a one-dollar bill. It's surprising how often this works when a cashier is busy or stressed. It's a quick, dirty, and dangerous way to make a fast $100 or so; making people see something that isn't there.

This is what I did. I moved quickly through the house, and when I was sure there was no one else I left the knife in the sink and climbed out the bathroom window. I got home in an hour, walking the whole way. I didn't see any blood on me, but I wouldn't be sure until I got home. I climbed back in the way I'd gone out, inspected myself, and stripped, tossing everything into the garbage.

After a hot, hot shower, I stepped into a robe and felt good. I peeked out a window and checked out the cops, reliable as the sun. I made myself a coffee, and the cops saw what I wanted them to see. It's what I do.

SCOTT WOLVEN

Vigilance

FROM *Controlled Burn*

THIS IS WHAT HAPPENED, the same story I gave to the investigators:

I never met Carl Larson before I rented a one-bedroom house from him in Potlatch, Idaho. I'd seen a handwritten ad tacked to a bulletin board at the University of Idaho and I called the local number from a pay phone. An old woman answered and said she and her husband were Carl's neighbors, just handled the keys for him. She'd be glad to show me the place, but I'd have to talk to Carl about renting it. Her name was Rose. She gave me a long-distance number to reach Carl. I dialed.

A woman answered and I asked for Carl Larson and she asked what it was about. The rental, I said. A man got on the line and introduced himself as Carl Larson. He didn't mention a lease or paperwork. Nothing for me to sign. He asked me my name. Ed Snider, I lied. The utilities — phone and electric — stayed in his name. The phone was restricted from long-distance access to prevent renters from running it up, and the bill went directly to him. Same with the electric bill. All I had to do was mail him the first month's rent, a five-hundred-dollar money order made out to cash. There was a garage I could use however I wanted and Rose and her husband, Dan, would explain that to me. The house heated with a woodstove in the living room and a pellet stove in the basement. The garage woodstove worked and the neighbors would show me about turning the water on, which valve was the pressure tank, and how to empty the tank, in case I went away during a temperature drop. Keep a close eye on the pipes in winter, Carl said.

The number I'd called was in the nine-oh-seven area code, Alaska, and the mailing address he gave me was Fairbanks. Everything was to be sent care of L. Matthews, and he told me on the phone the address was the house of a woman he knew, a shirttail relation of his. He spent as little time in town as possible. He'd built a cabin way out in the woods, far away, where he hunted and fished a good part of the year. His friends on the peninsula were all big fishermen, some commercial. His voice was deep and old, a little slow in coming. We drifted into a brief conversation about states with a single area code being the best for hunting and fishing. Montana, Idaho, and Alaska we ranked as the top three. Vermont, New Hampshire, and Maine in the East. Neither of us had traveled east in years. Carl said he liked the people out west better and I agreed. One time, he said, years and years ago, he shot a twelve-point whitetail in eastern New Hampshire, on the Maine border. He hadn't expected to see a buck that size, ever, and his rifle was under caliber, the shot a hair too long. The hit was a solid lung shot, but the deer took off. Managed to get over the state line, marked in the woods. Carl came to a clearing and a logging road. Three Maine game wardens had the buck halfway dressed in the back of a pickup truck. Too bad about your New Hampshire deer, the one game cop said, he decided to die in Maine. That's people from the East, Carl finished.

Like he'd said, his neighbors Dan and Rose held the keys and they'd explain the trash to me, answer any questions at all. He asked me not to move stuff around in the house and to be careful with the taxidermy and I said I wouldn't and I said I would. How long did I think I'd stay in Potlatch, he asked, and I said I didn't know. I understand, he said, don't worry about it. Go look the place over and let the neighbors look you over. In the meantime, I'd mail the money order, and once it got to Fairbanks, I could move in, unless Dan and Rose didn't like the way I dressed out. He told me if I had trouble with money to ask Dan, there was always extra work around. He wished me good luck and I said the same to him. We hung up and I walked across downtown Moscow to the post office a block off Main Street to mail the money order. I wrote "Cash" on the To line, "Snider" on the From line.

My brother and I had given up a scrap business in Nevada, so I carried a little money, but not much. Thirty-five hundred dollars and a truck that ran most of the time. My brother headed to Seattle after a girl, and in Seattle there were lots of girls in case he broke up with this one, so after a while you didn't even ask last names, because that wasn't important, you knew they would not be around long enough to worry about last names. Living in Potlatch put me close enough to two big colleges, Washington State and University of Idaho, both twenty minutes south. Plenty of dates if I wanted them. But I wasn't looking for that right now. I wanted to earn honest money and get on the right track. I wanted that a lot.

The one-bedroom house in Potlatch was fine. It sat fifty yards off the main road. Dan and Rose were an older couple who lived next door in a trailer with a redwood porch, and he showed me around the place. He wore a bright flannel shirt and a wide-brimmed Australian cowboy hat. He must have thought I was okay, because he let me keep the keys.

"You send the rent to Carl?" he asked.

"Yes," I said. "An hour after I talked to him."

We stood on the porch of the house. The one-bay garage was a concrete-block building next to the road. I had told Dan I hoped to fix some chain saws out of it, sharpen and sell chains to loggers.

"Do you need extra work?" he asked.

"Yes," I said. "Always."

"I can give you some work, but it's a little out of season, know what I mean? Still good work, though. Easy." He watched me.

"I shoot 'em when I see 'em," I said. "I worry about the regulations after. I've been known to keep one or two I shouldn't have. They taste the same."

Dan smiled. "You bet they do." He pointed at the garage. "See the pump behind the garage?"

I nodded. "It looks like an old gas pump."

"I'll give you the key for it. There's about ten or fifteen guys who come around and get gas from us, a dollar a gallon cash, we only sell one grade, unleaded regular, and we don't advertise."

"Where do you get the gas from?" I asked.

"A couple years ago, some big wheel from one of the universities' administration saw all the maintenance trucks pulling in and out of the gas station where both schools had their accounts. Apparently some of the boys were buying a lot of beer too, on the school card that was issued with each truck, and they were looking at the girls

— the point is they weren't working. Washington State is the biggest school west of the Mississippi, so that's a lot of gas and beer."

"That must have caused a problem."

"Oh, it did," Dan said. "The two schools got together and solved it by buying a mini-tanker, just five hundred gallons. And the schools bought their own big stationary tank and pump service, just to fill the mini-tanker."

"I can see where you're headed," I said.

"There are over a hundred trucks and vehicles that take gas in that fleet, not to mention lawn equipment, straight gas for the cans of mixed fuel, every single thing comes out of that mini-tank and they don't track it. They just pay the bill on the big tank and since it's less than the card system they were using, they're saving money."

"So the mini-tanker comes here once in a while?"

"Old friend of Carl's ended up with the job and as long as he's behind the wheel, we're golden. That's tax-free retirement, right there."

"How does the money work?"

"Never raise the price on the boys, it's always a dollar a gallon. Never take on any new customers, I don't care if it's your aunt Mabel. Let her get gas in town. Push the gas a little, if you've had a slow week, sell a couple cans to some loggers, just say somebody dropped it off or something. But every Friday, there should be an envelope on my porch with three hundred seventy-five dollars in it. Nothing bigger than a twenty, never take anything over a twenty and the boys know that."

"What about the driver?"

Dan smiled. "A couple years ago, he got himself into quite a fix with a woman and that woman's husband and Carl and some of Carl's friends sorted that out, so he's paying back, we're not paying him." He thought for a minute. "You know George Beck, the big fellow?"

"No," I said.

"You'll meet him, maybe. Anyway, he fixed it."

"And the rest of the money is mine?"

"Call it salary," Dan said.

"That sounds good to me," I said.

Dan patted the top porch rail. "Then welcome home," he said.

"As far as I'm concerned." He walked across the gravel back to his place and Rose waved to me through the window.

I turned the garage into a fix-it shop. It had the one-car bay, three stools, and a room in the back with a cot. Lots of tools and the woodstove on one side. I sharpened chains and sold new ones for the loggers and fixed their saws. Sold bar and chain oil. The garage air compressor worked and guys were always stopping by for air in their tires. The business brought in enough to pay the rent and the one twenty-five I kept from the gas business felt good in my pocket. I listened to the loggers talk about Montana fires and wealthy landowners who had set up their own fire stations and association. A sort of committee on wildfire vigilance. But the summer fires burned regardless and having spotters in homemade watchtowers didn't help.

At night I slept in the house and looked at the stuffed heads on the walls. Carl's small house was filled with antlers and wall mounts. A ratty-looking brown horse and a burro were penned in the field next door and behind. Sometimes a sleek black horse came out and ran through the field. I fed them apples. Dan and Rose were friendly. A warm apple pie sat on my porch two days after I moved in. I watched their lights go on and off in the night. If I got up early enough, I could listen to one of them snore through the thin trailer walls. I sent Carl's mail to Alaska for him, what little there was of it, and made sure the envelope was on Dan's porch every Friday.

She pulled in one Friday evening, right next to the garage. She had a tan cowboy hat pushed back on her bright blond hair. "Put this in the garage," she said. "Close the door. I'm Carl's sister Penny from Lewiston." She paused. "Is Carl here?"

"No," I said. "He's in Alaska."

"Lucky you." She winked at me. "He doesn't do me a damn bit of good in Alaska."

Her tits swayed in her denim shirt just a little as she shut the car door. Tight jeans with a big silver cowboy belt buckle that showed off her small waist. She was gas on the fire. She walked down the driveway, into the house, and I watched her the whole way and she knew it.

I put the car in the garage, turned the lights off, and made sure the place was locked. I went into the house.

"What's going on?" I asked.

Penny sat on the couch in the front room and took the cowboy hat off. "My boyfriend's after me," she said. "Boyfriend" didn't sound right, coming from her. She was a woman, not a girl, probably in her late thirties. "I'm staying here tonight."

"Okay," I said. "Do you want to go to Moscow for pizza? I was just going."

"You get it," she said. "I'm staying here."

On the drive to Moscow, I thought about my chances of going to bed with her and decided that they weren't good and that it might screw stuff with Carl. The whole arrangement, the rental with no paperwork, the gas business, the garage. I couldn't let that slip away for big tits and a hot ass. I got to the pizza place and ordered and watched the college girls while I waited. Penny ranked right up there. I put the pizza on the front seat and drove back.

When I got there, a big guy I didn't know was sitting on the front porch smoking a cigarette. He threw it into the gravel and stood up. I guessed he was six seven or more, close to three hundred pounds. The type of man you have to shoot twice. I figured it was Penny's boyfriend and this could get mean in a hurry.

"I'm George Beck," he said. "Good friend of Carl's."

We shook hands. I said, "What can I do for you?"

"You must be Ed Snider."

"That's right."

"You going to be here tonight?" he said.

"Yeah."

"Good. Penny's staying here until we can get a handle on her boyfriend."

"What's his name?" I asked.

"Tim Shipman," he said. "You don't know him, do you? We all call him Ships."

"No, I don't know him," I said. "What makes you think he'll come here?"

"You've seen Penny," he said. "If you thought she was here, wouldn't you drive up here from Lewiston?"

"Sure," I said. "I'd have already been here."

"You can see I came right away," he said, "and Penny and I broke up years ago. She'll look at you and fuck up your brain." He reached inside his coat and brought out a pistol, nine-millimeter, and tried to hand it to me. "Here," he said. "Ships is violent. This is in case he needs convincing." He held the piece out to me, butt first.

I wouldn't touch the gun. "I'll be here," I said. "And that's all that's necessary." Never touch another man's gun, because you never know what its bullets have hit. I was trying to get out of the habit of handling guns.

George slipped the pistol back inside his coat, "Suit yourself," he said, "but Ships will be strapped, so I'm just telling you." He scratched his head. Something about this wasn't quite going as planned for him.

"I'll be here," I repeated.

"Carl will appreciate that," George said. "I mean, the other thing you ought to know about Penny is that she probably did cheat on Ships or rip him off or whatever."

"I'll keep an eye out." I noticed that some makeup stained the shoulder of his jacket.

"Good," George said. "We've got some buddies in Lewiston and around and we'll take care of this." I stood looking at the ground and George went on. "Wouldn't have happened if Carl hadn't gone to Alaska." I wanted to ask why but didn't. "I'm the guy around here that gets shit done," he said. He took off and I went inside the house.

That night Penny stayed with me at Carl's place. As soon as George left and we ate the pizza, she wanted the lights off. We sat in the dark on the couch. There were only the cars passing on the main road. The lights reflected off the marble eyes of the stuffed animals. We sat there for two hours without saying a word. I watched the back field. The moon shone bright and full. The black horse was running around for some reason, but I couldn't tell which was the horse and which was the shadow. They both looked alive. Penny dozed off and I watched her small breathing, her lips and perfect nose.

Then a car pulled off the road. The door slammed and I heard footsteps over to the garage and then up to the door. The handle jiggled.

"Carl?" a man's voice asked the night. "Carl, it's me, Ships. Is Penny here?" There was a pause. "Penny?"

She was up now. She pulled me close and put her mouth on my

ear. "Pretend you're Carl," she whispered. "Use a deep voice, he won't know." Her hand was on my thigh.

I tried to use the voice I'd heard on the phone. "What?" I said in Carl's voice. "Who is it?"

"Carl," the voice said, relieved. "Carl, look, is Penny here?"

Now I was Carl. "What the hell's going on, Ships?"

"She owes me a lot of money," he said, "and she's going all around town talking."

"Talking about what?" I asked.

"About stuff she shouldn't be, is what, about you and me and George Beck and she needs to shut her mouth." He cleared his throat. "I didn't have anything to do with you guys, you know that, and she's all over town with it. She's loud wrong, is what she is."

I knew that I had been right not to touch that gun Beck had offered me. "Where is she now?" I asked.

"I thought she was here," he said. "Open the door, will you?"

"Ships, I'm busy," I said.

"If she's here, you better talk to her," he said. "And if not, I'm going to find her. She knows the whole story, I don't know why she's lying, unless she's just scared of George." He crunched gravel back to the car. The car sat there for a minute and then started again and spun out on the road.

I turned to talk to Penny, but she was already unbuttoning her shirt, standing up and pulling off her jeans. The plan I'd been following vanished and we barely made it to the bedroom. She straddled me and her whole body was smooth and tight.

The sex was fast and terrible. We sort of mutually stopped after a while. Just lay there. She was already pregnant, she said, which is the best birth control there is. She said it was why she was so horny. But both of us had other things on our minds. It really hadn't been worth it.

She sat on the edge of the bed, brushing her hair. "All this trouble is because Tim gave me a watch. That watch creeped me out. It was a present because I was always late. It was a man's watch, okay, but it was weird because every time I looked at it, it showed the same time. Twenty to six. It wasn't that the watch had stopped or anything, it just happened to be twenty to six when I looked at it."

She was fixing her makeup now. "Well, one month I came up short and pawned the watch. Tim and I were broken up, so what did I care? I had to write my address on the pawn slip and I bet it was a week later and two detectives and an officer came to my apartment about that watch. It belonged to an old man named Elmer Cooley from way up in the Panhandle. He'd been missing for about a month and they wanted to know how I got that watch. Cooley, they told me, had a grandson in prison who was head of a group of militiamen that live in the mountains and did I know a George Beck, they wanted to talk to him about a murder and where was my brother? So I told them the watch came from Tim Shipman and I didn't know anything else."

I had just half-fucked a woman who was involved in a possible murder, who was lying to me and lying to the cops and being actively questioned by them. She stood up to put her jeans on and I couldn't believe her body was that good, but now the whole thing was gone south. "I'd try not to worry about it," I said. "Bad coincidence." I was enough of a liar to know when I was being lied to. I'd leave at the first possible chance.

"It's on my mind all the time," she said. "What do you think Tim did?"

"I have no idea," I said. The room was much darker than the moonlit field.

"I tell people I'm married so they won't hit on me," she said.

"Does it work?" I asked. I shifted around to lean on my elbow.

"No," she said. She paused. "Men used to sit around and talk about me when I was gone. I used to be beautiful."

"You still are," I said.

"George Beck was the only man who could keep them off." She looked out to the black field. "I just didn't like some of the things he did."

It popped in my head that George Beck had been involved somehow in the disappearance of the guy named Cooley and that was what the cops were after. The watch probably came from him, not Shipman, who was trying to save his own hide.

"I'm going back to Lewiston," she said. "Tell George that's where I am and don't tell him we screwed."

"There's not much to tell," I said.

"I know," she said. "It just didn't click. We'll have to try again. I'd like to." She showed me a fake smile. "We just have to make sure George doesn't find out."

I knew she'd tell him the instant she saw him. I had half-fucked myself into a real problem. "Sure," I said. "Keep George in the dark."

"You bet," she said. "Count on it. Trust me."

When I woke in the morning, she was gone.

The next day I met Carl Larson. There was a knock and the door opened. I was sitting on the couch, having coffee, thinking about leaving.

"Hey," the man said. "I'm Carl. You must be Ed."

"That's right, that's right," I said. "I didn't expect you back."

"There were some problems." He waved his hand.

"That's too bad," I said.

"Is that your truck by the garage, the black one?"

"Yes," I said.

"How did that happen?" he said.

"What?" I asked.

"I think you've got four flat tires," he said.

I stepped onto the porch. My truck sat lopsided by the garage and the rims rested right on the ground. I wouldn't be running anywhere too soon. I went back in.

Carl walked around the place. I suppose he wanted to see if I'd moved anything. I hadn't. Then he came out to the living room and sat in the chair by the door.

"George Beck called me and said my sister Penny was in trouble."

"That's right," I said.

"How come you didn't call me? Or write?"

I shrugged. "It wasn't my place to do that, George said he was taking care of it. It only came about the other day."

Carl shook his head. "Don't do that again," he said. "If my sister comes to you for something, let me know right away."

"Okay," I said. "From now on I will."

"Thank you," he said.

"I didn't even know you had a sister."

"No offense taken," he said. "Now I'm going down to Lewiston to visit her and see if I can straighten this out."

"Okay."

"I should be back in a couple days and we'll work out some sort of arrangement when I get back."

"The garage is fine for me," I said. "As long as I can cut my rent in half."

"Go ahead," Carl said. "While I'm here sleeping in the house, just pay half. That should give you about a month at half rent."

"Fine," I agreed. "I'll pay it now, cash." I pulled a roll of bills out of my front pocket and counted two hundred fifty dollars in front of him and handed it to him.

"See you in a couple days."

As soon as he was gone down the road, I went out to patch my tires. It was no use. They'd never hold air again. Someone had taken a jagged blade and ripped each tire completely around the sidewall. Whoever it was had to have been a very big, strong man.

The next day the phone rang and I let the machine answer and it was Carl from Lewiston.

"Pick up," he said. "It's Carl."

I picked up the phone and he went on. "Is my sister there?"

"No," I said.

"Did you fuck her?" he said.

"No," I said. It sounded wrong.

"George Beck says you did. We'll talk about that when I get back. Go check the mail for me."

Sure enough, there was a letter from Penny. The postmark showed Portland, Oregon, and I told him that. He asked me to read it to him over the phone. And I did. It was a story about Tim Shipman, but completely different than the one she had told me. She'd been telling everyone that Tim Shipman might have murdered someone. She was doing that, she said in the letter, because George Beck had given her that watch and she knew damn well what was going on. George Beck was killing people in some rival gang, George Beck was moving speed. George Beck killed some old man Cooley in the woods near the Columbia River. George Beck had better pay her for keeping his name out of it, but if the cops caught Ships, he'd spill the whole thing. Ships knew about the watch and George Beck and Elmer Cooley.

"That's it?" Carl asked.

Vigilance

"Yes," I said.

"I'll be back in a while," he said. "Sit tight." He hung up.

An hour later, George Beck showed up. Two other guys pulled in, too. My truck just sat there, completely useless to me on flat tires. Mac, one of the gas customers, also pulled in with his rig. He eyed George Beck.

"Just come back tomorrow." I said. "I'll take care of you then, if you can wait."

He lowered his voice. "Never certain if tomorrow's going to show, with people like that around," he said. "You take care and I'll see you when you don't have company." He pulled back onto the road.

"Why don't you close up now?" George Beck said. "You're going with us."

"I don't think so," I said. "Carl didn't say anything about this."

"You can go with us," he said, "or never go anywhere again."

"Fine," I said.

We drove to a truck stop in Montana, seven miles over the Idaho border. George Beck and his two buddies sat in a booth drinking coffee and ordered food and Carl showed up and we sat there eating.

George waved to a trucker at the counter. "That's Speedy," he said. "You ride in his rig and we'll be behind you."

"Where are we going?" I asked.

"We're going to talk to Tim Shipman and straighten this out. He's hiding in a motel over here, but we found him."

"What's Speedy got to do with it?"

George Beck got bigger in the booth. "I don't know, you see, because I'm dumb," he said. "People expect me to do dumb things. For instance, you fucked Penny and I'm so dumb I just found out about it, just now, this instant. So we can all drag you out in the parking lot and in the middle of things, a gun goes off and dumb local boy George Beck shot the man who was fucking his woman behind his back and the jury comes in, local folks, and they see me, and they know what I'm about and who I'm friends with, and I go do two years. You think two years is going to bother me? I'll come out of prison with more friends than I've got now." He pulled his coat back a little to show me a shoulder holster with a stainless steel pistol. "It makes little holes going in, big holes coming out, and all I asked you to do was ride with Speedy."

I was trapped. We got up and I walked outside with the trucker who was hauling logs. I got in the passenger's side of the sleeper King Cab. It was an older rig. Speedy cranked it through the gears and we headed out of the parking lot.

"That George, he's a son-of-a-bitch, ain't he?" Speedy said.

I didn't say anything.

We curved through the mountain roads and in the side mirror I could see Beck and Carl and the others behind us. Speedy pulled over at a small cabin-unit motel. The big engine kept rolling as he put the brakes on.

"Lucky number seven," Speedy said. "Give Shipman a good talking-to."

I got out of the rig. George Beck and Carl Larson were sitting on the road in their trucks. I decided to try one last attempt at getting the hell out.

"I don't even have a gun," I said.

Speedy shrugged. "There's a pistol under the seat, take it if you need it," he said.

I reached under the seat and came out with a nine-millimeter and snapped the trigger twice at Speedy before the weight of the gun told my hand it wasn't loaded. He blinked hard, then relaxed. He smiled. It was the gun Beck had tried to hand me that night at Carl's house. I had screwed myself even tighter.

I got down out of the rig and I knew the security cameras were catching me doing it, walking with a pistol into room number seven. The door was open — I pushed it with my foot — and saw Shipman on the bed, the side of his head gone from gunshot wounds. He'd been shot less than an hour earlier. I sat on the edge of the bed for a minute, trying to draw them into the room, or within camera range. Don't throw up, I told myself, you always throw up. But nobody came, and eventually I just walked out. Speedy was gone. George Beck and Carl Larson had pulled down the road a ways. I walked and got in the back of Carl's truck and we rode all the way to Potlatch. This time I kept the gun.

After that George moved in with Penny and they were considered married by everybody. Shipman's body was found in a Dumpster ten miles from the motel, but the paper said the cops knew the body had been moved. Then I heard George Beck was being held in Boise on a federal warrant and was also wanted by the Mounties in Lethbridge on a gun charge and possible murder of a witness in a homicide case in Washington State. This just made me anxious. Penny had the baby, a girl, late the following spring. Soon there was another man living there with her, and I tried not to think about it.

Carl went back to Alaska and nobody really came to the shop after that, except the gas customers. I was in Moscow picking up a case of oil one day and saw Mac, the old logger, in the parking lot. He was talking to some men. He nodded at me.

"I could use some work," I said. "Maybe you could get me a job as a fire spotter. With the park service or private. Like you talked about that one time, that private association of landowners in Montana."

"No," he answered. "No thanks. The woods are all full. It'll burn with or without you. You should ask George Beck for work, he probably needs somebody to clean his cell or something."

I came back to the garage and Dan must have seen me pull in, because he came out of his trailer and over to the garage.

"Some men stopped by here looking for you. Knocked on my door. Frightened Rose." He handed me a business card. It was from an attorney in Spokane.

"What's this?"

"What is it?" he said. "It's fucking yours, that's what it is, but it ended up on my doorstep, how is that?" He didn't raise his voice, but he was clear. "Just because I don't believe in heaven and angels doesn't mean I don't believe in hell and demons. You need to get that shit straight in your head. Realize what you're involved in. Separate the concepts." He pointed at his trailer. "I've got a purpose here on Earth, which is to provide for and protect Rose. You seem to be about to sign on as a short-order man in the devil's butcher shop. You're on a bad path, with bad men. Those two things put us at odds. There might be a time when someone with a badge comes around asking questions about you and George Beck and Carl."

"And you'd rat?"

He shook his head. "Never. It's not the law that concerns me, not a single bit. I want to make sure you and I have an understanding. The law doesn't stop a thing. Consequences only come after and after is too late, far as I'm concerned." He pointed at the pen behind his house. "My brother's bringing me up a good dog from his farm and everything in my place is loaded with the safety off. Whoever buys the ticket will get an express trip if I can help it and I'm here to tell you, although she was a lot of trouble different times, I love my Rose and I love my job of protecting her. Knock on my door and I'll let Remington answer it. Both barrels."

"I understand," I said.

"See that you do," Dan said. "Or there will be pieces of you they'll never find." He started to walk back to his trailer. "We're not all hicks and cousin-fuckers up here," he said over his shoulder. "Do your business somewhere else. You mistook kind for simple," he finished. He shut the trailer door.

I called the Spokane lawyer from a pay phone and once I got past the secretary the first thing he asked me was did I still have that gun. Sure, I said, and it's keeping me alive. Because that's the gun that killed Elmer Cooley. Well, maybe it is and maybe it isn't, he said, and if I wanted to rely on that, put my whole life on the line for one ballistics test, then I could go right ahead. And I knew he was right, although I hoped otherwise.

The Feds were leaning on George Beck hard and he was going to inform on me, said the lawyer. His buddy at the motel had a videotape of me walking into Tim Shipman's room with a pistol and coming out and a Polaroid shot of Shipman lying dead on the bed. My name was going to be tied to all this, unless I could get Beck's lawyer some good information on the remaining members of the Cooley family who still lived in the Panhandle. The Cooleys ranked high on the Feds' most wanted list and usable information about them would loosen pressure on George Beck, would reduce his charges.

What Beck and his lawyer didn't know was that if the Feds got hold of my prints, my days as Ed Snider were over.

I wasn't going to take the rap Beck was ready to hand me. I'd get the information and be gone. I hid George Beck's nine-millimeter up underneath the dashboard of my truck, held by electrical tape to the fire wall. The truck stayed locked. That gun was the only thing that connected Beck to the murder of Elmer Cooley and I kept it for no reason other than desperation. I drove north into the Panhandle, past Priest Lake and further, headed to the Cooleys' house to do the best rat work I could.

I liked the Cooleys right off, which was tough on my brain. Over those first two winter months, I tried to adjust. It was them or me. They bought my cover without a question, just a guy up to log some adjacent land. No big deal. Pop Cooley and I ate dinner together a couple of times. One working man talking to another in the mountains. Talking about making a living in a place where that was real tough work. I liked him and I liked the kid. After sixty days, I had them on a talking basis.

The kid sat in a green plastic lawn chair in the snow behind my three-room cabin. Light was just corning. The kid propped his feet on an empty propane cylinder. He wore a dark blue jacket against the cold. Under his watch cap he had a home haircut. He was whittling a stick with the new pocketknife his father gave him for Christmas. I knew he was whittling weird little smiley faces, even though I couldn't see that far. I found the sticks everywhere; the kid did it to every piece of wood he came across. Small, crooked smiley faces and the word *Peeler,* his nickname. He couldn't have been more than fourteen. As soon as he heard me awake, banging and emptying ash from under the woodstove, he was at the back kitchen door. He was skinny, but tall with a man-size head.

"Well if it isn't Kid Cooley," I said, "bantamweight champion of the Pacific Northwest. How do you feel before the big fight, Kid, say something for the fans? Are you still single, the girls have been asking."

The kid half-smiled and then got serious. "No power, right, you got no power, no juice?"

I snapped the light switch back and forth. The kitchen ceiling light stayed off. "No juice," I said. I had rented the cabin from the Cooleys for two months now and the power was always steady, which is rare in the mountains and deep woods. It tends to flicker. A single light came from the Cooleys' house, further above me on the hill. "You got lights, though."

"Jap generator," the kid said. "Pop put it in a year ago, hard-wired it from out in back, so they couldn't cut power on us."

I sat on a folding chair at the card table in the kitchen. "How am I going to have coffee, Kid?"

The kid pointed at the rusted set of blue, white, and black camp pots hung behind the stove on what used to be the fireplace. "Pop says you got to give us a ride today. Pop says we're the soldiers and he's the general."

His father was standing right outside the kitchen door and raised his voice from there. "I did not say that, I most certainly did not, nobody has to give us a ride anywhere. I said catch him before he left for work if he was working today and see what he said. That's what I said." He cleared his throat as he came into the kitchen. "Seems we were vandalized in the night, somebody cut the tires on the Jeep and the power's out." The Cooleys used an old Jeep with its stick on the column to get around. The back fender was rusted except for a bumper sticker. MARINE SNIPER: YOU CAN RUN, BUT YOU'LL JUST DIE TIRED. Pop had been in the Corps, with Vietnam action under his belt. He mentioned it when I first moved in and saw the sticker. Pop's father, Elmer Cooley, had been involved in the white gangs that live in the Pacific Northwest. Elmer had been murdered, he said, in the woods of Eastern Washington, near the Columbia River. Elmer was buried up the hill, in the family plot near the house. Elmer had lived in the cabin I was renting and I knew Pop kept alert.

"Did you hear anything in the night?" I asked. "Did the dog go after anything?"

"I had the dog inside with me because of those big bears coming around lately, too close to the house," Pop said. "I didn't want Cannon getting mauled."

"Sure," I said. "Where do you need to go today?"

"Spokane," he said. "To the train station."

"What's going on there?" I asked.

"My younger brother's coming home," he said. "He just got done doing ten years of federal time. He maxed out."

"That's a long time," I said.

"I don't think they could give Jack enough time to beat him," he said. "When he was a kid, eighteen really, he did five years here state time for some shit. Now he's done ten more and he won't be forty until August. You'll see when we pick him up. Jack's a stone house, inside and out. Always has been, always will be."

"Hey, Snider," the kid said. "Let me wear your bulletproof, since we're going into the big city."

He had tried on my vest before and loved it. "Sure," I said. "I wouldn't want anybody to mess with you. Big city of Spokane, tough town." I tightened it on him, made sure he was comfortable.

We climbed in my truck, heading south through the woods and mountains, under the eyes of hawks and eagles, two hours to Spokane.

The lines were down because I'd dropped a limb on them. The tires were flat because I'd cut them. I wondered if Pop, somewhere in his mind, didn't suspect this. He wasn't a stupid man, when it came to hunting and fishing and fields of fire and decoy interest. All manner of blinds, lures, and smoke to fool the enemy. He talked hunting to Peeler as we drove. If he suspected, he never let on. He needed to get to Spokane and I was the only man available for the job, I had made myself that way, cut myself to fit. Purposefully become a piece of the puzzle. Cold sweat ran down over my ribs and bled into my T-shirt all the way to the train station. Jack Cooley wasn't a Girl Scout. He'd started out with the Hammerskins and moved up to the elite Eighty-eight Dragoons. Federal law enforcement blamed the Dragoons for a host of crimes, but most recently tied them to a shoot-out in Wyoming where five officers died raiding a meth lab and supposed Dragoon safe house. I knew any information I got out of Jack Cooley would be all George Beck needed to loosen his own state-held noose. George Beck had been in the woods of Eastern Washington the day Elmer Cooley died, and although they couldn't prove he pulled the trigger, they were applying pressure. When it comes to law enforcement, they prosecute deaths of their own kind hardest. Everybody else is just a scumbag to them anyway, or was involved in stuff that they deserved to die for. We didn't catch you at it, but you've got to be guilty of something, something you did before or something we don't know about.

The train station in Spokane is brick, a mix of new and old. Jack Cooley wasn't there yet; his train was late. The kid rode up and down on the escalators and had a soda. Pop sat on the wood benches and watched the people with their luggage, buying tickets. When I went to sit next to Pop, there on the bench was a small smiley face and *Peeler* written underneath. The kid went down the escalator again, back up. Then the train arrived.

Jack Cooley was one of the first ones to come out of the arrival door and start walking toward us. He was an inch taller than I was and broad in the shoulders. He wore an old army jacket and jeans and work boots. The kid went right over to him and hugged him and Jack hugged him back.

"Peeler," Jack said. "Fucking little Peeler. Jesus Christ." He hugged the kid again.

Pop went over and shook hands with Jack and hugged him with one arm. He introduced me. "This is Ed Snider, he's renting Grandpa's house while he does some contract logging over on the edge of old Freleigh's property. He drove us today."

Jack Cooley looked me up and down. "Thanks," he said. He motioned at Pop and the kid. "These are nice people to be nice to."

"Glad you're out," I said.

"You're never out after that long," Jack answered. "The cell just gets a little bigger." He looked around at the vending machines and pay phones by the door. "Come on," he said. "Let's get up in those mountains. I've been dreaming about them for ten years. Are they still there?"

"Nothing's changed," Pop said, "Nothing's changed."

The kid stopped to take a piss before we got in the truck and when he came out, he had another can of soda with him. He shook it before he got in my truck. He cracked the can open and sprayed Jack with the soda and Jack was laughing and shaking his head soaking wet. "I'll clean it," the kid said. "Pop told me we shouldn't use champagne, so I used soda."

"Peeler," Jack said, "you should never sleep too heavy." He was laughing as he said it.

I drove the Cooley family back to the tip of the Idaho Panhandle. By the time we got home, it was snowing lightly and the three of them walked up the hill to their house while I reloaded my woodstove for the night.

The next morning I had been up for a while when Jack Cooley came down for a cup of coffee. He was still wearing the old army jacket.

"How're you doing?" I asked.

"Fine," he said. "Same as always."

"How was it inside?"

"Brutal," he said and left it at that.

"Where'd you do most of your time?"

He sipped his coffee. "Kentucky. Pennsylvania."

He was right across the table from me, so I had to ask. "Pop said you might come out and go after some people."

Jack shook his head. He rubbed his chin. "I'm not doing anything to anybody up here, not a thing. I'm not involved in anything other than my own life."

"Do they know that?" I asked.

He put his coffee down. "Everything with you is a question," he said. "Who is they?"

"I didn't mean anything by it," I said.

"The only people here are you and me, Pop, and Peeler. Is that right?"

"Hey," I said, "I misspoke myself."

"I'm not moving off this mountain until yesterday is dead, do you get my meaning?" he asked.

"Yes," I said.

"I'm not hiding up here," he said. "I'm out."

"I believe you," I said.

"You ever see a nest of snakes in the woods? Sometimes they'll be in a rotted tree trunk or out in a field?"

I nodded.

"Crawling all knotted up with each other, biting each other, this one eating the tail of that one that's eating the head of another, sliding all around each other, so you can't tell which one is which one. Some poor people think that's life." He reached down and brought his coffee up, took a swallow. He was looking at the mountains. He set his coffee on the table and started for the door. "Solitary never bothered me," he said. "It was being in population that I didn't care for. Too many snakes." He went out and I watched him walk back up the hill through the ankle-deep snow.

The next day I drove to Spokane alone. George Beck's lawyer met me downtown and we talked near the water, in the park.

"What did you find out?" he asked.

"Nothing. Jack Cooley isn't doing anything in any organization, as far as I can tell yet." We walked along a side street and pretended to look at the shops.

"This isn't what we agreed on, this isn't going to help George. You've got to dig around and find something."

"These people don't trust me," I said. "And they don't talk much under the best of circumstances. Jack's still wearing his prison laundry army coat, for God's sake."

"Fine," he said. "Tomorrow, George is going to begin talking about Tim Shipman and you and that Larson girl and you can deal with the fallout from that on your own." He started to walk away. "The gun won't help you. We're going forward."

"That's no good," I said. "I need more time."

"Two days," he said. "And here." He handed me a pad and pen. "Draw me a map of where the Cooleys are, so if it comes to it, the sheriffs can get a decent address for the warrant."

I drew the map as best I could and if someone was really bent on finding it, they'd find it. I handed the pad back to him.

"That will buy you two days with me, but after that, George talks and signs statements and testifies and your name is on everything."

When I got home, there was a sandwich on my kitchen table and a small stick with a smiley face on it. As I went to put wood in the stove, I realized that several of the logs carried messages. *Peeler*, on each one of them. *Peeler*.

The next morning Cannon was scratching at my door and I came out. Something was in the road, about fifty yards from my house. I thought it was Jack, facedown in the snow. I recognized the army jacket. Cannon started back toward his house and when I looked up, Pop and Jack were running down the road toward me.

"They shot Peeler," Pop yelled to no one.

"I didn't hear a shot," I said.

"Nobody heard it," said Jack.

When we got close I could see a faint spray of blood around Peeler's head. I threw up into the snow. Not at any time had shooting the kid been discussed. Beck's people would push until something gave. Either me or Jack Cooley. I threw up again.

"Why the fuck did they shoot Peeler?" Jack asked the sky.

I realized Peeler had Jack's coat on.

"He drew the fire," Pop said. "He walked around in it the other morning. I thought maybe you had some cigarettes in there and he was trying out smoking."

When we got close, we could see Peeler was still breathing, even though there was blood coming out of his nose.

"Peeler?"

His mouth opened and his voice, scratchy and cracked, came out. "Pop," the kid groaned. "It hurts."

Jack rolled him over, pulled back the coat. He was wearing the Kevlar vest, my bulletproof. He'd been hit, twice, body shots. He was hurt, but he was alive, Jack carried him up to the house.

"What can I do?" I said.

"Keep an eye out," Pop said.

I took George Beck's pistol out of the truck, grabbed some shells Pop had given me when I first got there, and went walking. I went into the woods, to try to see if I could spot anyone.

Down the hill a ways, on the other side of the Cooleys' house, was a small family cemetery. I stopped for a minute. Pop had told me who was in there, where his family tree had branched. Outside the cemetery, I noticed a pick and a shovel. Jack must have been down there. It looked like he was getting ready to dig a new grave. Peeler had carved some sticks and one was in the shape of a cross. The stick read GEORGE BECK, SENT TO HELL BY THE COOLEYS.

I walked back to my cabin. Somehow, while in the shadow of prison yards and guards and friends and enemies, Jack already knew who killed his grandfather.

An hour later, Pop came down to my door. "Do you think," Pop asked me, "you could go into town and get some cigarettes and coffee and groceries — could you do that?"

"Sure," I said. "I'll do it right now." It was my only way out.

I drove through town and kept going. Maybe they were planning my burial, too. For such big country, things had closed in on me rapidly. I needed to get out of rifle range of these people.

That fall, in one of the big shipping yards out in Grays Harbor, a guy who looked a lot like me started running a forklift and a log loader. He didn't eat with anybody, didn't talk to anybody. He cashed his check in the bar across the street and lived in a two-room apartment over the pool hall. He walked to work. The name he gave people was Tom Miller and he worked at the yard for six months. He didn't miss a day.

Monday came, time to clock in, then noon, and the foreman noticed Miller's card still in the rack. He asked around, did anybody know where Miller was? One guy said he heard Miller say he had a sister in California. He never said that to me, somebody else spoke up. Said he was from right here near Tacoma, born and raised. He didn't want to go fishing Friday, someone said. We asked him to go fishing, said we were taking our kids and he was welcome, and he said no thanks.

I guess he quit, the foreman said when Miller hadn't showed by the end of the day. So if anybody knows anybody looking for work and can run a loader and show up on time, the job pays four fifty a week, you do your own taxes as a subcontractor and don't talk union here. Sitting behind his desk in his office, the foreman cut Miller's time card in half and threw it in the garbage.

Tom Miller hadn't quit. Somebody with sharp eyes and a long memory spotted him. The man who called himself Tom Miller couldn't report to work because he was being held in a little room in the basement of a Seattle courthouse. Held until the investigators arrived.

After I told this whole story to the investigators, they kept me in custody for a couple of days. They told me that the man who lived with Penny Larson and her daughter was fatally shot in a hunting accident in the mountains of Northern Idaho, not far from their house, but managed to struggle into Canada before he died. The Mounties found him. They told me George Beck had been released. They told me Carl Larson was missing. They told me that Jack Cooley might be dead but that Peeler was still alive. They told me they knew I'd been Ed Snider for a while.

Then the investigators approached me about being an informant down in Oregon, on the Rogue River, where a group of white supremacists was moving meth and dogs and guns. We want you to do this, they said. Not that you have much choice. Sure, I said, I'll do it. But all I wanted was out. The whole sky seemed covered with heavy-gauge mesh steel, one big prison. If I was lucky to be alive, I rarely knew it. Normal men get to be things. Sons and husbands, fathers and friends. I was not any of those things. I tried, but this is me telling you I failed.

So I went in undercover, and in the middle, the fucking middle of it all, there was an hour when nobody was watching me and I had a little money and I slipped away, on the ghost train out of there.

I can't even imagine how many people are looking for me now.

Contributors' Notes

Karen E. Bender is the author of the novel *Like Normal People*. Her short stories have appeared in *The New Yorker, Granta, Zoetrope, Ploughshares, The Harvard Review,* and other magazines. They have been reprinted in the Best American and Pushcart Prize anthologies and read on the *Selected Shorts* program on NPR. She teaches creative writing at the University of North Carolina at Wilmington and is working on a collection of stories.

- "Theft" began because I wanted to write something from the point of view of a swindler. Ginger was a great character to let out the id. It was fun trying to figure out how she would use people and try to figure out her own theories on how the world worked.

I chose a cruise ship because once I weirdly ended up on a cruise to Alaska, and the setting had to be used — the general sense of desperation and sequins and the constant eating opportunities, particularly the chocolate buffet, which was one of the most poignant and piggish experiences I have ever witnessed. A friend told me that he had heard of instances in which lonely people went on cruise ships to die and be found. That was incredibly powerful to me and somehow seemed to fit into Ginger's perspective — that was the container that would hold the story. So I put that in, too, which made the story darker and sometimes hard to write, but so goes the puzzling escapade of writing fiction.

C. J. Box is the author of six novels, the most recent being *In Plain Sight*. He is the winner of the Anthony Award, Prix Calibre 38 Award (France), the Macavity Award, the Gumshoe Award, the Barry Award, and an Edgar Award, and a finalist for the L.A. Times Book Prize. *Open Season* (2001) was a New York Times Notable Book and three of the novels have been Book Sense 76 picks. Box lives with his family outside of Cheyenne, Wyoming, and is currently writing a stand-alone thriller called *Blue Heaven*.

• When the editors of "Meeting Across the River" — an anthology based on the Bruce Springsteen song — approached me about submitting a story, my first thought was: I don't *do* urban. Then I read the lyrics with their vague, mysterious references to planning a crime, the girl Cherry, a $2,000 score. While contemplating how to put my stamp on a story with those elements, my family vacationed in Yellowstone. As we left the park, we witnessed an unexpected and somewhat jarring scenario — dark, leather-clad, menacing Eastern Europeans loitering on the corners and sidewalks of little Gardiner, Montana. They were wildly out of place, like a pawnshop in a cow pasture. Turned out they'd come to the United States for jobs in Yellowstone but couldn't get them. They had that look about them like they'd do just about *anything* for $2,000. At the time, my daughters were listening to Eminem. Suddenly, everything fit. Voilà: "Pirates of Yellowstone."

James Lee Burke was born in 1936 in Houston, Texas, and grew up on the Louisiana-Texas coast. He attended Southwestern Louisiana Institute (now called the University of Louisiana at Lafayette) and later the University of Missouri at Columbia, where he received an A.B. and M.A. in English literature.

Over the years he has published twenty-five novels and one collection of short stories. The stories have appeared in *The Atlantic Monthly, Best American Short Stories, New Stories from the South, The Southern Review, Antioch Review,* and *Kenyon Review.* His novels *Heaven's Prisoners* and *Two for Texas* were adapted as motion pictures.

Burke's work has received two Edgar Awards for best crime novel of the year. He is also a Breadloaf fellow and a Guggenheim fellow and has been a recipient of an NEA grant. He and his wife of forty-six years, Pearl Burke, have four children and divide their time between Missoula, Montana, and New Iberia, Louisiana.

• My best and oldest friend passed away three years ago, and I wrote "Why Bugsy Siegel Was a Friend of Mine" and two other stories in memory of him. The real "Nick Hauser" was a remarkable man and a great friend to have. Even though we were born in the Great Depression, the era in which we grew up was one that I do not think will come aborning again. The quiet tree-shaded street on which we lived was next to a horse pasture and a grove of live oaks that were perhaps two hundred years old. "Nick" and I had a shoeshine business, yard-service, and were masters at harvesting blackberries on property that was not ours and selling them in bell jars, door-to-door, for two-bits a jar. But our great loves were baseball and Cheerio yo-yo contests.

It was a grand time to be a kid. Minor league baseball players were celebrities and the Canadian men who set up street-corner yo-yo competitions all over town seemed possessed of magic. Even the gangsters with whom

"Nick" and I associated the word *criminal* had a Hollywood aura about them. I think the innocence of the boys in the story is a reflection of the mindset of the times. On V-J Day we knew with absolute conviction that our nation was on the right side of things and that the evil that had threatened our tiny microcosm on that dead-end street had been purged from the earth forever. Perhaps one could say that our national perspective was one of illusion, but I believe otherwise. I believe my generation will be the last one to remember what is called traditional America. We believed in ourselves. We were a united people. Each day was like waking to music and sunshine and the smell of flowers. Anyway, I'm proud of this story and the others I wrote about "Nick" and me. I hope you enjoy it.

Jeffery Deaver is a former journalist, folksinger, and attorney. The creator of the Lincoln Rhyme series of thrillers, he's the author of twenty-two novels, has been awarded the Steel Dagger and Short Story Dagger from the British Crime Writers' Association, is a three-time recipient of the Ellery Queen Reader's Award for Best Short Story of the Year, and is a winner of the British Thumping Good Read Award. He's been nominated for six Edgar Awards from the Mystery Writers of America, an Anthony Award, and a Gumshoe Award. His book *The Bone Collectors* was made into a feature release from Universal pictures starring Denzel Washington and Angelina Jolie. His most recent books are *The Cold Moon, The Twelfth Card,* and *Twisted: Collected Stories.* And, yes, the rumors are true, he did appear as a corrupt reporter on his favorite soap opera, *As The World Turns.*

- "Born Bad" is typical of my short stories. They don't come from real-life experiences and are meant to be pure entertainment; I simply sit down and came up with a scenario that I think will make a fun story. Like my novels, the short stories are carefully plotted and move along quickly to an unexpected ending. The difference, though, is that in a novel I strive to create an emotional roller coaster for my readers. Accordingly, I have to keep in mind the connection that readers have with the book's characters and never disillusion them. In short stories, that's not the case, since it's hard to form more than a marginal connection with the characters over the course of twenty pages or so; the payoff of a story is a gut-wrenching surprise. To stay with the amusement park metaphor: if novels are roller coasters, then short stories are like the parachute drop ride — when the parachute doesn't open.

Jane Haddam is the pseudonym of Orania Papazoglou, whose first language was not Greek and whose parents were both born in Danbury, Connecticut. She is the author of twenty-two Gregor Demarkian novels and, under her own name, of a short series about romance writer Patience Campbell McKenna as well as two psychological thrillers. She was married for thirteen years to the three-time Edgar Award–winner William L.

DeAndrea, who died in 1996. She lives with her two sons in Litchfield County, Connecticut.

• I don't think I would have written a story about a cat if the cat had been any other cat but Edelweiss. I'm not a cat-detective sort of person — all the cutesy half-humanness of detecting pets tends to make me climb the walls. So when Ed Gorman first asked me to do a story for a volume of cat-related mysteries, I was torn between my first reaction ("oh, for goodness *sake*") and the desire to have a chance to do a short story at all. I don't get asked to do them often, and I love the form. In the end, I opted for a story that wasn't anything like cutesy and that couldn't be mistaken for cozy in a million years. In the process, I gave Edelweiss — who was adopted after having been neglected and abused, and who had the most thoroughgoing case of shyness ever visited on a mammal — the sort of nonchalant self-confidence all cats are supposed to possess by birthright. She's a good cat, Edelweiss, even if you'll never get to meet her. If you visit, she'll hide under the couch or behind the recycling bin until she can be sure you're safely gone.

William Harrison is the author of eight novels — five set in Africa — as well as three volumes of short stories, essays, and travel pieces. He taught at the University of Arkansas for a number of years and still lives in Fayetteville.

• I usually begin with a character when a story comes to me, but sometimes a place — or even a single image — starts the process. I was driving down toward Dripping Springs, Texas, out of Austin when I saw this forlorn little real estate company in a squat building out there among the scrub oak and mesquite trees. My wife had once worked as a real estate agent and told me how women agents always traveled in pairs when dealing with male clients — especially in isolated rural situations — and my imagination just turned over. "Texas Heat" was the result.

Alan Heathcock has published stories in a number of journals. His story "Peace-Keeper," first published in the *Virginia Quarterly Review*, won the 2006 National Magazine Award in fiction. He is a native of Chicago and teaches at Boise State University in Boise, Idaho.

• Some friends of mine live in a lovely small town in Minnesota. I visited the town not long after a horrible crime — not unlike the crime in "Peacekeeper" — had been discovered. The town had palpably changed; everything felt different, somehow tarnished. I remember wondering if anything could be done to restore the town's peace and decided nothing short of having the crime erased from the town's collective memory would suffice. That, in turn, got me thinking on the nature of peace itself and how disrupted peace will always show itself, will be felt, will be ingested like fouled air, even if not seen by the community; peace, or the lack of peace, is a force of nature, is the very air we breathe. Around the same time I was working on a story about the Great Midwestern Flood of 1993, and it made sense that the two stories reside in the same fictive space. I owe a structural debt to the Christopher Nolan film *Following* for the disjointed manner in which Nolan unfurled his story, juxtaposing related but out-of-sequence scenes to enable a consistent tension — building multiple lines to a proper crescendo, was, for me, a key to unlocking this particular story's potency.

Emory Holmes II is a Los Angeles–based novelist, playwright, poet, children's storywriter, and journalist. His news stories on American crime, schools, and the arts have appeared on the pages of the *San Francisco Chronicle,* the *Los Angeles Times,* the *Los Angeles Sentinel,* the *New York Amsterdam News, Los Angeles Magazine, Essence, CODE,* the *R&B Report, Written By* magazine, and other publications.

• When my crime-writer buddy Gary Phillips called in the summer of 2004 and asked if I would contribute a story to *The Cocaine Chronicles* — an anthology of new writing he and novelist Jervey Tervalon were putting together addressing the effects of cocaine on American society — I jumped at the chance. I was eager to pen a twenty-first-century blues. I unearthed a motley gallery of killers I'd banked in an archive of traffickers and thugs, collected during my thirty years as a reporter and writer. Some of the characters and settings in "A.k.a., Moises Rockafella" got plucked from the novel I am writing about a meth epidemic (and murder) in 1980s Honolulu. I had done a page one story on this epidemic for the *San Francisco Chronicle* back in August 1989 and, a few weeks after that, *Vanity Fair* sent me back to Hawaii to do the story for them. Working on assignment for *Vanity Fair* is a writer's dream come true, and the experience was all that and more for me, but my Hawaii narrative never got published in *Vanity Fair.* It was, however, during this time that I first uncovered the remarkable crimes and characters that have become "A.k.a., Moises Rockafella."

I changed the settings from inner-city Honolulu to the outskirts of Los Angeles. My cycle of events takes place within the span of a few heartbeats, in a police interrogation room, a few miles from the urban hick town of La Caja, California (a fictional hometown I intend to revisit). To celebrate the invention of La Caja, I birthed an ambitious killer, Cut Pemberton, whose presence is a mere specter in this story. Nevertheless, he is my narratives' inscrutable engine. He is a quicksilver force and, I may as well add, a predator and a scoundrel and a merciless miscreant too who, for the moment, exists primarily as a mordent spook in the opulent, backtracking imagination of his gargantuan road-dog, his thoroughly guilty, yet somehow blissfully blameless — and hungry and thirsty and wronged! wronged! — pale-ass pussy of a sidekick, the roundly chastened and proportioned Fat Tommy O'Rourke.

"A.k.a., Moises Rockafella" is an inquiry into the mind of this man, Tommy O'Rourke. My story, frankly, suspects Moises is complicit in a monstrous crime. While negotiating the streams of Tommy's thoughts, I tried to make note of the reeling fluidity and momentum of subjective time as it whipped Tommy round and around in its rapids on that interminable day and night, while around him the grave machinery of fate ticked on. I looked for fun as well as art in this sad stuff. At a decisive point in Tommy's interrogation, DEA Special Agent Roland Braddock nails him with a slur, "Pale-ass pussy." Here's how Nietzsche, in *Thus Spake Zarathustra* (1883), critiqued the Moises Rockafellas of his day: "An image made this pale man pale. He was equal to his deed when he did it; but he could not bear its image after it was done. Now he always saw himself as the doer of one deed. Madness I call this: the exception now became the essence for him. A chalk streak stops a hen; the stroke that he himself struck stopped his poor reason: madness after the deed I call this."

My story is about exactly this: the *madness after the deed*. There's nothing funny about murder. True that. But, I won't get mad if readers think of this narrative as a comedy, even a slapstick comedy, and laugh out loud. That said, at the bottom of all this funny business, "A.k.a., Moises Rockafella" is a blues; a pale-ass, lowdown blues.

Wendy Hornsby is the author of seven novels and a collection of short stories, *Nine Sons,* that includes her Edgar Award–winning short story of the same title. She lives in Southern California, where she is chair of her college history department. Currently she is finishing the sixth Maggie MacGowen mystery

• One early summer evening, just before sunset, I sat on our front deck gazing out across Malibu Canyon, glass of good red wine in hand, thinking about a story for *Murder in Vegas,* the anthology edited by Michael Connelly. In front of me, a pair of magnificent red-tail hawks rose up out of the depths of the canyon, found thermals to ride, like kites, so they could shop the chaparral below for their dinner. Beautiful. I'm not a big fan of Vegas and whatever goes on there, but I do love the Red Rock Canyon area that rises from the desert floor just a few miles past the artifice and faux gilt of the Strip. Like the rugged canyons of the Santa Monica mountains where we live, that can be a very treacherous area for the unprepared. The elements of "Dust Up" began to emerge out of that place where stories lurk. By the time the last of the sun was gone, and with some help from my well-used copy of *Sibley's Guide to Birds,* the story was formed: bad guys, an excellent body drop, endangered wildlife, and Pansy Reynard, a character I thoroughly enjoyed getting to know. "Dust Up" was fun to write. I think Pansy Reynard and I may have some further adventures to explore.

Contributors' Notes

Andrew Klavan is the author of *True Crime*, which was filmed by Clint Eastwood, and *Don't Say a Word*, which was filmed starring Michael Douglas. He has just completed *Damnation Street*, the sequel to the Scott Weiss and Jim Bishop novels *Dynamite Road* and *Shotgun Alley*. His essays have appeared in the *New York Times*, the *Wall Street Journal*, and the *Los Angeles Times*, among other places.

• When I first finished "Her Lord and Master," my agent at the time told me not to try to publish it. He said its graphically sexual and politically incorrect subject matter would hurt my career. After a couple of venues turned the story down, I brought it to my friend Otto Penzler. I trust Otto, and I figured if he told me to ditch the thing, I would. Instead, he called me and said, "I'll get this into print if I have to build an entire anthology around it." It took him four years but he was, as always, as good as his word. The story first came out in Otto's anthology *Dangerous Women*. Then it got nominated for an Edgar Award. Now it's been included here. The moral of the story: when in doubt, call Otto.

Elmore Leonard is one of the most honored and beloved writers in America, a regular on the best-seller lists for two decades, and the winner of the Grand Master Award, given by the Mystery Writers of America for lifetime achievement. Among the motion pictures made from his books are *Hombre*, *Valdez Is Coming*, *The Tall T*, *Get Shorty*, *Jackie Brown*, *Out of Sight*, and *Stick*.

• Elmore Leonard has said that if he didn't have a good time writing novels and short stories he wouldn't have kept doing it for fifty-five years. According to Leonard, his ultimate pleasure is developing characters, giving them attitudes, and getting them to talk in scenes that he makes up as he goes along, without much of an idea how the book or story will end.

He was already working on his novel *The Hot Kid* when Otto Penzler called and asked if he had time to write a story for Otto's forthcoming anthology of suspense stories *Dangerous Women*. Elmore said, "You bet" and pulled Louly Brown out of the novel he was writing, but doesn't remember why he changed her name to Louly Ring. He also introduced Deputy U.S. Marshal Carl Webster, who later appeared in a fourteen-part serial called *Comfort to the Enemy* that ran in the *New York Times Sunday Magazine* and will be featured again in the book Elmore is currently writing.

"My characters," Elmore said, "are always on call, never knowing where they might have to show up again."

Laura Lippman has won virtually all the major U.S. mystery-writing awards for her Tess Monaghan novels. She also has published two critically acclaimed stand-alones, *Every Secret Thing* and *To the Power of Three*. Her short stories have appeared in numerous anthologies, including *Murderers Row*,

Tart Noir, Murder and All that Jazz, Dangerous Women, and *Baltimore Noir,* which she also edited. A former newspaper reporter, she lives in Baltimore.

• Much to my disgust, I have a bit of a "nice girl" rep in the mystery world and short stories have given me a chance to shake that up. I was particularly flattered when Gary Phillips and Jervey Tervalon asked if I would write a story for *The Cocaine Chronicles.* "What do you know about cocaine?" asked my parents, already mildly discombobulated by the recent revelation that I once wrote erotica. "More than I know about golf!" I said, referencing another story. But I also had a secret agenda. The cocaine trade in cities such as Baltimore would be much less lucrative if suburbanites weren't part of the customer base. I wanted to show an African-American drug dealer helpless in the face of true evil — two white girls on a diet.

Ed McBain, whose novels of the 87th Precinct, Matthew Hope, and other characters sold nearly 100 million copies worldwide, died on July 6, 2005. He had been battling throat cancer for three years. While he did not quite invent the police procedural novel, he refined it and popularized it, becoming a household name and winner of the Grand Master Award from the Mystery Writers of America. Under his own name, Evan Hunter, he wrote such memorable novels as *The Blackboard Jungle* and *Strangers When We Meet,* both of which also were successful films. Among his screenplays was the Alfred Hitchcock thriller *The Birds. Improvisation* was his last short story.

Mike MacLean is a faculty member of Harrison Middleton University and the author of numerous published stories. Born and raised in Arizona, he lives in Tempe with his wife, Bobbie, and their three dogs. Along with his love of writing, Mike has a passion for the martial arts and holds a black belt in Ja-Shin-Do.

Mike's short fiction can be found in the pages of *Thug Lit, Thrilling Detective, Demolition Magazine,* and *Plots with Guns.* His first novel, *The Silent,* is currently under consideration by major publishing houses.

• There is a mundane suspense that comes with getting a package. "McHenry's Gift" was an attempt to take that everyday experience and infuse it with tension. While many of my stories are quick and brutal, writing this one presented a different kind of challenge. I wanted to dangle the threat in front of the reader without resorting to overt scenes of violence. I wanted to make the reader sweat it out.

Walter Mosley is the author of twenty-four critically acclaimed books, and his work has been translated into twenty-one languages. Some of his characters have become iconic: from the reluctant detective Easy Rawlins to the ex-con philosopher Socrates Fortlow. His books encompass a wide range of genres: from his popular mysteries to literary fiction, nonfiction, young adult fiction, and science fiction. He has won numerous awards including the Anisfield Wolf Award; a Grammy Award for his linear notes accompanying *Richard Pryor . . . And It's Deep Too!: The Complete Warner Bros. Recordings (1968–1992);* an O'Henry Award in 1996 (for a Socrates Fortlow story); the Sundance Institute Risktaker Award; and a PEN Lifetime Achievement Award. Born and raised in Los Angeles, he now lives in New York City.

- I am so happy to have this story recognized in the crime fiction field. I was deeply satisfied with the world that Leonid McGill represents. I wanted to start writing about New York and about the toll working with crime has on both sides of the law. This story is the beginning of a long and convoluted literary relationship.

Joyce Carol Oates, a member of the American Academy of Arts and Letters since 1978, is the author most recently of the novel *Black Girl/White Girl* (Ecco/HarperCollins) and the noir story collection *The Female of the Species* (Otto Penzler Books, Harcourt). She is the 2003 recipient of the Common Wealth Award for Achievement in Literature and the 2005 Prix Femina for her novel *The Falls.* She lives and teaches in Princeton, New Jersey.

- Like most of my fiction, "So Help Me God" was evoked by some mysterious conjunction of place, time, and character. The setting is upstate New York in the foothills of the Adirondack Mountains, where young men like Luke Pittman, prone to violence, yet "attractive" as charismatic personalities, may be as likely to go into local law enforcement as into a life of sporadic crime. The attraction of such men to women, including even young women from "good" families, is part of the subject here, like the gradual awakening, in such a marriage, that the wife may have to emulate her violence-prone husband in order to save her own life. We've all had experiences with mysterious, unidentified telephone calls, especially women; the story's opening was suggested by an episode of some years ago in my life, which remained unexplained.

Sue Pike is the editor of *Locked Up,* an anthology of short mystery stories marking the 175th anniversary of the construction of the Rideau Canal, a navigable system of lakes and rivers joining Lake Ontario to Canada's capital in Ottawa. The canal was built as a defense against American invasion but now welcomes hundreds of boaters from the country each year.

Sue has stories in all six of the Ladies' Killing Circle anthologies and is editor of *Fit to Die, Bone Dance,* and *When Boomers Go Bad.* Her work has appeared in *Ellery Queen Mystery Magazine, Storyteller* and *Cold Blood V,* as well as *Murder in Vegas*. She won the Crime Writers of Canada Arthur Ellis Award for Best Short Story of 1997.

▪ I wrote this sitting on the dock at our cottage on Lake Opinicon in Eastern Ontario, feeling about as far away from Las Vegas as it's possible to be. I had a recalcitrant temporary crown at the time and began to wonder if DNA might lurk in its porous plastic. My dentist wouldn't commit on the subject but I notice he's been a little wary of me ever since.

Emily Raboteau is the author of a novel, *The Professor's Daughter,* and the recipient of an NEA Fellowship.

▪ I was surprised to learn that "Smile" was selected for this anthology because I didn't conceive it as a mystery story. My father, who is from the region depicted in "Smile," describes it as a horror story. I think of it more as a love story because it depicts my romance with the Cajun language. Who knows? Maybe it's all three. I've been thinking about the "mystery" designation, though. The thing that isn't said, the thing that's strategically withheld, is usually the thing that makes a reader want to turn the page. In a way, a lot of successful fiction could be referred to as mystery. Writing for me, like life, is also a mysterious process. I don't know how it's going to end and it's only through the blind act of doing it that meaning occurs.

R. T. Smith lives in Rockbridge County, Virginia, and edits *Shenandoah: The Washington and Lee University Review.* His stories have appeared in *New Stories from the South, The Pushcart Prize, Best American Short Stories,* and his new collection, *Uke Rivers Delivers,* published by LSU Press in 2006. He is also the author of several collections of poetry, including *The Hollow Log Lounge* and *Brightwood.* Smith is currently working on a novel about Sheriff Blaine Sherburne.

▪ When I read in *The Rockbridge Advocate* the reprint of a newspaper account of a crime outside Lexington at the beginning of the twentieth century, I began wondering about the gaps in the record and the feel of a suppressed subtext rippling through the testimony. Because jigsawing accounts, especially in criminal matters, often bring *Rashomon* to my mind, I decided to write a story that was distinctly Appalachian but that addressed questions of both motive and memory similar to those that interested Kurosawa. One of the Ryunosuke Akutagawa short stories that the film works from is titled, in Kojima's translation, "In a Grove." I joined the first three letters to get the victim's name and began looking at the evidence, as I imagined it, from disparate perspectives, in different voices. At one time or another in the process, every one of these unreliable narrators seemed to have some credibility and to arouse at least a little sympathy. Sherburne's name, by the way, is borrowed from the Lynching Bee section of Huck Finn's narrative.

Jeff Somers writes all of his stories on cocktail napkins while sitting groggily at local saloons, using felt-tip pens that produce blurry, indecipherable scrawls. He dreams of a society that does not consider pants required public attire, and swears someday he will wake up some time before noon, remain sober for the better part of the day, and compose a persuasive tract on the subject that will change society forever. He began publishing *The Inner Swine,* a personal zine, in 1995 and now has at least eleven loyal readers who actually pay him for each issue, assuming promissory notes and occasional alcoholic beverages count as subscription fees. His first novel, *Lifers,* was reviewed favorably by the *New York Times Book Review* in 2001. His second novel, *The Electric Church,* is forthcoming from Warner Aspect in 2007. He lives in Hoboken, New Jersey, where the ratio of bars to bookstores is roughly 344 to 1.

- Like many of my stories, *Ringing the Changes* grew from the title. I can't recall where I first heard it, but it evoked the opening scene of the story for me, the boring conversation endured for its cloaking purposes, the sly, steady grift that requires more patience and work than an honest job. From there, all it took was a bottle of bourbon and a few late nights, and Poppy was born, exhausted and unhappy. Every story requires a bottle of bourbon, so every story is slowly killing me. I think it is worth it.

Scott Wolven is the author of *Controlled Burn,* a collection of short stories. For five years in a row, Wolven's stories have been selected for the *Best American Mystery Stories.* In 2006, Wolven's stories will also appear in two other anthologies: *Murder at the Racetrack,* edited by Otto Penzler, and *Fuck Noir,* edited by Jennifer Jordan.

- "Vigilance" is influenced by the hard, beautiful geography of Idaho and Montana and Washington, where the story takes place. The great Western cowboy artist and writer Charles M. Russell titled one of his paintings *When Guns Speak, Death Settles Disputes,* and that is certainly true here. Jack Cooley sums it up when he talks about the snakes, and in the end my nameless narrator gets to live another day as a ghost dog. It's always night, in this story.

It's a serious honor to have my story appear here. Very special appreciation goes out to M, the great team at WSBW. Big thanks out to *Crimespree* magazine. Anthony Neil Smith and Charlie Stella and Victor Gischler—three aces in the writer's deck. For the art, inspiration, and support, Skylight Books and K, and nobody ever beats DMC Des Allemands and best brother Will.

Other Distinguished Mystery Stories of 2005

ANDERSON, KENT
    Elvis Hitler, *Pilots with Guns*, ed. Anthony Neil Smith (Dennis McMillan)

BAER, WILL CHRISTOPHER
    Deception of the Thrush, *San Francisco Noir*, ed. Peter Marvelis (Akashic)

BETANCOURT, JOHN GREGORY
    The Pit and the Pendulum, *Alfred Hitchcock Mystery Magazine*, July/August

BURGIN, RICHARD
    The Urn, *Antioch Review*, Summer

CARCATERRA, LORENZO
    A Thousand Miles from Nowhere, *Dangerous Women*, ed. Otto Penzler (Mysterious Press)

CHILD, LEE
    Ten Keys, *The Cocaine Chronicles*, ed. Gary Phillips and Jervey Tervalon (Akashic)

CONNELLY, MICHAEL
    Cielo Azul, *Dangerous Women*, ed. Otto Penzler (Mysterious Press)

DAUGHARTY, JANICE
    Going to Jackson, *The Ontario Review*, Fall/Winter

DEMPSEY, TIMOTHY F.
    Visit to a Chat Room, *Ellery Queen Mystery Magazine*, March/April

DENOUX, O'NEIL
    A Good Shooting, *Alfred Hitchcock Mystery Magazine*, January/February

DICKINSON, STEPHANIE
    Slave Quarters, *Story Quarterly*, Fall

Other Distinguished Mystery Stories of 2005

EDWARDS, SAM
   The Long Count, *Thuglit*, #1

FAHEY, GEORGE
   View from the Pines, *Glimmer Train*, Spring

FRANCISCO, RUTH
   Society Blues, *Ellery Queen Mystery Magazine*, March/April

GLATT, LISA
   What Milton Heard, *Small Spiral Notebook*, January

HOCH, EDWARD D.
   The Theft of the Rumpled Road Map, *Ellery Queen Mystery Magazine*, August

LIMON, MARTIN
   A Crust of Rice, *Alfred Hitchcock Mystery Magazine*, January/February

MEREDITH, DON
   The Greatcoat, *Texas Review*, Spring/Summer

MOODY, BILL
   Camaro Blue, *The Cocaine Chronicles*, ed. Gary Phillips and Jervey Tervalon (Akashic)

MEYERS, MAAN
   The Dutchman and the Wrongful Heir, *The Mammoth Book of New Historical Whodunits*, ed. Mike Ashley (Carroll & Graf)

NISBET, JIM
   Brian's Story, *Plots with Guns*, ed. Anthony Neil Smith (Dennis McMillan)

POLLACK, NEAL
   Pretty Good Vacation, *Mississippi Review*, January

PRUZAN, TODD
   No Fear, *The Insomniac Reader*, ed. Kevin Sampsell (Manic D Press)

RAMOS, MANUEL
   Sentimental Value, *The Cocaine Chronicles*, ed. Gary Phillips and Jervey Tervalon (Akashic)

RICHMOND, BRIAN
   Edwin the Confessor, *Alfred Hitchcock Mystery Magazine*, January/February

STANSBERRY, DOMENIC
   The Prison, *San Francisco Noir*, ed. Peter Marvelis (Akashic)

VIDAL, GORE
   Clouds and Eclipses, *Harvard Review*, #29

WARD, ROBERT
 Chemistry, *The Cocaine Chronicles,* ed. Gary Phillips and Jervey Tervalon (Akashic)
WATERMAN, FREDERICK
 Love or Money, *Hemispheres,* August

ZURUS, RICHARD LEE
 Runaway, *Story Quarterly,* Fall